The Time It Takes

Kaitlyn Johnson

Mme. Tové!
It's so good to see you
again! I promise I'll keep
in touch better than before♡
Thank you for being such an
amazing 3. inspiring teacher!
Love, Kaitlyn ♡

I want to say a HUGE thank you to my wonderful family and friends who have supported my writing career for as long as I have been writing! A special thanks to Andrew Clayton for helping me format my book and saving me from the brink of insanity more times than I can count. And lastly, the biggest of thanks to my cat, Fe, who constantly inspires me to be my best self. I love you all!

Chapter 1

It feels like I've been waiting hours for Denton. He's left me in here alone with his boring walls, even more boring desk toys, and his corny newspaper clippings on the wall. One of them reads, *Cop Delivers Justice to Local Pizza Parlour*, with a picture of Denton smiling, holding a free pizza.

It's hard not to roll my eyes every time I see that.

I check his ridiculously loud ticking clock, craning my head to see the neutral colours and plain numbers. It feels like it's been hours, but only ten minutes have passed. *Time is a tricky thing.*

Another merciless minute ticks by before Denton finally opens the door. I know that he's been doing nothing but chatting with his other cop buddies, the ones he's tried to pass me off to, but no one else will deal with me. At least, no one will deal with me how *he* wants me to be dealt with. No, he doesn't want his lackeys to take me seriously, he just wants them to shoo me away, and pretend to listen to me beforehand. I've gotten to the point where I don't even deal with the rookies anymore; I go straight to Denton's office and watch the time go by, ensuring he is well aware that I am waiting on him. He is not too fond of my tactics.

As Denton enters the room, he finishes a chuckle and tries to cover up with the clearing of his throat; it's no secret that a lot of the cops here laugh at me. Not that I mind. Not too much, anyway.

"Take your time," I mutter, not bothering to turn around and see Denton's half smug, half patient face.

"I was afraid you wouldn't make your weekly meeting," he replies, shutting his door, along with the blinds on the built-in window. I suppose he doesn't want his staff watching us. He putters to his desk, takes a seat, and flashes his eyes immediately to my feet propped up just next to his computer monitor. He swats at the air surrounding them until I set them down on the floor, and then he resumes his painful joke. "You came in last Monday, and now it's Thursday. That's ten days."

I shiver in his brisk office, a factor that I hate in coming here, and stick my hands into my hoodie's pocket. "Do you ever turn the heat up? It's winter, you know."

Denton narrows his eyes at me, one eyebrow arched just slightly. "You know, I am a police officer. I have things to do."

"It doesn't seem like it."

"...I am also the head of this department."

"And your other 'officers,'" I point back towards the door, leaning forward, "were playing blackjack. You can't have that much to do."

"They're on break, tell me what you saw."

I lean back in my seat, crossing one leg over the other, and gloss over more of the cheesy signage plastering Denton's walls. *Denton Promotes to Head of Department*, with a smiling, slightly younger and well shaven Denton shaking the hand of our lovely mayor, Andrew Layton. It's been a couple of years since I first met Denton, and I don't think I've ever seen him smile the way he does in his photo ops. Shocking. "You know what I saw."

Denton folds his hands neatly on his desk, observes them for a moment, and then shifts his eyes up at me. He develops a crease in his forehead, both skeptical and gentle, a look he's learned to perfect. The skepticism is the only truth in his gaze. "A plane."

I laugh at the notion and sit up a little more, arching my back. "Yes, a plane. A plane that's about six times as big as any plane ever built, that has blinding lights surrounding it, and isn't actually a plane at all." I squeeze my eyes shut for a moment, the good old song and dance taking its toll tonight. I am tired, and I suppose this could have waited until tomorrow if the urgency I constantly feel didn't exist. "For fuck's sake, Denton..."

"You could call me 'Officer,' you know." Denton is not too fond of the curse words, and it always brings a spark of happiness to me when I get under his skin. Not that it's very hard to do. "Or 'Chief.'"

"And you could actually listen to me for once."

"Look, Raleigh, when are you going to stop?" Denton rubs his face with both hands, and then covers his mouth, keeping steady eye contact. His voice is hoarse, his demeanor tired, a familiarity I know all too well.

"When you listen to me," I snap back. "Like Officer Andy."

Officer Andy is the only policeman in this station who has ever sat down and really listened to me. This was in my own rookie days, where I'd show up at the police station, and Denton would pass me off to others, in the hope that if he ignored me enough, I'd simply go away. He made the mistakes of handing me over to Officer Andy, who listened to me for over an hour and wrote down every little detail I said. Denton was not too pleased.

Denton's eyes drift shut, and he breathes deeply into his hands. "Well, Officer Andy is a rookie…" His eyes snap back open. "And you call *him* 'officer?'"

"It was over Pewter Elementary, by the way." I slowly begin chewing the gum nestled in the corner of my mouth that I had nearly forgotten about.

"Why were you even there?" Denton shifts a picture frame around so that it's closer to his monitor, further hiding it from my view; I've never seen what pictures he has on those desks. All I know is that, since I've known him, he hasn't been married. I couldn't really imagine him with a wife anyway. He's always struck me as the kind of guy who's married to his work, but what do I know?

I sigh. "…I was with a friend." A friend who's probably freezing his ass off outside.

"And you just so happened to see a UFO?" Once he mentions the term, we both grow silent. It's almost become a game, to see who can slip first, say one of the words we both know he doesn't want to hear. After that, we remain quiet, until Denton breaks the tension with an annoyed grunt and the crack of his neck. "You're wasting your time."

I clench my jaw, blinking harshly, trying to remain calm; one of these days, he's going to have to listen… "If you would ever just tilt your head up, and look at the fucking sky…"

"Okay, kid," he interrupts. *There's that flared temper again!* "Do you have a picture?"

"…No. But last time you wouldn't even let me show you!"

"You know, there are a lot of flight paths right above us." Denton lets his head slowly tip backward, letting his eyes gaze up towards the sky, only to be blocked by his ugly beige ceiling.

"You can't be serious," I grumble. Denton's gaze remains

forced and fixed on his ceiling. "They're not planes. There is something else out there." I inch towards him onto the edge of my seat, my fingers wrapping around the thick cushion. "Besides, don't you remember what happened the last time we discussed flights paths?"

Denton sighs, his eyes drifting shut, and then faces his head back to me. His eyes still closed, he kindly asks, "Why do you keep coming here?"

I've asked myself that question many times. Why do I keep bothering with this guy? Why do I think he'll just up and change his mind? Why do I think I'll be the one to do it? I am unsatisfied with the support of any online communities I've come across; I'm only considered a freak. "Because one day, someone could get hurt." He opens his eyes upon the mention of someone getting hurt; it is his job to protect and serve. Protecting, maybe, but he's sure as hell not serving me. "Or, we'll need to be prepared. People should know what's out there. Or, or,"

"Or, or, or!" he mocks, throwing his hands half-heartedly into the air. "Come on, cut the dramatics." He laces his fingers together once again and shakes his head to the ticking of his clock.

He's about to speak when I shoot back, "If someone gets hurt, that's gonna be on you."

Denton narrows his eyes. He's like every decent cop out there, haunted by the ones he couldn't save. I don't know if he's ever had anyone that he couldn't save, but the thought would frighten anyone. It frightens me.

I take a deep breath. "There are too many possibilities. We don't know,"

"Exactly, Raleigh. There are too many possibilities." He keeps eye contact and speaks slowly, not allowing his voice to waver in the slightest. "It could be a helicopter or a plane."

"It's not a plane!" I shout, unconsciously stamping my feet on the floor.

Denton smirks. "Well, I think that is my cue to tell you to leave." He snatches a pen from next to his keyboard, along with a folder from the stack of about eight plopped onto his desk, and he begins scribbling along the first paper he opens to. "You know your way out."

I don't say another word to him. I quietly get up, make my way to the door, and ignore the bullshit "work" he's doing to try to look busy. None of the officers give me any strange looks as I exit Denton's office. Most of them don't recognize me from previous visits, and the few that do barely glance up before returning focus to their blackjack game. Officer Andy isn't here tonight, otherwise, he'd be giving me a comforting smile.

I sweep past Kayla, the receptionist for the station, and she offers me her mandatory, disinterested nod before I step out into the brisk night. I stand a few feet from the door and breathe in the too cool air. I'm already shivering.

I turn to my left, seeing the figure I ditched out here some twenty minutes ago.

"You done?" the figure asks me, pushing himself back up to a stand from the concrete wall of the police station.

I sigh, only taking one step towards him, as he's suddenly right in front of me. I cross my arms, avoiding eye contact. "It's not a plane."

He chuckles mildly and places his hands on my hips. "I know." I instinctively grab onto his hands; they're warmer than mine, and he's been waiting outside in the frigid night. He pecks my lips and then draws away. "You okay?"

"I'm cold." I step closer, tempted to just steal his jacket from him. "Is your car warm?"

"You know the answer to that." His car, the shitty 1990's clunker that it is, takes about half an hour to warm up. But, a car is a car, and it beats walking, even if it is a short walk.

I groan. "Right."

Tristan drives me home after yet another one of our adventures at the police station. He usually tends to stay outside, and he says it's because he doesn't want to get in the way of my spitfire. I think it's also because of what happened a few months ago. That was the first and only time he'd met Denton, and neither were too pleased with the situation. Has it already been six months?

Even though Tristan doesn't come inside, I like that he waits for me; I like seeing his face after I lose yet another battle with Denton. I like seeing *him* altogether regardless.

The two of us drive back in silence and Tristan parks in front of my house. He turns off the still chilled car before I can see what time it is, though it's got to be nearing midnight. I don't remember what time Denton's clock said, all I know is that it was beating so damn loud.

We both take off our seat belts and wrestle into each others' arms, always presenting a challenge with the centre console blocking us. His warm touch sends shivers down my spine, and I can't help but smile against his grin.

Tristan only lives a few blocks away, making it easy to see each other. A lot. I thought that after we graduated from high school, we'd never see one another, but I'm pretty sure we see each other even more so than two years ago. Not that we were that close in school.

He slides his lips from mine down to my neck, and his hands slip under my hoodie and shirt, finding their way back up to my breasts. One hand begins to fumble with the hook in the back, and the other makes a beeline for my jeans.

I remove my hands from his body, and place them back on his chest, pressing firmly. "Not tonight," I whisper, a wave of fatigue flowing through me. I almost second guess myself and insist for him to come inside, but a yawn overtakes me.

He opens his eyes, smiles, and whispers back, "Okay."

We kiss our brief goodbyes before I brave the even colder weather outside his car, and rush into my house. *At least the house is warm.*

I shut myself in my home, leaning briefly on the door while I slip out of my boots. I stumble up the stairs and into my bedroom, collapsing onto my bed like a zombie. I wiggle out of my purse's tight grip and find my way underneath some of the thick sheets blanketing my bed.

And I fall asleep to the sound of Tristan's clunker struggling to make it down the street.

Chapter 2

Space Age, to my convenience, is but a short, brisk walk from the metro station. I follow the same transit route every day I go to work, which is about four days a week, and every day, it seems to take less and less time; I now have the buses and trains planned on clockwork, despite the inconsistent schedules. I know where to stand so that the train doors open right in front of me, perfectly centred, and which seat is, in fact, the best for the quick bus ride. It's been eight months since I first started, so I should know all the minute details.

I step into Space Age Comics and a shudder rolls down my spine thanks to the late winter wind. It only snowed once this year, but the air is still crisp and sharp.

"Hi," I mutter, noticing that one of my co-workers is hiding at the till, unsure who exactly it is.

"Hey," Michelle quips; her squeaky voice gives her away. She stands up straighter, revealing herself, and places her hands on her frail hips. "You on at one?"

I check the Superman clock hanging up above the Manga section and nod mindlessly; I have ten minutes. "Yeah." I take a few more steps towards Michelle and cross my arms over the counter. "Wait, don't you have school?"

"Pro-D day. Four-day weekend." She grins wryly, and her eyes sparkle at the mention of the glorious weekend.

"Nice." *And weird. I never had any Thursdays off when I was in school.* "Who else is working? Just you?"

"Lex is upstairs, and Rose is in comics." Michelle points back past the shelves of books and memorabilia plastering the fake brick walls to where Rose stands, flipping through a comic book. Below her comic book lay even more collectibles, surrounding her in glass display cases. The back half of the store, the section that Rose is currently monitoring, holds all the comic books and posters. Michelle has graphic novels and knick-knacks today, all properties accompanying the till. There is always something new at Space Age to find, and more often than not, I end up buying it. My forty percent discount isn't exactly helpful in that matter.

I start back towards Rose, but Michelle calls over my shoulder, "Hey, I watched *Super 8* last night."

I pause in my tracks for a moment; Michelle likes to poke fun at me, but I don't mind. Out of all the people working here, all seven of us, *she's* the outcast. So, I just smile and keep on walking.

"Good morning, sunshine," Rose greets, just as I'm stepping across the unofficial threshold to the back of the store. The floor changes from lovely and fake wood to linoleum in the comic section. When given the price for the renovations, Lex insisted on only remodeling the front half of the store to save money. It's mostly what our clientele sees, and the comic book readers don't really care how the floor looks.

Rose glances up from the latest *Rocket Raccoon* comic book and softens her eyes, drawing a smirk to her crimson lips. "Were you in a hurry?"

"No." I instinctively touch my hair, which, after my shower, was thrown up into a bun. It's still damp, which is probably why I was so cold on my way here. Even my wool jacket couldn't help me. "Am I working with you or Michelle?"

"Michelle," Rose says, returning to casually flipping through her comic; she's only skimming over the pages, not actually reading what's written.

I allow my eyes to drift over to Michelle; she's still in high school, in her senior year, and I'm pretty sure the primary reason that she works here is that her boyfriend, Tag, begged her to. I've met him a few times, and he's, surprisingly, quite the geek. Before I met him, I'd pegged her boyfriend as an athletic type who wasn't too keen on the intellectual side of school, considering all of my and Michelle's conversations tend to lead to the last party she was at.

I barely know Mike and Lin, considering I've worked with both of them maybe half a dozen times. They take all the same classes in university, so they only ever work together, as their schedules are very strict. Edward, Miles, and Kami are all fine, too. I've worked with my co-workers long enough to like them, and get to know them, but I'm not sure if I would call them my friends.

Except maybe Rose. And Lex. Maybe. They're not my friends like Tiffany, my high school best friend, but I suppose they are friends.

Rose, if I had to choose, is my favourite staff member, other than Lex. Rose is easy to talk to, and she doesn't take the job too seriously. She understands working retail.

"Go sign in with Lex," Rose adds, waving her free hand in the air, towards the technical second floor. It's more of a loft than anything.

I sneak past a few of the bookshelves until I'm at the stairs, and then creak up every single one. No matter how light a touch I might be, my shoes always pound, groan, and snap on these steps, like they're going to give away and collapse. I comfort myself with the fact that they're far too well built for that. Hopefully, anyway.

The upstairs, to the public, is merely a small balcony hung over the edge of the comic book section, and it holds records and postcards and still frames from movies. They used to be organized and tidy but have long been messed up. Lex used to let me re-organize them every week, but he eventually made me stop because it would take too long to do it properly.

I knock twice on the equally stable, equally sketchy door before accepting my unspoken invitation inside. From the public eye, the balcony begins and ends within the fifteen by six space, but there is a hidden office behind the camouflaged door; Lex has plastered the door with postcards, so much that at first glance, it merely looks like a wall. Except for the doorknob.

"Afternoon, Raleigh." Lex is facing my way, his eyes stuck on his computer screen. His office is always a mess; we once tried to clean it but got distracted by every photograph or postcard we found, and we conveyed a hearty discussion for each. We got through about eight topics before giving up on the room. "Did Michelle tell you she watched *Super 8*?"

I chuckle, shutting the door, and take a few steps towards Lex's desk, avoiding the scattered papers on the ground. "Is this suddenly national news?"

Lex smirks, shaking his head. He removes his hand from the computer mouse, his smile faltering just slightly, but returns even brighter as he strokes his four-day-old beard. "She was just so excited about it. She said her boyfriend made her watch it, but she really liked it."

"It was pretty good…" I stand next to Lex, waiting until he moves his old, broken, missing-a-wheel desk chair so I can sign in on the computer, but instead, he just hands me a clipboard.

"Computer's down," he says, shaking his hastily made sign-in sheet at me; his lines aren't even straight. "It's twelve fifty-five." I jot down my name and the time, and then hand the sheet back to Lex. "It's been down since yesterday since you asked. I can't figure it out."

"Just call somebody." I loop back around his desk to the corner of the room where all the employees dump their bags and coats, and I follow suit. I slide out of my jacket and toss it over my red cross-body, accidentally blanketing everyone's belongings. Lex has, allegedly, been meaning to put in some shelving unit here but has never gotten around to it.

"No…" I turn to Lex, expecting him to say more, but he just shakes his head and rolls his right shoulder, resisting the urge to give it a slight massage.

I find it hard to believe he's my boss sometimes. I'm fairly certain that all the customers who come in think Rose is the boss. Lex is a great manager, a fantastic boss, and a very lenient, accommodating person, but Rose still manages to capture the vibe that he can't quite grasp. She just has that look, even being ten years younger than him.

"Did you try turning it off and on again?" Before Lex can do anything further than send me a death glare from behind his desk, I scamper out of his office, shutting his door behind me.

I skip back down the steps to meet up with Rose again, to let her know she can probably get away with leaving now, but find her otherwise occupied with a customer.

"Let me know if you need anything," she says to the disinterested thirty-something man browsing through the *Fantastic Four* comic books.

"I'm just trying to find a present," he mumbles so quietly that I'm not entirely sure if he's talking to Rose, or himself.

Rose turns to me, now ignoring the customer, and asks, "Are you my relief?"

"Yeah," I reply with a decent amount of certainty. "Lex will just let you off." Lex is usually pretty relaxed with an extra few minutes here and there.

"Then I guess I'm off! I'll see you later."

Rose makes her break for the stairs and runs the rest of the way up to Lex's office. After only a few seconds of her absence, and my taking her place behind the glass cases, the man picking through the comic books checks his watch, and then makes his break for the door. He strides all the way through the store, not pausing to look at anything else, not even when Michelle calls, "have a good one."

I'm guessing lunch break.

Once Rose is back downstairs, her coat on and her bag strewn over her shoulder, she offers Michelle and me a curt goodbye.

I spend the next hour organizing the counter space, the comics within said counters, the t-shirts on the nearby racks and shelves, and a few of the figurines behind me. We have some handmade, specially crafted figures from a ton of different graphic novel and comic book characters, all of which cost well over a hundred dollars. They're collectibles; Space Age is known for that sort of thing.

Michelle has been keeping her silence, reading a novel she plucked from the shelf. However, even from the back of the store, where her features are blurred and fading, I can tell that she is disinterested. She keeps toying with the same few strands of hair in between her index and middle finger, twirling and entwining them around and around, and then smoothly swiping her fingers free, all at once. Her eyes begin to shift all around the store, scanning our different graphic novels and action figures. Losing yourself in the store is easy.

The bell dangling over the glass door rings as the door swings open, and Michelle greets our first customer of the hour. I can feel the air surrounding her fill with relief; she now has a reason not to be reading the suggestively un-entertaining novel. As far as I know, she's never been the kind of person to invest herself in these kinds of fantasy books.

"Hi there," she chimes sweetly, her high voice travelling throughout the building. I can hear the man asking Michelle something, as she slides her graphic novel further away from her, down the counter, but I'm not sure what he wants until, "Oh, comics are in the back."

He mumbles again; I assume he thanked her.

The man, reaching a height of at least six feet tall, saunters across the threshold into the back. He looks familiar, so I'm guessing he's been here a few times before.

"Can I help you find anything?"

"Um…" The man approaches me and leans on the glass case; I know that the glass is rather sturdy, and the shelves would not break under that kind of pressure, but I still get nervous at the thought of them shattering. "I'm looking for the new *Superior Spider-Man*."

"Oh, that comes out on Monday." I reach behind me, looking for my clipboard, and continue, "We can put one on hold for you and call you when we get it in."

"That'd be great." I draw my board out from inside a shelf, along with a pen, and wait until he says his name. "Darren Larrgo...six, oh, four...two, nine, five...seven, six, seven, nine."

"Seven, six, seven, nine," I repeat back to him. I place the pen down and meet his olive eyes with a smile. "All right, Mr. Larrgo, we'll call you on Monday."

"Thank you so much," he says with a stiff smile and begins to waltz towards the front of the store.

Within a moment, the store returns lifeless again.

Space Age is never busy on a Thursday afternoon; it gets more energetic in the evenings, and actually quite packed on the weekend, but I hardly work weekends, anyway. Most of the staff go to school, so I'm one of the few available during the week. I don't go to college, though I've been debating taking an astronomy class during the summer. I wouldn't say that I don't know what I want to do because I do. There are just too many ideas.

Part of me, a large part of me, would like to work here forever, or at least for another few years. I enjoy working here. I enjoy retail work. I have almost a year's worth of rent saved up in my bank account, which has been my plan before moving out for a long time. I can support myself on the paychecks I get now if I'm really "thrifty," but I also have that extra cash in case I need it. And this plan doesn't even include a roommate.

Maybe I could make it work.

I suppose my biggest passion, apart from master UFO spotter, is writing. I write down all my experiences with the third kind, and even write sub-stories, with theoretical backgrounds to each of the spaceships I see. My imagination likes to run wild; I'd love to be an author someday, preferably fiction. I have dozens of short stories taking up space on my laptop, ranging from romance to horror. What can I say? I like to imagine, and the possibilities are endless. It's the common denominator between all my passions.

As I'm daydreaming about the future, potential roommates or even just living alone, and having Space Age there to support my writing career, Lex finds his way back downstairs. He approaches me, all the while waving Michelle over. She bounds to Lex's side, her hands on her hips, and sways back and forth.

"What's up, Lex?"

"Computer news," Lex responds, starting out by locking eyes with Michelle and then gazes over to me. "It turns out the update is crashing our computer. So, we'll be manual for a while."

Michelle, puzzled, almost presses for more information, but thinks better of it. Instead, she asks a different question. "How long until it's fixed?"

Lex shrugs. "A few days tops. Internet is still working fine, everything else is working fine," he clenches his fists mid-air, "except this god damn program." He narrows his eyes at me. "And yes, I tried turning it off and on again."

I chuckle to myself, staring down at my scuffed Chucks, and then meet Michelle's still dazed eyes. She suddenly smiles, forgetting her brief lapse in memory, and says, "Maybe it's aliens."

"Yeah, maybe," Lex replies, without an ounce of hesitation. He brushes his hand back and forth across his head a few times, fluffing up what short hair he has left, and slights his body towards me. "Maybe one of those guys from Roswell."

"Do you think Roswell happened?" I still find that I have my doubts about Roswell. I'm not inclined to believe that it was merely a government drone, or whatever they want to call it, that crashed down there, but...I still find myself a little skeptical. It's not that I doubt alien existence; it's that I'm not sure this was an instance.

"I do," Lex answers matter-of-factly, now arching his back. He's not very tall, only standing at around five foot eight on a good day, but compared to a five foot three Michelle, he might as well be six foot four. He looks far less impressive next to me; I can't be more than two inches shorter than him. "Have you seen that interview? The one with the man who worked in the CIA back in the fifties, he saw the Roswell interview tape?"

"No, I haven't," I say, trying to remember all of Lex's words. It's something I'm going to be looking into once I get home. "When was it put out?"

"It was made a while ago, but it's only going viral now.

Compelling stuff, you should check it out. You believe in what happened now?"

I shrug, unsure of what to say. "I'm...not really sure."

Lex stares me dead in the eyes, his eyes darkened by how serious he is. "This will settle it. It happened."

"Um..." Michelle mutters meekly, staring absentmindedly at one of the comic books within the glass casing. "What's Roswell?"

Lex shifts his eyes back towards Michelle, appearing less impressed and more shocked by the second. "You've never heard of Roswell?" She shakes her head, glancing at me for help. My eyes merely travel back to Lex, my hands beginning to play with the elastic bracelet I have wrapped around my right wrist. It's a bracelet that I usually take off every night, but sometimes I just forget; it was a present from Tristan. There's a silver engraving tied onto the thick, black bands, reading the date Tristan and I first got together. "It was a flying saucer crash in 1947. With other life forms on board, not humans."

"Like, aliens?" Michelle purses her upper lip, unconsciously raising her left eyebrow. She drums on her unseasonably tanned arm with her fingers to the sound of the Superman clock; she's apparently a skeptic.

"Yeah, like aliens."

Michelle, quite badly, refrains from rolling her eyes, and a grin screens across her lips. "Do you actually believe in aliens? Like, actually?"

Lex, much like Michelle just a minute earlier, thinks better of it and stops himself before sneering back with a smart remark, and solely focuses on me, his unspoken favourite of the two of us. "Well, Mulder, looks like we got a Scully on our hands."

"What?"

"*X-Files*," I offer, but her bewilderment does not waver. She only blinks a few times before cutting eye contact.

Lex, now taking his turn to very badly refrain from rolling his eyes, whirls around on his heels and makes towards the front end of the store. Two o'clock is when he empties the cash register for the first time of the day, taking most of the money made up to the safe upstairs. He's paranoid about thieves and tends to take extra safety precautions.

I smile softly at Michelle's gentle blush as she asks, ensuring that Lex is out of earshot, "What's *The X-Files*?"

I feel like her boyfriend has already explained to her what *The*

X-Files is, and we do have some of their posters and t-shirts in here, but I still clarify, "it's a TV show about two FBI agents. One of them believes in aliens, and the other doesn't. That's Mulder and Scully. Mulder, the one who does believe, always says, 'the truth is out there.'"

"Like, the truth about aliens and stuff?" I nod. Michelle bites her lip and takes a step closer, visually concerned about Lex hearing her. She doesn't talk about it much, but I know it bothers her when she doesn't understand Lex's references. "Do you, um..." she clears her throat, "do you really believe in aliens?"

"You don't?" The words escape from my mouth before I even realize it. The word "alien" always seemed a little strange to me, but there are only so many words I can use. Martian? Extraterrestrial?

"I don't know," Michelle snaps back, avoiding eye contact. "It just seems kind of...scary." That idea has crossed my mind before but doesn't tend to stay for very long. I've never been afraid of their possibilities, but I could be confusing the feeling of fear with exhilaration. "Tag really believes in aliens, I know that." She cracks a smile, forgetting about her troubles from just a moment ago. Lex returns to us, clutching dearly onto an envelope filled with most of the cash within the store. He pauses near Michelle and me, probably hearing the word "alien" come out of her mouth. "He thinks they're going to take over the planet. It's crazy."

"Is it?" Lex chimes in, startling Michelle as she whips around to confront the voice behind her. He smirks, climbing a few of the stairs, and then pauses once again, ignoring Michelle's slightly embarrassed gaze. "Have a good shift, ladies. And remember," he smirks, arching an eyebrow just so, and subconsciously rolls his right shoulder, even shifting his neck along with it. His eyes widen as he bids us a final farewell, in a hushed whisper, "the truth is out there."

Chapter 3

The drive from my house to Tiffany's lasts a swift twenty minutes. On a good day when there's no traffic, or in the middle of the night when I hit all the lights, I can even make it in about twelve or thirteen, but it's only eight o'clock at night. Some people are still driving home from work.

I've driven to Tiffany's so many times now that at this point, the drive feels like nothing. Tiffany has driven to my house once or twice, but she can't do much with a learner's license. Not without her parents in the car.

I arrive outside of her 3-story dwelling a little later than anticipated, and I lock the bulky van into park; I text Tiffany to come outside. My fingers tap on top of the dashboard, my arms straining to reach as far as the front window, and my eyes drift off.

I was supposed to hang out with Tristan tonight. He called at seven, the time he said he'd call to finalize our plans, and then told me he had to take a rain check. He apparently has a huge test tomorrow, and has barely studied for half of the material, and needs the night. We agreed he'd make it up to me on Sunday; neither of us have school or work on Monday. I called Tiffany afterwards, and she just so happened to have the night free too, a rarity for her.

She suddenly appears at the side of the car, tugging her way inside. "Hey."

"Hey." I start the ignition and drive off down Tiffany's street, reaching the cul-de-sac at the end of the road instead of pulling a U-turn.

"So, what do you want to do?" Tiff asks, giving me a kind and generous look, the one that's always floating about in her eyes.

"I don't know. Anywhere you want to go?"

"Not really..." She purses her lips and then drops her head back onto the headrest. "I could go for some coffee, though."

I nod, taking a sharp right towards our usual coffee place, faithful Tim Horton's.

Tiff and I cruise through the drive-thru, ringing up our usual order of one coffee, one hot chocolate, and two donuts, and then Tiffany offers, "Want to just go talk somewhere?"

Neither Tiff nor I have been huge into the party scene, so us eating junk food and talking *is* our party scene.

"Sure," I reply and begin to take us up Maple Mountain.

Maple Mountain is probably my favourite place in the entire world. It's not a long drive from civilization, but feels endless along the terribly paved road, surrounded by gnarling trees and overgrown berry bushes. There's the occasional coyote or deer, even last week I saw a skunk, but most of the time there are only dark creatures of the imagination. I used to come up here alone, but I found myself driving up here with Tristan one day, and since then, it's become my go-to spot. It's where the whole ordeal with Denton happened.

After the rough stretch of road leading up to the peak, I park in the surprisingly empty parking lot. There tends to be at least a few scattered cars parked about, but there isn't even one tonight.

I switch off the engine but turn on the interior lights, so that Tiff and I can see what we're eating and drinking. We both take the lids off our too hot drinks.

"So, what's new?" Tiffany asks, almost daring to take a sip of her pure black coffee, but thinks better of it when she remembers the cream and sugar given to her.

"Nothing, really," I respond mindlessly, unable to help but search the star-speckled sky. I have been here many times since, but I can't help but be constantly reminded of what happened six months ago. I can't believe Tristan's shitty car managed to drag an entire spotlight up here; I didn't think we'd be able to fit everything we needed in the back seat. "You?"

"Nothing too interesting." Tiffany turns to me, her deep brown hair tousled around her taut cheeks. "Weren't you supposed to hang out with Tristan tonight?"

"He had to study."

Tiffany chuckles, facing forward again, but rests her eyes on her donut. "Yeah, midterms are this week." She takes a bite. "I finished my last one yesterday." She struggles to swallow rapidly, and when she does, she says, "I can't wait to get this semester over with. Working, even just a few shifts a week is not very fun. I can't wait to have the summer off to work, I'll actually earn a decent amount of money." I honestly don't know how Tristan and Tiff find the time or energy to work and go to school; working is plenty enough for me.

"More money, that'll be nice. You'll have a very nice summer." I take a bite of my donut.

"That's the plan," she chuckles. "Unfortunately, the more money I make, the more I'll have to save for school next year." Tiffany pays for about half of her schooling, with her parents paying for the other half. They had a bit of money trouble a few years ago, and couldn't afford to deposit money every month into Tiff's school fund. They bought a townhouse when Tiff was fourteen, and their landlord stuck them with a lot of unmentioned repairs. It wasn't an enjoyable time for any of them.

"At least you don't have to worry about rent, that's a plus."

Tiff laughs, finishing the last little bit of her snack. "Yeah, oh, my gosh. I'm so grateful that my parents haven't started charging me rent yet."

"Me too. I don't even go to school, but I'd have a lot less money to put into savings if my dad charged me rent…" I'm going to board the rent-free train as long as I can; I'm sure it'll end soon, but for now, I'll ride with it until the end.

"Yeah," Tiff mutters, her eyes darting all around the night sky. It's filled with clouds, so there isn't much in the way of stars to focus on, but Tiffany can't seem to focus on anything for more than a few seconds. Out of nowhere, she cracks a smile, opening her eyes with a blissful gleam within them. "Just a few more months. Then I'll get my break."

One of the things that I admire about Tiffany is that she can instantly pick herself back up. Even when she's venting about a class or some guy, at the end of the conversation, she always finds a way to motivate herself back into positivity. It's a commendable quality.

"This summer will be great," I reply, perpetuating the zeal. "Maybe we'll go on that road trip we talked about in high school."

"Wouldn't that be nice," she fantasizes. "A few years late, but better late than never."

"Better to actually have money to spend at the mall..." I notice a dozen lights dotting a wave in the sea of darkness, too low to be in the sky, and I get lost in the scenery. There's another mountain way bigger than Maple Mountain, covered in snow and decorated with ski lifts and chalets, where the lights are always on, and still visible from miles around. Thinking it over, I don't think there's been a time at night that I have not been able to see those shining bulbs.

"Oh, definitely. If we went then, we wouldn't be able to buy anything." Tiffany draws me back to the prospect of our potential road trip to West Edmonton Mall. It's no more than a twelve-hour drive from here and has hundreds of stores, not to mention an entire amusement park inside. Considering most of our high school afternoons were spent at a mall, a supermall would be a dream come true. Tristan and I ended up going after a few weeks of dating.

"Very true..." My phone vibrates in my purse, quiet enough that Tiff doesn't even hear it. I draw my cell out and take a peek at the text message that I had already figured out was from my father, bidding me a good night. I stow the phone back into my purse and unconsciously reach for my hot chocolate.

"Is that the north star?"

I follow Tiffany's now pointing finger, her print pressed up against the windshield, all the way to a bright dot, not too far from the moon. I need a moment to process the abrupt subject change.

"Actually, I think that's Venus," I answer casually, drumming my fingers on my slowly cooling cocoa.

"Seriously?" Tiffany leans back into her seat as I nod, and she drops her hands down by her sides. "You should look into astronomy classes. You'd probably really like it."

I chuckle carelessly. "Maybe. I was never good at memorizing things, though."

"I think you'd enjoy it. And I bet you'd do fine, especially with just one class, you'd have lots of time to study." Studying and I differ quite a bit; I'm not sure we ever really spoke in high school. "I mean, if you want. School does kind of suck."

"I have thought about it...maybe one day."

"Have you talked to Tristan about it?"

"No. I want to figure out what I want to do first." Tristan is a very supportive person, but I also know that he will pump me full of information that I won't know what to do with. I like to work on my own.

"Makes sense. How's Tristan doing, anyway? Still taking history, right?"

"Yep," I say. I readjust my seat, fidgeting with the levers until I'm in the prime position of seeing a few of the constellations, the moon, and Venus, and rest my hands on my stomach, palms flat on my gut. I try to push away the insecurities.

"I was always so bad at history," she notes, following my lead, and positioning her seat like mine.

"Me too." I find it ironic that my boyfriend is literally taking classes to become a teacher to teach my most hated subject. I always found it interesting, hearing about the wars and scandals of years passed, but it was taught in the most mind-numbingly dull fashion. The only reason I passed was because Tristan tutored me.

"How is work going, anyway?" I ask, realizing that I had yet to ask about her. Unlike myself, Tiffany has been working at the same place for three years now; I need more change than that. Space Age is the longest I've worked anywhere.

"It's okay. I only work a couple of times a week, which is great for school, but not so great for money." She finishes the last of her donut and takes a sip of her coffee. "Mm!" She makes an abrupt sound and rushes to swallow her drink. "Did I tell you about Kevin?"

"No," I say cautiously. "Wait, I think you mentioned some group project with a guy named Kevin. Is that him?"

"Yes, that's him! For English. Some report on this collection of short stories, we each read a story, write a report on it, read each other's reports, and then find something they all have in common. It's fascinating, I think you'd like some of the stories." Tiffany waves her hands in the air, giving her head a little toss. "Anyway. A couple of days ago, Kevin started hitting on me?"

"Really?!" I grin, holding my hands together on my lap. "Is he nice?"

"He's…a little odd. He actually asked me out."

"Did you say yes?" I blurt out. "Is he cute?"

"Oh, just wait." She chuckles, and even in this forgiving light, I detect faint signs of a blush. "I said no. Because he did this to another girl in our group, Mariah, he became fixated on her for like two days, asked her out, and when she said no, he moved onto me. Before Mariah, there was some girl named Liz."

"Oh."

Tiffany laughs at my disappointment; I know that she is perfectly happy to be single, and I was too, before Tristan, but I also want her to have a boyfriend that completely spoils her. She deserves it and much more than I do.

"Well, I don't blame you for saying no, then," I joke.

"Yeah, I'd rather have a guy who actually wants me, not just a girlfriend in general."

"Makes sense to me." *Good. She deserves that.*

The rest of our night flies by in a flash; we talk some more about Tristan, about university, about the future. The history teacher, the business major, and the dreamer. It appears in my head like a map, laid out before me with different coloured roads and options. There are so many things I want to do, but it all comes back to writer. I'd have to be a damn good writer if I wanted any sort of sustainable profit.

Tiffany tells me about her family and how they're doing, which is perfectly fine. Every second Wednesday night, they have dinner with one of their neighbours, but Tiffany doesn't usually end up making it. Her sister is graduating from high school this year.

A few cars come and go from the mountain until it is only Tiff and me once again. When the overwhelming absence of life becomes too noticeable, we decide to call it a night.

I offer her another snack, but she graciously declines, placing her hand on her belly; I'm stuffed, too. We drive home in near silence.

I park in front of Tiffany's townhouse and finally check the clock nestled into the dashboard; 2:14.

"It was good to see you," Tiff chimes, lazily sliding out of her seat. She rests one hand on the passenger side door and places her other hand upon the door frame. She smiles in my general direction, her eyes drifting shut. She doesn't handle being tired as well as I do. "Thank you again for the ride."

"No problem. It was good to see you too." We've come a long way from our high school days of seeing each other five days a week.

"Good night." Her slow smile turns blissful as she presses the door shut, giving it two pats before whirling around on her heels and shuffling back towards her house.

I wait a few moments until she's located her key in her small yellow purse, and when she's safely inside the house, I tear off down the street.

My favourite part about driving at night is driving home. I speed down the streets, keeping my eyes peeled for any wildlife about to hop in front of the van, blast the heat, and play my favourite mix of songs. The nights aren't quite complete without the pleasant drive home. The solitude soothes me.

The ride back home never quite feels like enough once I get there, though. I creep the van into the driveway, slowly inching forward until I'm as close as I think I'm going to get without hitting the garage door.

I park the beast of a vehicle, yank on the emergency brake, and slide the key from its slot. I open my door, only to be confronted and slightly startled by the sound of harsh beeping; I switch off the headlights.

Once back inside the safety my home I, for the second time, hit the lock button for the van. Even when I know I've locked it the first time, I always lock it a second time. My mild disorder really kicks in at night.

My shoes slide off my feet as I step carefully out of them, and I kick the pair aside, close to the front door.

I habitually flick on the entrance light, ignoring the glaring outdoor bulb. My dad always ends up turning it off in the morning. I switch on and off lights as I make my way through the house, but upon reaching the stairs, I find that there's enough light coming from Dad's office to see my way up without tripping.

When I first step onto the landing, it creaks so loud I can hear my father, in turn, squeal his desk chair in an effort to listen more carefully to what is just beyond his door. I rap gently on the wooden frame and nudge it open with my knuckles.

"Hi," I chime, barely stepping inside.

"Hey, Raleigh," he says, barely taking but a moment to glance up from his laptop. He continues clacking on his keyboard, and I take it upon myself to enter.

The walls of the office leading to my father's desk are lined with shelves and shelves of books, most of them being just for show. A few years ago, I had made it my mission to read all the books in his office, but I settled on just getting through a single shelf; most of the collection is academic, and there's not much room for creativity when concisely presenting facts. The library does contain some fictitious pieces, a few classics, and the occasional "steps to success" guides, but it's been a long time since I've even picked up a book. Mine and my father's tastes don't tend to match.

The back wall, which my dad has carefully planned his entire scheme around, has two tall windows, overlooking our gnarled mess of a forested backyard. He keeps the deep wine curtains shut most of the time, to cut out the sunlight from reflecting off his laptop, desk lamp, and the few picture frames with still frames of moments.

Other than his walnut desk, intimidating by its stature and vibrant hue, and his small desk chair, of tacky gray fabric, there is no other furniture in the room. He keeps planning on putting two chairs in front of his desk, should the need for someone to talk to him face to face in his office, but he's never gotten around to it. It's quite empty, but it feels full with all the books inside.

"Did you just get in?"

"Yeah," I mutter, striding towards the desk. I stand near my dad and glance down at the report he's writing; they all look the same to me, though he's assured me that they differ significantly.

"Do you need the van tomorrow?"

"No, I'm good, thanks."

My dad doesn't tell me extensive details about his work, and frankly, I don't ask. I don't suppose that our relationship is strained, but I've never been close with the man. We exchange pleasantries, assure that the other is satisfied, and then we basically live our own lives. I always wondered if he held resentment for me because my mother got pregnant, had me, and then left him to raise me on his own.

Dad nods mindlessly, typing a few more words, and then pauses. He takes a deep breath, places one hand to his mouth, and then uses the other to scroll up through his report. "You should go to bed."

I chuckle, briefly startled by the feel of the drapes brushing my hand, and I take a step forward, letting my fingertips graze the smooth surface of the desk. I don't doubt that my father cares about me, I actually guarantee it, but something unspoken remains. He's never talked to me about my mom, and the few efforts I'd put in, he had shut down immediately. We never really talk about much of anything, I suppose. "You should too."

He grins curtly and then nods, sinking back in his chair. The small pillow he uses to realign his back shifts as he leans back, reaching his hands above his head. "Yeah, I should..." With one arm extended, he scratches his head, feeling his receding hairline, and continues to stare at his laptop.

As he straightens up, the lateness of the night begins to hit me, and I make my way back towards the door. I don't work tomorrow, so I don't have to be up early, but I really should start going to bed earlier. I just don't know how to approach it... "'Night, dad."

"Goodnight," he responds, almost immediately resuming typing after I'd bid goodnight. I pull the door shut behind me on my way out; he usually leaves it open just a crack, but I always make a habit of shutting it when I'm going to bed. He never seems to mind.

My feet take me to my petite bathroom located just outside of my room, and I begin my usual routine; wash my face, brush my teeth, floss, mouthwash, count to sixty, and then stare myself in the eye, as if I'm staring at Life itself. During those sixty seconds, it's like the entire world has completely stopped. There's only me, this mounted mirror, and endless possibilities. It's an extensive regime, and probably the most relaxed part of my day. It always gets me in the mood to dream.

After the routine prep, I stumble my way into my room, out of my clothes, and into the first pajamas I can find in my drawers. Shutting my door, I slip into my bed and close my eyes.

I fall asleep to the moments of tonight echoing through my head, Tiff's soft voice, the desolation of the night sky, the possibilities that lie within. I can feel myself slowly losing consciousness, and my thoughts begin to wander around in my infinite mind, dancing, and spinning, and celebrating. I'm asleep within seconds, with a small grin stuck on my lips.

Chapter 4

Tristan and I have been silent for a solid twelve minutes. He's been typing away, finishing the last of his history paper on "The Most Influential Historian of the 19th Century," while I've been gazing up at his white ceiling. I don't want to interrupt him while he's writing; I know how important this paper is to him, as he's spent the past three weeks working on it, and I also know how hard it can be to get into even a decent writing zone. So, I glaze on.

"I'm almost done," he reassures, breaking the silence, but I'm not too focused on the background noise of his fingers tapping on the keys, nor the time that has passed.

After the lovely walk here, the icy winter weather travelling alongside me, I took it upon myself to enter Tristan's house, knowing he wouldn't yet be finished his paper. His front door is usually unlocked until his parents get home. I've been lying in his lumpy bed since I arrived, staring at the popcorn ceiling. The bumps and curves stretching across the top of the room almost look like they could be their own universe.

"Okay." Tristan sighs, drawing my eyes to his relieved smile. He shuts his laptop and then swivels his chair to face me. "Done."

I smile, kicking my legs over the side of his double bed, and I grip onto the edge of his mattress. "Yeah?" He nods, standing. "That's awesome. I bet it's great."

Tristan continues to nod, taking two long strides towards me before stopping in between my dangling legs. He places his hands on my cheeks, leans down, and presses his lips to mine. Slowly, he leans me further backwards, placing one knee by my hip, and lays me down on his bed. His body hovers above, gently releasing more and more of his weight on top of me.

I swirl my tongue around with Tristan's as his hands begin to lightly stroke my sides, shocking me with his cool fingertips once he's beneath my shirt.

In a moment of separation, he slips off my knit, and then his tee, tossing them behind him onto his silent carpet.

Our jeans are soon to follow.

Before I can even remind Tristan to grab a condom, he draws away, my teeth accidentally nipping at his lip from the surprise of him suddenly reaching towards his dresser. He fumbles for a few seconds, snatching one of the condoms from the box in his dresser drawer, and then turns back to me.

He smiles. "Were you going to say something?"

I bite my lip, eager to have him back in my arms, and I latch onto his shoulders, crumbling him down on top of me.

We slowly shift on the bed to fit more accordingly, now lying lengthwise with the sheets, and push most of his pillows out of our way, leaving just one for me. He jerks suddenly, gasping away upon feeling my hand through his boxers. With a quick grin, he's back at it again, this time more passionately with his hands everywhere at once. In turn, I let out a small huff with Tristan's touch. He always seemed to know perfectly well what he was doing down there and doesn't hesitate to tease me to the fullest extent possible.

He snakes his fingers onto the hips of my panties, and he tugs them off me, finally tossing them onto the carpet beside his bed. His fingers explore around, feeling for the right spot, and once he notices my body clench, he dives right in.

"Hey," I joke, gripping tightly onto his forearms. He shakes them off, giving me a quick kiss.

"I gotta get you warmed up," he whispers and kisses my forehead. He reaches behind my back and unhooks my bra in one swift movement, a rarity for him. "And besides, I think you like it."

He slips two fingers inside of me, and I chuckle, tingling. I try to think of some witty retort, but all I can see to do is shake my head and bite my lower lip. My eyes drift shut, and Tristan continues to make me feel good, and occasional fight off my wandering hands; he usually tends to leave me helpless, though.

It's not very long before I'm begging him to hurry up and put the damn condom on. Straddling me, he reaches over next to me and snatches the golden package. He tosses it onto my bare body, and I sneer, glaring at him while he strips down to nothing. He drops his boxers down to the floor. He's already hard, something I felt several times, and he holds out one hand. He's about to ask for the condom, but instead, he cups both of my breasts in his palms, rubbing them gently.

"Here," I laugh, throwing the wrapped condom at him. "Hurry up."

He smirks, a wicked look in his eyes, and rips open the contraceptive standing between me and pregnancy. Neither of us are even close to wanting that.

The first time we had sex was in his bed, like this, his naked body on top of mine, hands sliding all over as we kissed, while he prepared himself. He knew that it was my first time.

He kisses me a little more, mounting more comfortably in between my thighs. He draws his lips away, my teeth grazing his skin, and adjusts his position over me. He meets my eyes, a habit of his, ensuring that I'm doing all right.

I smile.

He easily slips inside of me, his hands just by my ears. Seconds turn to moments to minutes, his hips thrusting steadily to pick up the pace.

My hands fidget with themselves until they settle on his waist, my arms supporting his frame. I suck my lips together, and then exhale, releasing a tightly drawn in breath.

"Oh," I moan to myself.

Tristan begins to groan, his momentum grows and wavers slightly, and he pushes harder, deeper, taking the breath right out of my mouth.

"Oh," I repeat. "Oh..."

My teeth dig into my lips, my toes curl, my palms begin to produce sweat as I draw closer and closer to my climax. My hips tingle, his body rushing, more rapidly now.

My mouth opens, and my hands clench against his skin even further, my body nearly useless.

I let out a small gasp, and in an instant, my body rushes with relaxation, and my eyes rip open.

Euphoria floods through me all at once, and the tension snaked within my fingers and toes releases.

I peek over at Tristan, who is possibly unaware of my immense pleasure. He doesn't notice my subtle tilted head, my eyes meeting his own closed greens. Small beads of sweat line his hairline, and as one of the few falls, he glances down at my breasts, watching them briefly before pushing harder into me, locking both of our eyes shut.

I gasp again, the euphoria lasting, and I feel when Tristan comes. From the corner of my eye, I see his mouth gaped slightly, and his eyes squeeze shut. He grunts slightly, still pushing, and I place one of my hands on his warm back, feeling his shoulder flex. Instinctively, his hand presses down on my hip, but he quickly slides it down to my thigh, where he wanted it to land. He squeezes tightly, and firmly pulls my leg higher up, adjusting himself a little better. I tense my thighs tighter around his own, feeling his smooth skin stroke against mine.

To my surprise, he kisses beside my lips, missing by just an inch or two. He groans again after the butterfly peck, and he accelerates, keeping the elation within me further, letting me hold on for a little longer.

Just a little longer...

The tingles begin to fade, and the calmness sets in once Tristan slows down, and once he finally meets my eyes.

We smile.

Tristan pulls out, and rolls over me, flopping onto the space on the bed next to me. Almost immediately, I sit up, and in one smooth motion, I swing my legs over the side of the mattress and plop onto my feet. I hand him the box of tissues from his nightstand and make my way to his bathroom. After I'm done, I sneak under his blankets, familiarity returning to me, as he's tidying up the last of our intimacy. Despite the warmth radiating from Tristan, my body still feels thrills, and the sheets from our warm bodies only give me more.

Tristan slips off the bed and into his bathroom, disposing of the tissues; he's always a bit paranoid of his parents finding a condom wrapper and a thousand tissues in the trash, even though we're both confident that they know we're having sex. He gets more worried about that kind of stuff than I do. Tristan returns from his brief bathroom visit, and even though he's just seen my naked body, I habitually pull the covers up over my breasts, no longer exposing myself. He smiles, approaching me again, and places a lingering kiss on my lips, keeping his hands on my rosy cheeks.

"Did you...?"

I nod quickly, avoiding eye contact for a second. I wish I could say that he didn't need to ask, but that is most certainly not always the case. "Yeah. And,"

"Oh, yeah." I know I don't need to ask him. He chuckles mildly and kisses me again until we both hear a small beep coming from behind him. I peer around him, and he sighs, produces a small frown. "Sorry." He makes his way to his dresser and snatches a pair of pajama pants from his top drawer, and then plops himself down at his desk, and opens his laptop. "This might be about the project." He turns to me on his chair, swaying mildly back and forth. "I'm sorry."

"It's okay." I smile. "It's due in, like, two days, right?"

He nods. "Yeah. One of the guys said he'd put it together and e-mail everyone when he's done."

"Well, that's good then, that you got an e-mail." I peer over a little, only able to sneak a small peek at his screen; I don't see much.

Tristan shakes his head, his focus returning to his laptop. His finger slides along the trackpad in rigid movements, his eyes darting to and from different points on the screen. "He also said he'd e-mail if he had any problems."

"Oh..." I clear my throat and look around Tristan's room. The walls are bare for the most part, unlike my bedroom, but he has a lot of filled bookshelves, half with books, half with trophies from years past or souvenirs from his many travels. There are also a couple little gifts that I'd bought him over the years for past birthdays, Christmases, and "just because" occasions. "Is it a problem?"

"I don't know," Tristan admits. "So far, he's saying that he's done it, but it's a long e-mail."

"What exactly is the project about?" I smirk, feeling a little more playful and teasing. "You know, there are paintings from hundreds of years ago that have UFOs in them. That's history, right?"

Tristan cracks a smile; me talking about aliens always makes him smile. He's probably been the most supportive person about my interest, never genuinely making fun of me, nor trying to make me feel weird about it. "Well, the project isn't about that," he says. "And actually, that would probably be for an art student." I giggle softly to myself and draw my knees up to my chest, hugging them out of the blankets. "When do you think you're gonna give that up?"

I take a few seconds to process what he's just asked, but I just don't understand. My head shifts back to him. "What?"

"The whole alien thing." The words fall smoothly from his

tongue and out of his mouth.

"What do you mean?" I sit up further, a sinking feeling rising in the pit of my stomach. I wait in the silence for only seconds, but feeling like hours, before finally insisting, "Tristan?"

"Sorry, Jeremy is just..." He sighs. "I don't get what he's saying. He thinks he might have done it wrong." Tristan double clicks on the trackpad, his eyes drifting from the bottom of the screen to the top, and he begins reading.

"What do you mean?" I speak more slowly, articulating each and every word. Tristan and I have only fought a handful of times, so he's unfamiliar with my current tone.

He turns to me, arching one eyebrow just so, and then breaks eye contact. He shrugs one shoulder. "I mean, obviously they weren't all..." He sighs, shaking his head, and then returns to his laptop. He continues reading, his eyes jerking with the formatted lines. "You don't believe they were all...not all of them."

"Well, maybe they weren't, but I believe they were." I've looked over my pictures, some more feeble than others, my memories, my mental notes, and I've made the deduction that, statistically, they probably weren't all something. But I still believe that they were. Because, looking back, I can't find any evidence of doubt on my part. I remember how I felt, how I'd even missed out on some pictures because I wanted to decide that is was something before wasting a picture on an airplane. That's the last thing I need, to have subtle airplane influences destroy my case even further; Denton would have a field day with that one.

"God," Tristan mutters, shaking his head, and he rolls his eyes.

I scoff, heart blazing now. It would seem as though my previous thoughts about his support were misguided. "Did you actually just roll your eyes?"

"At this, not you." He takes a deep breath and holds his hands firmly before him, and clenches his fists. "Raleigh, listen, I just really need to deal with this right now."

I take a deep breath, matching his own sighs of forced relaxation, and I sit cross-legged on his bed, still wrapped in his sheets and comforter. "I understand that. But I also need to deal with this."

He glances over his shoulder at me; his eyes look exhausted, physically and emotionally. However, the reason behind the fatigue, me or his classmate, I can't tell. I'm leaning towards a combination of the two. "What?" he asks, pressing me to go on.

I shrug, the feeling of being naked beneath his sheets sinking in a little more than it had before. "Tristan..." I'm not even sure where I'm going with this. My grip tightens on the cotton blankets. "Do you...I mean, do you not believe in,"

"I don't know what I believe," he interrupts, leaning back in his desk chair. His bare stomach pulses, his breaths becoming shorter and slightly more agitated. His hands lay limp on his thighs, and he waits, staring.

I bite my dry lip, immediately moistening it to keep from further peeling. "You don't need to believe anything. I didn't mean it like that. I just need to know that you respect what I believe..." As I'm talking, my voice now trailing off, Tristan turns back to his project. I try to hold back, but I blurt out, "And clearly, you don't."

"You know I do." Guilt jolts inside of me for starting an argument while he's working on a project, but I can't help it. I'm not the kind of person who can very easily hide emotions. Not when I'm upset, anyway.

"How is asking 'when are you going to give that up,' respecting my beliefs?" Tristan slides his chair closer to his desk, and I catch a glimpse of my pink bra lying on the floor, almost being run over by the wheels. His foot grazes it briefly, and his toes feel the silky fabric, and then he kicks it gently aside. "How you asked it seemed like you were asking some kid when he's going to stop believing in Santa."

"That's not how I meant it, Raleigh. I respect your beliefs, I do, I just..." He holds both of his hands up and signals to his screen, his jaw set with annoyance.

"You just..." I take another deep breath. Calm down, take it easy. "Have you always just thought that I'm...that it's..." I try to find the right words, and when I turn to Tristan to see if he understands, he's still fixed on his laptop.

"Forget it," Tristan mumbles, and once again, I'm not sure what he's referring to. Either way, hearing those words don't help. He grunts, shutting his laptop, and presses his hands against the top of it. The fan speeds up as the computer rushes to cool itself before going to sleep.

"Maybe I should go."

That captures his attention. He rests, his forearms now just above his knees, fingers locked together, eyes fixed on mine. They waver for a moment, as he nods, slowly, but then more quickly. "Okay.

If that's what you want."

It's not what I want, but I find myself nodding anyway. I've always known what people thought of me, how it's odd to have this fascination with the extraterrestrial life forms, how I'm considered one of "those" people; I suppose I never even considered that Tristan would feel that way about me. I almost feel naïve for believing that he wouldn't. It was never the biggest of deals for me, I wasn't teased or bullied too much about it, just the offhanded comment here or there. I've grown a thicker skin about it now that I've realized I'm alone in this. I'm more than certain that there are other believers, but I haven't been fortunate to meet any of them. I've learned to go at it alone.

Tristan plops down at the edge of his bed, seated only two feet beyond my body. He manages a smile.

I'm not entirely sure if I send one back.

I slowly get dressed, putting on my underwear, and then my bra. I wriggle into my skinny jeans, and lace the belt back through the loops, buckling it at the front. I scan around the room. "Do you know where...?"

Tristan stands up and takes a few steps until he's next to me. He searches the room with me, and then quickly points, finding my shirt curled up into a ball just under his desk. "I thought I felt something," he attempts to joke, his voice muffled from facing opposite to me. He holds my top out to me before hopping back up to his feet. "You have everything?"

"Yeah." My body feels cold and rigid, something that I don't like feeling around Tristan. I feel distant. I'm sure that tomorrow after I've slept on it, I'll feel better, but until then, I'll sulk in the distance.

Tristan walks me downstairs, hanging right behind me until we reach the first floor. He veers into the kitchen upon seeing my coat, and I work on slipping into my boots.

"Do you ever tie those?" Tristan asks, producing my jacket for me. I'm not sure if he's offering to help me put it on or not, but I grab it from his hands either way.

I stomp one foot into my boot, throw on my coat, and then step into the other. "No. Well, once." I point down to them; the laces are tied, but I never bother untying them or tying them back up again. They're big enough to slip on and off, and snug enough to remain comfortable.

Tristan chuckles, and I reach for the door. "Look, Raleigh,"

"It's okay," I nearly whisper, gazing past Tristan at his stairway, letting my eyes focus on nothing in particular. "Finish your project."

He switches his weight from one foot to the other. "I don't want you to leave mad."

"I'm not mad." It's true, I'm not.

"Then I don't want you to leave upset."

My eyes meet his again. I try to think of something to come back to that, but I don't have anything. I swallow, only now realizing how dry my throat is "If you finish your project by tomorrow, maybe we can talk."

"Yeah. Yeah, I'll be done by tomorrow."

I nod, taking a step towards the door. "Okay."

Tristan reaches past me, his firm arm grazing my body, and opens the door for me. Before I turn entirely away from him, he leans down, as if to kiss my lips, but I lower my head and look down even further. He kisses my forehead in such a fluid motion that I'm guessing that was what he meant to do. "I'll see you tomorrow."

I nod, plunging into the bitter night, and I face Tristan one last time before leaving. With a thick, visible breath, I let out, "Good night."

He bears his signature half smirk, one that he seldom uses, but when he does, he uses it well. "Good night."

An airplane overhead roars on by, snapping my head up to the sky, but only for a moment before I walk down Tristan's pathway to the sidewalk. I hear his door shut once I'm in front of the next house over.

I pause for a moment and take one last glimpse back behind me, seeing my boyfriend's locked door. I force myself to keep walking, despite what I want.

I'm not entirely sure whether or not that was even a fight, but it was certainly not something that I enjoyed.

I usually walk home from Tristan's house scanning all the houses on my way, memorizing more and more of the smaller and smaller details of each person's home, but this time my attention remains fixed on the sidewalk before me. I'm having a tough time concentrating on anything else.

Does he really feel that way? I shake my head to myself, sticking my now chilled hands into my pockets, tightening my fingers into a fist in hopes of trapping what little heat they have left. I know that people say things that they don't mean when they're stressed, and me adding to his pressure probably didn't help. The thought never occurred to me that Tristan didn't support me. It wasn't something we needed to talk about because the support is mutual.

At least, I think it is.

I feel around inside my pockets, tangling up my fingers within my headphones, and I decide to draw them out and listen to some music. I listen to the first song my phone plays for me.

I walk to the beat of the music, the pavement crawling by, each break meeting my every second or third step.

I exhale deeply into the night, still too quietly to hear over my music, and paw around for my phone. I shake it a little, hoping that it will vibrate and tell me that Tristan has texted or called, but nothing. I tend to unreasonably hope that he will come back after I push him away.

You are overthinking this, Raleigh. This will be solved tomorrow, anyway...

I stop in my tracks, not only my thoughts, but my feet come to a halt, too. The coolness of my skin suddenly hits me when I stand still, and it sinks deeper, now into my bones.

A few dead leaves leftover from the worst of winter hit my boots and skirt around, disappearing into the darkness beyond the reaches of the streetlamp. I tug one of my hands free of my pocket and hold it out; I don't feel any wind. I've hit the patch in the houses where the entire block is an empty grass plot, awaiting development, without a single home.

I find myself, beyond my conscious control, gazing into the sky, only to be interrupted by the blaring light of the lamp post.

I wince, squeezing my eyes shut once again; I've only made it a few minutes from Tristan's house, and I still have a decent walk ahead of me. At this point, the police station is closer than my house. Denton is only just another street down, and a few blocks down the first crossroad.

I hear a small whirring sound that suddenly turns into a blast of what has to be some sort of machine, operating loudly in the distance. My eyes shoot back open, but almost instantly, they've closed once again. Across the street at Lion's Park is a blinding light, beaming nearly a pure white, but with a subtle tint of blue.

My arm instinctively shields my eyes, and I stumble slightly backwards, my boots losing their grip on the concrete, but finding it once again on the firm dirt. I lower my arm just slightly in an attempt to understand what's going on. It's far too bright, and blue, to be any kind of car.

My eyes widen; it's far too big even to be a truck.

In one smooth motion, unblinking, I look from the ground, through a few feet of air, to a massive hovering object, the whirring sound growing rapidly. There's a gap of shadow in the light, but I can't tell what shape it's forming.

My jaw drops, tears now forming from the burning light, and the shadow grows larger and larger, almost as if it's coming closer. I don't realize how short my breaths are until my throat catches itself on one, and a small cough escapes.

A sizeable metallic oval, at least fifteen feet tall, reveals itself as the shadow, and the size of this floating entity sinks it; it can't be any smaller than thirty feet long, and that is a very rough estimate. The notion of an airplane enters my mind, but it quickly leaves. It's somewhere between an airplane and a flying disk, too broad to be the former, too long to be the latter.

Words desperately try to escape my lips, and my heart pounds in my chest. My headphones fall from my ears, and I jump at the even louder sound, and a high-pitched squeal disrupts my senses.

Something on this...*thing*...is moving, and I can see it moving towards me. A tear strikes my exposed hand, sending a shudder through my body.

And then, in a single subconscious moment of panic, feet planted to the grass, body unable to move, everything goes black.

Chapter 5

When I first wake up, I force myself to keep my eyes shut. I feel the brightness just beyond my eyelids, and so I keep them closed, hoping that if I turn over, away from my window, there will be enough darkness to sleep. I roll slightly, confronted with discomfort that my bed couldn't bring me.

I'm not in my bed.

I open my eyes, expectedly getting assaulted by the white February sky. The sun is hidden behind some purely white clouds, which are probably worse than a bright, sunny day. I keep my focus down lower, where it's darker, where all I can see is grass. Short stubs of browning grass that are in desperate need of some care. At least it didn't snow last night.

I tell myself that I need to get up, though I'm unsure of the urgency; I don't move for another minute. I finally thrust myself up, groaning slightly, gently resting my forearms on my bent-up knees.

After I fully adjust to the sudden brightness, my hand instinctively reaches for my phone in my coat pocket, but it's not there. I quickly scan the area and see my small brick a few feet away.

"Oh, fuck." I crawl over to it; the screen is smashed like it was thrown onto the ground, and my attached headphones have broken. I hold down the power button, avoiding the broken glass, wishing for it to turn back on, but it doesn't take; I can't say that I'm surprised.

I slide the remains back into my pocket and groan quietly as I pick myself up off the ground. My legs begin to wobble the instant that I put my weight on them, and I scramble for the lamp post to help me stay on my own two feet.

It's daytime now. *Last night...*

The reality of last night sinks in. Me and Tristan and our argument. I moan to myself again, wishing that I could've had a few more minutes to not remember the fight. Was it even a fight?

What happened after the argument flashes back to my memory. Walking home, stopping, feeling the unnatural wind, seeing…

My head snaps up towards the police station; from this point, the station is closer to me than my own house, or Tristan's for that matter.

I wrap my arms almost all the way around the street light, supporting my feeble body. The thoughts of last night shake me. All I can recall is the bright light, the odd shadow, the large…*something*…

I take a step forward in attempts to ease myself, and I almost fall right back down. I peer down at my feet to find what I just about tripped over.

A book?

My hands quiver as one reaches down to pick up the book, the other still securely on the post. I stare at the soft cover for a solid minute, my mind still exploding with questions and exhilaration, but I don't know what the hell I'm looking at. Rounded symbols lie all over the cover of the book, symbols that I have never seen before in my life. They don't look like Mandarin or Japanese; they don't look like any language. My fingers graze the pages, but they don't feel like paper. They feel silky, like some sort of thin fabric. When I open the book, I'm confronted with even more unknown symbols, written over and over upon the strips of cloth.

What the fuck is this?

I shake my head, smirking a little; whatever this is, I bet it'll get Denton's attention. Maybe he'll listen to me this time.

I feel like I can stand and walk moderately properly again, and so I trek towards the station, the book pressed firmly against my chest; there's no way Denton can deny it this time. Now that I have something physical, other than the pictures he doesn't look at, or theories that I've spread.

My legs feel stiff, but I trudge onward, past Lion's Park and towards the station. I take a little more time than usual to observe the trees, reaching their tops with my head tilted way back. I haven't looked at the trees properly in a while because they seem taller than ever. A scream fills my ears, and my gaze shoots downwards to the park below the tall trees, where about a dozen kids are playing on a playground, accompanied by at least half a dozen parents. There are a few piles of snow in Lion's park, which comes as a shock to me that it's still there after more than three weeks of bright, or rainy, weather. I didn't think there was snow left anywhere, but there it is, with kids digging at the mounds. Most of the grounds are clear, other than the occasional chunk of white.

"I don't know," a female voice sneers, and I quickly regain focus to where I'm headed, and I hop out of the way of two passing strangers. The woman of the pair is giving me a strange look as if silently noticing my style, but I'm not sure whether it's in a good way or not. I arch an eyebrow, struck by the irony considering how her clothes aren't exactly what I'd consider to be everyday clothing. The man of the two doesn't even give me a glance, but there's something different about his style too.

Hipsters.

I press forward, now able to see the police station ahead of me. Throbbing slowly creeps up into my thighs from my knees, and I glance down to see that my legs are quivering. I can't tell if it's because I'm cold, or if it's just the stiffness from passing out on a grass and dirt field. Not to mention my head.

Three more people walk by me, two parents and their daughter, and the father gives me a cautious look, slowing as he does. It only makes me speed up towards the station. A strange feeling seeps into my mind, one that's starting to cause unease. My stare is fixed on my destination. Behind me, I can hear the man mention something to, presumably, his wife, but they're too far away for me to listen to what they're saying.

The throbbing pain turns into soothing aches, more tolerable than before, but just as uncomfortable.

Ahead of me, two girls around my age, probably a year or two younger, suddenly stop, one of them grabbing the other by the arm, and the two skip out of my path. The brunette, who caught her friend, has her eyes stuck on mine. She tugs her blonde friend closer and whispers, but not quietly enough, "is that...?"

I gulp, my mouth feeling dry as sandpaper, but I shake it off; my heart is pumping like crazy. Last night, I saw a giant shape in the sky, or in my face, with a light so bright that I passed out. How can my heart not be racing?

I finally reach the doors of the police station, shielding myself from the playground and everyone else around me. I keep one hand pressed on the cool glass and catch my breath. My legs are still trembling, my hands now joining in.

Sensation swiftly returns to my fingers, and I yank the door open, stomping to the front desk. There's a young receptionist who I don't think I've ever seen before, seated behind his computer. He doesn't even have the time to look up before I say, "I need to talk to Denton." He shoots me a brief, skeptical look, just based on the fact that I called him "Denton," and not "Officer Denton." Before he can add anything, I interrupt, "Is he here?"

"Yeah, he's here," the man, whose name tag reads Clark, spins in his chair shortly, glancing back at Denton's office, and then faces me again. "Do you have an..." His eyes grow twice the size they were before, and he leaps up from his chair so suddenly that I jump back. He knocks over his pencil holder but doesn't even flinch as all of his pens go flying. He lifts a hand to me, pointing with his index. "You...Denton!" He whirls around on his heels and breaks into a jog around all the other small desks filling the space. The cops at their desks seem to catch onto what's happening, and startle themselves from their seats, scattering around their small areas. They look like mimes in invisible confines. Clark bounds towards Denton's office, now yelling, "Denton!"

Clark rips open the office door, the only office door closed in the building and points towards me once again.

"What do you want, Clark?" Denton's thick, deep voice demands. It sounds a little raspy like maybe he's getting sick.

"She's here," Clark responds, taking a quick peek at me, and then back at Denton. "She's here!"

Denton is already out of the room before Clark finishes his sentence. I don't see a rushing Denton clearly until he's once again just behind the front desk, standing there, staring with as much awe in his face as I have in mine.

He looks...different.

His nonexistent beard has grown to cover his upper lip, chin, and part of both of his rosier cheeks. His eyes, along with deeper bags beneath them, have more wrinkles, crow's feet, and so does his forehead. Even his neck has more lines, with a subtle weight gain that could possibly be muscle. His hairline has receded.

He looks...older.

I shake my head, taking a step back, and I break my and Denton's gaze. All the officers, all twenty or so, have now sprung to their feet and are gawking at either their commanding officer or me.

"What..." I can only find it in me to utter one word. I look to my right, sensing movement, and I find another officer beaming in my direction. He's familiar but a stranger for a couple of moments until I place him. Andy?

Andy even has wrinkles now. The young twenty-something has faint wrinkles, just around the corners of his mouth, and just touching his eyes. I notice his hands most of all, seeing how rough and dry they are. How aged they are.

Denton takes a step towards me, holding his hand out. "Raleigh," he says gently as if he's trying not to startle a wild animal. I can't think of anything else to do but shake my head. "Raleigh?" He asks in the form of a question as if asking if my name is Raleigh.

"What?" I take a shaking breath and force eye contact with Denton again. I press the book even closer into my chest, my hands gripping on the edges as if this is the only thing normal in this new situation. I don't even know what to think.

Slowly, he turns to Clark, and says, "Call an ambulance."

An ambulance? Clark nods, reaching at the phone beside his boss, and one of the pencils rolls off the desk, hitting the floor. I don't realize how silent the room is until I hear that pencil drop.

"Why do you look..." I chuckle to myself, my brain working on electric wires trying to figure out what the hell is going on. I search around the office, and all at once, I notice minuscule differences. How the coffee maker has been upgraded to a single serve unit, how the carpets have been redone to their original colour, a deep blue, instead of a faded ugly pastel. A new stain is on one of the tiles of the ceiling, an extra fire extinguisher added to the opposite side of the room, several of the desks have been replaced, most of them have new chairs, as well. It all looks so different, now that I'm taking the time to really look.

I stare at Denton once again, my legs finally strong enough to cease the tremors. "What is going on here?"

Chapter 6

It has been five years. It has been five years since I passed out, just last night.

Hours after Denton first tells me, after I'm carted into an ambulance on its way to the hospital, the chief barely making any sense with his own sentences about years of being missing, and I'm still at a loss.

But, not the way I thought I would be.

Upon arriving at the hospital, everything instantly intensified. Everything began moving faster, and they wheeled me up to the second floor, to do a bunch of tests that Denton had ordered to be done. He was the only one who came in the ambulance with me, shouting at the other officers to continue their work while he's gone.

It's taken hours. My blood was tested, my blood pressure, my cholesterol, my iron, my calcium, I got X-rays, and emergency MRI scans, something that I had never done before, and had only seen on TV or in the movies. Technology I had never seen before presented itself, with three-dimensional screens, and motion sensor reports. I hardly pay any attention to it. Every possible thing I could think of had been done before I was finally returned to a private patient room. I still don't understand why I needed to go to the hospital and have all these tests done in the first place. I suppose I do from the rushed explanations, the constant need to treat me like glass, but...I don't. It doesn't make sense.

I spent the entire ordeal in a strange headspace. It felt like I was watching myself from a camera in the corner of the room, seeing this shell of a person be tested on, and not fully comprehending what was happening. I had reached a new point of confusion and fear that I accepted everything given to me.

The nurses caring for me, cautious of my state, insist that I ride in a wheelchair from location to location. Denton is waiting in my private room, complete with bed and bedside window, drenching half of the wall, when I arrive. He doesn't stand when we lock eyes, instead, he adjusts himself, arching his back, and tightening his grip on his pen and notepad, each in respective hands. Even after bothering him for so long, telling him about my many encounters or attempted contacts or random sightings, I didn't have a clue that he was left-handed. My hands start shaking.

That's what you focus on?!

"Just take it easy," one of the two nurses says to me as I slip out of the wheelchair. "Lie down, rest. Dr. Bailey will check on you later."

I transfer myself onto the white bed, not bothering to lie beneath the thin sheets. I know that those sheets won't help cure the emptiness and perplexity inside. I look over at the small table next to my bed, finding my inexplicable book of comfort, and some small gray sphere inside of a plastic bag. I reach for the book, bringing it onto my lap.

"Please, push the button if you need anything," the other nurse says, dropping my medical chart into the slot at the foot of my bed. The two women leave. I don't bother looking at which button she's talking about.

Old Denton plucks the clipboard and begins to look it over. I wince at his movements, slower and more concise than what I'm used to. He flips through the dozen or so pages, nodding reassuringly. "Everything is normal. Except for your iron, you have,"

"Anemia," I insert. "Yeah, I know."

"It looks like there's a small bump on your head, on the right towards the back, but there doesn't seem to be any actual damage. Might make remembering things a little difficult..."

Maybe that's why I don't have a clue what the fuck is going on.

His eyes meet mine again, and he takes a deep breath. "I just told my officers to call your dad, some of your friends. I wanted the chance to talk to you before they came." Denton bites his lower lip. "It's been five years." I don't respond. My gaze shifts towards the window, the brisk air outside; I don't know what to say. I just don't know. I glide the tips of my fingers across the silky sheets, taking a small comfort in the soft feeling. "Raleigh?"

"Yeah." I take a deep breath, attempting to conceal the quivers, but without success. "I..."

"Why don't you just tell me what happened?" He inches slightly closer in his chair, resting only about five feet away from me. I can tell he's eyeing the book, but I don't mention it right away. I should try to start from the beginning so that I can offer some explanation for this.

I nod, staring down at my boots that are plastered down flat on top of the stiff hospital bed. They let me change back into my clothes from the ugly, mandatory robes. "Okay."

"You can close your eyes if that helps you remember."

I shoot him a cautious glance but end up taking his advice. "Last night, I,"

"Last night?"

I almost rip open to blazing eyes, but I control myself. "February twenty-fourth, two thousand and eighteen. I was..." My eyes do flutter open, but not because of the date. Because of Tristan. "I was at my boyfriend's."

"Tristan Barnes?" Denton asks, taking me by surprise.

"Yeah...how do you know his name?" It's a thoughtless question, considering Tristan's name was undoubtedly on the arrest report from that night on the hill. I guess I'm just surprised he remembers after so long.

He shrugs bluntly and replies, "We're calling him too. Go on."

"Okay..." I return to my thoughts, trying to visualize what happened over again. "I was at my boyfriend's, at Tristan's. We...spent time together, and then we sort of had a fight."

"What about?" The question rolls off his tongue so smoothly that I'm sure he was expecting to ask it. I try not to let it concern me too much.

"About...about my beliefs. About aliens, just about that kind of stuff." His pen scratches violently against the compact paper in his hand, and I wait until it stops to continue speaking. "I walked home around midnight, I think. But on my way there, I saw something."

"You saw something?" I can hear Denton's attention being grabbed, and his head jolts up from his small pad.

"Yeah...well, I noticed the wind first."

"What do you mean?" He shifts himself in his chair, keeping one leg crossed over the other, and hunches forward a little more.

"There was wind, but there wasn't." I scoff at how stupid I sound, and I try the sentence again. "Things were blowing in the wind, leaves, but I couldn't feel any wind. And then when I looked up, I saw..." My hands float in front of me, carrying the basic shape of a three-dimensional object, but words escape me.

"What did you see?"

I'm about to explain what I see, but then I remember; this is Denton who I'm talking to. The most skeptical police officer on the planet. I utter a small chuckle, resting my elbows on my knees, the book kept safe within my arms. "You won't believe me." He narrows his older eyes at me, causing my emotions to spike. "You never believed me before, why would you now?"

"Because you were right." I stay in the moment as long as I can where Denton believes I was right. Where he at least claims that I was right. If there's any proof that things are very, very different, this is it. "Somebody did get hurt, and everyone who cares about you got hurt." He shifts again, clearly uncomfortable within the chair too small for his larger frame, and presses. "Please."

I bathe in the moment for just a few seconds longer before daring to continue; we both know I don't need an excuse to talk about anything out of this world. "I couldn't see what it was. It was just a shape. Maybe...thirty feet long?" I attempt once more to see it inside of my head. "And there might've been a figure, a silhouette." *I don't know.* "I don't know. The shape, it was more...it was flat, not really round or anything, just...wide. And it was floating, or it was hovering. It wasn't touching the ground." My head continues to shake, back and forth, as I speak, almost in time with Denton jotting every single note down. He's not even trying to doubt me or tell me that it was a god damn plane. He's just listening. "This is the first time you're actually listening to me."

Denton peers up from his little notes, a look on his face I can only describe as melancholy. His solemn eyes can't hide, even beneath the recently developed wrinkles. "It wasn't just your friends and family who got hurt, Raleigh."

I can't do anything but stare into his eyes. I want to say that none of it feels real, that it must be some weird dream, or alternate universe, or...something. But I don't believe that. I believe that this feels all too real. And that's what is scaring me right now. I think what's really scaring me is my reaction to it all. How does someone react in this situation?

I finally pry away my ocean blues and fixate on a coffee stain on the floor. "And there was a light." His pen is thrown into action once again. "It was almost white, but still a bit blue. And then I blacked out. And then I woke up this morning in the same place, and I went to your police station."

Denton freezes, mid-sentence. His aged fingers twitch unconsciously, along with his dry bottom lip. "Are you saying..."

"I don't know what I'm saying. Maybe I'm really in a coma, and this is all just an elaborate fantasy. Maybe I'm asleep, maybe..." I take a deep breath. "Denton, I don't know. I don't understand, why am I even in the hospital?" My body starts aching, growing restless from the hours of tests and poking and prodding, of being told to rest, relax, and take it easy.

"Raleigh, it's been five years,"

"What do you mean? How has it been five years? Where have I been, then? How do I not look any different if it's been five years?" I didn't truly understand how strange that was until I really looked at my reflection. As I was waiting to get my MRI scan, I stared at the window panes leading into the room with the giant monster of a machine. I stared at myself in the glass, the thought of five years going by in an instant stuck in the back of my mind, and it hit me that I looked the same. I even leaned closer, examining my face for any possible wrinkles, any differences. There were none. I look no different than when I was walking home from Tristan's house last night. I'm still in the same clothes.

"I don't know." The February sun slowly vanishes behind the fluffed clouds, darkening the room to the point where even the long and lean light bulbs above us don't feel like enough illumination. "Everyone thought you were missing."

"Missing, how?"

Denton snorts, refraining from rolling his eyes. "Just missing. We had posters up with your face on them, we still do. There's one at the station," he jabs a thumb in the general direction of the building, "hung up on the wall right now. Your dad, he thought you ran away, you were living somewhere else, travelling or something. He thought you just wanted to get away." Oh, my god, my dad... "But your friends, Tiffany, your boyfriend, Tristan, they...they were just worried something happened to you. You were just gone, not a single trace of you..." his voice drifts off, and he pulls his sleek cellphone out from his pocket, reading something on the screen. "Your dad is on his way, so is Tiffany. Haven't heard anything from Tristan yet."

"Denton..." my knees pull closer to my chest until I can wrap my arms around them. "I don't understand."

He offers the first sympathy smile of the meeting and shuffles his chair closer. "Is there anything else you can tell me? Anything?"

"I..." I sigh, looking down at the book. I clutch it in my hands, facing the cover to me, staring at the odd umber lettering. "This book. It was with me when I woke up."

I flip it over, revealing the symbols to Denton. "I saw," he mumbles cautiously. "One of your alien books?"

"No! Denton, I have no idea where this came from."

His eyebrows perk up, and he shuffles onto his feet. He leans over the hospital bed and stares down at the novel. "It's not yours?"

"No, it's not. I don't know what language this is, if it even is a language, I don't know what any of it says."

Denton plucks the book from my hands and skims through the pages, but, as I suspected he would, comes up blank. "You've never seen it before?"

I stare flatly into his eyes, sneering a little. "No. I have not." I emphasize every word, earning a glare in response. "Maybe it's hieroglyphics or something."

"It's not."

"How do you know?"

"I studied Egyptian hieroglyphics in university. These look more like letters than drawings."

"...are you serious? You studied hieroglyphics."

"It was an elective," he grumbles. "The point is, it's not Egyptian hieroglyphics. I don't know what it is, I've never seen anything like it."

"Then I don't know..."

"Thought it was from some movie you liked or something, like a movie prop." *That is something I would buy...* "We ran it for prints and DNA while you were getting your tests done, but only matches we could get were from you." But it's not your book." His statement is more of an inquiry.

"No, it's not. I bite my tongue. "Can I have it back?"

A startled look floods Denton's face, and I hold out my hands for it. I feel oddly protective of it. "Are you sure you've never seen it before?"

I clench my teeth, baring a toothy scowl. "Denton, I haven't seen the fucking book before, I just…" I sigh, straightening out my hands, waiting for the book. "I want to study it. See if maybe I can remember something by looking through it. Do I have amnesia or something?"

Denton sighs, shrugging his shoulders, something I do not want to see. "You said you passed out, you might have just hit your head, it knocked things around a little. Or…"

"…or, what?"

Upon examination, he is nervous. He seems unsettled and a little disturbed. At once, he clears his throat and regains his intimidating demeanor. "Or, who knows?" He draws out my medical chart again, flipping through the scribbles of Dr. Bailey's writing. Looks like you have a bump on your head, probably hit it, maybe messed something around…"

"Or what?"

He meets my eyes. "I've often seen in highly traumatic cases that the vic–," he catches himself, "patient will force themselves to forget, to keep from reliving the experience."

"I wasn't kidnapped," I scoff. "I'm not hurt. I mean, look at me. I'm fine. Just hit my head."

Denton finally hands me the book, and I keep it tight on my lap, tapping my fingers on the front cover. My mind is running in a thousand different directions, all these emotions piling up with nowhere to go.

"I have one more question for you." Denton pulls up the plastic bag from my small bedside table, the one containing the mysterious marble. "Have you ever seen this before?"

A shiver creeps through my entire body, quickly and an itch arises in my ear. "I don't think so," I respond, and lean a little closer to the metallic sphere. "What is it?

"We analyzed it, came back as just a metal ball. It was found where you said you woke up today, but it wasn't found in our initial search when you first disappeared. You've never seen it?"

I blink a few times; have I seen it before?

"Raleigh?" the chief of police presses.

I smile, exhausted and meek. "I just don't understand what's going on. And I feel so confused." I meet Denton's eyes, just as tired and humble as mine. "And so…" I try my best to finish the sentence, but I just don't know how.

I play it over and over again how one night, *last* night, has lead to this morning, where everything has changed. One night, one experience, one giant shape in the sky...

Denton, transfixed in my mindless thoughts, is interrupted by the vibration of what must be his phone. He doesn't even touch the screen while he reads a message. "Your father is here." He looks up. "I'm going to talk to him for a few minutes before he comes in, okay?"

I nod and begin rubbing my legs, still sore from their pain earlier on the way to the station. I allow my tired eyes to drift closed, and the familiar sound of my dad's voice enters my ears.

I take a few moments to enjoy the peacefulness of being alone within the walls of the small hospital room, just listening to the sound of my breath. I am soon disrupted by the two words circling inside of my head, the ones that have been there since Denton first said it, back at his station.

Five years.

Chapter 7

The hospital tried running even more tests for even more hours, under Denton's orders, to make sure that I was okay. And I am. I woke up this morning, barely technically morning, feeling fine, like nothing was wrong. Like five years hadn't been washed away in the moment of a night.

The chief of police and I debated again on why exactly I don't recall the events of February 24th, all those years ago, but we can't quite land on any reasonable explanation.

None of our theories explain why I don't look any older.

Waking up in the hospital this morning, to what apparently had not been a dream, made me absolutely sure of two things, the first of which being that it has been five years. Five years have gone by, whether I remember them or not, whether my body shows it or not. The past five years happened. The second thing of which I am positively certain is that whatever unidentified object I had seen two nights ago had something to do with it.

My brain is working on overdrive, pushing itself to remember something, anything more. But it's stuck in the same loop. I'm walking. I see the leaves. I see the massive, floating object. I see the bright light. And that's all. I play the scenario over and over in my head, but the outcome is always the same. I can't remember anything else.

The notion of alien abduction comes to mind, which isn't as implausible as one would think, considering the fact that I did see that vast flying phenomenon. But...

My dad came to revisit me today, and so did Tiffany. Tiff ended up staying longer again. Yesterday, my dad got to the hospital a little while before Tiffany did. He told me that he never thought anything bad had happened to me. He told me how everyone else seemed to think that I was in some sort of trouble, but he never thought I was.

"I somehow just knew that you weren't," he told me, sitting in the chair that Denton had previously sat in. I assumed that Denton explained, to the best of his abilities, the situation as we know it, or as well as we can all know it. My dad, like Denton, had developed more wrinkles, but overall, he didn't look too much older. He just looked like my dad. And he acted like my dad. He asked me how I could look the same and I told him the truth; I didn't know. He told me he thought I had just run away, and that he was glad I was doing well. He didn't tell me that he loved me.

I didn't know how to respond to him. It's painfully clear that he isn't very good with emotions nor dealing with things. It was clear as day growing up, and somehow even clearer now.

Dad visited again today, and it almost felt like the five years hadn't existed for him either. He didn't even ask about or mention what had happened, and it was all colloquial. It felt as if we'd traveled back to the day after I allegedly went missing, and he was, in a rare omission, telling me about his day. He asked how I was feeling, and then we sat in silence for a little while. He only stayed for half an hour, telling me he had to go back to work. It saddens me to know that the gap between us has just gotten bigger; it saddens me even further that I expected nothing less.

When Tiffany came to visit yesterday, she cried. She saw me and immediately burst into tears, throwing us both into a hug.

I was too in shock to really focus on the hug.

Tiffany definitely looked older. With my dad, with Denton, another five years doesn't do all that much. It was noticeable, sure, but with Tiffany, the gap from twenty to twenty-five...a lot happened. Her hair is longer and thicker, placed up high in a bun, a look that I never thought she'd go for. She's wearing jewelry, a matching necklace, and bracelet, another shocking revelation.

She never used to wear jewelry, anyway.

"Raleigh, I can't believe it's you," she said to me. "I mean...I thought you were..."

I told her that I was okay, but it only made her cry again.

She told me her side.

She told me how she thought that I'd been kidnapped or murdered, or something horrible. She told me that she thought my best-case scenario was death, because at least then I wouldn't be in any pain. She told me how my dad thought that I was off somewhere else, that I had simply run away, and how she didn't understand how he couldn't worry. She told me they considered him a suspect because of his behaviour, that it was suspicious for a father to regard his daughter in that sense, and that Denton had interviewed him several times.

I expected part of my heart to sting a little bit, hearing that, but it didn't. Once again, I expected nothing less.

Tiffany stayed last night until visiting hours were over and then came again today. She left around two today, arriving at eleven, just after my dad had left, and Denton ordered more tests to be conducted on me. I've never had a problem with blood, nor too much of a problem with needles, so the tests weren't too bad, but they weren't exactly fun. It was exciting seeing more touchscreen analysis reports up close, but I wasn't allowed to touch any; it was like looking at a giant tablet.

Once all the tests were over and done with, and I was in the clear, Denton told me that he'd drive me home. I'm not sure if he was at the hospital all night, but he was here when I went to sleep, and here when I woke up. If he was at the hospital all this time, I don't know where he was hiding, but I'm guessing as a police officer, he had his ways.

"I'll be downstairs, in front of Emergency," he says, after our small argument deciding if I need to be wheeled out of here. "Do you need any help?"

I shake my head, nestling myself inside of my soft black sweater. It felt nice to change out of the clothes I was wearing yesterday, and even nicer to have a shower this morning. I went through all my tests with wet hair, tied back into a bun. My dad had apparently told Tiffany to grab some clothes for me because he didn't know which ones I'd like. "I'm good, thanks. I'll be down in a minute."

"And you know where it is?"

"Yeah." This is the only hospital I've ever been to, so I know it reasonably well.

Denton nods and heads out of the room. I take a deep breath, looking at my few scattered belongings that Tiffany had brought me; clothes, toothbrush and toothpaste, a couple of magazines, a book, she brought everything that I keep on my nightstand at home. I guess she wasn't sure how long I'd be here, and she knows that I like to pack heavy.

I pack up my items, stuffing everything into the duffel bag Tiff brought them in but pause when I come across the foreign book. I graze the soft pages, still stunned by how soft they are, and I tuck it gently into my bag. I read into it a little bit yesterday, but I'm not sure where to start with it all.

As I'm leaving, the tiny marble catches my eye, locked away in the small plastic bag. I shrug to myself and end up tossing it into my tote as well; couldn't hurt.

I swing the strap over my body and throw the bag onto my shoulder. I massage my neck with my free hand, the weight of the duffel sinking in. My body is stiff; my joints feel tense and tight, and stretching has never felt so good.

I escort myself out of my temporary room and down the hall, past the other patients who have better and more logical reasons to be here, and into the elevator.

The elevator stops on the second floor before hitting the first, to let an orderly wheel an elderly lady on. I try to avoid eye contact and squish against the back corner, out of the way; I would have taken the stairs if I had known where they were.

The orderly wheels the woman to the right once we arrive at the main floor, out towards a different wing of the hospital, while I make a beeline for the emergency entrance. I'm only about ten feet away from the emergency desk when I'm stopped in my tracks by a man rushing inside the hospital. I see him as he clears the first set of sliding doors, but he barely makes it through the second. He swiftly turns to his side, placing his hand on one of the doors to force it open a little faster, and then stumbles inside to the front desk.

I'm about to continue past the clearly frantic man, not wanting to get in his way, until he commands to the woman behind the desk, "I need to see Raleigh Carlisle."

It is only then that I really take a good look at the man. Realization dawns on me that I'm not just looking at any man; I'm looking at Tristan. And I can't believe that it's him.

I don't know where to start. It's not so much the most noticeable parts of him; his hair is barely longer, just long enough to need to be styled, he's gained a little weight, but not anything distracting from his chiseled face, and he's only barely taller. Drifting down, I can see that his shoes have slight lifts. His shoes that are so well kept that they're reflecting the unflattering lights from above. That, or they're new.

It's not even the clothes that are throwing me off. Dark jeans, a brown sports coat, a button up dress shirt, all new to his wardrobe.

No. It's his face.

"I'm sorry?" the woman behind the desk nearly jumps at the sound of Tristan's voice, and she throws herself into a frenzy to log onto her computer.

"Raleigh," Tristan sneers, his teeth clenched.

It's his face.

His eyes are identical, just like I remember them from two days ago. But now...I'm not even sure I can describe it. His lips, his cheeks, his chin, his forehead, his nose, they're all the same. But together, he just looks older, like he is exactly five years older, not a day more, not a day less. There's something in his face that causes my brain to unable to formulate any words.

"And the last name?" the timid nurse dares to ask.

As Tristan is about to yell my last name through the E.R, I interrupt, in an equally gentle voice.

"Tristan."

His head whips towards me in a heartbeat. I'm surprised he even heard me. I drop my duffel bag after I say his name, its weight starting to ache. And from ten feet away, I watch him turn from angry and panicked to completely helpless. His jaw drops, and his casual grip on the counter tightens as his body sways unconsciously backward.

"Raleigh...?" He almost sounds like he's asking if it's me. I know he's not, but I nod.

Tristan charges at me and throws his arms around my body, squeezing me tighter than he's ever held me before. One arm snakes around the back of my neck, the other following along my waist. I barely had enough time to be able to free my arms to hug him back, but after a little squirming, I succeed.

"Oh, my god, Raleigh," he says, and his voice cracks along with my name. I try not to let my own tears escape, something he's failing at as well. I give up almost immediately. "Oh, my god." He squeezes me tighter and more tears fill my eyes. I can feel his own tears in my hair.

He uses his hand to brace my head gently in place, and he brings his lips to kiss the top of my head, keeping his lips there for a few moments. He then draws away and looks me in the eyes, tears streaming his cheeks, leaving damp marks of where they were and still are beading. He emits a small laugh and shakes his head. "Raleigh."

I smile, nodding, but my smile doesn't last long before I must bite both of my lips to remain partially calm. "Yeah."

He chokes back a sob and presses our foreheads together, letting his eyes drift closed. Mine do too, by habit. "I didn't get Denton's message until today," he whispers, now holding my head against his own. His skin is warm, almost hot, as it usually is, even in cooler weather. "I didn't check it until today, I would've been here...god, are you okay?" A part of me wonders where exactly Tristan was, that it took him so long to receive the message, but I can't quite bring myself to be anything but elated to see him. Tristan quickly pulls away, prying his arms off me, and caresses my cheeks, scanning my body and then my eyes. "Are you..."

"Yeah." I sniff, glancing over to my left, where I see Denton's police car outside. I ignore it and stare back into Tristan's eyes. A shape, which I'm assuming is Denton, is standing by the car. "I am."

"You don't..." He clears his throat, one last tear escaping from his eye. "You look...you look the same."

"I know..."

"How?" Tristan steps impossibly closer, still staring into my eyes. "How can you look the same? It's been five years, it's...I don't understand."

"I don't, either."

His hands drop from my face down to his sides, but one hand finds one of mine. He strokes it gently, feeling my skin. "It's been five years..." He meets my eyes again. There is so much hurt hidden within, so much pain.

And then it hits me why.

I knew that Tristan loved me, and that's a feeling that I never thought I'd feel. I never thought I'd experience that romantic love, that I'd actually know that someone loves me romantically. But I felt it. And I felt it hard. I don't imagine it would be easy for him, and I won't pretend to think it was a walk in the park, but my disappearance was made even harder by that night. For him, it didn't end two days ago, where it was a dumb argument. For him, it ended five years ago, in a fight.

I open my mouth, hoping to say something, anything, but Denton strides back inside the hospital. His boots clomp on the ground, drawing my attention to him. "Raleigh?" Tristan has to turn around for

Denton to recognize him and be a little less weary. The officer's shoulders relax as he sees Tristan, who takes only a small step away from me. "Hello, Tristan. Glad to see you got my message."

"I'm sorry I wasn't here sooner," Tristan replies, shaking Denton's extended hand. The two had only met in one circumstance before, and it was certainly not a setting where the men were shaking hands. A lot can happen in five years. "Work has been crazy." My mind jumps on his statement, and I can't help but wonder if he's working at a university right now.

"You got here just in time, she's ready to go home."

Tristan's eyes widen, and he turns to me, beaming hope from his gentle smile. "What, um..." He faces Denton again. "What exactly..."

"We don't know." Denton, instead of explaining more, faces me and says, "I'll be in the car. Take your time." He bends down and snatches my duffel bag from the ground, and then he saunters back out through the entrance. I stare after Denton, a little curious of his behaviour; he's visited every day, he's driving me home, he's carrying my bag. If I didn't know any better, I'd almost say that he cares about me, despite the usual harassment I bring with me.

"You don't know?" Tristan asks, capturing my attention once again. My mouth opens, but I can't find the right words. The entire situation, everyone who I am close to being five years older...I don't know what to say. I don't know what I can say.

"I don't," I conclude, wishing I had something more concrete to offer. "Barely. I..."

"What do you remember? Do you want to sit down?" Tristan searches the lobby for only a second before finding a vacant bench and guides me over towards it, but I shake my head.

"I'm okay. Um...I..." I don't know what to tell him. Our last conversation was about my beliefs. If I told him about this...who knows what he'd think of me. Looking at him, it's like I'm looking at a movie star who had gone into hiding for five years. He's recognizable but certainly different. A familiar stranger.

"No, it's okay." He holds out his hands in front of him like I'm an erratic animal he's trying to calm down. "You must be exhausted. We can talk another time. Just...rest a few days, okay?" He places his hands on my shoulders, meets my eyes, and wraps me in another hug. It feels awkward at first, at least on my end, but he doesn't seem to notice or mind. "I am so glad that you're okay, Raleigh."

I let myself sink into Tristan, remembering his distinctive scent as it surrounds me. He rests his chin against the side of my head, almost reaching the top, and he occasionally squeezes his hands against me.

I smile.

Me too, Tristan. Me too.

Chapter 8

My "few days" of rest condenses into one day. I called Tristan the evening I got home from the hospital and planned a meeting with him. I didn't feel sick when I returned home from the hospital; I didn't feel sick when I was *in* the hospital. I felt stiff and sore, increasingly and now decreasingly so, but not unwell.

I really feel the soreness when I attempt to jog down my flight of stairs. I almost immediately clutch the railing and steady myself before continuing down, slowly and carefully. I haven't taken any painkillers yet today, but the day has just begun. Something has definitely upset my body.

"Morning," Dad chimes from the kitchen. I can't see him until I get fully into the kitchen, where he's sitting at our kitchen island, a cup of coffee on one side, an empty plate with bread crumbs on the other, and the newspaper in his hands.

"Morning." I glance at the clock on the microwave; eleven is still technically morning. Without a word, my dad points at the golden bus pass on the counter, and I swipe it up. "Thanks...where is the van, anyway?" The lack of van was one of the first things I noticed when I got home yesterday, but my mind was elsewhere before I could think to question its absence.

Dad glances up from his newspaper and stretches a bit, shrugging one shoulder. "In the shop. It's getting old."

I chuckle, leaning against the bar. "Maybe you should get a new one." The van was eight years old when my dad first got it, and it's been another four years since then. Another nine years, technically.

He frowns, licking his dry lips. "Maybe..." I guess a joke isn't the right way to go about this. He clears his throat, breaking away from his haze, and asks, "Do you have your phone?"

I nod; my phone was broken. It wouldn't turn on because I completely obliterated it somehow, which the lovely people at Telus truly appreciated. My dad got me a new one yesterday as a surprise. I'm still adjusting to it; it's a lot bigger than my old phone and has a lot of strange command technology that I'll probably never use. "Yeah. Thanks." I pat my purse, feeling my massive phone, and then slide the bus pass alongside it. Bus passes still look the same, but now have a barcode feature on the back, something I don't quite understand yet.

I take another look around the living room and kitchen; barely anything has changed. We have a new blender in the kitchen, and a new, bigger television, but I can't tell if anything else has been updated. My room is identical. It's easy to forget that it's really been five years. I sometimes doubt it. I sometimes think that I might be legitimately insane and that this is all some delusion inside of my head. I think about that possibility, and others like it, yet I don't believe it. I don't know what I believe, but something tells me that…

"I'm sorry I can't drive you," my dad offers, holding firm eye contact with the paper. I can't help but notice the date on it. He has this week off from work. Once they heard about what happened, about his daughter reappearing, they insisted he take time off. I'm sure he tried to fight it a little.

"It's okay. Thanks for your bus pass..." Another gaze at the microwave clock. "I should probably go. I'll see you later."

He grumbles some kind of acknowledgement and continues to flip through the newspaper pages. I glance at the cover, and notice the words "Prime Minister," and a new face that I've never seen. He's surprisingly handsome.

I shut and lock the door behind me with the same old set of keys I got when I was eleven, and grip onto the knob tightly. I have an odd feeling in the pit of my stomach; my keys reach for the door again, but I force myself to step away from the house. My thoughts return to the mysterious book. It'd be ridiculous to bring that book everywhere with me, but my mind seems to keep coming back to it. It apparently means something to me...

I try to forget about the book, now hidden in my bedroom, and I trek out to the bus stop. It doesn't hit me until I arrive, and wait for a solid twenty minutes, that the bus routes may have changed. The pole is still the same, albeit with a newer looking sign, but the bus was supposed to be here almost ten minutes ago.

"Shit."

I fumble through my purse for my phone, hoping that I can still text the bus stop and find out when it comes, just as the bus, the good old 236, rears its way around the corner. I didn't even consider that the bus routes might have changed, and it still managed to work out, so I can't complain too much.

I meet Tristan an expectedly ten minutes late at our most frequented Starbucks. It's not exactly near either of our houses, but it is near our old high school, which is why we would also go to it. The bus route is all surrounded by residentials, so there isn't too much difference to notice, which is a nice feeling. I can almost slip back into five years ago.

The bus lurches to a stop, just outside the cafe, and I hop off with a hefty "thank you," towards the bus driver. I don't realize how cold I am until I step through the glass doors and a quiver pulses through my body.

Tristan, sitting at a small table near the back of the cafe, stands when he sees me approaching and smiles. "Hey, Raleigh." He draws me in for a tight, brief hug.

"Hi," I say, my mouth muffled by his shoulder. Tristan chuckles as he draws away and points me to the seat across from him, sitting himself back down. "I'm sorry I'm late, the bus came a bit late."

"You bussed?" I nod. He shifts uncomfortably in his seat. "You could've told me, I would have picked you up." I smile, feeling slightly at a loss for words. I'm about to say that it's fine when Tristan slides a cup and a small paper bag over to me. "I got you breakfast."

I smile again, chuckling a little. "Thanks, Tristan." My smile brightens when I see that he's ordered me my classic favourites. Five years and he remembers.

He nods one single nod, a brief grin on his lips, and the two of us begin to eat. He also bought a sandwich from Starbucks and a sharply scented coffee drink. I knew he liked coffee, but I didn't think he would ever go for Starbucks specialty drinks. He'd take his coffee black.

I devour my sandwich; I'm glad Tristan and I don't speak much while we're eating so I can fill my empty stomach. My appetite has been lacking the past few days, so I guess now I'm making up for it. I normally eat about half as slow as Tristan, and I've been keeping up with him pretty well, confirming to myself how hungry I really am. I finish my last bite just after he finishes his.

"Oh, have you talked to Tiffany recently?" Tristan asks, pointing his index my way. "She called me the day after you were..." He waves his hand around briefly, not sure of how to word it, so I fill in the rest.

"Yeah, we've talked a few times now, and we're meeting up on Saturday." Tiff is crazy busy with work, though I haven't even gotten the chance to ask what she does yet, so she offered Saturday to see me again. Technically I offered Saturday, because she told me she could meet up any day of the week, and I would have loved to meet up every day, but I didn't want her to miss any more work. She already missed two days because of me, and I was starting to feel oddly guilty, even though she assured me her boss was more than okay with her ducking out for a few days. When I talked to her at the hospital, she barely told me anything about herself; she kept asking me questions and telling me about all of the theories that people had surrounding my disappearance, about all of the precautions that were taken to try and find me. I still don't know how to respond to that.

"Good, good...Raleigh, what happened?" I arch my eyebrows, just slightly, a little startled by how flat his tone is. He grips onto the seat of his chair with both hands, and pulls in tighter against the small table, closer to me. "Denton told me that you were wearing the same clothes you were wearing that night when we..." I take a deep breath; I can place calm in his voice, and something along the lines of urgency as well.

"I was," I reply, attempting to add other words to fill the void, but none come to mind.

"And you look..." Tristan uses both hands to signal to my sitting body. The body of the girl he knew five years ago. "I don't..."

"I don't either, Tristan," I confess. "I can tell you what I remember."

"Please, do."

I open my mouth, about to speak, but then I recall, once again, our argument. How is he going to react when I tell him this? Instead of explaining what little I can piece together, I take a sip of my hot chocolate. I prepare myself again, maybe a warning for him to keep an open mind, but then I pause for a moment and reconsider. He can think what he wants.

"I was walking home from your house. And I was just about

halfway home, and this giant," my hands, without my conscious consent, begin to create an object within the air, "*thing* just appeared. Well, first, it got windy. I didn't notice at first, but it was windy, and then the thing," my hands twitch, "was there."

"What was it?" Tristan asks.

I meet his eyes, seeing that urgency again. "I don't know. It was...massive, I don't even know how big. And it was hovering." My nerves start to get the better of me, and a tinge of worry shocks through my veins. "And then there was this bright light, and...I passed out. I guess. Because I woke up there the next morning...but I guess it wasn't really the next morning."

"Do you think it was a UFO?"

My ears perk up when I hear Tristan ask that. I didn't expect him to jump to that conclusion so quickly. "I think it was, yeah. I don't really know what else it could have been, though."

"Do you think you were ah–"

"No." My words come out before my mind even has the chance to process what he was asking. The thought of it has entered my mind, but it has never stayed around very long. I don't know why I'm so adverse to the idea. I hate to say that it's a "gut feeling," but there are no other words to describe it.

"No?" Tristan mimics back, disbelief lining his voice. I can tell how badly he wants answers for what happened. But I'm not the one who can give them to him.

I shrug both my shoulders, my mind getting clustered and frustrated. "I don't know. I don't think so, but I don't remember." It's all feelings. I remember how I felt more than the actual events. "And when I woke up, there was this book,"

"A book?"

"It's in another language. I can't read any of it."

"Can I see it?"

I hold back my retort for a moment and stare Tristan in the eyes, finding it difficult to recognize him right now. He's speaking with such urgency, and I can't comprehend why it's coming out that way. "...it's at my house. You can see it the next time I see you." My possessiveness of the book shines brightly. It's sitting at my house, hidden in the back of my closet. When I got home yesterday, I sat on my bed, holding the book for a solid twenty minutes. I kept flipping through pages, seeing recognizable numbers at the bottom, unable to identify anything else.

After I had exhausted myself enough with it, I felt compelled to hide the thing, as if someone would want to take it from me. As if it's even my book.

Tristan must sense my firm tone because he leans back in his seat and takes a deep breath. "Sorry."

Neither of us says anything for a few seconds, and I almost break the silence with the metallic marble found where I reappeared; I think better of it. The marble means nothing, so much so that all the tests came back revealing it as just a small metal sphere. Denton informed me that they chalked it up to something in the grass, unrelated to my "case."

We stew in silence until two curt beeps come from Tristan's blazer's pocket. He fumbles to retrieve his phone from his inner pocket and checks the screen.

"Do you need to get back to work?" I tap my fingers on my hot chocolate cup repeatedly, to an unknown tune floating from my head down to my fingertips.

"Eventually," Tristan sighs, shaking his head, but manages a small smile.

"What do you even do now?" I ponder out loud. "Did you finish school?"

His smile grows. "Yeah, I did. But not for history."

"Really?" The last thing I know, is that he was avid about his history classes, studying hours on end and even doing the optional work, in hopes of being the top in his class, in all of his classes. "Then, what do you do?"

He checks the screen of his brick again, one similar in size to mine, and his expression turns wicked. "I can show you." To my surprise and minor concern, he grins wryly, the same grin that I've come to know and recognize. "I think you'll find it interesting."

I arch an eyebrow, my interest already peaked. How he dresses, more formally than I've ever seen him dress, excluding our high school graduation, I expected him to be some college professor or even a high school teacher with a secure job. However, apparently not.

Tristan stands, signalling for me to come with him, and I hop to my feet, grabbing my nearly untouched hot chocolate. I trail after Tristan outside, the two of us tossing away our trash in the meantime, and he leads me to a car that is not even remotely similar to his old beat up mess. I don't believe it's genuinely his until he flashes the headlights, unlocking the doors.

Even though I know the answer, I still ask, "What happened to your other car?"

"Broke down," Tristan says, chuckling along. "About four and half years ago."

"And you got this right after?" This car is beautiful. It's sleek and silver and looks about the cost of my house. I hardly know a thing about cars, but I know this one is gorgeous. I slip inside the car, feeling the inside of the door, lined with strangely smooth fabric. Even the interior is beautiful.

"No way." Tristan puts his coffee down into the cup holder, and I follow suit; he didn't care about his other car getting spills or food crumbs, yet I'm pretty sure he cares about this one. It's in pristine condition. Tristan pushes two buttons just below the dashboard and then adjusts the heat. "I bused to work until about a year ago, finally had enough to buy this."

"Wow." I know that he had "inherited" his old car from his uncle after he had bought a new car. It was only a matter of time before the thing fell apart. It was about thirty years old. "Wait..." I place my hand in front of the small heater to my left and grin, turning to Tristan. "There's actually heat?"

He laughs, revealing his pearly whites that he used to be self-conscious about, and throws the car into reverse. "Yeah, I've got to say, heat is pretty nice." Within a few minutes, tingles begin to surge throughout my body, starting from my seat, and I realize that the buttons Tristan had pushed were seat warmers. It's a pleasant surprise on an unseasonably chilly February day.

This car, in all its glory, is a vast improvement over his last car. Part of me misses that car a little, but not enough to wish for Tristan to have it back. It was a really shitty car.

Tristan and I don't talk very much on the way over, and if he does, I don't hear him. I'm too fixed on all the changes around. Leaving the housing areas, and entering more modern and urban places, the developments stick out like a sore thumb. A Dairy Queen that I used to go to when I was younger has been renovated, and the light up sign that has been there since it first opened late in the fifties or early sixties, is now gone and replaced with an even uglier sign. It lacks the vintage charm.

Driving along the highway, I can't help but notice the new

shops; there seems to be this new recurring fast food restaurant called Hamm's, where I'm guessing they specialize in hamburgers, and what I think is a clothing store named Kate's. The sign makes it seem like a quaint boutique, but it's about the size of a department store.

There are significantly fewer trees and a lot more buildings to begin with, but the further along we drive, the more the opposite ensues. I'm pleasantly surprised at how many more trees there are along this stretch than there used to be.

After a solid twenty minutes of driving, Tristan takes a quick left, and we cruise for another five minutes. We've switched from highway to a more secluded mountain, going up a slight incline throughout all the twists and turns.

And finally, I see where we're headed.

A tall, thick building with a curved roof appears over the line of the horizon and reveals itself to be attached to a more rectangular structure near the base. I noticed too late the sign telling me where I am, and so instead turned my focus back to the monster building. I spot an uplifted part of the rounded roof, lining its centre, as if it could open up, or if something could move along those lines.

Tristan drives up towards the building and draws to a slow stop. I peel my eyes away from the marvel of the impressive concrete mansion to find that we're already stopped in a parking spot. Upon gazing forward, there's a sign that reads "reserved for Tristan Barnes."

"You have your own parking spot," I joke, following Tristan's lead and getting out of the car.

"Yeah, right next to the door." He points to the doors, two sliding glass doors in between two lean glass windows, stretching the same length as the doors. "Nice on cold days."

"Right," I mumble to myself.

We stride through the front doors into what seems to be a lobby. Warmth hits me like a wall when I step inside from the chilled outdoor weather, not just in the physical sense. The lobby has a light, welcoming feel to it. Nearly sparkling off-white tiles cover the floors and lead up to a large wooden desk with a gentle curve towards the man sitting behind it. He strikes me in his mid-twenties, but from the way he quickly glances up at Tristan with hopeful eyes, it looks like a younger brother looking up to the older one. Two small ficus trees are planted on either side of the room, one of which has a black leather couch alongside it. I take a second to gather my thoughts; this building looked more like a strangely shaped warehouse, I didn't expect such an elegant lobby.

"Hello, Mr. Barnes," the eager receptionist beams at Tristan. He glances at me for only a second before facing Tristan again.

"Hey, Jack." Tristan seems a lot more casual with Jack than Jack does with Tristan.

Before Tristan can say anything else, Jack takes another look at me and his jaw drops. "Is that...I mean, I heard on the news..." *The news?* He makes eye contact and promptly stands, extending his hand to me. "It's an honour to meet you."

My eyes widen immeasurably, and I chuckle, shaking his hand. "Hi..." I send a cautious glance to Tristan who smirks and tosses his head towards the door to our left that I hadn't noticed when we first came in.

"I'll show you."

I follow Tristan once again through another doorway, but behind this door is something more spectacular than I could have ever imagined.

It's just amazing.

The door leads to a giant office space, all with slightly arched desks leading towards the furthest wall of the room. There must be about two dozen of them, along with the two dozen workers behind each desk. My eyes trail along with the desks, which are all focusing towards a wall filled with computer screens. The screens stretch about ten feet tall and wide, with a large, what I can only assume to be, control panel, with dials and notches and buttons, including a vast set of keyboards. There must be about twenty or so screens, each showing different...

I take a step forward, towards the magnificence, not really believing what I'm seeing.

All the screens are looking at different celestial bodies. Different stars or planets or meteors. They're all scanning the skies. They're all different sizes, with slight variations of colour, and they're all being monitored by a group, by a *team*, of people taking notes on clipboards and discussing their findings with others.

Tristan takes a step forward, in front of me, and throws his hands in the air, just around his shoulders. "Welcome to NETRAD."

"NETRAD..." I mimic back, still transfixed by all of the monitors. Seeing all the images of outer space, as if they're right here in the room with me...I had only ever used a telescope a handful of times and had been saving up for one, but I'd never gotten around to buying one. This is better than any telescope I could ever afford. It's only then that my eyes find their way upward and discover a beautiful, ginormous telescope about thirty feet up above the desks, suddenly explaining the rounded rooftop. Along the edges of the curved ceiling, there's a grated metal pathway leading from a small door around the roof, and straight to the massive telescope. It's tilted on its side, towards the back of the building, explaining why I didn't see the telescope when I first saw the building. I'm surprised nobody is up there now. I force my attention back to Tristan and repeat, "NETRAD?"

He arches an eyebrow, making me think that he probably just explained it and I wasn't paying attention. "National Extraterrestrial Theory, Research, And Development."

A thought then strikes me, and I freeze, pointing one arm towards Tristan. I didn't hit me until this moment how high up Tristan is here. "Is this...*your* company?"

He hesitates, shrugging his shoulders, and topples his head from side to side. "Partially mine, yeah." I take a glance back at all the busy workers to find that they're not so busy anymore. More than half have turned to face their bodies in my direction, and only more keep joining.

"Um..."

"Partially mine," Tristan repeats and then points straight behind me.

Turning around, slightly worried about what I'll find, I'm confronted with...me. I cautiously step towards a smiling picture of myself, unease washing over me. The image of me is blown up to be about a foot tall, and is, now that I'm seeing it again and reminding myself, my most recent Facebook profile picture. It's nothing special; it's a picture of me from my shoulders up, smiling, that's about it. I notice that there's a description below the picture of me, which is in a display carved into the wall. There are even two small light fixtures shining down on me.

Raleigh Elizabeth Carlisle. If it weren't for the determination and bravery of Raleigh Carlisle, The National Extraterrestrial Theory, Research, And Development team would not be here today. Thank you, Raleigh, for your courage, and may your truth one day be discovered.

I read over the passage about six times, refusing to turn around and face Tristan. My heart is pounding inside of my head, cheeks flushing red, hands quivering just so. I can't really be given credit for something that I had nothing to do with. This can't all be because of me.

"Oh, wow."

I finally turn around, hearing an upbeat female voice. I find myself not only face to face with Tristan, but the entire team who were just looking at the computers, mere moments ago. Three men, two women, with one of the women, a preppy redhead, perched next to Tristan.

The redhead beams a wide, toothy grin. "Raleigh." She extends her hand, which I cautiously take, and she instantly snaps the other on top, gripping my one hand from all around. "It is such a pleasure to meet you. I've heard so much about you from Tristan..." She glances up at Tristan, and the sides of her lips curl up towards her cheeks, and her pupils even dilate. I know what she's thinking. "I can't believe I'm actually meeting you, Raleigh."

"This is Peggy," Tristan says, and Peggy's cheeks bloom.

"Right, yeah, I'm Peggy, co-founder of NETRAD." She chuckles nervously, shooting another glance at Tristan, and then finally releases her tight grip on my hand.

I smile. "Hi. This place is incredible. You and Tristan have really made something amazing..." Her smile brightens even further, spreading across her pretty face, but I find myself cautiously gazing at Tristan. The thought has been burning through my mind. "But I don't get it. Why would you just randomly switch your field from history to astronomy, or business, or...whatever you took?"

"Um," Peggy says before Tristan's face can even begin to come up with a reaction. She chortles again, and takes a step back, holding her hands out in front of her. "We'll get out of your way." I lock eyes with one of the young men observing this interaction, and Peggy answers my question before I can even ask. "We take in students, interns, in astronomy, just to, um..." She waves her hands in the air. "Yeah. Anyway, again, it was so great meeting you."

"You too." I smile at her and the four interns.

Tristan waits until the five of them are back to where they started, in front of the mesmerizing screens, before continuing the conversation. He's avoiding eye contact with me, something he's rarely ever done, and shifting his weight from side to side.

"What?" I press on; I don't understand why he's so nervous.

"Raleigh, after you went missing," he says, words that still confuse and intrigue me, "all I could think about was the last time I saw you. When we fought." I sigh; I was wondering when this was going to come up. "About your beliefs." I sigh, crossing my arms, trying to ignore the nearby giant picture of me. Even after that fight, argument, whatever, I still didn't doubt my beliefs. I'm not sure if I ever could. "And after a few weeks, even after a few days, I could feel you..." Tristan takes a deep breath and closes his eyes for a moment, "It's like you were slipping away from me. Getting further and further, and I was starting to forget things. And thinking about the fight, my last conversation with you, it made me want to learn more. To feel more connected to you." All this time I've been staring deep into Tristan's eyes, but he's barely even glanced into mine. He finally locks eyes with me and smiles. "So, I switched my field. I met Peg, she had similar interests, we found other people. She was in a few business classes, I took a few, some of my credits transferred, and the rest is history. We're one of the biggest organizations in the country. We have over a hundred million followers on Facebook and Twitter, we have a website, a magazine, all because of you."

"No." My gaze hardens. I don't deserve credit for creating this place, even as much as I wish I did, it's all Tristan and Peggy. "It's not because of me."

"You gave me the reason to, Raleigh. If it weren't for you, we wouldn't be here." I can't argue with that, not after hearing Tristan's story. But a thousand other things could have changed this. "We have tons of posts online, letters, emails, all asking about you."

"What?" The words "one hundred million" then really sink into my brain, and my jaw drops a little. "Why?"

Tristan cracks a smile and shrugs playfully. "Raleigh, Peg and I based this corporation on you. Every follower, fan, subscriber, they all know your story."

"But what even is my story?" I stifle a laugh as I ask. "Did you think I was abducted, or something?"

"We wrote your story as we knew it, that you dedicated your life to proving the existence of aliens, and one day, you were gone. There were a lot of theories. Abduction, leaving to pursue a career in the craft, government conspiracy,"

"Government conspiracy." I can't help but smirk.

Upon seeing my skeptical expression, Tristan bites his lower lip, choosing his words carefully. "You have a lot of fans, Raleigh."

"But this..." I look around the building space and wave my hands around, attempting to signal to everything, "how did this even happen?

"People are more willing to believe what can't be explained." I have to take a second to let those words really flow through my mind. They bring me this strange sense of warmth and comfort, and undeniable happiness. I guess I wasn't sure that the day would ever come when someone could say that and really mean it. "A lot can happen in five years."

"Apparently," I mutter.

"It was all you, Raleigh. No one heard a story like yours before, a young girl trying to prove that aliens exist, suddenly goes missing without a trace? It got people to believe in something they'd never seen before. It got people to look in the skies like you did. It's a different time."

I find myself drawn back to the blown-up picture of my grinning face; that picture is only a few months old. I close my eyes, sighing deeply. I don't know how I'll get used to this. Millions of minutes, thousands and thousands of hours, five entire cycles of Earth around the sun, just gone. I don't know how I'm dealing with it now. I have an eerie sense of tranquillity filling my mind, something that scares me even more than the fact that five years have gone by in the blink of a night.

"I'll show you around the rest of the facility," Tristan offers, breaking my train of thought.

I nod mindlessly, taking in the giant office space once again. The calmness, I think to myself once again, and the lack of panic, as if I knew what was coming, as if I was expecting this, on some kind of level, as if I was at least somewhat prepared. That's what scares me the most.

Chapter 9

Last night, I, Raleigh Carlisle, ended up on the six o'clock news. I never watch the news, but yesterday evening, Tiffany texted me and told me to turn to the news channel. When I asked which one, she said any of them.

And there I was. My picture, the same picture hung up at NETRAD, was plastered behind the face of a Botox ridden newscaster. I took Tiffany's word literally, and I switched around to different news channels. I was on every one of them. And all of the channels had that same picture. I browsed minutes at a time, the headlines making it obvious what the news reports were about. *Girl reported missing five years ago, found.*

I couldn't peel my eyes away. For the first time in my life, I watched the news for the entire hour. I couldn't stick with one reporter either, I kept switching, catching their different takes on my situation, my story, but they're all the same; glad she's safe, but what happened?

What really struck me was when one of the women telling what she knows of my story mentioned Denton. She said that the Chief of Police, Clay Denton, refused to give a statement other than that I'm safe and have returned home. How odd it is to think of him with a first name.

I just sat there and watched, not uttering a single word.

A few of the moments I saw mentioned NETRAD and all the support that Tristan talked about before. It showed snippets of messages and tweets, including a new hashtag called NETRADRaleigh.

The moment the hour was over, I went upstairs and stayed in my room for the rest of the night. I didn't sleep until well after three, but that was fine with me. I needed time to think. My brain has not processed since this ordeal first began, just one short week ago.

Until this morning. Well, early afternoon. I wake up, and it feels like none of it has happened. I get up, expecting Tiffany over in an hour, and I have a shower, a long shower. I throw my hair in a bun, not wanting to deal with the gnarled curls, and I head downstairs for breakfast.

Only when I see the newspaper, the one my dad still expects delivered to his house every morning, does it all rushes back to me, and I have to ask myself the question; did I really forget, or is it already normal?

The headline of the Saturday paper reads, "Girl missing for five years found, unharmed." It doesn't immediately sink in that the "girl" is me. I read the first few lines of the story, which includes that same picture of me that was plastered all over the news last night.

After vanishing five years ago, Raleigh Carlisle, 20 at the time of her disappearance, has been found. Police have neither confirmed nor denied the possibility of foul play, but–

I throw the paper down onto the counter, not wanting to read anymore. Next to the paper is a scribbled note from my dad, saying that he'll be out for the day, not striking me strangely at all. He does that.

My phone, silently in my pocket, flutters into a vibrating frenzy, startling me back to focusing on the fact that Tiffany will be here within ten minutes. It's probably her calling.

"Hello?" I answer, without checking caller ID.

"Raleigh?" a deep voice says on the other end of the line that is definitely not Tiff.

"...yes?" My stomach begins to churn in knots, adding to the emptiness left from not eating for the past fourteen hours.

And then it flushes away. "It's Denton."

"Oh!" I don't bother containing my surprise. "Hi. How did you get my number?"

"Your dad gave it to me a few days ago." He answers as if he's already expecting the question. I take a deep breath, glancing at the clock; I have a few minutes. "I called you yesterday."

"You did?" I interrupt, not realizing I've done so until after it's said and done.

"Yeah." He sounds so blunt. "It went straight to voicemail."

"Oh..." I quickly check my phone, seeing if anyone called, but it comes up blank. "My phone died around six thirty, that might be why..."

I can't tell if Denton grumbles knowingly or if the connection wavers a little, but he continues. "I just wanted to talk to you about the press. Did you see the news last night?"

My eyes fix on the newspaper, and I take a deep breath. "Yeah."

"Okay, then you know that we haven't told them anything regarding your disappearance, other than that you are safe, and you shouldn't either."

It had never occurred to me that I would be questioned by reporters and "the press" about any of this. Even as I was watching the news last night, it felt like I was watching myself in some alternate universe, like it wasn't really happening to me. "Would people want to talk to me?"

"Some do," Denton casually admits. Listening to him, his voice sounds older, more tired. The realism is surreal. "I think this happened after you disappeared," the normalizing begins, "there was a law put into place a few years ago banning anyone working in the press or media to approach a victim that they deem newsworthy. It has to go through the police department where, if said victim wants to speak to a public figure, they tell the police, the police post a notice, and they are then allowed to speak to you."

My end of the conversation shrinks in silence for a few moments while I attempt to digest that ugly word. Victim. I don't like that at all.

"Raleigh?"

"I'm not a victim," I spit out, feeling extremely defensive. "Nothing bad happened to me."

"Raleigh, we don't know,"

"No, I know that I'm not a victim. I don't know a lot about what happened, but I know that I'm not a fucking 'victim.'" I glance up at the clock on the microwave; in three minutes, Tiff is, for the first time since I've ever known her, going to be late. The word victim is for someone who something terrible happened to; I don't feel this is the case.

"Look, Raleigh, my point is not to worry. If anyone bothers you, tell me, and I'll deal with them. You know what I meant, just take it easy."

I reflect for a moment, one arm crossed tightly across my abdomen, and I begin to relax. Denton has been quite the hero of late, I should really cut him some slack. "I will. Thanks. Why'd they pass that law anyway?"

"Breach of privacy, I don't know, some shit that should have been passed a long time ago."

Since I've met Denton, I've seldom heard him swear, so this is a bit of a field day for me.

"Well, no one has talked to me yet. Not that I know of."

"Perfect. I'm not too worried about the press, to be honest."

"No?"

"I'm more concerned that a few aliens nuts might try to contact you because of that whole space thing, the one your boyfriend made."

Contact.

Create contact.

My heart starts pounding in my chest, and beads of sweat begin to form along my hairline. The words "create contact" echo through my head, along with the visual words displayed before me. There's a book, the book that is currently hidden upstairs in my closet, in some kind of encasement, I think, but it's somehow in English. I can't get all the details from the brief flash in my head, but I'm confident that those words were written in that book.

Create contact…

"Raleigh?" Denton's voice snaps me from my state, and I physically shake my head.

"Yeah?"

"Are you okay?"

I blink a few times, unsure of what just happened, but remembered a critical point that Denton told me. There could be triggers for my memories. Was that something that actually happened?

"Yeah. Yeah, sorry, I just…" Should I tell Denton? I decide that I should wait until I have something more to offer than an incomplete concept, something more concrete. "I think I'll handle the alien nuts just fine."

A few seconds of silence go by before Denton clears his throat and speaks again. "Is there anything else you remember from what happened?" It's as if he knows. I can't deny it now.

"Um…I don't know if it's anything. I remember the words 'create contact.' Like, I read them in that book that I had with me."

"But the book was in a different language. You said you couldn't read it."

"I can't. I saw the words in English. And the book was in this…" I try my best to visualize it, but it's fuzzy. "Like, some pedestal or something. I don't know, it's hard to remember."

"Interesting..." And even through the phone, I can tell Denton is nodding his head, bobbing it gently up and down. I hear a small scratching sound; it must be the sound of his pen on paper. He must just carry them around with him everywhere. "All right...well, you let me know if anything comes to you, if anything becomes more clear."

"I will." I'm tempted to make another attempt at humour, but I drop it. Time and place.

Denton hangs up before I do, my phone beeping to signify it, and I place my cell down on the counter, on top of the newspaper. I don't get the chance to take more than three steps towards my fridge, let alone even think about breakfast before Tiffany comes up knocking on my door; I never feel that hungry for breakfast, anyway.

I open the door, surprised at the girl waiting on the other side. I saw her only a few days ago, but I still can't help but be shocked at how different she looks. Her clothes, though slightly more mature, aren't so different, and her hair only has a vaguely different shade and style to it, but her entire demeanour just feels so much older and more mature. She's always had that sophisticated side of her, though it was only a small part of her; now, it appears to be dominating.

"Hey," Tiffany coos, immediately reaching in for a hug.

"Hey." I hug her back, mixed emotions washing over me.

Tiff only hugs me with one arm, and I find out why when she draws away; she holds up a McDonald's bag. "I'm guessing you haven't eaten yet."

I smile wryly, chuckling a little. "You're guessing right."

She grins and then steps inside my house, letting her luscious curls bounce in unison along her shoulders. She's only about three feet in the door when she halts and begins to look around. "It looks...the same." She turns to me, a small smile upon her lips. "Your dad hasn't changed a thing."

"Yeah..." He really hasn't. It all looks the same.

Tiff takes it upon herself to find her seat on her side of the couch and drops the fast food bag, which is infecting the house with its intoxicatingly delicious scent, onto the coffee table. I find my seat, sitting on the opposite end to her, and she draws out a large carton of fries from the bag, holding it out for me just as I settle down. "Thanks."

"There's some cheeseburgers in there, too," she chirps, and pulls out some fries for herself.

"Thanks, Tiff."

She smiles, gives a quick nod, and the two of us start eating. It's not long before she begins conversation, though. "Your dad really hasn't changed one single thing, has he?"

"The TV," my voice is muffled with fries, and I use one to point, "and a couple new things in the kitchen. But I think that's it."

"Your TV is different?" Our eyes fix to the blank screen.

"Yeah, it's just a bit bigger," I confirm.

"Hm... where is your dad, anyway?"

"Oh, just out. Grocery shopping, I think."

Tiffany bites her lip and looks off towards my door as if my dad is about to walk right in. I'm not even entirely sure where my dad is; he could be out grocery shopping, or he could be at work, trying to catch up. He'd often go in on Saturdays to catch up, and especially after staying home for the week, I can't imagine him wanting to stay home today. "How is he doing?"

I shrug, about to dismiss it, but I can tell that she really wants to know. I clear my throat and readjust on the couch, swallowing the remnants of the fries in my mouth. "He's okay..." I try to think of more to say, but the words just don't come to me.

Tiffany faces me further, drawing a leg up onto the couch, lining her arm along the back. "I haven't talked to him since...well, obviously at the hospital, but before that, it had been years...I came a few times to say hi in the months after you were gone..."

"He's okay," I repeat, finding those words hold a lot more meaning that they seem. There really isn't much to say about my dad. He's more of a roommate than anything. I can tell in her eyes that she's asking to be polite, because I saw the disconnect between her and my dad at the hospital. They were always cordial and kind, but after my and Tiff's conversation, and how unimpressed she was that my dad wasn't too bothered about my situation, she skirts a little around the topic.

Tiffany smiles, seeming relieved that she did not, in fact, step on my toes, and relaxes a little more on my familiar couch. "And you, how are you?"

I chuckle, trying but failing to refrain from stuffing my face with food, "I'm okay, too...I'd rather ask about you, how are you? What are you doing now, where do you work, do you have a boyfriend?"

A cheeky smile arises on her lips, and I know the answer to my last question. "I'm doing pretty good," she begins, "I do have a boyfriend."

"And when did this happen?" I can't help but smile, nostalgia creeping up on me; is it still nostalgia even if you don't remember the years between a memory? All the hundreds of times we spent talking about boys in our high school years, how amazing our future boyfriends would be, it all rushes back to me. It must be nostalgia.

"Two years ago. We met up two and a half years ago, decided that we'd just be friends, and then started dating six months later."

"How did you meet?" Another flood of memories, brainstorming the fantastic ways we'd meet our amazing boyfriends.

"Online. That's how everyone meets," she jokes, but I can tell she's serious. I guess even more romance has turned to the internet for help.

I inch closer, eager to hear more and to eat more; I've managed to demolish my fries, and so I reach into the paper bag to grab one of the burgers. "Well, tell me about him!"

Tiff blushes and avoids eye contact, biting her lip to keep from grinning. I've never seen her this shy before. "His name is Cole. He's the same age as us, a month younger than me, and he's...great. He's going to school to be a vet right now, he loves animals. And he really wants to meet you."

I arch an eyebrow, a little thrown off, and swallow the remainder of my burger. "Oh, really?"

Tiff nods then chuckles a little. "Well, who doesn't?" I force a neutral expression, and my stomach finally beginning to feel full, but I still reach for my second burger. Sensing my discomfort, Tiffany continues, "And, yes, I have a job. I finished my four years of school, and, as dumb as it sounds, I am a secretary."

"Well, do you like it?" My voice is muffled from the burger in my mouth, but she hears me.

"Yeah, I really like it."

"Then it's not dumb."

Tiff smiles again, this time much more humble, and she allows herself to say, "You haven't changed at all, Raleigh." I can't help but feel warm inside. "I don't know, it just kind of seems dumb. I have my degree, and I'm a secretary. I mean, I love it, I really didn't think I'd love it so much, it sometimes just feels silly to think that I went to school for four years to end up here."

"What did you get your degree in?" I ask. After hearing about Tristan's 180 and changing career paths, I don't want to assume Tiff has done the same.

"Economics, same as before," she says. "I interviewed for this company downtown, Fairfield, and instead of offering me an internship, they offered me a secretary job. I didn't think I wanted to take it, but I did anyway because I thought maybe I could climb up the ladder that way, but I like just being a secretary, as weird as that sounds."

"That's not weird. That's awesome, I'm glad you found a job you like. Nothing worse than working at a shitty job just for the money."

"Tell me about it." She rolls her eyes, shaking her head. She hated her first job and judging by the look on her face, I'm guessing she's had a few other hated jobs in that time as well. "You seemed kind of surprised that I was still in econ."

"Oh, no, just..." I crumple up the paper my burger was wrapped in, and toss it onto my coffee table. I still feel hungry, but I'm not about to start eating Tiffany's food, too. She's onto her first burger now. "The whole NETRAD thing."

"Oh, yeah, you know Tristan switched his studies."

I nod mindlessly, still drawn back from the fact that an incredible corporation like NETRAD exists. "Yeah, I actually went there on Thursday."

"To the building?" I nod. "Really? What did you think? I only went to the grand opening, and that was, what, two years ago?"

Two years. "It's...wow. I mean, it's amazing."

"Yeah," Tiff stifles a laugh and gazes off, scanning in my house once again. "I have to admit, I'm less skeptical than before." She meets my eyes, smiling softly, but it begins to slip away. "And you?"

"...me what?" I draw my knees up onto the couch, sitting cross-legged, my palms resting on my knees.

"I mean...with what happened, how you described it, it sounds like it was–"

"I know." I don't try to interrupt her, and I shoot her a gentle glance as an apology. "I... I don't remember what it was, but–"

"What else could it be?" Tiffany returns the same glance. I can't argue with that. "Do you think it was–"

"Yeah." I have given it a lot of thought. The possibility of it being something extraterrestrial was a thought I almost couldn't believe, because I wanted to believe in it so deeply. I was so reluctant to think of it as a spaceship, a flying saucer, a UFO, in case my mind was playing tricks on me, and I was only seeing what I wanted to see, what I believed I was seeing. But I know me, and I know that this was not a terrestrial occurrence. "I do." I pause for a moment, trying to read her expression. I'm about to ask if she does too, but that doesn't really matter to me. It doesn't matter if she believes me or not; I'm not the type of person to sway easily, or at all.

"Aren't you scared?" Tiffany suddenly blurts out, her voice closer to yelling than anything else. She laughs nervously and then gazes off, about to reach for her second burger, but she draws back. "I mean...it scares me. The fact that you were gone, that you don't look different, that there could be actual..." She raises her hands up towards the ceiling, towards the sky, unable to say the words. "Aren't you scared?"

I take a deep breath; I've asked myself this question a lot. I've asked myself this question more in the past week than I have at any other point in my life. The answer is always changing. "Tiff," I begin, unsure of where to go from there, but my mouth seems to have other plans, "it's...hard to explain. I have this strange," I draw my hands up; I have the habit of using my hands to get my point across, even though I know it's completely useless, "feeling, this strange, calm feeling deep down that just...not remembering what happened, of course, that scares me sometimes. But at the same time, I feel almost comforted. Subconsciously, I don't feel scared, it's almost like, deep down, I know nothing bad happened. I wasn't hurt, look at me, I'm not hurt." I've even checked for anything that could possibly be an injury; not a scratch or a bruise. Nothing. "I'm okay. And maybe I'm stupid for believing this feeling, this instinct, but I feel like I've been okay that entire time, during all that lost time, I was fine."

"Raleigh?" Tiff interrupts my thoughts, and the things I want to say to her, the scenario I wanted to act out. I know what I feel, but I also know how it sounds; naïve.

I meet her eyes, her filled with concern and wonder. "Yeah, sometimes," I say, finding that those two words can sum up all of the things that I'm feeling. Upon seeing Tiffany's face though, even more worried than before, I add, "I'm not hurt, Tiff. I'm okay."

Almost as if her mind was somewhere else, she snaps back to smiling and shrugs heavily, all the while shaking her head. "I know."

Her voice is so smooth, it almost convinces me that she's not nervous for me.

The day drags on, and Tiffany and I talk late into the night. My dad eventually comes home, but only gives a quick hello, puts away groceries, and then heads upstairs, all within five minutes flat, and doesn't disturb us again. He's never really felt the need to really get to know my friends, so he takes it upon himself to make himself scarce.

Tiff, now with her own car, leaves around midnight after she asks me five times if I want to go to sleep. I'm surprised at how tired I am, and I finally indulge her and decide to head to bed. Tiff promises that she'll text me tomorrow, which I know she will, and that we'll hang out sometime soon. I'm already excited to hang out again. She's my best friend, and even though it hadn't felt five years since I'd seen her, I missed her.

It's not too long after Tiffany leaves that I head off to bed. I'm not sure why I'm so tired, considering the time I woke up and the amount of sleep I got last night, but I still take it as a sign to head to bed. I lock the door after Tiffany leaves, and I listen to her car, her mom's old Toyota that Tiff bought from her, speed down the street. How odd it is that Tiffany can drive now. I slowly turn off all the lights downstairs, and creep up to the second floor, careful to avoid the creaks on the stairs. While I'm ascending, though, I notice that none of the stairs are making any sound at all. I guess my dad fixed the stairs?

When I pass my dad's office, I can't help but peek inside, through the small sliver of the barely open door, and find a sight that I've rarely seen before; an empty office. The lights from the neighbours, outside of the giant windows, are just enough to illuminate the room to see that my dad isn't inside. I glance at his bedroom door, closed. He must be asleep.

Before ducking into my room, I stop in the bathroom. I brush my teeth and wash my face, not bothering to floss tonight, and then migrate into my room. With each step I take, more and more fatigue washes over me; by the time I'm in my pyjamas, I'm ready to collapse.

However, when I lay down, I can't sleep. I toss and turn, shifting the blankets for cold spots in the unseasonably warm weather, I flip my pillow around, and adjust a thousand times.

And then I reach the state where I'm not even sure whether or not I'm awake. I feel like I'm floating just above my bed, my sheets barely touching me. My eyes are so heavy, I can't open them, even when I try. My body is stiff, almost lifeless, unable to move.

I'm standing up, outside, wind flowing around me but not touching my skin. Leaves flutter by my feet, my boots. A large object is hovering in the sky, near the patch of grass with the one streetlight. I can't find my voice.

I still feel the heaviness, like something is weighing me down, I feel dizzy from the feeling. Within the object, the massive metal thing that has sharp edges, not cylindrical at all, abandoning all rules of aerodynamics, a silhouette appears. Another rectangle within the rectangle, within the, dare I say, *ship*, and slowly floats outwards, towards me. I quickly learn that it is a door, opening, not toward me, but towards the ground, a sort of ramp. And within that doorway, one that extends feet above the average human height, a figure–

My eyes, no longer weighted, shoot open. All my bones, my muscles, they all seem to turn to jelly, or even to nothing, and a sickening feeling rushes through me.

I'm going to be sick.

I start dry heaving as one hand fumbles for my lamp, my arm still nearing limp, and the other for something, anything, that could substitute as a bowl. I have nothing within reach.

The light from my lamp stings my eyes, and I throw up a little inside my mouth. I instinctively swallow it, almost regretting my choice. I lie in wait to see if I'll be sick again, or if not moving will help calm my stomach, tears filling my eyes.

I don't move for a solid minute, keeping my eyes pressed shut.

I finally force myself to sit up, swinging my legs to the side of my bed, and I grip the edge of my mattress, taking in gulps of air.

I don't think.

My feet leading me all the way, my vision slightly blurred, I find my way downstairs, to the kitchen, with a glass in my hand. I fill it halfway with water and swish it around in my mouth before spitting it into the sink. I do this six times.

When I finally feel calm enough to really concentrate on anything, I check the clock on the microwave; Tiffany left two hours ago. It's 2:18 in the morning.

I don't know if I was asleep or not. I can't say for sure that that wasn't a construction of my dream state, as opposed to a real memory, though it could even be both. A memory disguised as a dream, how poetic.

I fill my glass with water, after a quick rinse, and drink the entire thing in under ten seconds. I head upstairs again, clutching a new cup of water, wanting only to return back to bed. In the hall, almost to my bedroom, my stomach lurches again.

I'm immersed with the giant craft again, the shape levitating in the sky, the door lowering, the figure showing through, reaching tall, taller than a human...I think.

It only lasts a few seconds before I stumble onto my own two feet, in my hallway, dry heaving again. I rush into the bathroom, ignoring the accidentally spilled water from my cup. I slam the cup down onto the counter next to the sink and grip onto either side of the porcelain bowl. Just as it dawns on me to throw up in the toilet, I vomit into the sink.

After a few minutes, I consider myself safe. Once again, I rinse my mouth out, this time only five rinses, but adding mouthwash to the mix, and I stare at myself in the mirror. My pallor has dropped significantly, which doesn't even seem possible. My lip is quivering, my entire body is shaking. The only thing holding me up right now is my arms, my hands, planted firmly on the marble counter. My legs are useless, wobbling uncontrollably.

I force eye contact with myself in the mirror, shifting from one eye to the other.

I don't ask myself what's going on. I know what's going on. Somehow, I'm remembering.

I'm remembering that lost time five years ago.

Chapter 10

It's 7:23 in the morning when I first wake up. I immediately attempt to throw myself back into a deep sleep, but after an hour of lying in bed, I give up. I'm stuck, awake, in the morning. I've never been a morning person, though I've always admired the idea of being awake for the entirety of the sun being up.

I force myself to sit up, blankets still draped on and around my rapidly cooling body, and I try to plan my day. Dad is off at work, his first technical day back after his "insisted" week off. We spent some time together, we spoke, which is what his boss's intention was, but he doesn't really get the relationship my dad and I have. And how we can apparently go five years without a thing happening and only have a few moments, mere seconds, of conversation and be moderately content. It's one anomaly after another.

The thought of hanging out with Tiffany briefly enters my mind, but then I remember that she has school. And then I remember that she's done school, and not only has a job but a career. At her old job, at my old jobs, we could visit each other and just talk for a solid fifteen minutes without anybody caring. I can't exactly do that at a corporate office, as far as I know, but I don't know the courtesy of a business setting.

I think of my other friends, the ones whose Facebook messages and emails have gotten lost in the notifications of NETRAD fans and followers, reporters, and random people I can't even be sure that I'd met but apparently attended a school of mine, the friends who I scarcely talked to before the five years even flew by. I look back and think about those high school friends but feel them rapidly fading away. They're already gone.

There is only one person who I both can and want to go see today.

I toss my comforter and sheets off my body, and after my initial regret, I hop out of bed and find something to wear. I go through most of my wardrobe, but I end up back wearing my go-to outfit.

I stare at myself in the full-length mirror in my dad's bedroom, stroking my skirt; my style hasn't changed, but it feels older to me. I never really dressed for my age, never wore those sweaters with animals on them, the ears on the hood, never got into plastering my shirts with "clever" quotes, I've always just tried to find nice pieces of clothing. Some things never change.

After doing my makeup, I skip down the stairs and find some my bus pass from my purse. Rumbling fills my ears, startling me, which is when I realize the downpour happening outside. It's almost enough to make me want to stay home, go back upstairs and curl into my bed. The temptation grows when I hypothesize that my sheets are still warm. The attraction fades, and I raid the coat closet for a suitable jacket. I can't find a waterproof one, so I stick to a wool coat and grab my pink umbrella.

It's not raining as hard as I thought, but still harder than it usually does. I'm pretty sure we're the city with the most rain in the country, though often drizzles and showers, as we scarcely see any sort of storm. Or, maybe the weather has changed over the past few years.

Global warming must be taking even more effect by now.

The bus stop, thankfully only a few minutes away, doesn't provide any shelter for me; only a single pole stands, bearing five single digits.

The entire bus ride, including the transfer to get me to my destination, I set the music to shuffle and let the randomness serenade my ears. For once in my life, I'm not micromanaging what song plays next, or when a particular song ends or begins, or playing any songs on repeat. I let the songs randomly present themselves. In all honesty, though, I barely hear the songs on my journey. If anything, I hear the hopefully never-ceasing rain and my own thoughts, all of which revolve around NETRAD.

My first and only visit to NETRAD was terrific. I was overwhelmed; every aspect of that facility interests me, from the many screens to all the desk work, to the giant telescope peering up into the sky. I can't begin to imagine how beautiful it would be to peer into a telescope like that one. An outside view of a planet pops into mind, curved glass the only thing separating the planet and I. The sky surrounding it is dark and speckled with stars, and I can feel my eyes twinkling at the thought. The planet almost looks like Earth, except with more brown than I would imagine. I open my eyes; I must have seen whatever planet that was through the telescope I borrowed from my high school.

On the second bus ride, I rest my head against the ever-moving window, occasionally flinching at individual drops of rain hitting the window, but keeping my gaze focused on seeing the facility. I've gotten a few stares on both buses, more so on this one, and hushed notes on who I am. It's a strange feeling. I'm grateful that no one talks to me about it; I don't have a clue what I'd say.

The bus begins to ascend a gentle slope, and I know that I'm almost there. Over the line of the horizon, I start to see the bulge of the tallest part, the telescope hidden just beyond my view of the roof, and soon the rest of the building reveals itself. I hadn't noticed that the colour of the place is just plain white, but it really stands out against the gray sky. It doesn't blend in with white fluffy clouds as it did the first time; this white is vibrant, alive, and much more noticeable.

I hop off the bus at the nearest stop, only a short walk from the door, and immediately wrap my arms around myself. The weather has cooled down considerably, but I might just be thinking that because of how warm the bus was. It drives away, leaving me standing alone, destroying any hopes of me returning to said warmth.

I march along the sidewalk and into the parking lot of the facility, passing by Tristan's new car; it feels so odd without the clunker.

The doors, automatically opening upon my entrance, introduce me to the still new lobby. A receptionist, a different man than last time, hardly takes a second to glance up and greet me. "Hello," his chipper voice rings.

I produce a basic grin, and cautiously approach the intimidating desk. I place my chilled hands atop the counter, and I'm about to speak when I look behind the receptionist's desk. There's a picture, or rather an abstract painting, of a forest, but a forest with only a few trees. It's not a print, as far as I can tell, and behind the glowing green trees, there is a sunrise. However, I notice the moon as well. Its light is fading, but it is still noticeable enough, just about being cut off by one of the trees, and the edge of the canvas. It's the kind of art I would love to have in my future home.

I'm not sure why I didn't notice it before.

"Hi," I chime back. "Um..." I cautiously eye the door that I entered through last time, unsure if I can just walk in or not. "I'm here to see...Tristan." The receptionist pauses, his baby face frozen, and he slowly raises his eyebrows. "...Barnes." *Is there more than one Tristan here?*

"Do you have an appointment?" He eyes me carefully, suspiciously. I wouldn't be surprised if it was a rare occurrence for visitors to simply drop by.

"...no. I'm his friend." I glance at the door again, debating whether or not I should make a run for it. I didn't see any security guards last time I was here, but I really wasn't looking for them.

"I'm sorry, you'll need to make an appointment."

I shift my stance, taking a tiny step towards the door leading to all the wonder of desks and screens. "Well, can I make an appointment for now?"

He chuckles briefly, though I can't tell if it's because he's unimpressed, shakes his head, and takes a quick peek at his computer screen. "Appointments need to be made with at least twenty-four hours notice."

I lean against the desk, pressing my forearms to the smooth top, just next to a small candy bowl with Werther's candies inside. "Look, if you just told him that I was here, he'd probably let me in." As I'm speaking, it does cross my mind that I should have called him, or at least texted, beforehand to give Tristan some warning that I'd be showing up.

"I'm sorry,"

"It's fine, Jeff," the devil's voice interrupts, suddenly appearing in the doorway leading inside the facility. I meet his eyes, and he smiles, and then transfers the contact to the receptionist. "She's always allowed in. This is Raleigh."

A small sound similar to the letter R breaks free from Jeff's tight lips, and then his eyes widen madly, and his mouth drops to a small O shape. "Oh, my goodness." I can't help but grin politely. "I am so sorry, Ms. Carlisle, it is an honour to meet you." He stands, flinging his chair back against the wall, and extends his arm out to me.

"Just Raleigh is okay," I say, shaking his trembling hand, and he smiles, exasperated, and then takes a step back. I can tell that he's not going to call me Raleigh.

I turn back to Tristan, and he holds the heavy looking door, along with his arm, to lead me inside. "Come on in."

I don't hesitate to head towards Tristan, letting myself into the facility that seems much more familiar than I thought it would after only being here once. I suppose it makes me feel like home to be surrounded by outer space.

"Sorry about that," Tristan says. "Jack is out sick today, we have Jeff who comes in as a cover sometimes."

"That's fine," I mutter, more distracted by my surroundings.

Marvelling at the massive office space, recognizing the screens and seeing what must be planets up close in a few of the televisions, I don't even hear the door shut behind and Tristan appear behind me until he speaks up, "So, what are you doing here?" I quickly turn around, finding myself confronted with Tristan, a soft look in his eyes and a gentle smile on his lips. "I didn't expect to see you today."

"Yeah, sorry...I kind of just showed up." I try my best to keep my eyes focused on Tristan, but the telescope seems to be my primary focus. I do a double take over the screens, trying to see if any planets look like the one I saw in my head earlier; no dice.

"It's fine! You're welcome here anytime you want." He sticks his hands in the pockets of his blazer, and sways gently back and forth. "So. Any reason for your visit?"

I shrug, following suit with the swaying, and allow my mind to take it all in for a second time; words cannot describe. "Not really...I just wanted to visit." The thought of remembering only a little more of what happened flashes through my mind, and I bit my lip to refrain from telling Tristan about it. I meet his eyes. "Do you..." I clear my throat. "Do you know anything about what happened when I just...disappeared?" His calm grin and demeanour fade and he shifts uncomfortably in his stance, but I press on. "Any...I don't know, I mean,"

"Some."

My eyes widen; I'm not sure what I was expecting his answer to be, but it was not that. My heart flutters a little, even hearing a possibility of explaining what exactly happened and why I can't remember. "You have something?"

"Well...it's not much. We have a video feed from the night you disappeared on Edgar Street."

"So, you can see what happened?"

Before I get my hopes up too high, Tristan shakes his head solemnly. "No, we can't. The video was facing just at the corner of Edgar and Caulfield, but–"

"Edgar and Caulfield." My hopes begin to rise again. "In front of that empty lot, Tristan, that's where it happened!"

"Denton told me," Tristan mutters, his expression crushing my spirits. "There's nothing that we can see. No ship, no light, no anything."

"Can I still see it?"

Tristan nods quickly and extends his arm towards the many screens surrounded by employees. "Of course!" He steps past me, placing his hand briefly on my back to urge me forward, and then takes me through the rows of desks, all the way to the screens. Two metal steps are leading up to the raised platform, where Peggy, who I recognize by her hair, and a few interns stand, watching the interactive planets. There's another man along with them who I don't recognize, in his late twenties, pointing to one of the screens containing nothing but stars and constellations within them.

"Peg," Tristan says, distracting from the other man's speech.

Peggy looks over and smiles widely upon seeing me. "Raleigh! Welcome back." She sounds excited, but her voice is still hushed out of fear of interrupting the other man.

"Thanks." I glance at the interns; their eyes are plastered to the screens. I think the interns are the same as last time, I recognize one of the boys. *Men*, I guess, considering that he's older than me...

"She wants to see the tape," Tristan says, and he and Peggy staring into each others' eyes. It's not exactly hard to place what look is in her eyes, and possibly Tristan's; I can't tell from the angle I'm at.

"Oh, I'll show you where it is." Peggy turns, now fully interrupting the older man, and says, "I have to step away for a while, so Mr. Peters will be teaching until I return." Mr. Peters, the older man, nods, barely giving Peggy a glance, and then continues as if nothing had stopped him in the first place. Peggy smiles. "Come with me."

Peggy leads, and I trail with Tristan on my tail along the raised platform with matching silver rails, towards a lean hallway. The office begins to close off, with doors on either the left and right side of the hall; the soft cream colour of the entrance, decorated with nothing but the off-white pallor, almost looked like an entirely different building compared to the open, busy space. The sound is nearly sliced once the two walls close us in.

We take the first door on the right, already walking past one on the left, into a room with a large table in the centre, comfortable looking chairs, and a projector facing an empty wall. Peggy turns on the faint light, takes a glance at the projector, and then turns around so quickly that she almost runs into me. She averts her startled eyes to Tristan. "Do you have the key?"

He only hesitates for a moment before digging through his pocket and then drawing out a set of about a dozen keys. He flips through a couple before plucking out the right one and then hands the full set to Peggy.

I meander towards the projector, grazing my fingertips along the top of the smooth table until I find that there's a laptop attached to the projector. It looks a bit bigger than my own, but otherwise, not so different; I'm surprised, considering specific advancements in technology five years ago were moving so quickly...

"Second drawer, right?" Peggy is crouched down next to the smaller of the two filing cabinets of the room, each on either side of the empty wall. As she's asking Tristan her questions, she's already unlocking the second drawer.

"Yep." Tristan appears beside me and presses the power button for the projector, and then opens the laptop. It's only then that I see the more significant differences between my and this laptop. The keyboard is nonexistent; the entire bottom half is flat, only with lights illuminating the outlines and symbols of where the keyboard should be. It's almost like a touchscreen keyboard.

Once the laptop is all set up, after Tristan has also revealed to me that the screen is in fact used by touch as well, Peggy stands beside me and holds out a USB to Tristan.

"People still use USBs," I mutter to myself, but manage to turn both sets of eyes onto mine.

"Better than hard drives," Tristan mumbles back and sticks the stick into the port.

The folders load within a few seconds, and there are dozens of them. Maybe even hundreds, all labelled with different dates, different time stamps. I don't get the chance to read them all, but there seems to be at least one every few days. Tristan searches for the date of my disappearance and then clicks on the folder. Even within the folder, there are still dozens of files. Different text documents, pictures, types of files that I don't even recognize. Tristan scrolls down, my mind fixed on the fact that computer mice and trackpads have become entirely obsolete, until he stumbles across a media file.

"Take a seat," Tristan says, giving me a glance, and then gazing over to Peggy. I take the seat closest to the projection of the video that, as it's loading, I grow more and more nervous to see. Tristan and Peggy take seats across from me, Tristan turning the laptop so that he can still control it from his position.

All at once, a video feed without any sound begins playing, plastering the wall, of a sight that at first, isn't even familiar. It takes me a few seconds to place where I am, where Tristan said I would be; on the corner of Edgar and Caulfield. From the video camera, I can see the light post where I stood only a few feet from, probably just out of the focus of the feed, and part of the vacant lot, where houses were allegedly going to be built.

"What time is this?"

"Just past midnight, says at the bottom right." I follow Tristan's index to find the small time stamp, showing the hour, minutes, seconds, and milliseconds. It is just past midnight, literally only a couple of seconds.

My shoulders grow tense. That night, I left Tristan's house just after midnight. Within a few minutes, I should be seeing myself, watching that object brighten the entire neighbourhood. But I don't.

In my mind, I'm transported to a place where my body freezes; I feel like an outsider in my own skin, goosebumps crawling across my skin. I haven't been back to that spot since I first woke up. I don't think I'm ready to go back there yet.

Definitely not ready, a voice inside me chimes.

I think a small part of me might even be scared.

The video ends after a solid fifteen minutes of nothing. The file closes, and I'm confronted with the folder of my disappearance once again. "It's over?"

Tristan sighs, shrugging, leaning back in his swivelling chair. "That's it."

"I should get back," Peggy says. I had almost forgotten she was in the room with us; granted, I had almost forgotten anyone but myself was in the room with me. She stands, and gives Tristan's shoulder a tight squeeze, offering an even tighter smile. "I'll see you later." She looks at me, her hand still squeezing, and smiles. "It was nice to see you again. I'm sure I'll see you again soon."

"Nice to see you too," I grin back, but I can't keep my grin to last very long. The second Peggy leaves the room, I'm in my slump again. "I don't understand. How was there nothing there?"

"That's where it happened, right?" Tristan has always been a reasonably level person in general, but he seems more level than ever right now.

"Yeah. Literally, right there, I was, what, four feet from that streetlamp. How is it not...are you sure this is the right night?"

Tristan cracks a small smile and nods slowly, averting his eyes to focus on the modern laptop. "Very sure. I've checked about twenty times and had it analyzed by professionals. It's the right moon cycle, the right amount of darkness for that time of night, it's the right night."

"The leaf..."

"What?"

I face Tristan, his thoughts intrigued. "There was a leaf," I recall, "that blew by me, right by my feet when I stopped. A few leaves. They should have..." I hold my hand out to the video, at a loss for words. I don't even know how to respond at this point. Before I can think of any other suitable response, I find myself asking, "Can you play it again?"

And he obliges. I sit on the edge of my seat, being careful not to even blink too many times, and I observe. I keep my head focused on finding anything, literally anything, within the video. Minutes go by. And then I do see something. For what can't even be an entire frame, what must be a small, small fraction of a frame, the feed goes dark. "What was that?" I shoot up in my seat and point, looking to Tristan to see if he noticed. It's easy to tell by his reaction that he has.

He pauses the video, and switches to the folder containing the video, and then clicks the media file next to it. It's only five seconds long. On the fourth second, I realize that this is the original video played in very slow motion, and the feed goes black. Tristan pauses it. "This only lasts about two milliseconds." I meet his eyes. "Per the electricity company, this was apparently a power outage."

"A power outage?" I look at the time stamp. This has to be around the five or six-minute mark after leaving Tristan's house, when..." I hold my hand out to the screen. "This is when,"

"That's what I figured," he says, and then rubs his face with his hands. "Our best guess is that the camera had some sort of malfunction.

This isn't present in any other video from that night at that time."

"Malfunction?"

Tristan shrugs. "We don't know. No visible tampering has been made, the camera had been untouched, there was absolutely nothing out of the ordinary or wrong with the camera, except this glitch. What we've thought is that something made the camera turn off, even for a second..." He notices my smirk. "What?"

I can't help but try to identify the man I used to know, who didn't even think about if he believed in life forms outside of planet Earth. I can barely recognize him today. He couldn't possibly lie within the man who's dedicated his career towards proving, though moreover finding, extraterrestrial life. "What do you think it was?"

Tristan holds his hand close to his face, his first two fingers along his hairline, his second two across his lips, and his thumb supporting his chin. His eyes glaze over, and he seldom blinks, gently shaking his head. He swiftly throws his hand up, shrugging along with it, and manages a smile. "Aliens!"

I chuckle, drawing the joking side out of him, even if it's just a little bit. "And what do you mean by aliens?"

"Beings not of this world." He says the words so bluntly and flat, I let my smile crack a little further. He clears his throat and rolls closer towards the table, closer towards me, and rests his forearms on top of the wooden table top. "What is it?"

"What is what?"

He flaunts his level smile, the practiced yet natural smile of a working man. "What's troubling you?"

I laugh, scanning the rest of the darkened room. "The fact that I can't remember. The fact that it's been five years, and the fact that I don't even know why what happened did, in fact, happen."

Tristan, a calm look on his face, waits a minute of staring into my eyes before reacting. He rolls closer to me until our knees are almost pressed together, and then gently pats one of my own, tightening his grip around my kneecap. He then captures my attention once again and removes his hand from my leg. "Raleigh, you were the craziest alien nut I'd ever met." I narrow my eyes at him; I'm not sure what he's trying to do here. If his mission was to slightly annoy me, he has succeeded. Feeling my seething frustration, he continues, "Nothing could stop your beliefs. Nothing could change your beliefs. It was really...impressive." He briefly strokes his stubble with one hand, and then laces his fingers together, resting his hands neatly on his lap. "Really, I know it must have been hard."

"It wasn't," I blurt out. He arches an eyebrow, just slightly, and I shake my head. "It didn't seem like a lot of people understood that it wasn't as hard to be open about what I believed. It was harder not to be." I think of a way to even begin to explain how that involves the judgements, the misconceptions, the overall paranoia, but I really have nothing else to say. I don't need to say anymore. Sure, it sucked when people made fun of me, but it was a whole lot worse denying who I was and what I wanted to do.

"Well, that's great, Raleigh." Another genuine smile flashes for just a moment. "That's great to hear you say, but...now, with all that's been happening, it almost seems like you don't want to believe anymore."

I bite my lip. It took me days of endless thinking to figure out why I felt so unsettled about the entire situation, and my conclusion only gave me some clarity. I did, for a brief time, consider that fact that all my beliefs had just gone out the window and I refused to believe it, but that's not true. "I do believe." I pick my words very carefully, plucking them from the vocabulary inside my brain. "But the idea of an abduction? That is the part that I cannot process. That I was abducted, or taken, or whatever you want to call it, it doesn't..."

"You can't control that stuff, it's beyond you."

My sensitive side gets the best of me, and I tense up, biting my lip once again, harder, to exert some anger. "I know that." My teeth grind slightly, and I force a deep breath to calm myself down. "I understand that. But...it doesn't seem right."

The entire time that I've been speaking to Tristan, I haven't looked him in the eye. And now that I do, I realize why I haven't. Because he doesn't get it. I don't know how to explain it, and he doesn't understand it because I don't know how to explain it. I suppose the purest form of it is saying that it's a "gut feeling."

Tristan is looking at me like I can't accept what happened, and he is right because I can't, but not for the reason that he thinks.

He swiftly claps his hands onto the table, changing the somber mood of the room, and while he asks, "Do you want to see something cool?" he rolls over to his laptop and begins sorting through the hundreds of files again.

I inch a little closer to him, and the thought strikes my mind,

"How big is that USB?"

"You wouldn't believe it," he replies with a smirk. Suddenly, a video begins projecting onto the empty wall, and Tristan returns to his side of the table, clearing the way.

And the video shows...a UFO. People are gawking at the spacecraft in the sky, trying to zoom in on it with their limited camera. It almost looks like a giant disk, without the top bulge that a traditional UFO might have.

The clip suddenly switches to a night sky, and people speaking what I can only recognize as Spanish. There is a glowing orange light in the sky above, and a few mutters giving their personal commentary of the sighting. The light doesn't look like too much, but all of a sudden, a bright blue light fills the sky surrounding the orange circular dot and displays the silhouette of an object that must be at least a hundred feet long. A few of the people scream, a few remain silent, but the majority gasp and then drop to a hush.

"Oh, my god."

The clip switches again, but Tristan speaks to grab my focus. "They're different types of UFOs, aliens, flying saucers, from all over the world." I laugh, placing the scene of this next video by the highest tip of the illuminated Eiffel Tower. "People send these to us to examine, see if they're real, to help us." I can't peel my eyes away from the different spaceships, each more amazing than I can even imagine. "And it's all because of you."

My throat goes dry upon hearing those words, and that instant of terror that I had last night returns in full swing. The night, the ship, the figure. *The figure.* It disappears as quickly as it appears, and I take a deep breath.

My eyes grow warm, and I know what that means, but I don't want to admit it to myself. I can't help but get a little emotional. People all over the world are sending NETRAD videos of sightings in hopes of helping research and discovering more about what we don't yet know. They're helping. It brings a smile to my face, not only the fact that these people are doing all that they can with one camera and a postage stamp, but how much it reminds me of me, of my attempts at picturing the sightings, proving them. All these people...it's just amazing.

And it's all because of...

Chapter 11

Once again, my efforts to sleep in have been foiled. I wake up early to an odd sensation, the feeling of wind barrelling down on me as if pushing me into my bed. It's almost like my body wants to float away from my warm blankets, and is being forced down by the strong gust.

It's an unsettling feeling.

I stay in bed for a while, squeezing my eyes shut, trying to remember what dream I could have had to bring upon those feelings. I know it wasn't a dream, though, and more of a memory. I've only felt wind like that once before.

My stomach churns in knots, my body feeling like it's free falling into space until I open my eyes again. My room returns to me, and all my surroundings gain familiarity.

I won't be falling asleep again after that.

I slip out of bed, not bothering to change out of my pajamas, and I head downstairs to a rare sighting; my father. I can't remember the last time I saw him getting ready for work if it's ever happened. He leaves by 7:30.

As if this is a common occurrence, my dad looks up from his paper but sticks his nose right back into it after making eye contact. "Morning, Raleigh."

"Morning."

I approach him at the bar and take the seat next to him, eyeing his neglected coffee and toast. His hand absentmindedly reaches for the bread slathered in peanut butter and jam, and he eats it in an impressive four bites.

7:23.

"How'd you sleep?" Dad asks through his last mouthful,

swallowing with a quiet gulp.

"Good," I humour, "you?"

He nods curtly, now downing his coffee. After a few seconds of silence and his chugging, "Good. Do you want some toast?"

"Yeah, sure. Thanks."

Dad sets himself to work, drawing out butter for my plain toast, and places it on the counter before me. He instinctively pours me a glass of water, and then begins working on the bread. I've never really seen him in the mornings, but he seems to take them pretty casually. I think he gets up an hour early, giving him time to lounge around, compared to my fifteen minutes of getting ready in the morning. His work, despite its aggression towards the business world, does take their employees in a more relaxed manner.

I sigh quietly, quiet enough so Dad doesn't hear, and let my mind think about the topic that has entered my brain and left it just as fast; work. I haven't asked my dad, or Denton, or anyone about what happened to my quaint and perfect job after my disappearance, though I can assume. Work hasn't exactly been high on my priority list when it comes to the extraterrestrial experience. Any time I've even thought of Space Age, and those have been rare, I immediately stick it to the back burner. I never had the energy to think about work and all the repercussions.

As the thought of my past job encircles my brain, I think about all of my co-workers; are any of them still working there? Rose, Michelle, is Lex even there? I can't imagine him wanting to sell his own business, considering how much time and effort he's put into it, but five years...that can do a lot. Everyone there, whoever is still there from five years ago, must have heard about me. They must have had their own theories, kidnapping, abduction, traveling.

I should visit.

Within an instant, I decide on my plans for the day; I should pay Space Age a visit. If not to see the people I'd been working with for almost a year, to see how the store has changed. All the products are all still there in my head, in their proper places, in glass displays, on the shelves. Perfectly placed.

Dad slides the plate of toast in front of me and then hops up to his feet.

"I need the car today, staying late at work," he announces.

I take a bit of my toast as he speaks, and I chew thoughtfully.

Taking public transit has never been a problem for me.

"Okay," I respond.

He doesn't look me in the eye at all, instead makes his way to the front door, and snatches his briefcase up along with him. As he reaches for the handle, I find myself interrupting his groove.

"Dad?"

He stops himself. His fingers grip into a fist, just in front of the knob, and he swiftly turns around to meet my eyes.

"How are you doing?" I ask meekly, rouge flushing my cheeks.

"I'm fine. How are you?"

"I'm okay." I gulp down the mouthful of bread in my mouth, reaching for my water to soothe my throat. "It's just all a bit...weird."

"I agree," he states.

The two of us stand in silence for a solid fifteen seconds, and I don't know what to do or say. I've seen all these TV shows of parents being reunited with their kids after years, all the tears and hugs and memories flooding back of better days. That never really happened with my dad and me. Even my feeble attempts at any kind of small talk don't seem to be working.

"I have to go. I'll see you later."

I sigh. "See you." I turn back to my toast, taking a slice and a massive bite. He strides out of the house and shuts the door behind him, locking it as well. I'm not sure there's much more I can do until I figure out what's going on. He used to be distant, sure, but this is a cavern of space.

I push aside the thoughts of my father, unable to sink in so much more energy. There's nothing I can do while he's not here.

I devour my toast, and then make myself another two slices before heading back upstairs to take a shower.

My shower lasts exceptionally longer than usual, only because it's earlier in the morning; when it's cold out, my showers grow longer and hotter. Nothing feels so good. It takes me an extra ten minutes in the shower to will myself to leave the damp hug of warmth, but when I do, I immerse myself in towels. I pick out the outfit I had in mind last night, throw my hair up in a wet, drawn back bun, touch on some makeup, and get all my things together.

I skip down the stairs for the second time today, and immediately head straight out the door, ensuring for the third time that I have my bus pass, phone, headphones, and wallet. It's all there, nestled in my fading purse.

It feels strange going to work again; I've always loved my job, I love working at Space Age, but I've rarely shopped there outside of work hours. Any time I've ever bought anything there was when I was on shift; it's an odd feeling heading to work, knowing that there's no chance of me being late, or needing to rush, or even the concern of being too early, and then being stuck with Lex in his office. It's not exactly bad to be waiting with him to open the store, Lex is just awkward early in the morning. Despite owning a business that opens at 9:00 am every morning, except weekends where he gives himself an extra two hours, he is not a morning person.

The bus ride isn't as strange to me anymore; I've been on it quite a few times since the mark of the five years, and most of the minor difference have become natural and familiar to me. The new shops, the lack of trees, even the slightly tweaked bus route, adding a stop in between two lengthy stops, are all normal. It's as if I've been here all this time.

What is strange, however, is my train route. The train, being over roads and trees for part of my trip, gives me the chance to see all the differences on my way downtown. I almost can't believe it. All of the trees cut down within the past five years is already shocking enough, but the amount of personal developments made is astonishing. There are high rise buildings left and right, a nearby mall had been torn down and rebuilt, reaching even farther than before, and there are consistently new developments in the tiniest of corners. Every single place possible along the strip that follows the train is now a coffee shop, or a small cluster of homes, or a forced patch of garden or trees. I supposed forced nature is still nature.

The last thing I see before my train delves underground for the remaining eight minutes of my journey is yet another gas station; I can't even process the new gas prices. I guess I'm going to need a new job soon...

The thought strikes me of working at Space Age once again, but...I'm not sure if that's what I want to do. I almost feel like it would be wrong just to pick up where I left off. I haven't even begun to think about what I'm going to talk to Lex about. Thinking back, I've never really known where our conversations would begin or end, and now is no exception.

My stop finally arrives, and on comes the walk of sure changes that I'll notice walking down the street. To my surprise, it's not so different. Downtown is still downtown, all inclusive with the same old holes in the wall, the random sparse trees looming around to give a simulant of nature, the busy buses and packed traffic, pedestrians illegally crossing the streets, but still, no one will really do anything about it. There's not much anyone can do here. The pot industry has grown, and that is probably the most significant difference. More places openly sell pot; is it legal here now?

One of the things I do notice, however, is the homeless population. It's very clearly gone up. I suppose the gas prices just reflect the state of the economy. I guess the bubble has not yet burst because prices just keep going up and up.

I shove the thought of the economy from my head and trek on to work, or what used to be my work. Not the first job I've ever had, but definitely one of the best.

I arrive at Space Age and press my palm against the cool metal rimming the glass door. I take a peek inside; a lot of the older fandoms have grown. *Firefly* is still becoming evermore popular. *The Walking Dead* refuses to cease, as does *Game of Thrones*. I guess Winter has come and gone, but that might have happened when I was here in the first place.

I don't allow myself to think anymore, I just do. My fingers wrap around the rectangle of metal, and I yank open the expectedly light door. Stepping inside, my olfactory senses nearly kill me. Floods of memories of working here return to me in an instant, just after one short breath. I find myself gasping at the quickness of it all.

"Hey," a deep voice croaks from the desk next to me. I glance over, finding a surprisingly young man flipping through a comic book. Upon my silence and staring, wondering who he is, he offers a simple nod, grin, and returns to his book.

I swallow deeply and look around my old workplace. It has the same layout, and a lot of the same products, like a timeless classic that's just been updated to high definition. Before I can even think about it, my tongue slips, "Um..." bringing the young man to look up at me again.

"Are you looking for something?"

I chuckle to myself and approach the desk he's at. I rest my arms on the glass, taking note of the collectibles inside the transparent cabinet. "Yeah. Um...is...Rose here?"

His eyebrow arches just the slightest bit, and he shrugs, shaking his head. "Sorry, I don't know who that is."

"Oh." I blink. "Okay. Um...Michelle?"

Another blank stare.

I clear my throat; I can't expect all my old co-workers to have the same retail job five years later, but this is still weirding me out. "The twins, Mike and Lin?"

"I'm sorry, um..."

"Who's the manager? Owner."

"Oh, that's Lex," the guy answers, eyes now beaming that he can help me out. I let out a huge sigh of relief; at least Lex is still here. I could never picture this place existing without Lex, despite the number of times he'd said he hated it and wanted to sell. He never really would. I am surprised that no one else is here, though I suppose the retail turnover is very high... "He's upstairs if you want to see him."

"Cody," Lex's all too familiar voice rings out, followed by heavy stomps down the wooden stairs. Cody, as I learn his name, and I both look up. It didn't even register that Lex would look older, but seeing him now, not much has changed. A few more creases, but still the same hard attitude, same blazing personality. It's all in the walk. "You're on your half."

Lex finally removes his fix on the fascinating stairs he's descending and makes eye contact briefly with Cody before noticing me. It registers slowly for Lex, and the realization in his eyes slowly unfolds. He shifts his weight on the stair, shrilling creaks filling the store, and crosses his arms. I'm expecting some quick remark about being late for a shift from five years ago, or some witty, sarcastic comment about how he can't believe I didn't even bother to pick up my last paycheck. But instead, all he says, with not even all that much disbelief in his voice is, "Raleigh." He doesn't question me. He just says my name.

He sways carefully on that stair, still looking over his past and present employees.

"Should I still go on my break?" Cody asks gently. He seems like the sort of person who doesn't handle authority very well, considering how shifty he's being. He's like me when I first started; I'm sure after a few weeks, maybe even a few months, he'll be treating Lex the way I treated him. He was more a co-worker than a boss.

"Yeah," Lex says, taking another step downwards, still guarding my gaze. "Just flip the sign on your way out."

Cody nods, and without even an ounce of hesitation, makes a break for the door. Lex doesn't say a word to me until his employee has grabbed the key, flipped the sign, and is out the door, and even then, he merely stares.

I can't help but notice how unsurprised he looks. "Were you expecting me?" I ask, shoving my hands into my coat pockets.

Lex shrugs one shoulder and subtly shakes his head. "Saw you on the news." Oh, right. "Still shocked to see you here in person, considering...but seeing you on TV softened the blow." I force a smile and glance around the shop, once again taking note of the similarities and changes that have taken place. "Talk in my office?"

I trail up behind him on the stiff wooden stairs. I tactfully avoid the creaks, where I've instinctively remembered them, but new ones have developed; I'm not sure there's a safe spot left on these stairs.

In a rare omission, Lex allows me to enter his office before him. He only tends to do that with customers; I guess I'm not exactly an employee anymore.

His office hasn't changed at all. The pile of papers still floods his desk, beyond the point of overflowing, his laptop nestled perfectly between the stacks, and his same old chair remains, despite the fraying edges, much more frayed now, and the ripping cushion. Staples didn't restock his chair then, and they apparently haven't now. Even the old posters on the walls remain, with hardly further noticeable wear and tear. I never thought that I had the best memory, or even a good one at that, but now that everything looks different...I guess it was all inside of my brain somewhere.

By habit, I sit in the chair in front of Lex's desk, not even bothering to ask for permission. I meet his eyes, which is when I hesitate and almost stand back up; he looks a little concerned. Instead, he seats himself behind his desk, clears his throat, and meets my eyes again. He laces his tan fingers together; I know he never wanted to get married, which I'm not surprised that I don't see a ring, but I'm wondering if he's still dating the same woman. Lolita is her name, I think.

Lex puffs out his cheeks and then releases a loud breath, shaking his head. His eyes are fixed on the armrest of my chair. "I wasn't sure if I'd ever see you again, Raleigh." He meets my eyes. "Wasn't a kidnapping, was it?"

I try to retain my grin, but the edges of my lips curl up ever so slightly. Leave it to Lex to find the conspiracies. I explain what little I know, capturing Lex with every word.

"What do you think it was?" Lex asks, at the end of my spiel. I spared no detail with Lex, and he didn't interrupt me once. I stare blankly at him, almost surprised at the fact that he hasn't immediately jumped to the A word.

"What do you think?"

He shrugs, cracking his back as he sits up in his chair, removing his feet from their rest upon one of the drawers from his desk. "It doesn't sound like you just ran away." He inches his chair closer, eyeing me cautiously, enough to make me wonder if he was concerned for my absence at all. "Or that you were kidnapped." He chuckles, but not out of amusement, more out of spite. "Horrible minds, people have. Brutal theories."

"Did a lot of people just think I was dead?"

He shrugs again, avoiding eye contact. "Eventually...I think it was just easier to deal with. After months, people forced themselves to believe you weren't just locked up in some basement." A shudder rolls up my spine. "There was just no trace of you, you know? Of course, that didn't stop the cops."

"Really?" I unintentionally raise my voice out of confusion.

"Yeah. Not even that long ago, about four or five months, one cop came in here, telling me my statement, all that stuff, asking me if there was anything else. I guess he went through everyone else."

I bite my lip, licking along where it had accidentally split yesterday. I really didn't expect Denton to care so much. I understand, in the sense that I too would be terrified if someone I knew just suddenly disappeared, without a trace, but I'm still thrown off. It seems more like a father trying to find his own daughter than a cop trying to find some annoying girl who bothered him with aliens every other day. It's almost the opposite, how my dad and Denton are reacting...

"You left something here, too. On your last shift, before you disappeared." I'm glad that Lex can fully say it; not many people know what to call it, or how to put it, but Lex just says whatever comes to mind. "A sweater."

"My brown one?" my mind immediately jumps. I've been wondering where that was, and now hearing about it reminded me that I'd left it at work.

"I think it was brown." He scratches his ear, squinting his eyes. "That friend of yours picked it up, the guy. I think you were dating back then."

"Tristan." Lex nods. "He has it?"

"He should. He said he would keep it for you."

I take a deep breath and adjust in my comfortable seat. "Lex...what do you–"

"I'm pretty sure you know what I think," he interrupts. "The truth is out there." Amused, he smirks and meets my eyes. "You know they rebooted that show."

I match his grin and nod. "I was actually here for that."

"...oh. Did you watch it?"

"Not yet."

"You should. Lot of complaints about it as a standalone, but the fact that it's *X-Files*..." He clears his throat, and his eyes pierce into mine. "What do you think happened to you, Raleigh?"

"Nothing else makes sense," my mouth speaks before my mind can clearly comprehend my response. "Nothing makes sense. But this makes the most sense of the nonsense."

"Why doesn't it make sense?"

"The entire situation is so messed up, and confusing."

"Why?"

"Because,"

"No, Raleigh. Why?"

I take deep breaths, not wavering from Lex's hazels, and I slowly nod. "Yeah. Why? Why then, at that time, just...why?"

Once again, Lex's charms lighten the mood, and his lips twitch with glee as he thinks what he needs not say.

The door downstairs suddenly slams shut, and the slightly familiar voice of Cody rings up, "I'm back from my break!"

"'Kay."

I point in Cody's general direction, down the stairs, and my mind formulates the words that I'm trying to say. "Is... does anyone still work here who did before?"

Lex chuckles, shrugging one shoulder effortlessly. "No, don't think so. Most quit for school, or careers. The twins, Miles, Kami, uh...that other boy."

"Edward." Lex nods. "What about Michelle?"

He arches his eyebrows. "She actually just quit not too long ago, maybe a year, a year and a half. She really liked it here, I was sad to see her go..." Lex shifts in his seat, almost seeming a bit uncomfortable. "She talked about you a lot."

My eyes grow. "Really?"

He nods, and even his eyes are skeptical. "Really. I didn't think you two were that close. She even said you two weren't that close, but she always really respected and admired you. Said she almost thought of you as an older sister, how you'd look out for her and all that."

I blink a few times, trying to take it all in. Looking back, I guess I sort of did treat her like a little sister. If she didn't have lunch, I'd split with her, buy her coffee some mornings, call her to the back of the store when some guy came onto her, and she clearly didn't appreciate it. I never really realized it before. "Where is she working now?"

"Oh, um..." Lex begins to look around on his desk. "She told me where, I wrote it down in case I ever needed to contact her."

"Why did she even quit?"

He shakes his head, fumbling through all of the contents of his desk drawer; thumbtacks, sticky notes, tons of pens and pencils, small cartons of staples. Essentials. "She moved, more towards the smaller cities, even further than where you live, and the commute was getting to be too much. Here!" He tosses a pink crumpled up sticky note onto the desk, showing just her name. I unravel the note, finding that she works not too far from my place, at one of the malls. Down and Out is a store pretty similar to Space Age, but with less comic books and more collectibles and accessories. It wasn't at the mall last time I went there; there was one downtown, not too far from here, but I guess they're expanding. The "nerd" market is flying.

"Thanks." I slide the note back over, and I respond to his confused glance, "I know where it is, I'll stop by sometime."

"I'm sure she'd love to see you." He smiles gently, and the thought suddenly hits me that I haven't even asked about the one co-worker I had considered an actual friend, not a sister or work associate.

"Where's Rose?"

All at once, Lex tenses, pupils dilating, and he bites his inner cheek, something I've seldom seen. I don't like this...

"...Rose died."

My mouth dries up; *no.* "What?"

He clears his throat and laces his fingers together, diverting his attention to them. "A couple years ago. Not too far from here, crossing the street, got hit..." He sighs, shaking his head. "Horrible. The woman driving just wasn't paying attention." I don't really want to hear this. "Apparently, her kids were in the back seat. Young kids." *Stop.* "The official story is that the girl was trying to deal with her kids, wasn't looking at the road, and apparently 'Rose came out of nowhere.'" Lex snorts, oblivious to the fact that my body is shaking. "She's in jail. The woman is. Don't know for how long, though...I'm sorry, Raleigh." I meet his eyes. "I know you two got along really well. I didn't think you were that close..."

"We weren't," I interrupt, sighing along with my words. "I mean...we talked during work, and whatever, but...we weren't really close. Just the fact that I won't get to see her again." My mom and dad had me young into their early twenties, which gave me access to grandparents, and even great-grandparents. Death isn't a new concept to me. But it seems to hit me a little harder every time it happens... No one ever knows when someone might disappear one day, never to be seen again.

Lex sighs himself, humming a little, and then leans closer to me. "I'm sorry, Raleigh."

That's all he can say. That's all I can take. "I'm sorry too, Lex."

He smiles softly.

I think about Rose the entire walk and train ride back towards home. It's hard picturing someone and knowing you can only see them again in pictures or hear them in videos. I guess a lot of people felt the same thing about me.

I squeeze my eyes shut, sinking into my blasting music. When I open my eyes, thoughts still swarming around Rose, I find a young girl, probably just a few years younger than me, the twenty-year-old me, staring into my eyes. She quickly looks away, and then draws out her phone, and begins fixing her lip gloss. I just stare at her; I could swear that I'm staring at Michelle.

Michelle.

All these thoughts about Rose, now leading to Michelle. She apparently talked about me a lot. She cared about me. If she feels half as helpless about never seeing me as I do for Rose, then I need to talk to her. I at least owe her that.

I arrive back at the bus loop and rush off to another bus that takes me to Woodland Centre, the mall with Down and Out. Music still blasting, I settle in for my lengthy journey, tapping my fingers along the back of my phone, picking at my nails, biting my cheeks, bringing back all the nervous habits that I believe are due to boredom. Waiting. Anticipating.

I can't tell why exactly I'm so nervous. Maybe because Michelle is more of an outsider in my life. She was the odd one out at Space Age, for the mere fact that she was more concerned with high school popularity than whether Batman ever does avenge his parents. The thought of people thinking of me when I'm not there...it's unsettling, to say the least.

Nine songs later, I'm at the second bus loop of the day, the one just across the street from Woodland Center.

Ignoring all the recent construction, the renovations made on every other building, the additional high rises, and the fact that there is a train running from this bus loop to the one I was just at thirty minutes ago, *I guess I should pay more attention,* I walk by memory, feeling confident in my unwavering steps. It feels normal, despite the screaming alterations telling me otherwise. Once inside the mall, however, I have to stop. All the stores have changed around, except for The Bay.

Two long strips of stores face me, and two shorter strips of stores snap to my right. The entire mall is made of a rectangle of strips, with large department stores at three of the four corners. The fourth corner has, naturally, a Starbucks.

I take a few steps in the door and head towards a small booth showing one giant map, with more modest pamphlets for the taking; at least the directories remain in their same locations. Instead of snatching up a map, I search Down and Out on the list of stores, finding it under "specialty stores," and discover that it's almost directly below me. I hop on the nearest escalator, another commonality still in place, and as I descend, I see Down and Out's blue and white bubble-lettered sign. Butterflies trickle in my stomach, and my feet plant in place, not wanting to leave the escalator. I'm not sure I have the power to make them walk towards the pop shop until I'm forced to.

I barely look up from my shuffling shoes until I'm inside the colourful store. The merchandise all instantly appeals to me, as I'm a collector of knick-knacks and figures, but I still divert my gaze towards the cash register, where a guy stands.

I take in a quick search of the store, but I can't seem to find anyone else. Maybe she's in the back, if she's even working today.

Before I can skirt out of the store, kicking myself for not even thinking of that possibility, the standing guy notices me and speaks.

"Hi!" he says cheerfully, baring a toothy grin. He looks more excited than I thought he could ever be; I guess, like me, he looks miserable until he smiles. "How are you today?"

"Good," I smirk back, biting my drying lips. "How are you?"

"I'm doing good, thank you," he comes around from behind his cashier's desk, and leans against it, crossing his arms. "Can I help you find anything?"

"Um..." I glance around, finding a cute *Teenage Mutant Ninja Turtle* wallet. "That's cute," I point, and upon his chuckle, I regain my focus. "I'm actually looking for...Michelle." His expression changes to surprise and possible confusion, so I throw in, "she works here, right?"

"Michelle, oh, yeah," the words roll off his tongue. "She does, she's just not here today."

I really should have thought this through before making it my mission to waste my time coming here. At least I know for sure that she does in fact work here, and hasn't moved to a different workplace. "Oh...do you know when she'll be in?"

The guy, whose nametag reads Lloyd, inhales sharply, and I recall that it is a rule that employees aren't allowed to share their co-workers' work schedules. I'm not sure if it's an official rule, but it's an unspoken one. "Uh...well...I'm not sure...do you want me to tell her you stopped by?"

I shake my head. "No, no, um..." the wallet catches my eye again, but I shake it off. "I'll just come back."

He nods, smiles again, and then returns to his desk. The store seems dead, but it's the middle of a weekday. Nothing is busy this time of day at the mall, except probably the food court.

I walk out of Down and Out and stop just beyond Lloyd's possible line of sight; I don't bother looking back to see if he's watching. All I can think is that I want to go home. The mall, though familiar in structure, feels completely different. Home, thanks to my unassuming father, hasn't changed a bit. It's still the same.

I just want to go home.

I make my way to the bus stop, check when my one bus home is going to arrive, a whopping twelve minutes, and I take a seat at the empty bus bench. There's a loop, just across the street from the mall, with about ten stations total, and mine is the only one empty. It is mostly a residential route, excluding the two malls and transit stations it travels between.

I close my eyes and bury my face in my hands, breathing in the fresh air between my spread fingers.

I'm just waiting. That seems to be the case for most things, just waiting. I feel like I'm longing for some place where I wasn't waiting, where I was enjoying life to the fullest. Maybe not even enjoying, perhaps just accepting my present state. Where I was jealous of myself in the moment, because I knew that it would end. Where I missed those times before they finished happening. I'm waiting to not feel strange; I hate myself for not feeling strange, which is in itself strange. I'm waiting to feel like I'm back, and like I belong, and I'm waiting to find out what the fuck happened to me. I'm just waiting.

I'm longing for a state of mind that might not have even happened to me. I feel like it did, but...what do I know? I want a state where I'm happy and lovely, something that I know I experienced, but I can't place when. I don't know how to get there.

I hear the wind rushing as my bus draws into the loop, and shivers run through the entirety of my body. I look up.

I guess I'll just have to wait and see.

Chapter 12

After spending an entire night tossing and turning, I have finally achieved my goal of being able to sleep in again. It was partially because I could not sleep, but also thanks to my phone's alarm malfunctioning. Either way, I am proud.

However, I am not awakened by the gentle music of my alarm, I wake up to the shrill vibration of my phone, rattling on my small wooden dresser.

I throw my arm over my night side table, catching my phone against my wrist. I guess someone is calling me. My eyes adjust to being open, and I notice the small notification at the top of my screen, telling me that my alarm did, in fact, go off nearly two hours ago for the final snooze.

"That's great," I hiss at myself, hating the fact that it's already 12:30. I wanted to sleep in until maybe 10:00, not waste half my day, but this middle ground apparently does not exist.

I swipe to answer the call, the area code from somewhere I don't know, and muster up a slightly raspy, "hello?"

The noises on the other end of the line almost electrocute me even more conscious, between a sharp scratching against what must be the receiver, and two muffled voices beyond the scribbles. I force myself to count to five before saying hello again, unable to make any sense of the mumbles, but I only make it to four. "Hello?"

"Is this Raleigh?"

"Yeah." A small part of me jolts from the fact that an unknown woman is calling and asking for me, but the stronger part of me just wants to know why they're calling.

"Ah...Raleigh Carlisle?"

"Yeah." I squeeze one of my eyes shut, rubbing it with a fist, trying to get the sleep out. My dad almost told me once what the sleep in my eyes is, but he said it was gross, and I told him not to tell me. I'd rather it just be a mystery.

"Hi, Raleigh. This is Dorothy Kendrickson, I'm here with my husband, Arthur." Kendrickson. Are they serious? "Our daughter is Marissa." Yep. That's Mom.

I sit up in my bed, resting the arm not occupied by my phone on one of my bent knees. I stare off at the wall, processing the fact that anyone on my mom's side of the family is trying to contact me. I think that was the initial attraction between my parents, that they, and their entire families, are so distant. I don't know where I fit into it all. "Oh...kay..."

"We're your grandparents. I believe we met when you were younger." Grandparents. What an odd thing to hear. When I hear the word, I think of my dad's parents, who I see at Thanksgiving, Christmas, and who send me a card with cash in it for my birthday. Then again, *they* never called. And my mom's parents are.

"Yeah, a few times," I mutter, inviting in all the vague memories of these people who I hardly know. I remember they bought me a doll once, and that they don't smile. "What, um...how are you?" I'm not very good at small talk with the remote family that I haven't seen in over a decade. It's closer to two, now...

"We're doing just fine, Raleigh. Your mother actually wanted to call...well, she wanted *us* to call to see how you were doing." I blink a few times, and in the background, I hear another woman's voice. Not an older woman, though. I'm guessing it's my mom. The scratching fills the phone again, something Dorothy, or Grandma, or whatever I'm supposed to call her in this situation, must be doing in attempts to block my efforts at hearing anything. I can almost see it in my mind, the unclear silhouette of an elderly woman clutching dearly onto an ugly beige spin dial phone. My grandparents on my dad's side used to have one of those; it's long since been in storage.

"Um...I'm okay." I'm actually feeling a little fucking confused; I should change my answer. "I mean, I'm fine."

More etchings. I hold the phone further from my ear and wait patiently, hearing the mumbles between Dorothy and my assumed mother grow slightly louder and more coherent.

"Hello, Raleigh, it's Arthur," his voice suddenly rings through the phone, crisp and clear, with just the slightest bit of a speech impediment. "You say you're doing fine?"

"I am, yeah." I close my eyes and tousle my own hair, feeling the unruly curls swell up between my fingers.

"That is good to hear," Arthur states. "We are glad that you are safe." I just sit there, blinking, not knowing what to say. I hold my hand to my forehead, and my eyes lazily wander throughout my bedroom. "Your father told us about the incident a few years ago." The incident? "He never explained fully what happened..."

"He doesn't know," I say bluntly. "Neither do I."

I half expect Arthur to protest or ask how I could possibly not know. And for a second, I think he might. For a second, I think that he thinks that he might. I can almost hear his mouth open and close right again.

As far as he knows, me and my mom, we're one in the same. Leaving all of our friends and family, without an explanation. Like mother, like daughter. Except I came back. And my mom can't blame her absence on lack of memory. I don't know what she blames it on, if she blames it on anything at all. The most I've gathered, from my careful research over the years, is that she has chronic anxiety. My dad would sometimes let words slip as he spoke to my mother, or her parents, on the phone, words like "medication," "doctor," or perhaps the most obvious one, "chronic anxiety." I'm not sure if that's why she left. But I'm sure it's why she's not speaking to me on the phone. Getting her parents to call, it must be some form of progress, facing fears, something of those sorts. I don't hate my mom. But I don't know her enough to like her. I'm not against getting to know her, but I'm not going to try. It's an oddly neutral feeling. Maybe it's because I've always lived with the idea that we can't help the people who won't help themselves. Maybe she's the reason I grew up with that lesson.

She's the reason for another important aspect of my life...

As I'm thinking, unsure if Arthur has spoken any words again or not, I can't help but wonder if my dad felt the same way after I left, as when my mom fled. I can't blame him if he did. I'm sure he did, thinking it over. Even if he believed that I was kidnapped or dead, in the few seconds I've realized it, any shred of doubt in my mind has gone. It's in his eyes. That same look as when my mom first left. I'll never forget it. It went away with Mom, eventually. But I don't know if it will go away this time.

"Did you say something?" I ask boldly, snapping myself back into the conversation.

Arthur clears his throat, and I realize that, other than him, his side is silent. I guess Mom and Dorothy left the room. "Yes, I said that we should probably go...we are glad to hear that you are all right."

I nod to myself, biting my upper lip. "Okay. Thanks."

"Yes, well...have a pleasant day."

"Thanks. You too."

He hangs up before I do.

I lie here, on my bed, still holding the phone to my ear, even after the ending beeps. I'm having a hard time comprehending that that conversation just happened. That was the closest I'd come to talking to my mom in about ten years. Give or take another five. Slowly, I place my phone back on my bedside table, and I roll to my back, lacing my fingers together on top of my chest. I feel myself breathe. And I let myself think about what my mom might look like now. And, once again, as I always do, I allow myself think about how it's okay that it doesn't matter anymore. And that I'm not even sure I care anymore.

I squeeze my eyes shut, pressing my palms into my chest until I can feel my heartbeat within my hands.

I need to do something today.

My eyes shoot open, and Tiffany enters my mind; it's Wednesday, which means that she only has one class today. Even though I just saw, I snatch my phone and recheck the time; it's nearing 1:00. Her class ended at noon. Through my fatigue, I text her asking if she wants to meet for coffee.

And then my head starts to spin.

Through my head, the dizziness begins to spread through the rest of my body; my neck, shoulders, following down my arms, flowing through my torso, and it doesn't stop until it reaches the tips of my toes. When it does end, it begins to overflow my senses. I force myself to sit up and immediately throw myself into the past.

I'm standing.

I'm waiting.

I'm back on that street, back near Lion's Park, back where the giant craft is hovering before me.

It's standing.

It's waiting.

My mouth drops ever so slightly, and my eyes fill with tears, blinded by the bright light. The silhouette of a creature, bigger and longer than I've ever known, and only grows in size as we shrink closer. I can't tell whether it is the one coming towards me, or if I'm moving, levitating, towards it. I can't help but feel the former.

My feet remain planted on the concrete sidewalk, and the distance between us withers.

I try to make a sound, but only a small squeak escapes.

The darkness of the creature looks infinite, deeper than any shadow I've ever seen; I'm finding colours within it. Reds, blues, yellows, purples, greens. I'm finding them swirling around within the shadow's core, but whenever I try to focus and pinpoint, the darkness consumes once again.

The arm of the shadow raises, now being only several feet away, and I can formulate the shape of a hand reaching towards me. Its palm faces up, its fingers closely knit, but remains open.

All at once, I've moved, and all I can see is the sky. I'm looking at stars blanketing the darkness, but I don't recognize any of the constellations. I don't think I've ever seen it so dark.

Legacy.

The word echoes through my head, but I don't take my eyes from the clusters of lights.

Legacy.

I'm not the one saying the word, I'm not even the one thinking it. It's a voice inside my head, but not a voice of my own. It's neutral, in the sense that I can't find a single word to identify it. Not high, not low, not male, not female, not…anything. Just like the voice I'd heard before.

All at once, the infection of dizziness congregates in the pit of my stomach, and I can't calm the acid stirring inside of me. I lean over, thankfully now equipped with a small garbage can next to my bed, and vomit inside. I tip myself over, onto my carpet, producing a significant thud; at least my dad isn't home. I partially miss the trash bin and groan even further, my body not ceasing.

It takes a solid five minutes for my breathing to even begin to regulate again.

I collapse onto my carpet, digging my nails into the fibres in desperate need of a vacuum, and close my eyes. The darkness, the shadow that I'd just felt is seen within my head, the colours all there. I've never seen a black so dark before.

I need to get up.

I press my palms down in hopes of pushing myself up, at least onto my knees, but I barely make it a few inches off the ground.

I lie there, motionless, my heartbeat sinking into the floor until I can feel it across all my muscles and bones. I try, and fail, to slow the beat. I've never been good at that.

Motivation rushes through me, and I curl upwards, on all fours, and grip onto my bed. Faithful bed.

I sit atop my thrashed sheets, my head in my hands.

I need to get up. I need to do something. My brain is on fire right now.

I check my clock; a wasted twenty-something minutes. And no response from Tiff. I then realize how stupid I am as she does not have classes on Wednesday since she is no longer in school. She has a full-time job. For that time, I forget any time had even passed.

A small grin unfurls at the corners of my lips; I certainly can't bother Tiff at work, but there is someone I can.

Denton called a few days ago to check in, and it's not like I have anything else to do. And I know there's no chance in hell that Denton would ever dare to use a sick day. I can't help but wonder how many forced vacations he's taken.

I find myself in the bathroom, washing my face, rinsing out my mouth. I'm too lazy for makeup; my skin isn't even that bad today. I throw my hair up, stumble back to my bedroom, and begin to search inside my closet. I grab the easiest and warming clothes to wear, but in the process, I find a book down below, hidden by a small box of mittens and toques and winter items. I crouch down and take the book in my hands, observing the elusive title once again; the book.

I've been actively ignoring any thoughts of this book. I thought that if I stopped thinking about it, I could come back to it with a fresh mind and solve it once and for all.

It's a naïve thought.

I try to put the book back in its place, behind the container of seasonal warmth, but I can't quite seem to part with it. I keep staring at it, my mind flooding with the hundreds of different scenarios in which someone finds and takes the book from this particular spot. It becomes overwhelming. In the moment, I make the conscious decision to take the book with me, everywhere I go. I can't find it in me to leave it here anymore. I'm not sure how to describe the protective behaviour of an inanimate object; all I know is that I can't let it go. I discover a bag in my closet, big enough for my purse essentials and the book, and I slip the novel inside, my fingertips glossing against the fabric pages.

What does it mean?

With my new, larger bag in tow, I make my way downstairs. To my surprise and relief, I catch a glimpse of the van seated in the driveway, sun sparkling along the silver sides. After this morning's little fiasco, I'm not really in a walking mood. I check the fridge for something to eat, settling on a trip to Tim's later in the day, snatch the keys from my tote, and I embrace the sunshine for a few glorious seconds before slipping into the van.

And I sit there. I don't move for a while, I just stay there, staring at my always shut garage, the paint still peeling.

I don't feel in control anymore, my mind wanders. My life, five years of it, anyway, have already come and gone. I used to be in control. I never even minded not being in control, as long as it still felt like mine. But it doesn't feel like mine anymore. It feels like I'm an opening act for someone else, for this person who won't be there until I find out what happened…

I shake my head, physically hoping to shake away all the angst and frustration. Control has always been a tough issue for me. I need a precise balance between what I can and cannot control, and they have seldom clashed, but now, it's hitting me hard.

In a dream state, I drive over to the police station. I glide from my car all the way inside, face to face with the all so familiar scene of my recurring teenage years. Which, I guess, are still kind of happening.

Kayla, the receptionist who I remember from my first day back, greets me with a sort of eerie smile. It's very pleasant, too pleasant, but doesn't feel fake.

"Oh, hello," she says, holding straight eye contact. "Raleigh, is it?" I nod. "What can I do for you?"

"I'm here to talk to Denton," I mutter in response.

"Sure thing, go right ahead!" Kayla must notice the highly skeptical expression plastered on my face, and she chuckles. "Special orders, he's always free to see you."

It's odd, but even more so oddly comforting, how the times have changed.

I stride past Kayla, attempting to offer a smile half as genuine as hers, and I suppose I manage, considering her brightening, squinting eyes and slightly shrugging shoulder. At Andy's desk, where Andy should be seated, holds another officer. Where the fuck is Andy? I saw him the first day I was here. I thought I did, anyway. Was he in uniform?

Before entering Denton's office, I knock on the durable wood, rapping a satisfying sound.

"Come in."

The sense of déjà vu rushes through me; the scene is the same. The same desk, the same, yet different in content papers sprawled all about, the same file cabinet holding dozens, hundreds of open cases around the city. The only difference is the man running the show looks just a little older. Like the older brother of the man who had initially run the show.

He glances up, and for a second, I think he's going to do a double take, but he doesn't.

"Take a seat." I pull up one of the chairs. One of the files, in a surprise twist, is facing me and describes of a man's car window being smashed. I've talked to Denton before about cases like that; it probably won't be solved. "I've been wondering when you'd come in." He stacks the papers he'd been working on back on top of a seemingly random pile and starts eye contact. He must see something that I'm not intentionally conveying because he adds, "Do you remember anything else?"

I clear my throat, nodding a little. The part that makes me the most uncomfortable is that Denton seems more invested than ever in actually believing what I have to say. It might just be the biggest adjustment I'm facing.

Denton, clearly surprised, allows his stern expression to drop, and he even leans in a little closer to me, as if we're sharing a well-kept secret, even though I know every word I say will be written down and stuck in the large file of me. I saw the file once; my sightings reports, no matter how reluctant any given officer was, were written and stuck in that file. My disappearance must have doubled the size. "Well?"

I lean in myself. "I've been having this weird thing, where I'll almost zone out, but then I'll remember bits of what happened that night. I end up getting sick afterwards, or at least feeling like shit," I bite my tongue, unsure if Denton will mind the curse, "and every time it happens, I'll remember more." Before he can ask, "I don't know how it happens, it just does. And then these words keep repeating in my head,"

"Start with the first part, where you say you zone out," he says calmly. "We'll work our way there."

One thing at a time. "I was standing back on that street, back by Lion's Park. And there was this...that giant...craft. Ship." I wait for the eye roll, but it doesn't come. "And then, a door, I suppose, opened."

"How big was this object?"

"About..." I hold my hands out, as if I could measure it with my hands. "Thirty feet across, I'd say. I don't know how far back. It was like a rectangle, I think. Or a rounded box."

"How did this door open?"

I wondered for a moment why Denton wasn't writing anything down, but then I saw his little recording device. There's a sign on the door, one I hardly notice anymore due to habit, warning anyone coming into the office that they may be recorded. It should say *will*.

"Down," I say. "Like, a platform, almost, coming down from the top and resting just above the ground."

"Not touching the ground?" Denton asks.

"No. Nothing was touching the ground." No further acknowledgement. "So, the door came down, pretty slowly. And this figure appeared."

"What kind of figure?"

"I don't know, human-shaped." I try not to scowl. "Didn't I say this before?"

"Just making sure," he says. "Did you see anything behind the figure?"

I take a few seconds to think of it, but I come up mostly blank. "No... I saw some sort of wall behind him, I think. Like, ten feet behind him."

"It's a him?"

I blink, not even realizing that I said that. I've sparked his interest. "I... I mean, I don't know, I guess it looked like a him? It was bald, I think. Or had short hair, if any, its head just looked like a head, no hair. And I couldn't see any facial features."

She's learning, I almost hear Denton think.

"And it...it reached out to me."

"Like it was grabbing you?" Denton asks, a small clicking sound following. Only now do I notice the ballpoint pen in his hand. He's tapping the end lightly on his desktop.

"No," I say with conviction, "it wasn't. No. Its hand was face up, like, offering it to me."

"Are you sure?"

I nod, ignoring the skeptical look I've come to know splattered across his face. "It wasn't trying to grab me. I don't think, anyway," I add. "And I didn't feel scared at all...it had four fingers."

Denton's eyes narrow, his top lip curling up just slightly. I lied; *that* is the look I've come to know. "Four."

"You know. Like *The Simpsons*." My joke falls flat, but I can't help but grin. He rolls his eyes, but I can see the small part of him that accepted the lightened mood.

"And the words, what words do you keep hearing?"

I shift uncomfortably in my seat, glancing at the same ugly clock perched above Denton's head. "They're not in my own voice. It's like hearing it in someone else's voice. Some weird monotone voice."

"What words?"

"..." I shy around telling him, desperately unsure of what I'm even hearing. "'Create contact.' And 'legacy.'" Those are what I've heard so far."

"Do you have any context?"

"No, that's what I'm saying." I grow more frustrated; this isn't going anywhere, I don't even know why I'm telling him. No one else was on that ship. No one else can remember for me. This is all me. "Look, that's it. I don't know what else to tell you."

The both of us lean back in our respective chairs, the formal part of this meeting drawing a close. He gently tosses his pen onto a short stack of papers, only about fifteen or twenty pages in that one. There's a stack that must be six inches tall.

"Ready to get rid of me for the day?" I press, not wanting to be here anymore. It's a first, my wanting to leave before he wants to kick me out.

"How are you doing? How's your adjustment?" Denton asks. I can't help but wonder if that's what he asks all of the victims of kidnapping, or whatever the hell he classifies this as.

"It's okay." He has two clocks in here. I didn't notice that before. It must be new; it's sitting to my right, on a completely different wall. I guess one is for him, and one is for his visitors. The clock has one of those seconds hands that doesn't make jerky movements every second, it's a smooth circle. I like the older clock better. "I mean...it's still strange. But I think I'm doing okay." *Sometimes I think that because I'm not in a constant state of panic, something is wrong with me,* I don't say.

"I'm glad," Denton says, a genuine smile, and then glances up at the clock hung next to my head. "I'm afraid I'll have to cut this short, I do have a meeting. But I'm glad you came in."

"Me too," I say, scooting my chair back so I can stand. He smiles, patting his hands on his slacks. "I'll see you...soon, I'm sure. I'm going to start scoping the skies again."

"Fantastic," he grumbles, but once again, that light shines through. "Be safe out there, Raleigh."

"I will. And you too," I add ominously. He clears his throat, offers a brief smile, and then I am on my way.

Purposefully, I avoid eye contact with Kayla, to save her from my insincere smile, and save myself from the thoughts of dealing with that, and I head outside, a small chime rising from the door. *Is that new?*

Since I first entered the building, twenty minutes ago, it's started to gently rain. I step out into it, feeling the harsh mist on my skin. I close my eyes; I missed this, how it feels, the smell, the environment, the all-around atmosphere. I suppose it's been a very long time.

Chapter 13

I check my phone for the sixth time since I first got to NETRAD. I've been here for a total of twenty-one minutes, and I'm getting more and more nervous by the minute, even though I have a feeling I have no need. I know Tristan will say yes.

Last night, after visiting Denton, I decided that I needed to be more active in figuring out what happened to me. I was waiting, hoping that my memories would return to me with just a little prompt, a little push. Now I realize that they need more than a shove. No one else can remember my lost memories for me. Only me. And the one, clear direction in my life is pointing straight at me; NETRAD. It only makes sense that the more I surround myself with the external universe, the more chance I have of figuring out what happened to me. Not only that, I want to know why I forgot. Did something make me forget? Did *I* make me forget? Is it really just trauma? I shudder to think.

A small sweat breaks on my forehead; the room is a little too hot for my taste, especially considering that it's March now. It's still chilly outside, the rain is coming and going, the wind joining in as well, but the room feels too humid, too warm. A quick glance up reveals that there is an air conditioner near the top of the back wall, but it is not turned on.

The phone, the fourth time it rang since I first arrived, is answered by Jack, who has been casually eyeing me. Every time I catch him, he smiles, always startled. When I first got here, he instantly welcomed me and almost began resuming his work, assuming I'd just walk right in. Tristan had instructed him to do so. However, I formally informed him that I was actually there for a meeting with Tristan, and I had arranged it for 2:00 o'clock. Surprise didn't begin to describe his expression. He has a very, almost overly expressive face, the kind I'd expect from an actor.

"A…you have an appointment to see Mr. Barnes?" he asked, puzzled.

I nodded. "It's to discuss business."

Even with my curt explanation, he didn't quite understand, but nonetheless, he paged Tristan and told him that his "2:00 o'clock," was here and waiting. He just didn't know that it was me.

At 2:27, Tristan finally emerged from the back of the building, wiping his brow. He exhales deeply and just about walks past me before noticing.

"Oh!" he says, braking in his tracks. "Raleigh, hi." Without missing a beat, he leans down and gives me a tight hug. "I'd love to chat, but I'm late for an appointment. You know you're welcome anywhere here, though, right? You don't have to wait for me."

"Actually, I am your appointment," I say.

He draws his eyes from the other empty chairs and plasters them both onto mine. He cocks his head ever so slightly to the side, like a bewildered puppy, and chuckles. "You're my appointment. I thought it was..." he eyes me carefully and grins a little. "Ah. Ms. Kendrickson. Your mom's last name. But...why?"

I smile wryly. "Shall we go into your office?"

He discontinues questioning my unique methods, and instead, takes a step aside and holds his arm out for me, inviting me to his office. I graciously accept. I hop up to my feet, and following his instruction, into the back. We walk past all the students learning from Peggy, who doesn't notice the two of us sneak by. She looks like an incredible instructor, how she carries herself, how she moves, speaks, dances with her words. It's lovely.

Tristan and I walk by the computers, the eager and studious employees, researchers, all of them enthralled in their work. We get to the right side, hop up the few stairs, and take a sharp right down the hallway. It isn't long before Tristan and I are shut within his office.

"Take a seat, Ms. Kendrickson," he says smoothly, drawing out one of the guest chairs for me. I smirk, sitting across from his imposing desk.

"Please, call me Raleigh." I take the few seconds before Tristan is seated at his desk, and I look around the room to observe his office. It's a little on the small side, but it is also packed with furniture. There are three separate file cabinets, stacked neatly next to each other, nestled on the left wall. He has a large plant snug in the back right corner, and his desk is more than imposing. It's a deep coloured wood and seems to have drawers lining one side. He has a computer perched to his right, at about the same angle as the only window, half covered by the cabinets, blinds partially drawn. I'm in one of the two chairs facing him, and his chair looks much more comfortable. His desk is almost bare, given the computer.

Tristan plops down in his seat, clears his throat, and reconnects with my eyes. "What can I do for you, Raleigh?"

"Well..." I'd been considering this for a while, maybe even ever since NETRAD first opened. NETRAD was my dream. It was the dream, the one I wished to create. I suppose, in a way, I did. Not that I will ever take credit for it. I'm like the Winnie bear that Christopher Robin first met in the zoo. The inspiration, the reason, but never the creator who instigates. "I want a job."

"...here?" Tristan asks, neither his tone nor expression changing. He's unintentionally good at hiding his emotions. I don't even need to confirm. "And why's that?" Before I can even answer, Tristan is laughing absentmindedly to himself. "I already know the answer to that, don't I?"

He stands up, lacing his hands behind his back, and peers from his window. The ground to the right side of the building almost plunges downwards, giving the window in Tristan's office a beautiful view of a miniature valley, it seems. The grass is green, trees are dotting the hills. It's lovely, but gray from the drizzling rain.

"Of course I can give you a job," he says. I chuckle mindlessly, but it soon turns into a sturdy laugh. Tristan stares at me with inquisitive eyes. "What?"

"Well, last I knew of you, you wanted to be a history professor," I say. "Now you're working for a company that chases aliens. You own a company that chases aliens, where you'll hire some girl just because she's your," and it kills me to say, "friend."

An odd look washes over Tristan, and his grin fades into a neutral, indifferent expression. "You are not just 'some girl,' though." My smile disappears. "You know that you're the reason that all of this is possible."

"You can't say that."

"But it's true. All of this. If you hadn't disappeared...NETRAD wouldn't be here, Raleigh. I'd be some TA in some nearby college or university if I was so lucky. Unpaid internship at a middle school, maybe even elementary school, would be most likely, if not completely unemployed and out of work." He sits back down in front of me again, and I take the time to study him. Is this the man who gave up his dream for someone else's? Or the man so riddled with inapplicable guilt that he changed his dream? Did he force his dream to change, or did it just change on its own? I don't know. What I would give to know what's going on in his mind. Tristan, the TA. Tristan, with the unpaid internship at the middle or elementary school. I would have adored seeing his transition to who he is now, just as much as I fear it. Is this what he really wanted? For the first time in a long time, I realize that I don't know him as much as I used to. It seems as though it should be obvious, of course I don't know him anymore. But it just hits me, right now, in this moment. "I wanted this, Raleigh. I wanted to understand, I hoped that somehow, some way, this could help me find you."

My hands quiver upon my lap. My heart is heavy. My eyes are stones. My entire body is crisp with excitement, but not in a joyful, positive way. In a new way, in an adrenaline rush. "Did you want this?" I ask.

Tristan looks up, quick and surprised. "What? What do you mean?"

"I mean," I adjust in my chair, "did you really want this? Is this, is NETRAD, what you wanted to do with the rest of your life? You say you did it because of me. I wouldn't want that. I'd want you to do it for you. For your happiness, not because of me. I want you to do what makes you happy. Does this make you happy?"

His eyes, hard at first, soften once again, soothing my worries and fears of him becoming strange to me. "It does, Raleigh. I wasn't sure about this at first. It was just one class. But during the first week, being immersed into that world...why the reality that we constantly see before us, I see why that bored you."

"But–"

"Raleigh, I know. I know you worried about that, about me being a pushover, about me not taking enough risks. This was my risk. And it made me happy."

I sit there, stunned into silence, blinking. He remembered how often I pushed him to do the things he liked. He remembers our relationship vividly like I do. I glance down to my hands; the shakes are thankfully gone. I arch my back, cracking it with ease. "Okay." I shut my mouth. I can't push the guy into something that makes him happy and keep pushing. "So. Am I hired?"

"Of course you are." He doesn't hesitate. "What do you want to work in? Research? Intern?"

I blink. "I... uh, I haven't thought that far ahead."

"Well," he says, smiling warmly, "we'll figure it out." He stands up abruptly and offers me his hand. "Raleigh *Kendrickson*, I'd be honoured to have you here at NETRAD."

I stand as well, shaking his hand. "Thank you, Mr. Barnes. However, before I accept the position," I lean in closely, smelling his minty fresh breath, and an odd but satisfying whiff of pine, "what exactly is the pay?"

He grins. "Oh. You won't be worrying about finding a minimum wage job anymore, my darling." My heart skips a beat as he calls me "my darling."

"I also have another request," I say as Tristan walks around his desk to my side.

"Yes?"

"I'm not sure what department this falls under, but..." I flatten out my black skirt; I even made sure to dress formally for this. I think he appreciates the thought. "I want to find out what happened to me. I know you do, too, I know a lot of people do." Who better than me to find out, right? "So, I–"

"Research," Tristan says clearly. "We'll put you on the payroll as research. Or an analyst."

"Analyst?"

Tristan nods and leans against his desk, gripping the edges in his tight grasp. Being this close to him, this platonic to him...I think it's getting harder every time. "Every day, we are sent pictures of possible sightings."

"Really?" Part of me still hasn't quite grasped how big NETRAD is. How a corporation based on chasing the unknown, especially something that isn't currently affecting the general populous of the human race, is getting so much attention, not to mention funding. I read on one of the few plaques dotting the facility that they are partially government funded.

"Really. Some are airplanes, some are photoshopped, and some are the real deal. We've been meaning to hire an analyst to differentiate the real from the fake, so you actually came at a really great time. We have a software, a division of Identify," *what the hell is Identify?* "that you can use. Some of us here at the office, we've been alternating and checking out pictures, but none of us are all that good. None of us have experience first hand, night after night, like you. You could tell if some light in the sky was an airplane, and what type of plane, in five seconds flat."

"I'm not the best with computers," I admit, deflecting the compliment, but having flashbacks to the Boeing 788s flying about. In a flicker, Tristan gazes down to my breasts, and a blush flushes into my cheeks. The only white button-up shirt I have is a little small for my chest. The push-up bra doesn't help. Not in looking professional, anyway...

"Trust me, you'll get it."

"And really? No one has more experience than me?"

He shakes his head. "Really. A lot of people, this is their job, nine to five, ten to six. With the exception of a few of us, me, Peggy, Roger, who I don't think you've met, it's a job. Of course, everyone we hire is devoted to finding out the truth, and everyone works very hard. But at the end of the day, it is just a job." I smile, almost as if I know what he's going to say next. "Unlike us, where it's a way of life."

I'm briefly distracted by the grass and lined trees, but I regain myself. He is right about that; it has become my way of life. "Okay. Let's do it."

"Fantastic." He fills with glee. "We have a conference room where you can work for now, the room we were in before. I'll try to figure out an office situation for you, as well. I think you'll really like it here."

Before I can refuse my own office, he begins to usher me out the door, escorting me to this conference room. We exit his private room and pop into the room next door, bearing the same wooden fixture, but a very different interior. Going from one room to the next, it's hard not to pick out the differences. The place is broader and longer, extending much further back than Tristan's office, and plopped in the middle of the room is that long, ugly, tan coloured table, surrounded by eight office chairs, all equal in stature. Above the table hangs a projector, one point I didn't notice in my previous visit, directed at the far back wall; I'm not sure if the room has two projectors, or if the one I saw before is now suspended from the ceiling.

"It's not much in the ways of an office," Tristan offers. *It's a conference room*, I think to myself. *It's not supposed to be an office.* "We have a lot of renovations to do. We haven't done many since we first opened, so it's a little old-fashioned."

"It's fine," I comfort. "It's a bit cold, though."

"Oh." Tristan steps out of the way to reveal a portable heater nestled behind the open door. "Yeah...the building is in a constant state of cold, which is great for summer, but not so great for winter. And we know how much it rains here." I pity laugh at the cliché. "Which is where the heaters come in."

"Ah." I clear my throat, observing the room once again. In the middle of the table on the far end, lies the laptop. "Does this one have Identify?"

"Oh, yes!" He scurries over and adds a chair to face the computer. I join his side and follow his careful hands as he flips open the screen. He clicks on the user named NETRAD, enters a password, for which I instinctively look away, and a solid black background pops up. One by one, little icons pop up in a very timely manner, unlike my own faithful laptop, and within ten seconds, Tristan is opening a folder titled "Images." I glance up from the screen and notice another item that I'd neglected to see, a scanner and printer, mirroring where the heater stands. I'm guessing that might be very useful in this situation.

"Every day, we are sent pictures of possible sightings. We accept them from anyone, in either e-mail or snail mail, or in person." My heart leaps at the mention of the word "sightings." "On our e-mail," he pulls up a browser which defaults to an e-mail page, and he almost presses on one of the folders named "blocked," but instead reaches into his pocket and pulls out a pen. When he taps on the screen with it, I learn that it is a stylus, "you'll notice that we have a list of blocked e-mails. Any time they send us a message, they are sent an automatic response notifying them that they are blocked."

"Why are they blocked?"

A small smile along with an arched brow rises upon Tristan's handsome, curious face. "A lot of people still mock the thought of the unknown," he says, cautiously picking and choosing each word he vocalizes, speaking slowly. "It is much more widely accepted and has peeked much more interest, but not fully." Nothing is ever fully accepted. Not even simpler things, things that are easier to believe. "So, of course, we have some lovely fuckers," I nearly jump at the profanity, solely because I haven't heard this new and refined Tristan say such a word, "who like to send pictures from Google, *X-Files*, you name it."

"I see," I say. "Makes sense why you block them."

"Yeah." He returns to the e-mail screen. Forty-six e-mails waiting in the inbox. "The people who send in snail mail, and the people who come and bring pictures in for us, they're usually much more sincere. It takes longer to write and send a letter or drive all the way here than it does to write an e-mail. Anyway, the people that do come in, we try to get as much information as we can from them, when, where, how, even what kind of camera they used, if they know. A lot are on cellphones, and with the ever-growing quality of cellphone pictures, it's not such a bad thing."

"Hmm..." I glance at the e-mails again. A lot of them have the same title, "UFO Sighting," followed by the date. I suppose that's a suggested title. "Is this e-mail specifically for sightings?"

"Yes. The majority of pictures come through e-mails, but they also have the highest chance of being unreliable. Most people don't respond to our e-mails asking for information, they just ignore it, and a lot of them are photoshopped, people either playing a joke or trying to get some fifteen minutes of fame."

"Which is where Identify comes in," I say.

Tristan's eyes twinkle, just a little. "Which is where you come in, as well. I know you like organizing, so I think you'll enjoy this." An odd sensation flows through my blood, and my body feels colder than ever. I really miss him. "I'll show you, briefly, how the program works."

Using his stylus, Tristan closes the browser and opens Identify. It appears just like Photoshop, a highly updated one. He returns to the Images folder and enters another mini folder, one labelled "Tests." He picks the first of the three pictures inside.

"This, as far as we can tell, is a real picture." The picture loads onto the screen. It's quite dark, with trees scattered along the bottom, silhouetted against the thick gray sky. A small pyramid-like shape is hovering in the sky, with even smaller blue lights dotting the bottom. It looks strange and foreign, and is most intriguing.

"Wow," I mutter to myself, filled with wonder.

Tristan nods, and his body tenses. I meet his eyes, and his cheeks are a bit flushed. Maybe he's not handling this as well as he thought, either. He looks back to the screen. "Yeah. See here, at the bottom," his stylus draws to the right, a button that reads "scan image." He clicks it, and where the button once was is a brief percentage bar that goes from 0 to 100 very quickly. The word "done" flashes, and the original "scan image" button returns. "That scans the image."

"For what?"

"For any inconsistencies. It is very, very rare that it will automatically be scanned as clean right away. Even when the pictures are genuine, it is rare. This was a rare one, which is why it is our test."

He closes the image, and resorts to his next model, bringing it up onto the program. It's similar, dark, but without trees. It appears to be above a large lake, maybe even an ocean, just some kind of body of water. It looks cylindrical, almost like a giant toilet paper roll, but thicker. Lights line along the edges, and spot within the craft. The moon shines in the background, illuminating the scene. Tristan presses the scan button once again, and along the way to one hundred percent, parts of the image are coated in red.

"Red means bad, I'm guessing," I mumble.

"Right. It means there are a few problems. So, look here," he zooms into a problem lying along the body of water. A red oval coats the supposed problem. "If you click on it, it will explain." He clicks on the oval, and a small word bubble pops up. Law 19.

"What is Law 19?" As I speak, my heart is racing. As I listen, I can barely breathe. All of this feels so wonderful and astonishing. This is what I've been waiting for, the "big break" as it were, finding a community so accepting. Part of me hoped I would be a contributing factor, in the sense that everyone wants to feel like they did something that really mattered, but a bigger part of me knew that statistically, that wasn't going to happen. Yet, here we are.

"That is why we go here," Tristan says. He clicks on the "file" tab near the top, and scrolls down to the word "Laws." He clicks, and in another document, a long list of laws pops up, reading "Law 1," "Law 2," and so on in numerical order, each carrying a description of said law. "Identify has a set of laws that allow it to diagnose problems and whatnot. If the picture is real, the fewer laws it will have, if any. Though, as I said, it's rare to have a completely clean picture right off the bat, just because of all of the precautions Identify takes. Technology is far from perfect. Law 19," he scrolls, "describes a reflection law." Before I can read the law, he closes the document and shows that there is no light reflection from the spacecraft, however, there is a reflection from the moon.

"So, it's fake," I say, but then change my own mind. "What if the distance is just off? So no reflection?"

"Good." Tristan beams, and shows me to another problem in the photo. The spacecraft itself. "So, you keep looking." A small, minuscule, red circle appears just next to the object along the left. Tristan zooms in. "Law 1. Distorted appearance." The sky wavers around the ship.

"So, it was edited."

He nods. "Right. So, you now know that you don't have to keep looking for signs that it's a real picture because you know it's not. Because this is a test, to show people how the software works, but with real pictures, we delete them. Now, here comes the fun part."

Tristan opens the third image, a very clearly photoshopped image. It's a classic disc-shaped flying object, with a yawning ginger cat placed on top of the craft, shooting lasers from its eyes.

"Obviously real," I joke.

"Oh, we told the police right away, it was a danger!" We laugh together as Tristan scans the image. "But we jumped the gun. We should have scanned it, because something pretty obvious snuck by us." Nearly the entire image is coated in red, with one big red circle in the middle, circling the UFO, the cat, and all the lasers. Tristan clicks on that circle, and it breaks off into smaller red shapes, ovals, triangles, squares, diamonds, all of the smaller issues within that one big one. "We'll click on the cat." He taps on the cat, and something truly incredible happens.

The picture breaks apart, flipping to its side. Each layer of the photograph separates into one, revealing five different layers.

"What..." I'm awestruck.

"When a picture is altered, it will not get past Identify. It has never happened. With this picture, there are only five layers. The background, the UFO, the cat, the lasers, and the topper. Some real sighting will come in and will have a few layers, as the photographer may have edited the light, the colours, to see things more clearly. Which is where..." Tristan clicks on a layer and drags his stylus across the screen, revealing the entire layer, "this comes in." A code pops up on the right side, filling the no longer empty space. "Not only can you see what's been edited, but it will also tell you everything in this code. There is another log, underneath 'Laws,' called 'Codes,' which will ask you to input the code, and it will tell you everything you need to know. You can input it, or just compare with the log. Either way, it'll tell you."

"Tristan..." My eyes are dazzling. They feel like they're going to well up at any second. I never realized how much I wanted some form of true acceptance until now. I never understood. I knew it would be nice, but I never grasped the magnitude of how magnificent it feels. Tristan has always been good at teaching me to understand. "This is...amazing. I mean...incredible."

"I have you to thank," he jests lightly, but I shake my head.

"No, Tristan,"

"Yes, Raleigh," he interrupts. He leans a little closer. "It's all you."

"You did all the work, though." I find myself being drawn to him, rolling my chair just slightly, slightly closer.

"You pointed me in the right direction. I won't take all the credit." His eyes, just for the briefest of moments, leave mine and glance back down to my breasts. Some things really never change.

"I won't, either." I can't help myself. Not with Tristan. He knows that. He knows how vulnerable he makes me, how he can tell me anything and make my head spin, how with one, only one look, he can shake my whole world and turn it upside down. He knows. And he also knows that I can do the same to him. *You have this stupid charm,* he once told me, *this fucking charm, that's so...intoxicating. You flutter your pretty lashes and I'm there. And you know this, don't pretend like you don't.* At the time, all I could do was laugh. Now, all I can do is patiently wait.

"Partial credit," Tristan says smoothly. "Fifty-fifty."

"Maybe..." He looks down to my lips, and my heart skips a million beats. I feel breathless, overwhelmed, and most of all, safe.

Just a few inches, only a few inches more...

...

...is all I would have needed had not a lovely knock rapped upon the door. Snapping back into reality, Tristan and I both draw back as if strings were attached to our backs, trapping us back against our seats.

"Come in," Tristan says, without missing a second.

In walks Peggy, adorable Peggy. Her hair precariously curled into fiery locks, her lips a sultry pink, her eyes a brilliant hazel. "Oh!" she exclaims, seeing me. "Raleigh! Hello, how are you?"

"I'm good," I say, forcing a kind smile. "How are you?"

"Oh, fine, thanks!" Peggy shifts her gaze to Tristan and grows warmer.

It's no secret that she likes him. For those few moments there, I had completely forgotten about her; are the two of them an item? I wouldn't be surprised, I'd seen them together at times, touching hands, shoulders, hair. What was I thinking? The last thing I want is to be a part of any cheating, least of all something that I could prevent. Learn to think, Raleigh. Just because you want to be with someone doesn't mean that the universe has to cater to you.

"Tristan, we're just heading out to grab some food, would you like anything?" Peggy asks sweetly.

"Where are you going?" he asks.

"Just to Thurlow's."

Tristan turns to me. "Are you hungry at all? Thurlow's is a little bakery, sandwiches, cookies–"

"I'm okay, thanks," I accidentally interrupt, shifting my focus between Tristan and Peggy.

"I'll get a ham and Swiss sub," Tristan responds. "You have the card?"

Peggy scrambles into her pockets and pulls out a credit card. "I do. The staff will appreciate it." She grips onto the doorknob, beginning her exit, and turns to me. "It was nice to see you, Raleigh."

"You, too," I say, the words coming out like sludge. Not because I dislike her, not at all. It's because I feel terrible.

A solid minute passes after Peggy leaves. During that time, I try to think of something clever, witty, or just subtle to say about them, that they're cute together, or that she seems very nice, in hopes of getting some information on the two of them. But, in the end, my blunt side wins.

"Are you two dating?" I blurt out, much louder than I had anticipated. Tristan literally jumps at the question.

"Oh." *I KNOW WHAT THAT MEANS*, my insides are screaming. "It's..." *don't you dare say it*, "it's complicated."

I can't help myself from rolling my eyes. "Tristan,"

"And what I mean by that," he expands, surprising me, but he seems perfectly fine with continuing the conversation, "is that we dated back in college. A bit. Nothing serious. A few dates, here and there, just...nothing serious. Once we started NETRAD, we stopped, focused on work, and haven't established what we are. Neither of us wanted anything serious. Her ex joined the army. They decided to break up because of it, he didn't want her waiting for him. That was when I met her. It's..."

"Complicated." I hate myself for saying it. I chuckle to myself. "It's, um...it's weird. I mean, you and me, we ended...five years ago, back when I 'disappeared.' That's what it was like for you, anyway. For me, it was,"

"A few weeks ago." His voice cracks as he speaks. "Yeah. It's..." he laughs to himself, breaking out his smile, "it's all very complex."

I nod, smiling at his smile. "Yeah." I clear my throat, gripping onto the edge of the chair, and push myself to my feet. "I really should go, though. You've been nice enough to give me a job, and spend an hour teaching me the basics."

Tristan stands up, chuckling. "You're really the one doing me a favour. We could use you."

I meet his neutral green eyes; I'm glad I will be seeing him more. It has been five years. I need to get to know him all over again. I know that I'm still the shadow of who I was all those years ago, but something feels different. I feel changed. I feel more relaxed, more mellow, more...at peace.

"Thank you for coming in, Ms. Kendrickson." Tristan offers his hand to me. I graciously shake.

"Thank you, Mr. Barnes. We will be in touch, I'm sure?"

"We sure will, Raleigh," he chuckles. He releases my hand and throws his arms into the air, looking around the room, beaming. "Welcome to NETRAD."

Chapter 14

At half past three, I arrive at Woodland Centre. It's my second attempt to try and find Michelle, and this time, I think I'll be more successful. I hope so, anyway. The odd sensation of butterflies flutter around in my stomach, but I don't understand why. Michelle and I were never that close. Or maybe I was looking at it all wrong.

I sigh, sitting in my car, watching the minutes tick by on my dashboard. I remember Lex's words that she thought of me as a sister. Did I think of her that way? Maybe I did. Looking back, I sure acted like it. I'm an only child, and as far as I know, Michelle is as well. Neither of us know what it's like to have any sort of sibling. That doesn't really matter, though, does it? What matters is that she talked about me a lot, and that I have butterflies going to see her. The pages we're on are not as different as I had initially thought.

You could have called to check if she was there. Left your number with that other guy, Llyod. This is all on you.

I make the decision to go into the mall after another five minutes. All that nervousness spent on someone who may or may not even be there.

I glance for cars and then trot across the street and right into Hudson's Bay. I walk through the overpriced women's section, the perfume, the makeup counter, and make my way into the mall. Down and Out is just around the first corner, a few stores down. Eddie Bauer catches my eye, but I return my focus to my goal. There is only one reason why I am here. I can't even stay for all that long; I have plans with Tiffany later tonight. She lives with her boyfriend, Cole, and he apparently wants to meet me; I'm convinced that he doesn't really care all that much, but is probably at least intrigued by "the vanishing girl."

I've seen some ridiculous articles, including one about me being referred to as such. Before all of this, I used to Google my name in hopes of finding any trace of my existence and usually finding nothing. Now, I'm a suggestion in the search box. How the times have changed. Oddly enough, more of the articles began to resurface after I was "found," for lack of a better word. It's a little creepy; I only remember a handful of times when people would directly take my picture, glances from the corner of my eye, but I have seen the occasional picture of me online, taken at unsuspecting times. All of the photographs I've found have been me on my way to the hospital, me leaving the hospital, me at the police station. At least none have been at my house.

I'm standing still in front of Down and Out, searching the employees. Only two people are working, a man and a woman, and a group of three teenagers are in the store, looking at some of the collectables. I'm about to walk away when the woman catches my eyes. I'm shocked, to say the least, that it is Michelle.

I'm surprised that I even manage to recognize her; she's so different. Her hair has gone from blonde to a deep purple, popping her always shining green eyes. Her nose is pierced with a matching purple stud, and her eyes are plastered with eyeliner, with an interesting class to them; it seems like it should be overkill. She's gained weight, but she is most certainly not fat. She used to be tiny, and now she's rounded out with an additional twenty to thirty pounds. She looks healthy and fit. She's smiling and looks a lot happier than she did when I knew her, which is odd, because she was happy then, too. She's radiating happiness now. It brings a smile to me. She's standing behind the counter, counting some papers, probably receipts, and very deep in thought.

I step inside the store, and a sensor gives off a curt ring, drawing their attention. The man, whose name tag I can't read without my glasses, smiles, while Michelle's lips drop open.

"Oh, my god," she says, placing her hands on the counter before her. She rushes around and throws herself around me. "Oh, my god!"

I let out a small gasp and hold my stiffened arms up at my sides, trying to hug her back. "Hi," I manage, grinning. I can't believe how relieved I am to see her; I honestly didn't expect it.

In a heartbeat, she jerks herself back and stares me up and down. "Raleigh, I can't believe it's really you! I saw online that you were found, and..." she examines me up and down. "Fuck, you really do look the same."

The three teenagers, the two girls and one boy that are in the store make a beeline around Michelle and I, giving us, but mostly me, a peculiar look in the process. Neither Michelle nor unnamed co-worker bid them farewell.

"How is that possible?" Michelle adds. "I mean, you can't have aged that well." Ah, there she is.

I chuckle to myself, finding it a little funny that no one else has seemed to consider the possibility that I just age really well. I laugh even more when I realize how stupid that sounds. "Good question."

"Hey, are you that girl?" the co-worker approaches Michelle and me, pointing a finger at me. "I think I've seen you online."

"I'm going to take my break," Michelle says before I can respond. She slips out of her lanyard and tosses it to the newly identified Kevin. "Take care of the store."

"But...I'm still in training, should I really be left alone?"

Michelle looks around the empty store and holds her arms out. "I think you'll be fine, Kevin. If anything goes really wrong, text me. Okay?" He nods, and Michelle chuckles at his skittishness and takes my arm, leading me out of the store. "He's new. He knows a lot about comic books, not a lot about people."

"Are you the manager?" I ask, not even trying to pry my arm away from her. I usually hate walking with arms linked to another person.

"Assistant manager. Supervisor. Whatever, something." She turns to look up at me, smirking. "It's pretty great. And a lot more convenient than Space Age, though I do miss it at times. Have you seen Lex?" I nod, and her expression turns somber for a moment. "He told you about Rose?" Another nod. "Yeah. It was really sad. A lot of people were at her funeral, I saw her parents...man, it was sad." She shakes her head, shaking off all that sadness. She's always seemed like the person who can bounce right back up again. "Anyway. Holy fuck, you're actually alive!"

"I am," I confirm, hiding a wry grin. "Weird, huh?"

"Very. At Space Age, we all thought it was aliens. Like, some weird alien abduction." She stops in her tracks as if just realizing this, "what did happen? I mean, your ex, he founded that NETRAD thing. I took a tour, it was really cool, actually, have you been?"

My mind is still trying to wrap around the word "ex." Tristan?

Ex? I don't like the sound of that at all. "Tristan...yeah."

She blushes, another realization hitting her. "Oh, right. I guess...I mean,"

"I get it," I save her. I drag us a few feet out of our direct path, so we hit up the food court. I grab the first table I find, a small one, with two chairs face to face. "It's been five years for him. I can't expect him to wait." That doesn't mean I don't secretly want him to, though.

"What do you mean, five years for *him*? Was it not five years for you?"

"Well..." I clear my throat, thinking back to all of the blurry moments I've had. The pieces are there, the pieces are coming. But they haven't all fit quite yet. Not quite. "I don't...I don't remember the last five years. And, like you said, I don't look different, and I couldn't have aged this well."

"So, alien abduction?"

I wince at the word. "No. Not...not abduction. I don't think they did anything to me..."

"But...look at you. You're the same, and it's been five years. Like..." She sighs, running her hands through her plum hair. It's amazing seeing the exact same personality in a different shell of a human. "Like...I don't know..."

I sigh; she could be right. I keep acting like I must know that those aliens, those beings didn't hurt me. But what if they did? What if they experimented on me and made me forget? What if a billion other things? I still can't shake this feeling that nothing bad happened to me. I wasn't hurt, I'm still okay. But...

"I know what you mean," I say. "I... I do. And I know that it sounds stupid, but I just know that nothing bad happened to me. I don't know what, but I know it wasn't bad." I lean in a bit closer and clear my throat, giving the room a quick scan. "I've been remembering some things. And... fuck, I don't know."

"What? What have you been remembering?!"

"It didn't...there was this figure thing, and it didn't try to grab me or anything."

"So, what does that mean?"

I laugh. "I have no idea. Your guess is as good as mine." It means something. It means that there is a chance that I didn't willingly consent to being on that ship, maybe some kind of weird mind trick took place.

Michelle frowns, and that cheerleader spark that I once knew is still there. It makes me happy. A lot of the people I've reconnected with, they don't have the same spark. Maybe it's a different spark or no spark at all. But I'm glad to see Michelle preserved, maybe in a different body, but one lighting the world just the same.

"Well...how are you even doing?" Michelle asks. "How are you and Tristan? He used to come by the shop sometimes, say hi, he took all of Space Age and Down and Out on a tour. We all really liked it, it was pretty cool. You've seen him, I'm guessing?"

I nod, gazing around the mall. It's another strange adjustment, and there have been so many, going from a committed relationship to absolutely nothing and having no control over it, no say, no nothing. "Yeah, it's been weird. I don't remember what happened, but to him...I don't blame him for moving on. It was five years. It's just hard." I chuckle lightly, trying to brighten the mood. "As if any of this would be easy." Before Michelle can ask any follow-up questions, I switch the subject, "What about you? Still dating that guy?"

She shakes her head, smiling. "Nope. We weren't going anywhere. It ended about a year after I last saw you...maybe only six months. Either way. I dated one guy, Isaac, from England, but then, of course, he had to move back. He didn't know when he'd be back, so we broke up. That was a year ago. Two months ago, I started dating Darren, and he's really nice, I'm pretty into him. Part of me still misses Isaac, but more of what we had, just the memories. I've moved on...I've really missed you." I raise my eyebrows, a little confused. "I wish I could've talked to you after my breakups. I feel like you would've known what to say to cheer me up..." She blushes, staring down at her hands. "I lost a lot of people after high school. Which is okay, I mean, they all kind of sucked." *That's high school.* "And I still have some good friends. But I've really missed you."

My heartstrings pluck, and it shows all over my face. "I missed you, too," I find myself saying, and genuinely meaning it. Maybe I didn't realize it until now, but I did miss her.

She smiles, glowing with excitement. "I'm glad. Well, I mean, you don't even remember being gone, but still. It makes me happy to hear. Do you remember anything else that happened?"

I shake my head, wishing that I did. I should have paid more attention to Michelle before this whole explosion of confusion. There must have been so much more than met the eye, and I was too dumb to notice. "A giant spaceship appeared while I was walking home, and some kind of being on it reached out to me." The more I tell the story, the easier it becomes.

"Like, to grab you?" Michelle asks.

"I don't think so."

"Why do you think that?"

I'm just about to answer, my mouth gaped and everything, but I shut it right back again. I honestly don't know why I think that. Unfortunately, all I have are some odd and sickening memories that may not even be true, and my emotions, my gut, all telling me one thing; it wasn't hostile. "I wasn't scared," I say, ending my thought process with that small statement. "I don't remember being scared at all, in anything that happened, I wasn't scared that night. I know that it's not much to go on, but all I can say is that I don't think it was an abduction. I don't think anything bad happened to me. I just have a feeling, I guess."

Michelle, staring at me in a peculiar way, licks her sultry lips. She's resting her chin within the palm of her hand, tapping her fingers against her cheek, her pinky finger grazing her bottom lip.

"Well," she says, in a matter-of-fact sort of way, sitting up straighter than before. Her hands slap down gently on the table. "Sometimes that's enough to believe." She smiles madly. "I'm sure you've believed on less."

A smirk breaks out, and I roll my eyes, nodding. "I suppose that's true."

"Give yourself time," she says, growing more serious. "It's only been a few weeks. Don't rush anything. You'll figure it out." She pulls out her phone and checks the time; I'm guessing it's been half an hour, if not more. "You always do."

Michelle stands up, and I follow suit. "Break time over?"

"It's been over for a while, unfortunately. But he'll understand. I'm so glad we caught up." Michelle draws me in for another hug, but I've prepared myself this time, and I wrap my arms tightly around her. "Can we hang out again?"

How she asks the question, it's almost like a young girl asking a friend if they can join their group at recess and play foursquare. It's adorably charming.

I find myself beaming, checking my phone. I have to leave soon, and it has definitely been more than half an hour for Michelle's break.

"We definitely can."

She smiles gently, her spark illuminating the entire food court, and then walks away. I smile away all the nerves I felt before actually meeting her again. It all seems so silly now, to worry about seeing someone from the past. I can't control anything, anyway.

I sit back down where Michelle and I sat and take a few minutes to myself. I reacquaint myself with this mall. Most of the food court is unchanged, but a few new restaurants have popped up; Chronic Tacos, for instance, along with Bourbon Street Grill. Neither used to be here. My eyes find their way to the Dairy Queen/Orange Julius, on the far end of the court, leading into a shopping corridor; a blizzard sounds great right now...

I check my phone again. I need to be at Tiffany's in less than an hour, and it is now entering the worst part of rush hour. Not to mention that I'm going to her house for dinner, so I probably shouldn't eat anything before I go. I've never had Tiffany's cooking, so I'm curious to see if it's good or not, and more than interested in meeting her boyfriend. He apparently grew up in Alberta, where the land is mildly flatter and the farmlands reside, so I'm somewhat expecting a bit of a country boy. I'm invested, to say the least.

I idle a few more minutes in my seat, feeling the familiarity flow back through me, and then I make my way back towards my car. In five years, so little has changed. I've noticed two new shops on my way out of Woodland Centre, and only a few other shops swapped around to bigger locations. When I get back to my car, I scroll through my text messages to Tiffany and find where she wrote her new address. It's a townhouse nestled into a small community; she says there's a public pool, hot tub, and full gym for all the residents of the neighbourhood. It sounds like my kind of place, excluding the gym. But it's always nice to dream.

I quickly Google my way to Tiff's place, just to be sure that I know where I'm going, and I set out on my way. Under my breath, I mutter the directions over and over, so I don't forget. "Left on Sherwood, left on Guilford, right on Durant. Left on Sherwood, left on Guilford, right on Durant..."

I was wise to leave when I did; despite the complex being relatively close to the shopping centre, the traffic drags out my commute an extra twenty minutes, arriving just on time. I slowly find the address, and then circle back around to find the nearest visitor parking, only a few numbers away. Parked in the driveway of her house is a light green Honda, which must belong to Cole, considering she doesn't own a car. I'm honestly a little surprised at the state of her townhouse, and how nice it looks, but Tiffany was always very good at saving money long term. She did just move in three months ago, too.

I step out of my own van, pressing the door shut behind me, and examine all the townhouses. I always did like the idea of living in a charming townhouse; it's close enough to others, but still feels relatively private, like a house. Depending on the complex, there's often not someone above or below, and the walls are thick. I like them.

I take the few steps up to Tiffany's bright red front door and knock gently. Within five seconds, she's at the door, fully decked out in an apron and oven mitts.

"Hi!" she beams widely, leaning out of her door to give me a hug.

"Hi," I chuckle back; the entryway is small and lovely. Just a coat closet, a small table with a bowl for keys or cards, and a picture that I'm pretty sure Tiff painted back in high school. It's a quaint little windmill overlooking a grassy knoll.

"Come on in!" Just after Tiffany invites me inside, I hear a sudden sharp, but relatively quiet barking sound. It's still enough to make me jump. Tiffany turns towards the stairs leading upstairs and barks right back. "Murphy, no!"

"You have a dog?" *And she hasn't mentioned it?!*

Tiffany turns to me, surprised. "I haven't mentioned Murphy before?!"

I giggle. "Nope. Not as far as I know..." I peer up the stairs and see a small black and white dog, wagging his tail viciously. I'm allergic to dogs, but not severely. I'll survive. "He's so cute."

"She belongs to Cole. He wanted to get a dog and name him after his grandfather, and then he met this little girl and fell for her...and still named her Murphy."

"I think it's cute." My name is Raleigh, which is not a typical name, so I may just have a soft spot for Murphy.

Tiffany nods and holds her arm up towards the stairs. "Shall we?"

I nod, squeezing my hands together. I'm a little nervous, I suppose. She's so serious with this guy that they've moved in together; I just hope that I like him. Not that my opinion will make or break their relationship, but it's always much easier when the best friend actually *likes* the boyfriend.

Once reaching the second floor, all I see is Tiff; her Shakespeare play collection, all of her favourite Disney movies, the snow globes she collects from various airports. There are few things I don't recognize; it doesn't take a genius to see that Cole is smitten with her, considering her stuff is plastering the place. I step into the living room which, to the left, leads into the kitchen. The walls in the kitchen are a soft pastel yellow, Tiffany's favourite colour, and the living and dining room a rich green. It's classy and unique, and it screams my best friend's name. Plopped onto one of the two couches in the living room is Cole, who Tiff has shown me pictures of, and... some other guy. I can only see the back of his head, but the fact that anyone other than the three of us is here is a surprise. I'm still wrapping my head around the fact that she has a dog and didn't mention her.

"Raleigh, this is Cole," Tiff says.

Cole turns to me and flashes a truly award-winning smile, just like in the pictures she's showed to me a hundred times. He stands quickly and holds out his hand, striding in my direction. "Great to finally meet you, Raleigh. Though I gotta say, I never thought I would."

I can physically hear Tiffany's annoyance. She clears her throat, and I catch the death glare radiating from her eyes.

Cole, in a panic, adds, "But, I am thrilled to! Tiff really went on about how great you are."

I can't help but blush. "Thanks. It's great to meet you, too. Tiff has also gone on about how great you are."

On cue, Tiffany giggles, and lightly slaps my arm. "Oh, stop. Oh, and Raleigh, this is Cole's brother. Bradly."

Bradly turns around, peeling his eyes from some football game that he and Cole had been watching, and flashes his own Oscar smile. He also stands, about half a foot above me, and offers a small wave. Murphy jumps up into his spot, and settles down, surprisingly quiet for a dog. "Hi. Nice to meet you."

"You too..." I reply wearily. Something is going on. And when I briefly notice the glance between Tiff and Cole, and then her wryly grin, I know exactly what. "So, Tiff, you need help in the kitchen?"

She nods quickly. "Sure!"

"Need Brad or me in there?"

"Oh, no, you boys watch your game." She waves her hand,

dismissing the question. "Let me know if you need anything!" I usher Tiffany into the kitchen, muttering curses for all these new open floor plans, and before I can bare my fangs at Tiff, she's already talking. "You want a drink? We have some wine, beer, juice, water..."

"Water is fine, I drove. But I know I'll be wishing for drinks later."

"What?" To my shock, she looks...well, shocked. She almost looks scared that she did something wrong, and I almost feel bad for it. Until I realize that she did do something wrong. "Why? What's wrong? You don't like Cole? I know, he gives off kind of jerky vibes, but,"

"Not Cole," I snarl. "Bradly. Why is Bradly here, Tiffany?"

She forces a smile, wincing just the slightest at her full name. "Well...he's Cole's brother, and he's in for a few days. He flew in the other day, from Edmonton."

"And it just so happens to be the same few days that you invite me to dinner?"

"...yes. You know, Cole is from Edmonton too, actually." *Really, two brothers from the same city?* "He moved here to go to school, he went to UBC,"

"Tiff!" I snap, and she jumps. "What are you thinking?"

"I just think, because..." Tiff really doesn't have to say anything else, I already know what she's thinking. "I just want you to be happy."

My expression softens a little, and hers fills with relief. Did she overstep a boundary? Yes. Was it completely wrong? Probably not. "I know. And I appreciate it. I'll..." I take a quick peek back at Bradly. "I mean, he is cute." He really is. Most of my adult life, I've been single; I guess I should get back to my roots. Realistically, Tristan, my first serious relationship, isn't who I'm supposed to spend the rest of my life with, even if I want to. This could be a good thing.

"Good!" Tiffany squeaks and gives me a light nudge. "He's really nice. And, you know, Cole has another brother, but I picked the best one for you."

You better have.

I head back into the living room, water in hand, and take a seat next to Bradly, who has moved accordingly thanks to Murphy. The pup is already lightly dozing. I take a deep breath and rid my mind of Tristan and try to focus on my date for the night. Admittedly, he does smell pretty good.

"So, Raleigh, do you go to school or anything?" Bradly asks, looking a bit skeptical.

"I don't," I say. "I…work." I forgot that I now have a job again. And a decently paying one at that. "Do you?"

"No, I'm done with school, thankfully. I work a boring office job, nine to five, off on weekends."

"What do you do?"

Tiffany returns to the room, plops herself down next to Cole, and leans awkwardly close to Bradly and me. It's like she's my mom, hopelessly trying to set up her lonely, spinster daughter.

"I work as a computer technician. I fix computers."

"Oh, Raleigh, you said a while ago that your computer had a virus, Bradly could help."

I turn to her; it's literally like the years never happened for her, either. "Tiffany, that was five years ago."

Bradly laughs, "well, I hope you have a new computer then!"

My eyes are fixed on Tiff. "Does he not know?"

Her cheeks flush, and she smiles sweetly at the both of us. "Know what?"

Oh, my god. I look at Bradly; suddenly, the night seems young and full of hope. Cute guy from Edmonton, utterly unaware of the mystery surrounding my life, who doesn't seem immediately put off by me. This could work.

"Nothing," I respond, smirking the awkwardness away. "Don't worry about it."

After that little escapade, Bradly seems a lot more at ease. He doesn't like to be called "Brad," though deals with it at work, and he has two cats are home, both calicos. He shows me pictures. I try not to reveal my inner crazy cat lady, not just yet. I start to let myself enjoy the evening, and I don't even have to try. The time flies by while Bradly and I bond over West Edmonton Mall and its many fascinations. He tells me that I should check it out again one day, and I let myself enjoy the moment. I tell him about how I live with my dad, and that I am only twenty. The age difference doesn't seem to bother him, though, nor does it bother me; it's only four years. He thought I was Tiffany's age, and we both silently agreed not to try to explain it.

How refreshing it is to meet someone like him.

Tiffany finishes dinner about an hour after I arrive, and we all sit down at her small, round table. It's covered in a lovely lilac tablecloth, and she even has a burning candle in the middle. It's very classy, but I'm not surprised. Tiffany has always been very sophisticated.

Bradly and I sit across from each other, with Tiff on my right, Cole on my left. The table is absolutely packed with food, with only small places for our plates and glasses; garlic bread, a whole roast, mashed potatoes, gravy, cooked carrots, beans, and turnips. It's all so delicious. None of us even talk very much during the meal, but I suppose that's what happens when dinner plans at six change to dinner plans at seven; Tiff misread the cooking instructions for the roast and had to turn up the heat. It still came out fantastic. Throughout our dinner, Bradly gently rubs his feet against my own, running up my leg. He doesn't go so far as to touch my skirt, but it's nice all the same.

To be completely honest, the rest of the night is a blur. I don't spend the time picking apart every single detail. I don't overthink every single word. And I don't think about what a worldwide oddity I've become every single second. It's so refreshing, so relaxing, so...normal. All I know is that Bradly has his arm around me shortly after dinner when we move back to the couches. Tiffany begins playing some movie, and I'm not sure if it's any good because Bradly is quite a distraction. I laugh a lot, smile a lot, and I allow myself the comfort of a near stranger. It is all so typical that I lose track of everything I'd spent so much time trying to solve. It is liberating to take a night off.

Before I know it, it's eleven o'clock. Cole and Tiff have work in the morning, and Bradly is going with Cole to see what his older brother really does. Part of me wants to invite Bradly to spend the night, but considering I live with my dad, and he's staying with Tiff, I'll have to pass. The thought, however, is exhilarating.

Tiffany walks me downstairs on her own. As I'm slipping into my boots, she leans against the wall, crossing her arms over her chest. "So, is my cooking terrible?"

I chuckle, shaking my head, as I secure my foot within my boot. "No way. It was seriously delicious, Tiff, you gotta have me over more often."

"Good, good..." I can tell that Tiffany is smiling, maybe even blushing. "And...the other meal?"

I accidentally, and quite unattractively snort from her terminology, and stand up straight. Before I can respond though, the "other meal" comes skipping down the stairs. Now that he's standing, I get the brief chance to admire his lean body. He's definitely in better shape than I am, but I definitely do not mind.

"Hey," Bradly says smoothly, "can I walk you to your car?"

"Sure," I respond, giving Tiff a gentle smile.

Bradly reaches for the door and opens it for me, holding his arm beyond the doorframe. I follow his hand outside, but not before I hear the distinct sound of Tiffany's voice hissing, "text me." Oh, the days of dating.

"Did you have a good night?" Bradly asks, sauntering next to me towards my closely parked van.

"I did," I answer, nodding. "I didn't know Tiffany cooked so well."

"Yeah, it was delicious. And me?"

I laugh, trying to hide my rouge in the darkness. "It was very nice to meet you."

"Yeah?" Bradly takes a step closer, raising his hands.

"Yeah…" He places his hands on my hips and tugs at me, stumbling me against his firm chest.

"Yeah?" I can feel his breath tickle my lip, and before I can even think of an answer, we're kissing. And it's good. It feels like I haven't kissed anyone before; it's new, exciting, and really, *really* good.

He alternates between tensing and loosening his grip on my hips, and after a few minutes, one hand slips further down my waist.

The kissing ends too quickly, and he swiftly pulls away.

"I should probably go, before Tiff and Cole…"

I giggle; as if they don't know. "Right. They have no clue."

He grins briefly and plants his hands back on my hips. "I…I live in Edmonton."

I bite my lip. "I know." I'm not expecting anything of this, not even a word after tonight. And part of me is okay with that, and happy for it. I know that I am not over Tristan, but there's no harm in some fun, right?

"Maybe when I get back?" Bradly offers to my surprise. I'm not sure if he's just trying to be polite or not, but the shock must show on my face because even in the soft moonlight, I can sense a gentle blush.

"Sure," I reply, a little uncertain.

He nods, smiling, and walks around my van to open the door for me. We bid our goodbyes, and he kisses me again.

On my way home, I replay the romance a couple more times, but I feel confident that I am never going to see Bradly again. I actually smile about it; Bradly is very nice, very sweet, and an excellent kisser, but nothing more will come of tonight. It almost comforts me to know that he is temporary, just as is my current situation. I will meet people who don't know me as a missing person, and I will surely meet more as they come. Or, maybe I will meet people who don't think I'm a freak. My life will stabilize. For the first time in a while, my destiny is not set, and that is a feeling that I truly enjoy. I haven't felt this way since…

Well, since that night, a voice speaks inside my head. *You were free that night. Nothing could control you. You had endless possibilities ahead of you, and you had the choice to do whatever you wanted. You made a choice. You searched for your path.*

I slam my foot on the brake, snapping back into reality, and I find myself parked just before hitting my garage door. I throw the car into park, remove the keys from the ignition, and switch off the lights.

You seem to have found one, a voice echoes through my head.

I force myself out of my van, eyes blurry. Before I even make it to my front step, I kneel over and vomit in the bushes, just beneath a side window.

Choice, the voice repeats. *Choice, choice, choice, choice…*

"Shut up," I hiss to myself, and then vomit again. For the briefest of moments, I am no longer throwing up.

I'm standing, staring at a pedestal of sorts, holding what appears to be a book. The book. The book is held open to a page, written once again in illegible scribbles, but there is glass protecting the scripture. I am staring intently at the pages, somehow inside a type of room, with metallic walls beaming behind the podium, appearing to curve.

No. I'm not staring at the pages. I'm reading words written on the glass.

Before I can fully identify a word, I stumble backwards off the front step leading to my door, and into the clean bushes behind me. I lie there for a minute, staring up at the lightly dotted sky, and hold my breath. I count to twenty. I let it out.

I don't waste any more time thinking; out of pure habit, I march my way to my front door, inside, I slip out of my shoes, lock the door, continue upstairs into my room, and I collapse down onto my bed. I change my mind, though, and I go to my bathroom to rinse my mouth of the wretched taste, and I brush my teeth. I avoid eye contact altogether with my mirror.

As I'm about to hop into bed, my foot catches on my messenger bag on the floor. I didn't take the book with me today and instead tucked it beneath my bed, wrapping in my bag. I didn't want to leave it in the car during dinner, and I certainly wasn't going to take it in.

I crouch down, tugging at the fabric pocket of the tote, but I jerk my hand away.

I stand up and force myself into bed, and I erase the previous two minutes from my mind; they will not ruin this night, they will not ruin this moment. I will have my mind at peace, even if it's temporary. Just this one night.

I have never felt more at ease since returning from my unknown journey. I feel confident and renewed, from seeing Michelle to the possibility of another romance, to the inevitable fact that I will not always feel so unsettled. This will pass.

I feel refreshed.

I take a deep breath and shut my eyes, focusing on the facts that I know right now. I'm getting closer to finding out what happened, and this clarity is only helping. The clues are there and have been there since the beginning. I just haven't remembered them all yet. I understand that the choice was mine to enter that spacecraft. I willingly stepped aboard. I willingly made a choice.

But…why?

Chapter 15

For the first time in my life, I arrive to a doctor's appointment on time, and I am taken into an exam room on time. I'm not sure if this is just a weirdly slow day for the hospital, or if I just got lucky with timing, but I am thankful either way; it's always been a long, long wait to be seen by a doctor, no matter what the appointment time. Maybe now that I'm in the future, they've perfected the ratio.

The door to the small room I'm enclosed within rips open, and a slightly familiar-looking doctor enters, wearing a pristine white coat.

"Ms. Carlisle?" he says, and glances at my face.

He's already nodding to himself before I say, "Yep."

The doctor, maybe in his late forties, plants his feet before me and gazes into my eyes. He has a warm expression, a face that I trust. "I'm not sure if you remember me, but I'm Dr. Bailey. I was your doctor when you came in here in February."

I rub my hands together. "Yep, I remember." I remember more of the idea of him, rather than his quirks, his soft smile, and his rough hands. I remember a doctor, but I was a little preoccupied as to why I was there as opposed to who I was with.

"Good to know. So, it's been…" Dr. Bailey checks his chart, "yes, six weeks. How have you been feeling?"

"Okay…" I glance out the window and find a crow sitting on the landing just outside the window, a few feet away. I'm on the main floor of the hospital, not being rushed to the third floor like I was when I first arrived almost two months ago. This is the hospital that I've been coming to all my life, but the walls always feel stiff and cold.

This morning was less than stellar. I'd gotten the call a few days ago, for my mental and physical evaluation, and Dr. Bailey even set aside a date and time for me. So today, like any other, I dreaded forcing myself out of bed in the morning, had a quick shower, and headed downstairs, with the full intention of skipping breakfast.

And then I saw my dad.

Seeing my dad, as unfortunate as it is, is the one thing that has not become increasingly easy, normal, okay. It's gotten more difficult, awkward, and not okay. It's not as if either of us are tense, but we hadn't really talked; I'm not sure if we had the intention to speak to one another, either.

"Morning," my dad said to me, not actually facing me. "You need the car?"

"Yeah, if that's okay," I responded, stalling myself after slipping into my boots. He nodded, and turned around to face me, but revealed a paper in his hands. That was when I decided that we should talk. He is my dad, and I am his only child. It makes sense, right? "Dad?" He nodded again. I sighed, crossing my arms. "Dad."

He looked at me with impatient eyes. It's like he didn't even want to speak to me. Silent roommates, that was enough. "Yes?"

I chuckled, out of pure discomfort, and twirled my wet curls behind my neck. "Um…" I knew what I had to do. Anger brings out the worst in people, but at least it brings out *something*. "Mom called me the other day."

I swear that time actually stopped in that moment. I stared at my father and couldn't see any sign of life. He didn't blink for a solid twenty seconds, maybe even more. "Your mother."

"Well, her parents," I corrected. "She wanted them to call, I think."

"Why?"

"To see how I'm doing, I guess."

My father scoffed and turned around, shaking his head all the while. He didn't look at me. He stood there, hands clenched around the cliffs of the counters, head swinging back and forth. "That bitch."

My eyes almost popped out of my head. I'd never heard my dad swear before, let alone call my mom a bitch.

"Are you mad at her?" I asked boldly.

"Yes." I don't know what I was expecting.

"Are you mad at me?"

He sighed, and I saw the tension rising and falling from his shoulders. "Raleigh, you…you and I, we've always had this," he waved his hand in the gaping space between us and turned around to face me again, "relationship. I love you, as a father loves his child. I am happy that you are back. But you were gone for five years." In his eyes, I saw only emptiness. No emotion lies within. None.

"I didn't try..." I don't even believe that it was beyond my control anymore. It was my decision, my choice. Mine. "Do you want a closer relationship?"

"Raleigh, listen to me." I stiffened. "Your mom left, and I raised you. And then you left." My entire chest caved in on itself. "You were gone. It's just something that happened."

I stood there, speechless. Part of me was in absolute shock, and even fear; this is the plateau. The fundamental, natural love from a father to his child is as far as our relationship is going to get. The bare minimum. I attempted to protest, but the bigger part of me was yelling, *screaming*, that he was absolutely right. What felt wrong to me is that it felt right to go back to nothing. I'd always thought that we both wanted more, but it was always forced. He never came to recitals. I never gave him any "best dad ever," mugs. It just didn't happen.

It clicked, in that moment, why my parents first got together. The emotional distance, the forced validation, the plea for total independence. I could see it all pan out in front of me, why they got along so well, giving each other space. They never told me, but I assumed I wasn't planned. I don't think they ever wanted kids.

It clicked that by leaving for five years, whatever did or didn't happen in that time, had put a wedge in between us that I can never take away. I can't do anything about it anymore, not with who he is. We're clashing. I don't know where I got my emotions from, but it wasn't my parents.

It clicked that my dad now views me as my mom. Another woman who up and left one day, no explanation. Maybe if something terrible had happened to me, my dad would view me differently; we'll never know. He can see in my eyes that I believe, that I *know* nothing horrible came my way during my absence. I wonder if he recognized the look from my mom, if he ever saw her.

The third worst part of the morning was the fact that it was the only conversation we'd ever had about our emotions. The second worst part was that, other than this morning, I don't know the last time my dad told me he loved me. The absolute worst part is that I used that as closure.

"I'm okay," I repeat to Dr. Bailey, his eyes now fixed on his clipboard.

"Good, glad to hear. Nothing unusual?"

"Nope." I squeeze my eyes shut, squeezing out the tired.

"Good. Now, we're going to have to do a blood test, just to compare from last time. I'll check your heart, ears, a basic check-up."

Dr. Bailey's version of a "basic check-up" is a little different than what I thought it to be. It's only been five years, yet there are strides to prove it. From the ceiling, the doctor pulls down a large sheet, one that looks like iridescent plastic with a small row of buttons on the side. He positions me on an examination table, lining the sheet with my torso. He switches off the lights and pushes a small button along the row. All at once, the sheet illuminates with what I can only describe as a live X-ray. I jump upon seeing my own bones, my own heart, in real time.

"Amazing isn't it," Dr. Bailey mutters, fixating on my beating heart. "Technology these days never ceases to amaze. This one is new, just got it in last month. Love using it." His smile when he speaks is the smile that I aspire to have at a hypothetical career. It is joy, and it is so wonderfully pure.

To check my ears, there is something called an "earogram," as an unofficial term, according to the kind doctor, that look like large, over-the-ear headphones. They're kept merely in a padded drawer, and like most doctor's tools, are cool to the touch. Apparently, though, you can see through the ear canal with perfect ease, and my ears just happen to be perfect.

The last test, as he mentioned, is taking my blood. I've never had much of a problem with my blood being taken, but I don't particularly enjoy it, either.

The entire time, I'm thinking about my dad, and how he's right. It doesn't matter how much I wish it wasn't true, he *is* right. I should be twenty-five right now, and so he's acting like those five years happened and I just wasn't there. I suppose that's how it felt for him. We are just too far gone, because there's no changing his opinion on the facts he's been given. I just don't know what to think anymore.

"Are you sure you're okay?" Dr. Bailey asks, slowly tugging the needle from my arm. The tool he's using is something I recall from five years ago; it's a sort of light that highlights my veins, to prevent aimless stabbing. "You look a bit pale. Don't like needles?"

"Don't mind them…just tired."

"Well." He pats my arm gently where the thick needle struck and presses a small cotton ball to the mark. "Get lots of sleep tonight. You're young, you still need sleep."

I bend my arm at the crease, trapping the cotton as a blood capture. "Exactly how young?" I ask.

Dr. Bailey hesitates, eyeing me carefully. "I'm not sure that I know what you mean…"

"I mean, how old am I?"

He blinks a few times, flustered, and begins to shake his head. "I don't…"

"Because, as you know, it's been five years. But I don't look any different." I can feel my desperation showing; I know that he nor any other doctor knows a damn thing about what happened to me, and they can't explain it either. I just wish that they could. "Has this ever happened? I'm identical. I haven't aged. Is that possible?"

Dr. Bailey leans back in his small rolling chair, rubbing one hand against his stubble. Two vials of my blood sit next to us, watching me. "As far as I know, no, it is not possible. To not age, it's what folklore and fairy tales are made of. Perhaps an advancement of the future, but to my knowledge, Raleigh, you've merely aged splendidly." His joke comforts me, and I chuckle, but I find myself quivering. "However, I've compared samples. Not too long before what happened, you came in and had blood taken. I've compared the two samples, and not much has changed, it's strange, to say the least. With technology today, we can tell stages of life through blood, it's really incredible. But as far as your blood is concerned, you, my dear, have not aged those five years. I'm stumped."

"Okay." I try to hide my disappointment. One last attempt to see if science and biology can help figure out what happened. "Thank you. For all of this, I mean."

"Not a problem." He strips off his plastic gloves and tosses them into an open garbage can near the door. I have vague memories of all of this happening two months ago, but I really don't remember much from then; the shock was still so fresh. "You should tell that police officer."

I turn to him, bewildered. "Denton?" Dr. Bailey nods. "Why?"

"He seemed very concerned for you when you first came in. I thought he was your dad at first, from how he was talking."

My dad? That one train of thought had never struck me. Yes, Denton and I did see a lot of each other, but all we ever did was bicker. It is more meaningful than merely acknowledging existence and being grateful that someone was not brutally murdered, though.

"Huh. Yeah, maybe I will."

"Good!" Bailey stands and signals me to the door. "Send my regards as well. He's a nice man."

I stand up, grabbing my coat and purse from the guest chair near my seat. "He is…" I mutter, leaving the room.

Dr. Bailey escorts me to the elevator, past the few other examination rooms, and takes me all the way to the nearest exit. "Have a lovely day, Raleigh. Enjoy the sun!"

"Thanks, you too," I say, peeking outside; it's sunny out, but it is definitely not warm. It's the uncomfortable, blinding sun that only appears on the cusp of spring.

"I don't care, tell me!" an urgent sounding voice growls from behind me so viciously that I turn around immediately, tongue in cheek. A man is standing at the ER reception desk, most likely scaring the poor receptionist; his body is blocking her entirely.

The pressure, the fear, the shock in the man's voice, it's all reminiscent of Tristan and his time here to see me. The first time I saw twenty-five-year-old Tristan.

I whip around and march straight out the door, not wanting to give it another thought. I've thought of him so much, and thinking never really does all that much good. Unfortunately for me, Tristan does happen to provoke a lot of thought. Bradly was a lovely break from that.

I stride out of the automatic sliding doors and into the parking lot. There are about six patients, most of them appearing to be here indefinitely, smoking away. One man, probably in his late seventies or even early eighties, is plopped in a wheelchair, a morphine drip in one hand, cigarette in the other. Smoking is a real nasty habit.

I slip past all the smokers and find my car, the ticket presented beneath the windshield not even close to expiring; this may have been the quickest hospital visit of my life. Inside my car, I pull the ticket from the dash and lean back against my seat. Denton as a father; crazier things have happened.

Before I'm even out of the parking lot, someone has taken my parking spot, and even waves me off in gratitude. The hospital is about a twenty-minute drive from Denton's station, maybe even less considering the lack of people on the road. After a quick stop to Tim Horton's, I switch through radio stations, singing along to several songs, and the occasional asshole enters the road. I am the first to admit that I have a mild form of road rage, prompting a few snarky comments, but nothing too extreme.

My mind briefly dabbles in the memories of Bradly, but that quickly fades. He is back in Edmonton and will be for the next several months. We haven't spoken since.

I pull into the visitor parking lot next to the police station, grab my extra donut, and slip out of the car. The lot is relatively empty, but it is a Tuesday morning. Everyone working here has their own reserved spot, so this parking lot is solely for visitors, and today, that includes me and two other vehicles.

As I'm approaching the parking registration machine, the thought hits me that Denton might actually be busy. I'd never made an appointment to see him before, but then again, he's never asked me to make an appointment, even before I disappeared.

I punch in my license plate into the machine, and a ticket pops out, showing my license plate number and the time that I've logged in; the parking here is free but lasts only an hour, which is often plenty of time. I crumple the ticket into my pocket and head for the small, square building. Upon seeing its shape, I realize that I haven't honestly seen the entirety of the station. I've seen the central office, where the officers have their desks, Denton's office, and only glimpses of meeting and staff rooms, lining the rear of the building. The left side is lined with a few jail cells, I think, probably mostly used as drunk tanks. Coming here in the morning, it all looks different. It's much tidier and neat, and everyone is lively and ready to tackle the day.

Kayla, already recognizing me, offers me her courteous smile and then returns to her work.

"Hey, Raleigh," Andy's voice greets cheerfully, and he stands up behind his desk. He gives a small wave, capturing my attention. "Here to see the chief?"

"Yeah, thanks." I detour closer to his desk before heading to see Denton, and I can't help but glance at the plethora of pictures on his desk. "How's it going?"

"Can't complain," he says. "My wife just had our second last week, a boy, so we're pretty happy."

I stand there, subtly shaking my head in shock. I didn't even know that he was married. "Congratulations! That's great."

"It sure is," a small, involuntary grin sneaks across his lips, and he chuckles to himself. "Denton's been great about it, too. Gave me a raise and cut my hours to part-time so I can stay at home more." I never pictured Denton as a family man, but I guess he could have kids. He's got to be around fifty or so now, so his kids could be all grown up.

"That's really great," I reassure, finding myself with the same dopey smirk. "I'm happy for you guys."

"Thanks, Raleigh." He sits back in his chair, stretching his lanky body. "And you? How are you doing? Adjusting to the real world?" I bite my lip, and Andy explains further, "I've heard how you don't remember much. Must be weird."

I laugh a little louder than intended, and a few heads briefly turn my way. "That's an understatement. It's...very weird." Andy offers a consoling expression, and before he can say another word, I beat him to it. "Well, I should see Denton. Nice seeing you."

"You too," his voice trails off behind me while I make my way to Denton's office.

I knock on the wooden door, blinds drawn, and step inside upon invitation.

Denton has his eyes fixed to his computer, and a pen stuck in his mouth like Sherlock and his pipe. He swirls it around, gently gnawing on the plastic. I'm worried it's going to explode and get ink everywhere.

"Hi," I say, my voice coming out much more shy and small than I'd hoped. Denton's eyes spark up, his expression spooked, and he swiftly removes the pen from his mouth.

"Oh, hi, Raleigh. I wasn't expecting you."

"Right, I meant to ask, should I make an appointment to see you, or..."

"Up to you." He rolls back in his chair and laces his hands on his belly. His clothes hang a little more loosely on his body, but he is still well rounded. "I'm usually here. It'd be more for your benefit, in case I'm ever busy...but my line of work, I'm often here doing the paperwork. Only called out for the harder cases."

Like mine, I think to myself. "Good to know." I sit down before him, as I had done so many times before, and scoot my chair closer to his desk. "I had a checkup today. A six-week thing, make sure I'm fine."

"And?"

I shrug. "I'm fine. Hospital is…weird. Not used to that kind of checkup."

"A lot can happen," Denton says warmly, nodding slowly.

I observe his hands, finding no trace of a wedding ring, but the shadow of one looks like it remains. Two picture frames are facing him, but I'm not sure what's inside them, even after all this time. His desk is cleaner than usual, less case files thrown about, less scattered papers. More room for other office tools; a new three-hole hole puncher is lining just behind his monitor.

"I'm glad you came by to let me know," Denton says, sitting up straight. He hunches his back forward, resting his elbows on his desk, pushing his weight onto them. "I appreciate it. You are my longest, unsolved, active case."

"How are you going to solve it?" I ask. Upon his perplexed eyes, I continue, "I mean, all evidence points to it being something extraterrestrial. How are you going to write that?"

His eyes grow thoughtful, and he drops his head from side to side in quiet contemplation. "That is an excellent question. Any suggestions?"

I can't believe I don't know whether he has any kids or not. "Maybe. I actually came by to tell you something else."

"Yeah?"

"I…remembered a bit more." A wry smirk crosses my lips. "I don't think you're going to like it."

He purses his lips out and then shakes his head, glancing around his office. "You know, people come in on a weekly basis telling me of alien sightings. All with your same principle, 'we need to let people know,' or, 'we need to be prepared.' I've heard it all, at this point, and it's mostly because of you. Your, for lack of a better word, *quirky* personality has prepared me for the brunt of it. And your unique case, it's the talk of the town. Hell, of the country."

"The country," I repeat.

"Yeah. But it's interesting, don't you think? You have all these articles written about you, all these TV stories, specials, the documentaries, you've traveled the world. Many have heard of you. But what's interesting, really peculiar, is that all of them are speculation. It's a touchy subject, aliens," the word slips out of his mouth like thick mud or cement, heavy and unwelcomed, "all these theories of what happened to you, what these creatures did to you. They took you, experimented on you, hence you've never aged." My heart starts to beat faster and faster, and the harsh reality flows through me that I have absolutely no idea what people are saying or thinking about me. I knew of some stories, but I have basically stayed off the internet since my return, a refreshing new life. "But no one has contacted you, have they?" I shake my head, a blush rising to my cheeks, but I'm not sure why. No one has asked for an interview, for "insider information," for anything. "No. Part of that is the law in place, so they can't legally contact you. But some would still try. Hardly anyone has filed the paperwork here to try to talk to you because they don't know what they want. They saw that you're alive, heard police statements, and that's all they need to know. They don't want you to come on their show and tell everyone that aliens are real, and there's a superior race plotting our death. They don't want *that* crazy. But they also don't want someone to deny all their theories. Everyone wants to be right about you, and what happened, but even more so, they don't want to be wrong."

"It's…" my voice quivers, "it's like if you buy a lottery ticket. If you don't scratch it, you could be a millionaire, but if you do, then you'll know. I guess people rather wouldn't know for sure."

"Exactly." Denton scratches along his receding hairline and then rubs his hand along his fine hair. "It's a strange world we live in."

"Is that what you're trying to say?" I ask, the redness in my cheeks settling. "That you don't want to know?"

"No, no," he responds, eyes deep in thought. "I just thought it was interesting that I'm the only one who really gets to know."

My heart skips a beat and becomes more burdensome. I smile, narrowing my eyes. "Officer Denton, are you saying that you believe every word I say?"

His smile matches mine, and he leans forward. "I'm saying that I listen to you. And that I'd like to hear what you have to say instead of basing my theories on my own knowledge."

"This is a very, very different Denton than the one I know."

His expression grows a bit more serious, but prudent all the same. "And then a girl went missing and came back five years later without aging a day, and no memories of what happened. I've learned to accept the strange."

I nod carefully, biting the words on the tip of my tongue. It is strange, to have this altered version of Denton. His roots are the same, without a doubt, since he's always been the type who has to see something with his own two eyes, not through the lens of a camera, to believe it. I guess I'm his million-dollar shot.

"I wasn't taken," I say flatly, holding firm eye contact. I visualize that night, like a movie I'd seen hundreds of times. I know the scenes, the lighting, the sounds. But for the life of me, I can't remember the end. I consider the thought of going back there, but that voice says, once again, *not ready.* "It was my choice. The alien *figure* thing gave me a choice. He invited me on his ship. He didn't force me."

"It was a male?"

I flash out of my subconscious trance. "What?"

"You said 'he,' 'his.' It was a male?"

"I don't know," I unintentionally snap. "I don't know if it was a gender. I'm just saying 'he,' because,"

"I understand," Denton interrupts. "Continue."

Looking back, I referred to the thing as male several times while explaining my story over the months. Its black silhouette resembles the typically genetically male body, with a few tweaks here and there. I didn't even realize it until now. "I went on that spaceship voluntarily. I wasn't drugged, or physically forced, I just know that I did it on my own." The figure is before me, holding out its hand, and I can count the four fingers it has. It has a thumb, like us, but the rest of its fingers are all the same length. The thumb falls in slightly shorter. I watch the fingers move independently on their own, as if the joints aren't as connected as ours are. I can't move all my fingers on their own without at least twitching another. The creature's hands don't have that problem.

"Why?" Denton asks.

I shake myself back into the room, the image being thrown into the back of my brain. "Why what?"

He chuckles, but more out of mild confusion than anything else. "You said, 'but, why?' As in, why did you go?"

I said that? My mind scrambles around, trying to find some sort of quick-witted response, but ultimately comes up blank. I can't think of anything, but the answer to that question could be the key. "I…I don't know."

"What made you go on that ship? If you say that it was your choice," I watch Denton's hands float through the air, visually describing his thoughts, "then you knew what was going to happen. What would make you go on that ship for five years, away from all of

your friends and family, leaving everything, everyone, behind? Were
you promised money? Eternal life? The book?"

My hairs raise on end when I hear mention of the book, and I
flash back to the messenger bag under my bed, holding that sacred text.
I haven't opened it in a while, but I check on it every morning when I
get up, and every night before I go to sleep.

"I don't know. I don't have an answer for that. But I think that I
did know what was going to happen, I…" I clear my throat, and regain
myself, attempting to hide my confusion from Denton. During my
frequent check-ins with the book, I'll have quick flashes back to the
glass display case, holding the book, seeing quick snips of words in
plain English, but I can never fully think one through. "I went willingly.
But I don't know why."

"I think that's a good question," he says. "If you really believe
that you went of your own volition,"

"I do."

"…then, you need to answer that question for yourself."

"I think you're right." I look down at my lap and find the Tim
Horton's bag, still filled with a donut. "Sorry, this is yours." I toss the
paper bag onto his desk, and Denton peeks inside.

"A honey cruller?"

"Yeah. Thought I should I get you something for putting up with
me."

"It's a good start," he says, sliding the donut out of the bag. He
takes a bite and holds up the remains as a thank you.

Two knocks suddenly rap upon the door, and before Denton can
answer, the door is thrown open wide, rattling against the wall. I jump
at the sound of it and whip around just in time to see a teenager, maybe
fifteen or sixteen, scrambling inside. He has a cheap black backpack,
which seems too big for his small frame, slipping off his slender
shoulders, and is holding a thin, plastic binder. From my angle, there is
a distinct "X" across the binder.

"Hi, sorry about the door," the boy says, panting. "I sort of
tripped."

"Get out," Denton snaps, and my attention focuses from the
fresh-faced blonde back to Denton. He does not look happy. "I am with
someone."

"Weird," the kid says, and I can feel him glancing at the back of
my head. "You're never busy. The guy out there said I can come inside.

Where's Andy? He wasn't at the front desk." *He's on a personal level with Andy?* I avoid eye contact, trying to keep my gaze fixed on Denton; I don't want to interrupt whatever is going on between the chief and this kid.

"Probably on a short break. And clearly 'the guy' is wrong. Liam, get out." I have no idea that Denton had other regulars, especially not random teenagers. I'm barely out of the random teenager field myself, but it's still odd to me that there are others.

"Sorry…" Liam says, and I can hear his footsteps getting closer.

"Liam," Denton warns.

"Sorry to interrupt." I glance up to my right to find Liam right next to my chair, nestled in between the two visitor chairs. He's making direct eye contact with me, his eyes a vibrant, almost obnoxious, green. He smiles politely and then looks at Denton. "I'll be out…" He suddenly turns back to me, eyes on fire, and his jaw drops. "Oh, my god!" In an attempt to take a step back, he gets twisted up with the chair behind him, just about losing his footing, and then steadies himself. "You…you're Raleigh Carlisle!" My eyes widen, and if I could back away, I would. I end up leaning away from him in my seat. The excitement level is way too high for the morning.

"Hi," I chime, glancing at Denton. His head is resting in his hand, shaking from side to side. *Who is this kid?* "Nice to meet you."

"Nice to meet you!" he squeals, and my eyes enlarge again. "I kept following along with your story, it's so interesting."

"My story…" My voice trails off.

"Yeah, about the aliens and stuff."

I chuckle out loud, smiling brightly. *Aliens and stuff, you know how it is.* "Yeah, the aliens and stuff, it's pretty intense."

"Incredible, I'd say. You're one of my inspirations. I can't believe I'm meeting you!" Liam subtly hops up and down, and the two of us find ourselves staring at Denton.

"Liam, you really shouldn't be here."

"And who is Liam?" I ask, pleased with the fact that Denton looks almost as annoyed at Liam as he did at me whenever I'd bring in all my alien proof. *Does Liam…?*

"I do what you do. Well, I mean…what you did. I'm not sure if you still do it. I take pictures of UFOs and bring them in to Denton!"

I blink, staring at Denton; he almost looks a little embarrassed, rosy cheeks, but the light could be deceiving. He meets my eyes and rolls his own. "Liam, leave the girl alone."

"It's fine," I encourage, half because I'm curious, and half because it intrigues me to see Denton back in his natural habitat.

"You're the one who got me into it," Liam says. "I was ten when you were abducted."

"Liam!" Denton snaps, drawing a weighty tone into the room.

"And I heard about it in the papers, on TV, everything," Liam continues as if Denton's snap didn't mean a thing to him. I have to say, it's entertaining to watch. "And I remember I saw an interview with Chief Denton, and he said that you'd often come in reporting alien or UFO sightings, pictures, videos, anything and everything. And he said that you wanted people to know the truth. Real Mulder." I giggle. "Is that true?"

I'm thrust into a question on the spot, and I find myself fidgeting in my seat, adjusting and readjusting, rubbing my hands together. "Well…I guess. I mean, it wasn't so *X-Files*, it was just more to get the knowledge out there. If someone was confronted with a UFO, they should know what to do, who to tell, they should know that it's a possibility. Not just some sci-fi crap that people get made fun of for."

"Wow, that is so cool." Liam's eyes are sparkling, holding tightly with mine. "And you're so pretty. Prettier than in pictures."

I blush; I never thought that I'd be associated with that word. "That's sweet, thank you." I slip off into another train of thought, the one leading to Denton doing interviews on TV about me. I wanted people to know "the truth," apparently.

"I can't believe this," Denton grumbles, and swiftly takes another bite of his donut. "I can't believe that this is actually happening in my office."

"I didn't know I had any…fans," I say, already feeling my head swell. It's an oddly bittersweet feeling, but that could just because Liam flattered me.

"Oh, you have quite a few of them. For weeks, months, after you were gone, people would come in with any information. Some of it complete bullshit," he winces, realizing that Liam is, in his eyes, too young for swearing, "but, lots of people came in. Liam is by far the most consistent, you should see the pictures he has. Hundreds. Maybe even thousands. He could give you a run for your money."

I smile nostalgically, but then my heart stops. Pictures. He's been taking photos for the past five years. He's seen ships, maybe even ships that I've seen, and he has photographic evidence. Not only that, he probably has a better camera than anyone had back then. "Liam, you have pictures?"

He nods enthusiastically. "Oh, yeah, tons! Not all of them here. But that reminds me..." He reaches over and pulls his backpack onto his lap.

"Not now!" Denton growls, and Liam zips his bag shut, frowning.

"Liam..." I mumble, not even fully sure of what I need to say. All I know is that I need to see those pictures. My heart is racing, my stomach filled with butterflies, fluttering so much that I'm in pain. "Have you heard of NETRAD?"

"Have I?!" He nearly jumps out of his seat. "You bet I have! It's so cool, it's your company!"

I don't bother arguing for the sake of urgency. "I'll make you a deal. I'll give you a tour, the whole tour, of NETRAD if you bring me all of your pictures."

"Really?!" Liam squeals and I swear, the mug resting on Denton's desk just about shattered.

"Really." I smile, excited and exhausted. "How about tomorrow? Can you get them all together by then?"

Liam bounds and nods, his hands shaking like mine, but for an entirely different reason. "I can! Definitely! Oh, my god!"

"Oh, my god," Denton echoes.

"Great. I'll give you my number..." I pull a sticky note and pen from the desk, and jot down my number, then hand it to him. "Text me later today. I can drive you tomorrow, if you'd like, you can tell me your address." I'm not going to make Liam take the bus to NETRAD with his potential thousands of pictures.

"Thank you so, so much!" Liam screams, his hands quivering violently, holding the sticky note. "I can't believe this, this is amazing!"

"I think you should be getting back to school," Denton chimes in, clearing his throat. The donut is now gone.

"Right...okay, well, Raleigh, or Ms. Carlisle, it was so nice to meet you!" Liam springs to his feet, and practically grabs my hand into his, shaking it viciously. "I will see you tomorrow!" He skips out of the office, binder tight in hands, and shimmies his backpack over his shoulder.

Denton and I sit in silence for a while; my mind is stuck on the fact that I was called "Ms. Carlisle" by a fifteen-year-old, but I'm not sure what's on Denton's.

"He has school tomorrow," Denton breaks the silence. "It's Tuesday, tomorrow is Wednesday. He has school."

"He also has school today," I mutter casually, trying to cover up the fact that I genuinely forgot that anyone under the age of eighteen does, in fact, go to school. "And yet, he was here. It's just a day."

"Why are you doing this?" His tone is rough, but his eyes are brimming with wonder.

"He has pictures," I say flatly. "He has pictures that could help me. He reminds me of me, out every night, even if it's just for a little bit, taking pictures, videos, trying to get you to listen." I face the chief head on, and in that moment, and that moment alone, he looks small to me. Not my inferior, but rather shy around me. It's unsettling. "I think he could have pictures of the ship I was on. And maybe, maybe if I could see it, I could…"

"Remember."

I nod solemnly, and Denton sighs, leaning back into his inflated chair. He laces his fingers together, resting his hands on his stomach, and takes slow, deep breaths. I cling to the edge of my seat, the thought of possibility racing through my veins, and I plan my day for tomorrow. I'm honestly not sure how I'm going to get to sleep tonight, simply thinking of tomorrow, and what it could bring.

I'm so close. I can feel it on the tip of my tongue, right there, waiting.

My eyes drift closed, partially due to the fact that I didn't sleep much last night, partially that Liam speaks a mile a minute, and I try to let myself relax in the ever-familiar visitor chair.

Waiting…waiting…

Chapter 16

For much of last night, sleep eluded me; I couldn't fall asleep with the potential of Liam's pictures in the back of my mind. Just as I would slowly drift off, I'd think of another picture that I might see tomorrow, and my eyes would jerk back open.

It was a long night, and despite my unrest, I am well energized today. It all feels so close.

I'm parked in front of a park, apparently located near Liam's house; our meeting place is this park, and I'm assuming it's because he hasn't told his parents that he's skipping the day of school. I don't blame him.

Liam appears out of nowhere, and slips into the passenger side of the car, tossing his backpack near his feet. "Whew! It's cold out!"

While he shivers dramatically, I blast the heat. "Sorry if I kept you waiting long," I mumble, starting up the van.

"Oh, not at all! Sorry if I kept *you* waiting."

Is this weird? I mean, I just drove by a park and picked up a kid in my van.

"You didn't," I mutter, and pull back into the flow of traffic; I'm bewildered, actually, at the lack of people on the road right now. It is just after 9:00, but there really aren't many cars out driving, considering it's a Wednesday. "Are you hungry? I was going to stop at Tim Horton's."

"That sounds great to me," Liam responds, and adjusts the backpack at his feet. "I brought all the pictures. They're all on a USB, I hope that's okay."

"That's great. I really appreciate you bringing them all."

"Are you kidding? You're taking me to NETRAD! NETRAD! I

can't believe it, I've been wanting to go there for years."

"Why didn't you ever go?" I ask innocently, and he meets me with a loud snort.

"They don't do private tours. I've tried. I went in once, and I only saw the lobby. Apparently, you have to book a group tour, or just know someone there."

"Oh." I had no idea. I thought that NETRAD was open to anyone since Michelle and the Space Age staff all got to see behind the scenes, but I guess it makes sense that it's closed to the public. People are trying to work, and they probably don't want many journalists or bloggers in there... I clear my throat and change the subject. "So, you started taking pictures when you were ten?"

"I did, yeah, because of you!" I will never get used to that. "My dad was watching the news one night, and they were talking about you, and how you were missing, without a trace. There was one camera on the street you were walking on, and you're not in it at all. Like, you literally vanished. And then everyone started talking about how you believed in the 'extraterrestrial,' and that you took pictures, and had been in consistent contact with Chief Denton." It's like he's quoting precisely what a news report would say.

"Wow," I respond, feeling a bit dumbfounded. "That's just...wow."

"Sorry," Liam says, and I glance over to find him blushing. "I've seen the news reports a lot. I know I'm a bit weird, I just find it so interesting. I mean, they are out there, and it's just fascinating. I'd love to learn more about them."

I smile warmly, reminiscing about 'the good old days.' "I know exactly how you feel. I felt weird, too, taking pictures, bringing them to Denton," I turn into the Tim Horton's parking lot, and make my way towards the drive-thru. There's a five car wait, but I don't mind, "It was sometimes scary, and I felt stupid sometimes, and at one point I even tried to hide it," I find myself confessing everything to this kid, "but sometimes it shone through. But I knew that it was what I liked, and I wanted to learn more, like you."

"It's hard to explain when someone hasn't experienced it."

I turn to Liam, meeting his eyes. It's like he's reading my mind. "It really is."

I drive up to the ordering machine at the drive-thru, ordering both what Liam and I want, and then pull forward to the window. I pay for both of our bagels, drinks, and donuts, and then we set on our way.

"Thank you," Liam says shyly, and he actually seems to be at a loss for words. "I can pay you back, if–"

"No, it's fine. Consider it a thank you for the pictures."

Liam nods, taking a bite into his bagel, and finally asks the question that's been burning on his mind. "So, Raleigh...Ms. Carlisle..."

"Raleigh." I don't want to be called Ms. Carlisle by a fifteen-year-old. It makes me feel ancient.

"Raleigh. What happened? Was it aliens?"

I glance over, spotting the marvel in his eyes, and I clear my throat, shrugging. "I don't know. I mean, I know that it was aliens. I'm slowly remembering more and more, and I'm almost there. I figured out that I wasn't abducted, it was voluntary."

"Really? Are you sure? What if they want you to think that?"

I chuckle to myself, a wave of nostalgia and paranoia washing over me. "I don't think that's the case. It's just what I remember, and a strong gut feeling, so I could be wrong, but I don't think I am. But I don't remember much, I only remember the ship appearing," my mind flashes back to the night, "and a door opening, and a figure coming towards me." The silhouette reaches to me. "And it held out its hand, and I think I must have taken it. But I don't know why. That's where you come in."

"Me?!" His loud startled voice almost swerves me off the road. "How so?!"

"Your pictures. Liam, if anyone has pictures of the ship I was on, it's you. And I'm hoping that seeing it will trigger some memories, or...or something." I squeeze my hands tightly on the steering wheel. I know that it's a stretch, but this is all I have to go on; hope. I just hope that I'll remember, hope that Liam has some pictures, hope that all the pieces will fit...

You're reaching.

I know.

"So, where do you go to school?" I ask, shifting the subject over to something lighter; we're going to be talking about aliens all day, I might as well get to know the kid.

"Candish High," Liam replies.

I find myself smirking, thinking back to my high school days and how we used to compete with the Candish kids like crazy. They were our number one competition, even though it was unspoken competitiveness. "And your school let you take the day off?"

I can feel the temperature rise inside my van, and Liam sputters out, "Well, I mean...no. This is for a good reason, though, so I'm hoping that they'll go easy on me."

"Is Candish strict?" The last I'd heard, they're one of the more relaxed high schools around here.

"I'm not worried about Candish, more my parents."

The mention of parents plucks one of my heart strings. "Do your parents—"

"Oh, they support me fine," Liam interrupts and then blushes some more. "I mean, they support me no matter what, but they don't want it to interfere with my school work. Usually, it doesn't, because I go searching at night, but today is a special occasion. They'll be mad when I tell them, but I think they'll be okay with it. My mom will, anyway. My dad might not be, but my mom will talk to him."

Oh, to have a two-parent household. I wonder what that's like.

"That's really great that you have parents like that."

"Yeah, I guess I'm pretty lucky. My friends think I'm a bit nutty, though. Some of them think the alien thing is cool, but they still think I'm a bit weird."

My eyes widen, and I smile softly; *it gets better.*

The more I get to know Liam, the more I like him. He's very eccentric, but he's so passionate about what he's doing. It's inspiring, ironically, since I'm apparently the one that inspired him.

We get to NETRAD soon enough, and I find a spot in the staff parking, near the end of the lot; Tristan recently told me that he wanted me to have my own spot closer to the entrance, and that he's "working on it." I really don't care where I park either way, it's only an extra thirty seconds. I gather all of our garbage from breakfast, cram it back into the Tim Horton's paper bag, and grab my hot chocolate from the cup holder. I trail behind Liam as we walk the length of the building towards the front entrance.

"This is NETRAD," Liam states. "It's huge! I forgot how big it is! That's the giant telescope, right?"

I nod, not bothering to look up to where he's pointing; the sun is bright enough for me, and I'm not even looking at the sky. "There's a lot," I respond, tapping my fingers on my cup. "Look, while you're taking the tour, I'm probably going to be going through your pictures.

Is that okay?"

"Definitely! I'm just happy to be here!" Excitement radiates from him; his smile is lighting up the entire parking lot. It warms my heart to see him so excited to be here. "Who's going to give me the tour?"

"Not sure," I respond, trying to hide my nerves. Nobody even knows I'm bringing Liam in. A wicked smile pops onto my face, along with a similar thought. Considering my history with Tristan, and the things I've done for him in the past, it shouldn't be a problem. "We'll see who's free."

I step inside, greeted by the usual chairs, tall indoor plants, desk, and receptionist, and I make my way towards the "Authorized Personnel Only" door.

"Good morning, Raleigh," Jack greets.

"Morning."

"We have a guest this morning?" Jack glances at Liam, flashing a quick grin.

"Yeah, he's going to take a tour," I reply, reaching for the door.

"How nice. Enjoy." It seems like I could get away with anything around here.

"Oh, thank you, I will!" Liam exclaims; his body is vibrating, unable to contain himself.

Just as I'm about to throw open the door, leading Liam to utopia, a voice calls from behind me, "Raleigh!"

I turn around, and Tristan bounds up behind the two of us, smiling. He's wearing a blue button-up shirt that I'm certain is the exact shade of my eyes.

"Hi," I chime, blushing a little.

"Running late," he says, chuckling, and then holds up the coffee in his hand. "Purposely, though, I suppose. Do you start today?"

The other day, Tristan and I spoke on the phone for about an hour, ironing out the details of my employment. He very well overpays me, and I, like him, only work four days a week. It's a hell of a bargain. The difference is that he has set days that he can work, whereas I can come in any weekday of the week I please since my job is a little different than most; my position is now called "technical analyst," but really, I look at pictures. Part of the contract states that my first day isn't supposed to be until next week, but I don't think I could've waited.

"Technically, I start on Monday, but…I couldn't wait."

Tristan nods, seemingly doing some mental math, and then smirks. "I think we can work with that. Who's this?"

"Oh, I'm Liam," he responds, holding out his hand.

"Tristan Barnes. Nice to meet you."

I can see the spark in Liam's eyes fan into a full-on fire, but he forces himself to remain calm. "It's nice to meet you, too. I'm very excited to see NETRAD."

Tristan nods, and reaches over me to grab hold of the door, and holds it open for the three of us. Once inside the central facility, Liam is gone. His shaking has settled, and I think he might even be in shock; he's not even speaking.

"Raleigh?" Tristan says. I turn to him, and he takes my arm, gently dragging me a few feet away. "What's going on?"

"He has pictures," I blurt out, not thinking properly before I speak. "Every day, since I've disappeared, he's been taking pictures. He says he has over a thousand pictures of possible sightings. I told him that I'd give him a tour of NETRAD if he gave us access to those pictures, I–"

"Hold on, a thousand pictures?" I nod innocently. "Right now, we're only sitting on about twenty-five hundred pictures. Another thousand in our repertoire…" Tristan chuckles, and he actually looks excited, too. "That'd be huge. It would give us so much more to compare, different angles, it'd give the development team a lot more to work with."

"What do you mean?" I thought I was the one who now analyzed the pictures.

"We have a team of us, down the left corridor," he points, and my eyes follow; opposite my little conference room office, "who have multiple pictures of ships. They're comparing the pictures, finding out the size, even what technology they use. We have simulations, I can show you…" It just now hits me that my job is probably the lowest of the lows here, considering all I do is figure out if the pictures are real or fake. But the thrill of seeing a picture and discovering that it's real…that's truly priceless.

"Maybe later," I respond, suddenly feeling restless myself. I'd be dying to see that research on any other occasion. "I really want to get my hands on those pictures."

"Fair enough. What do you think you'll find?"

I smirk, shaking my head, and glance off at Liam; he's still, remaining in shock. "I don't know. Something, I hope. It's a long shot, but I have never met anyone like this before. This passionate about it, this devoted, this–"

"He's basically you," Tristan interrupts. "Minus the eccentric behaviour."

I stand there, blinking, flashing back to my photography days. The hope that I'd felt back then, it all rushes over me at once, the hope that someone would find my pictures useful, someone would notice, someone would believe me, and not dismiss me as "quirky." Maybe my gut feeling is wrong. Maybe I just want this kid to feel the way I never really did.

"I guess so," I agree.

"This…this is amazing," I hear Liam sputter from a few meters away. "I can't believe I'm actually here."

"We're glad to have you," Tristan chimes in, and walks back towards him. "Listen, I'm going to get a friend of mine to give you a tour. In the meantime, you think we can get those pictures from you?"

"Oh, yes!" Liam throws his backpack to the ground and begins to scramble through it, rushing past textbooks and stray papers, and the binder that I'd seen just yesterday. He produces a USB and hands it off to Tristan. "They're all organized by date. I mean, their names are their dates."

"That's great. Thank you very much, from all of us at NETRAD. Your pictures could really help us make some research advancements."

Liam's face turns bright pink, and his jaw drops. He's done a lot more than he realizes, a lot more than I had realized he would do. "R-really?"

"Really. You'll see on the tour. Oh, perfect timing." Tristan waves to someone off to my right, and when I turn, I see that it's Peggy. She grins and strides over, tall and wonderful.

"Good morning, Tristan," Peggy says. "Good morning, Raleigh."

"Hi," I reply awkwardly.

"Peggy, I need a favour. This is Liam." Tristan places a hand on the boy's shoulder; I never realized how mature Tristan is in his work environment. It's kind of sexy. "He's brought us hundreds of pictures for our archives."

"Really! That's amazing!" She smiles brightly, and I can tell that Liam is smitten with her. She is a beautiful redhead. "Thank you very much!"

Before Liam can mutter out a response, Tristan says, "so, the least we can do is give him a tour. I think you'd do a great job at that."

"Oh, definitely."

Tristan leans in close to Peggy, and mumbles a few sentences; I only catch a couple of words or phrases, like, "show him...research...pictures...will do..."

She nods obediently, flashes me a smile, and then shifts it towards Liam. "Well, let me lead the way! There is a lot to see, so if you want to take a break–"

"I don't think that'll happen," he interrupts, and Peggy chuckles. The two disappear towards the million screens, Liam only reaching just below her nose. He's not very tall, but he's only fifteen. His growth spurt could be just around the corner.

"So, do you really think you'll find anything?" Tristan asks, grinning.

I shrug to myself. "I don't know." I snatch the USB from him, matching his lips. "But I should get to work."

I start my way towards the conference room, and feel Tristan's presence behind me, feeling his footsteps shadowing my own. "Let me help. A fresh set of eyes could help."

"You don't have anything else to do?" I ask, trying not to sound harsh. I'm still not entirely used to him being this interested in my unique hobby.

"Not more important than this. I should oversee our new additions."

We take the few steps to the higher level, and then make a sharp right, heading down the hallway. "Whatever you say, boss."

His chuckle echoes in my ear, and I enter the conference room, finding an empty table, apart from the laptop at the end, waiting for me. The cord is plugged in; I'm guessing they leave it to charge overnight, maybe all the time.

The steps I take towards my seat are heavy and feel short, like I'm not getting any closer. I'm nervous, and it is all over my face. It's in my hands, how they're clammy, tight, and frozen. It's in my blinks, rapid and unfulfilling. It's in my eyes, scared. I get a shock the moment my hand touches the faux leather office chair. My bones nearly rip out of my skin.

"This is really great," Tristan says, breaking my concentration.

He draws up a chair beside mine and plops down. "We are really behind on our picture analysis, but that's where you come in. And this, at first, will put us more behind, but it'll be so great in the long run. I'm so excited."

I turn my attention to Tristan and find changed mannerisms about him; his hands are fidgeting, fingers stretching, picking at his nails. His blinks are steady, calm. His eyes are captivated. The thought that this Tristan is very different from the Tristan I used to know seeps into my brain, filling every crevice of memory, slowly overwriting the old, stable thoughts I used to have about him. I don't remember seeing him this excited about anything, ever. And now he's excited about something I love, too. I never thought that he and I would break up because of our respective hobbies or passions, I always thought we fit together quite well. However, seeing him so genuinely enthralled in a similar fascination…it thrills me.

"I'll try my best to keep up," the words slip from my mouth.

"Oh, I'm sure you'll do great." His response is quick. "Take your time, there's no rush, really. Traditionally, examining the pictures from the earliest to latest date of being sent in is how we're trying to do it, just to keep it organized, give priority to whoever sent it in first. But today," he rolls his chair closer, "is a bit of an exception, don't you think?"

I nod, tapping my fingers on the USB stick. I get a small grip onto the laptop and flip it open, sign into the NETRAD user, recalling the password from before, and fit the USB in its slot before the start-up dings have even finished.

"I hope you find what you're looking for."

I don't respond to Tristan. I wait patiently for the pictures to load; all there is right now is an empty folder, without any indication of anything else. I dig at the skin on my thumbs, tugging and tearing, waiting, waiting, waiting…

All at once, the photographs load. All named by their date, just like Liam said. All thirteen hundred of them.

"Holy shit," Tristan mumbles, signalling to the number of pictures. "This kid…. fuck."

I shrug my shoulders, arch my back, and stretch my neck. "Let's hope there aren't too many airplanes," I joke.

"Well, you never took pictures of airplanes, did you?"

I make eye contact with Tristan for the first time since entering the room, and grin. "Me? No, never."

He laughs, inches his chair closer to me and the laptop, and we set out to work. While it is great, having all these pictures, Liam started this when he was only ten years old. And there are a lot of airplanes. Upon our first hypothetical UFO, three months into our journey, Tristan produces another laptop and tells me to transfer the file over to him. He then shows me that if you place two laptops side by side, you can copy and drag a file directly over to the other laptop, yet another technological advancement that overwhelms me.

Another ten pictures go by, and Tristan tells me that our first possibility for life was a satellite.

Airplanes continue flying around my head.

Over the months, we find some genuine photos, different crafts that aren't airplanes and aren't satellites. They're something else. The discovery of other flying objects slows our progress in the number front but sparks our minds. Whenever Tristan confirms that he believes, and has analyzed a picture of a real sighting, I take a long look at the object. Nothing has clicked in. I suppose it might be stupid of me to think that this will actually make me remember, but that's how everything has come to me; slowly, in a dreamlike state. A small trigger can make me recall a previously forgotten memory, and sometimes nothing but time can help me remember. I don't have much control over what comes back to me, but I can try everything within my power to try to change that.

We almost reach a year of progress, only into about fifty pictures, nearly in complete silence, both so subdued in our work, before Tristan pushes his laptop a few inches away from himself, and hops to his feet. "I'm going to get some coffee," he announces, his voice sounding a little raspy. "Do you want any?"

I shake my head; I don't look up at him.

"You sure?"

Yes.

"Do you want anything?" he presses.

"No, thank you."

He hovers for a few seconds and then sneaks out of his chair. "I'll grab us some water, too. Maybe a snack."

"I'm not hungry, I just ate. But thanks."

"Raleigh." I don't reply. He insists, slower this time, "Raleigh." We make eye contact. "It's 1:00. It's been a few hours already."

"What," I moan skeptically, and check the time in the corner of my laptop; I'm startled by this truth.

"I'll see what I can find." Tristan leaves the room, shutting the door behind him, shutting me in alone. I throw myself back into it, licking my lips, feeling my sandpaper tongue. Maybe water wouldn't be so bad.

Only a few minutes go by before I reach a year. There are significantly fewer airplanes, which is pretty great, and I start transferring some pictures to Tristan's laptop. As I'm sorting through the one-year mark, I'm holding my breath. The naïve, impractical side of me hopes, and maybe even expects that my ship will pop up, solely based on the fact that it's been a year. Those hopes disintegrate when the year comes and goes. I try my best to hold on, but I can't hold back any longer; I skip to the end. I told myself that I could wait until I reach the date of my return; I was wrong. I scroll through the hundreds of pictures until I reach the ones titled "February 24th, 2023." There are eight different pictures. I debate back and forth inside my head; *do I skip ahead? Do I go back and start again? Do I really want to know?* The last question is obsolete; I know my answer.

I click on the first picture and begin my search. The first three reveal themselves as airplanes, a real disappointment, and then number four pops onto the screen.

And I'm back standing in front of the beast of a ship, the metallic chrome reflecting the moonlight, my eyes hot and blazing. The creature, in his seven-foot glory, holds high above me. Suddenly, I'm inside the ship, and I see the pedestal containing the infamous book of my haunting. I don't yet see words on the glass. I only see then that there are two other creatures aboard, huddled near one of the craft's oval windows.

Panashlue.

The word and its syllables echo in my head, but I can't find any semblance of a word I understand in there.

Panashlue.

The same voice, that same unidentifiable voice utters the word. My heart leaps at the possibility of it being the voice of the creatures.

How do I know it's real? I ask myself, but it feels as though it's more of a memory than a present thought.

I feel my body transport again, and I'm inside a glass dome, the entirety of space surrounding me. It's the flicker of a match before I'm back inside the conference room.

"It's here," I say to myself, holding onto the cheap table to steady myself. "This is when I came back."

The emotions caught in my throat slowly churn into today's breakfast, and I feel the food rising back up to the surface. I swallow hard and search for a trash can, but the urgency has passed. I stick my face back inside the computer, and I stare at the picture, eyes fixed; *is this really it? Or am I just convincing myself that it is?*

The door opens silently, and Tristan enters, holding two bottles of water, a coffee, and a small paper bag of something.

"How's it going?"

"I…" I laugh, a chuckle at first, but then I really start laughing. "I found something."

"Really?!" He scrambles back to his seat, tossing our sustenance onto the table. One of the bottles rolls to the middle of the table. "Of course, when I'm not here. What is it?"

He peers in closer to the picture, bringing his face inches within the screen. He furrows his brow, rotating every aspect he can, taking it all in.

"I got on this ship."

"*This* ship?!" His voice almost cracks.

"I skipped ahead. I went to the date I came back. And I found it. This is the ship." The words feel like sludge out of my mouth, but I can't say it enough. My heart is killing me, beating so hard that my chest is aching a little.

"Oh, my god," Tristan slips and flops heavily into his chair. "Oh, my god."

Neither Tristan nor I touch our food. We sit there in silence, looking at the pictures. Five minutes go by. My heart still hurts.

"I…" I clear my throat. "I remembered a little more. Just bits and pieces, seeing more than one of the aliens," how odd that word sounded, "there were three that I saw. And the book was there, and, and…" Visions of a planet, one with lots of blue and white, enters my mind. It reminds of pictures I'd seen back in high school of our little blue world.

I hold my hands at my temples and squeeze my eyes shut as if that will expel my lost memories. I know that me remembering this is purely incredible, but the more I get, the more I want. I keep feeling closer and closer, and I keep wanting more and more. It's like a drug.

"Why, why did I get on that ship?!"

"They took you," Tristan says smoothly. I jerk up from my own mind and look to him, confusion plastered across me. "It wasn't your fault."

"It was, though." It's time that I finally confess what I believe to be true. I never realized that I'd been hiding this from Tristan, but looking back, I never gave any clear indication. I had never mentioned how I went on this ship on my own. Probably because I know how much it could hurt him.

"What?"

I swivel to him, holding his gaze. "I got on that ship voluntarily. I know that I did. I'm…remembering things, and I remember that it was my choice."

"You wanted to go?"

I nod and close my eyes. I don't want to think about the hurt in his voice. For the first time, I don't want to think about why I left. If I don't know why I left, Tristan can't be angry for the reason. It's silly to think that way. "But I don't know why. I don't know what would make me go, I'm still trying to remember."

Tristan doesn't say anything for a while. He sits there, holding his own hands atop his stomach, his neck bent forwards, his chin resting just above his chest. The clock behind my head ticks away, unaware of the tension it's adding to. I try to get anything out of Tristan, a quiver, a glance, *something*. We've reached a stalemate, his response pending.

It takes ten minutes.

"You wanted to leave."

My eyes that I had subconsciously drifted shut shoot open. I choose my words very carefully. "I wouldn't say that."

"Then what would you say?" His words sound harsh, but his tone is gentle, curious.

"I'd say that…I wanted to go. That doesn't mean that I wanted to leave."

"I don't understand why you would,"

"I don't either," I interrupt. "I'm trying to figure it out. I'm close, I can feel it, I…I think."

The book, the words, the echoes, the planets, the stars, the creatures, the technology…it's all right there. Tears sting my eyes, and I fight them back, holding onto my composure the best that I can.

It's right there, my mind speaks to me. *It's right there, right fucking there, and you can't see it. Why can't you see it? Figure it out!*

"I'm sorry," I find myself saying. Tristan perks up, his expression softening. He doesn't know that I was talking to myself. I face him, head on, and clear my throat. He deserves a real apology. "I'm sorry."

He rolls himself closer to me in his chair and slips his hand on top of mine. His strong fingers wrap around my hand, and he rests them both on my own knee. He takes a deep breath, and his thumb strokes the back of my hand; my skin is a bit dry from the cool weather, but he doesn't seem to mind. He might not even notice. It doesn't matter.

"I'm just glad you're back."

He inserts himself closer to me, in a way that enables me to lean on his shoulder. We sit like that, the two of us, Tristan holding my hand, me resting my head just along his neck. I close my eyes. And I don't know this for sure, but I'm pretty sure he closes his eyes, too. I sigh gently to myself, a smile plucking at my cheeks.

For the first time in a long time, this feels like home.

Chapter 17

Tiffany and I meet at Subway at 12:00pm sharp. As usual, I thought I was running a bit late, but the traffic surprised me, and I arrived just as she did.

"Hey," she greets me, the two of us coincide just before the front door.

"Hey."

We hug briefly, and then migrate towards the sandwich bar, only populated by the man behind the glass; it's odd, considering the universal lunchtime.

"How's work?" I ask as the employee approaches the two of us. Tiff and I have both been busy lately, with Tiffany's potential promotion, and my mind being caught up in the lives of extraterrestrials, so we both found lunch to be the perfect time to see each other.

"Not bad," she mumbles, her thoughts definitely hung on something else.

"How can I help you?" the cheery worker asks. He takes our orders, and Tiff and I continue.

"Busy," Tiffany resumes. "I hope I get promoted soon, a raise would be nice. I mean, I'm more than happy with what I have now, but a little more might help…" She turns to me, grinning from ear to ear. "I think Cole might propose."

My heart skips about five beats. *Propose?!*

"Propose?!"

Tiff nods enthusiastically, swiftly agrees to have her sandwich toasted, and then turns back to me. "I think so. He's been asking about where we want to live if we ever get married, and I've seen that he's been looking at bigger houses, and on his email, he's subscribed to a bunch of jewelry websites. I haven't been snooping, he just leaves his computer open all the time."

"Wow, that's…" *insane*, is my first train of thought. But I remember that I'd ideally want to be in a relationship near marriage by the time I'm twenty-five. This isn't odd at all. I think back to Tiff and I planning our weddings, me certain that she'd be my maid of honour, her wanting me as a bridesmaid, but knowing that she wants her maid of honour to be her cousin; they grew up like sisters. My heart starts racing, and I get excited for her. Tiffany married…I'm glad she's found such a great guy, "amazing. That's awesome, I'm so happy for you!" We hug again, and I too agree to have my sandwich toasted.

"I mean, nothing is set in stone, maybe he's just doing all this coincidentally, but he's been bringing up marriage a lot lately, too. I think it could happen in the next few months. Definitely this year."

"You want to get married, obviously, right?" I confirm.

"Oh, god, yes! I'd love to. For years I wanted to be a housewife with the kids," an electric jolt shocks me upon hearing that word, "but now with my job, I'm not sure I'll want to leave. I have time to decide, though…"

"Oh, tons of time!" I reassure, setting my own panic about the future aside. "Tiffany, that's great! That's so exciting!"

"Thanks." She blushes, smiling widely. The happiness is radiating from her, and I can't help but smile, too. I'm so happy for her. She has always been so sure about her future, about wanting the husband, the kids, the dog. I had a vague idea of my future, but I was always open to change. I wish I could be so sure. I place my doubts on the back burner and focus on the present moment.

We finish up ordering our food before conversing anymore, and then take our foot longs to the table I had been eyeing.

"You'll tell me, like, the second he asks, right?" I prompt as tiny thrills pump throughout my body.

"Of course! I mean, I don't want to get too excited, I don't want to jinx it. I can't stop thinking about it, though, like, when will he do it? Where?" Before I can provide any kind of response, Tiffany shakes her head. "No, too much. Just gotta calm down. Let's talk about you!"

"Are you sure?" I ask; I don't think I'd be able to shut up about a potential marriage proposal, it would constantly be on my mind.

"Yes, definitely. So, how about you? How's work for you?"

Tiff inadvertently triggers the waterfall of aliens swarming my head, making it relatively easy to switch topics, and I think back to yesterday; Liam adored the tour. He managed to stretch the tour out the entire work day, and even further beyond when some of the staff had gone home for the day. I saw him at the end of the day, and the drive back to his house was all about everything he had learned. It was heartwarming to see him so interested in the immersive world of the extraterrestrial, and NETRAD makes it even better.

While Liam was on tour, I saw some of the technologies that I hadn't the faintest idea even existed; Tristan, as promised, showed me some 3D projections of ships they had, being lit midair, hovering in blue light. They had imitation ships made with tiny blue dots converging into lines, and it merely looked like a projection, one reaching four feet long. I thought it was for show until Tristan began to turn the model with his hands. My jaw dropped. It was the stuff I'd seen in movies brought to life right before my eyes. Tristan let me turn the model myself, and it was the oddest sensation. My hands were greeted with warm air around the model, and naturally grew warmer the closer I got to the ship, but my hands could go straight through the blue lines. It was an indescribable feeling. Tristan first took me to see the technologies as a break from staring at the pictures; we had made it through two years before he forced a break upon me. After I'd recovered some memories, my head went into overdrive, and I sorted through pictures faster than ever, hoping to find a matching ship. It only took a few hours for Tristan to insist the break.

I think back to the end of the day when Peggy pulled Tristan and me aside and told us about Liam. The word "excited" came up a lot, but she seemed very cool about it. She gives off the vibes of someone who is extremely good with people of all ages. Tristan then told Peggy about the discovery we'd made, and then it was her turn to get excited. She and Tristan hugged, and she kept a hand on his hip.

"It's been good," I conclude to Tiffany, my head swirling. "I just started, but it's been busy, and really good."

"That's good." She smiles, chuckling. Conversations with Tiffany about UFOs and aliens have always been a bit odd. Honestly, after all this time, I'm not sure if she believes in them, but her support has led me to not care. It doesn't matter what opinions we differ on; she's the most supportive person I know. "You said in your text yesterday that you found some pictures?"

I chomp down on my sandwich, the hunger tinging at my stomach. "I did. I think I found the ship I was on. When I saw it, a bunch of memories just came flooding back." With most people, I worry about the small judgements they have, but with Tiff, I know they're not there. It's wonderful.

"That's really great, Raleigh! I'm happy you found something." She takes a bite of her sandwich and then struggles to chew and swallow fast enough to keep up with her words. "Oh, before I forget, thinking of you being happy. Cole said that Bradly mentioned you."

I arch my eyebrow. "Oh, yeah?" He was the last person I expected to hear about.

"Yeah. He said that you're very nice and that he's glad he met you."

"That's nice."

Tiffany chuckles. "I mean, I already got all the details from you, but it's just interesting to hear it from Bradly. Too bad he doesn't live here."

"Yeah..." Bradly has been residing in the back of my mind as a fond memory, and that's all he'll ever be. My phone chimes from inside my pocket, and for a moment, I think it's somehow Bradly, knowing that we're talking about him. It eases my mind when I see that it's Michelle.

"But hey, Tristan."

My heart flickers a little from Tiff mentioning his name, and I put away my phone, too distracted to respond. She knows mine and Tristan's history almost as well as I do at this point. She might even know more about Tristan now than I do.

"What do you mean?" I ask.

She snorts and then quickly swallows her bits of sandwich. "I mean, *Tristan*. Have you guys talked about it?"

"Um..." My mind scrambles to find the right words to say, along with flashing back to all the conversations we've had since my return. "I don't know. Not really. I think he and someone at NETRAD are dating?"

"Really?" Tiff asks while I continue to devour my sub; my hunger has yet to satiate. "Oh, is it the girl he started NETRAD with?"

"How did you know?" I try to keep my tone as level as possible; I think Tiff has been to NETRAD before but does she really remember Peggy?

"Well, it makes sense, they opened a business together. You don't just become business partners with someone you don't like."

"Makes sense," I mutter, now taking a swig of the chocolate milk I got with my combo. Tiffany both know that my snapping at her simple statement is just further proof that my feelings for Tristan are nowhere near gone, but she humors me.

"How's your dad?" Tiffany asks after a minute of silence, easing into a different topic.

My mind dances back to the lovely conversation we had last night, rooting from that darling conversation we had a week ago. It was curt, as most conversations with my father are, about how I am welcome to stay at home as long as I want, and he can pay for any amenities I need. It feels like I'm not actually his daughter, I'm more like a sad roommate who just lost a job. I don't know how much longer I'll be at home since I honestly haven't given much thought to moving out. The biggest pro to living at home is that I can save as much money as I want. The biggest con is that it is an emotionless abode.

This morning, I wanted to say something to my dad, and I tried, but all that came out was the statement to have a nice day. After he left for work, I tried to think of what I wanted to say and realized that it was nothing. There was actually nothing I wanted to say to him, there's nothing more to say. My head aches for the lost time.

"Good. My dad has been very…"

"Yeah," Tiffany responds, smiling evenly. "So, it's been weird."

"As always."

The rest of the meal goes by without a hitch, but my mind is a little distracted; it's caught between Tristan and the urge to get back to work. I've been haunted by the pictures I've seen, not just of the ship that I think I was on, but by all of them. They all have their own stories, and I want to know them all. This is the first time that I've worked anywhere where I've felt like I'm actually making any kind of difference, and it's barely been a day and a half. I had to set an alarm just to drag myself out of the place to meet Tiffany today.

Tiff and I finish our sandwiches, and as we're walking outside, she asks me, "What time do you have to be back?"

"One," I reply, approaching my car. She mumbles something and then checks her phone, finding it to be quarter to one. "Why?"

"I was thinking, if it's okay with you, I'd love to stop by NETRAD."

"Really?" My mind draws a blank; I didn't expect her to have any time today. "Don't you have to get back?"

"Well, yeah, but it's pretty much on my way, just a little detour. I'll just stop in for a few minutes, see how it's going. Haven't seen Tristan in years, might be good to see him."

"Sure," I blurt out, excited to share my world with her. My heart steadies a little; I'm still not exactly used to NETRAD existing, in the sense that it is such an open topic. If I mentioned any of my possible alien sightings five years ago, most of the reactions would be that I'm a loser who has too much time on my hands. Now there's a building in my own town completely dedicated to that exact research. "Yeah, for sure. Do you want to follow me there?"

Tiffany nods, and the two of us say our brief goodbyes before heading to our respective cars. Tiff follows me for the fifteen-minute drive to the facility, and I park further down towards the visitor parking.

"This can't be on your way to work," I yell to her as both of us get out of our cars. It's a desolate road with hills and trees and teeming with grass.

"It kind of is. The road we were just on, it loops back around and takes me near the next highway exit."

"Oh," I mutter and look off to the direction that she's pointing. The road disappears behind a small mound, and from there, I'm lost. This whole area is apparently lost on me, except for my one way to work.

"So, this is it," Tiffany observes and falls in stride next to me. "I keep forgetting how huge it is. I remember when it opened, they had a ribbon-cutting ceremony." She giggles to herself. "And there was a picture of you! Like, a blown-up picture of you, and Tristan made this speech and mentioned you about a thousand times."

"How did you see it?" I'm a little shy about that, despite my outgoing personality. Taking credit for anything good is not really my forte. Not to mention hearing that Tristan mentioned me so many times, my mind is drawing blanks.

"Oh, I was here. I stopped by to see it. But it was on every news channel, they had like hundreds of millions of people watching."

"Was it really that public? I've heard stories," I tug the door open and hold it for Tiff, "about how people knew me all over the world, but…"

"The world is different now," Tiffany replies carefully, and begins to take in the lobby's atmosphere. "It's weird, how quickly it changed. You never notice that it's changing, and suddenly, you look back, and it's all different. After you, it took, what, four months? People loved hearing about you."

I sigh, stepping past Jack, and into the main building. "People love a mystery," I conclude, and Tiffany follows me inside. Denton's words come back to haunt me, reminding me that the mystery is more interesting than the conclusion. The possibilities are endless; the truth is not.

"Woah. This is really a lot bigger than I thought." She takes a few steps around, gawking, and stuffs her hands into her coat pockets. She shakes her head and chuckles mindlessly, the sparkle shining in her eye. "This is really cool. It definitely wasn't this well established when I first saw it. And the giant telescope." She points to the door reading the word "Observatory," and places her hand back in her pocket. "I saw it outside, but I didn't realize it was so central. Everything kind of branches off from this main area." It hits me that I haven't even looked through the giant telescope, just because of how busy I've been trying to figure out my own world. Maybe I'll look further once I can focus on what's in front of me.

"Another visitor, I see?" Tristan's voice chimes from behind me. Tiff and I turn around, and he expresses even more surprise. "Oh, Tiffany. Wow, long time."

"Hi, Tristan!" She walks up to him and gives him a hug, which he smoothly reciprocates. "It's been a really long time. What, two years? Since NETRAD opened."

"Yeah, really." For some reason, though I'm not sure why, Tristan is blushing. It could be because he just hasn't seen her in a while but still strikes me as odd.

"I'm guessing you're happy to have our Raleigh back." Tiffany turns around and flashes me a smile, and suddenly I know why she wanted to see NETRAD. Sure, the facility is great, but she's back at it again with her little hints on Tristan and me. All throughout high school, she would drop hints to both of us to ask the other out, and eventually, years later, I followed through. But this isn't high school, anymore and that's not going to work. I narrow my eyes at her.

"Oh, uh, yeah. Of course," Tristan sputters, and produces an uncertain smile.

"Well," Tiff claps her hands together, "I have to get back to work. Sorry I can't stay longer. Nice to see you, Tristan, and Raleigh, I'll see you soon."

"I'll see you later. Have a good day at work," I reply, crossing my arms. She got the hint that she needs to leave, and she can see that she'll be hearing about this later.

"Thanks, you too!"

"Bye, Tiffany," Tristan says, and I'm pretty sure that he can tell what's going on, too. In high school, he didn't have a clue. He takes a few steps towards me but only speaks when Tiff is out of the room. "I haven't seen her in years. I'm glad you two are in touch."

"Well, yeah, of course. It's been hard, but…of course." The thought of Tiff and I not being friends honestly doesn't even compute with me. I clear my throat and point towards my office. "I should get to work. I'll see you later."

"Right. Sure."

I stride past Tristan, holding my head up; I feel defeated. Tristan isn't mine anymore, no matter what teenage hints Tiffany makes. He's Peggy's. Well, maybe not Peggy's, but I sure as hell know that he isn't mine.

I head into my conference room office and throw myself back into work. Pictures, pictures, pictures. I don't receive any emails with images today, so all I'm doing is sorting through more of Liam's pictures, into real, photoshopped, or mistaken sightings folders. There aren't any fake photographs, though, I doubt Liam even knows how to use photoshop.

The hours fly by.

I can't stop; it's like an addiction, trying to find all these different ships, carrying different cargo, or living beings, or anything. I can't get through them fast enough, no matter how many pictures I get through. I even know that when if I finish all the thousands of photos in the system, I'll still feel empty inside, maybe even more so, because I'll know that there will be nothing more I can do. I'm rushing to meet the loneliness.

Around 8:00 in the evening, I have to stop myself from going further. Since it's just me today, not the dynamic duo of yesterday, I've only gone through about a fifty pictures. It will never be enough. I slam the laptop shut, much harder than I should have, and I roll a few inches from the table. I stare at the technology still somewhat foreign to me; I can't do this.

I stand up and march right out of the room, heading for the bathroom. Upon entering the main room, though, I discover that everyone is gone. All the computers are off, everyone has left and gone home. It's just me.

I'm all alone.

In the bathroom, after using the stall, I perch myself in front of the mirror and stare into my eyes. I fixate on the colours of my iris as if I can see forgotten memories inside; as if the small hazel splotch can tell me why five years went by; as if the green around my pupil can inform me of the creatures I'd seen; as if just hoping enough can make me remember. I growl to myself, growing angry.

It will never be enough.

I quickly wash my hands, and then rush back to my conference room office, going through pictures as fast as I can accurately analyze them. I return with a newfound emotion propelling me forward; anger. Each picture that goes by, it feels like I've somehow failed, like there's someone on that ship who was lost to the Earth, just like me, and all their friends and family miss them and want them home, but because I can't figure it out, I'm fucking them over.

My heart rate is through the roof.

By quarter to midnight, my brain is fried. Mid-analyzation, I save my progress and once again, roll away from the computer.

I'm so close, I tell myself. That, or I'm just an idiot, who doesn't know what the hell she's doing.

The latter is probably right.

The latter is *definitely* right.

I rub my face in my hands and tug at my hair, snarling once again to myself. I am not the kind of person who can simply accept not knowing the truth. There's a reason why, for years, I was out scouring the skies for that ship I'd seen when I was fourteen. There's a reason for the massive light. Flashback to me at fourteen, doing Wikipedia research on UFOs, aliens, astronomy in general. Sitting at my computer, thinking of all these things, making charts and posters to plaster my walls and drench in scrawls. Thinking about how aliens always interested me, since I was a little girl, but I never knew why. Jump to fifteen, watching the entire series of *The X-Files* and relating to Mulder in the sense of believing so hard that it consumes. Sixteen, learning to keep my habit to myself because kids could be mean. Seventeen, learning not to care what those kids thought. Eighteen, putting all of my efforts into doing even more research and finding likeminded people, finding a new family at Space Age, now only Lex, misguided memories of Michelle, and the hollowed shadow of Rose. Nineteen, the skylight, and sharing my passions with anyone who would listen, and finding the people who supported me. Twenty, my first physical encounter. Twenty, and five years go by. Twenty years old, and I still don't feel closer. It doesn't sit right with me, I feel wrong.

I always need to find an answer, some kind of response, just...something.

SOMETHING!

It's been over two months since my return; I guess I'm due for some frustration. I've never been one to hide my emotions well, but I've also never been one to stay angry for very long. Just relax, it'll soon fade away...

The door suddenly bursts open, and I jump, so startled that my chair hops with me. Tristan appears at the door and stumbles back a little.

"Oh! Shit, Raleigh, you're still here."

I smirk gently. "I am. And so are you."

"Yeah, I..." Tristan glances back towards the main area, runs his fingers through his hair, and takes in a deep breath. "Boss' work is never done. Why are you still here?"

"Just..." I signal both hands to the laptop and smile; *that's right, you're fine. Relax.* "Trying to figure everything out."

Tristan takes a few cautious steps from the door. "Raleigh, you shouldn't be here this late. You gotta go home, at this rate, you won't get enough sleep. And I know how much you sleep."

My grin returns with a vengeance, and I shake my head, slowly sinking into my chair. "I can't leave. Not when there's all these pictures, all these possibilities, how can I just leave?"

"You'll be back tomorrow." He pulls up a chair next to me.

"That's not good enough." I need to finish this as fast as I can, despite how true his words are.

"There are thousands of pictures, Raleigh. And analyzing them is just the first step of many."

"But,"

"I know exactly what you're going through." Tristan pauses, waiting to see if I'll object, but his words shut me up. "Ironically, it was also about you. I felt like everything had to be finished right away, so that way, I could find out what happened to you faster. I barely slept. I barely ate, I barely did anything else."

"When did you give up?" I regret my phrasing the second I ask it. My jaw drops from how blunt and harsh I sound. Part of me is catty as hell. "I meant, when did you stop putting so much pressure–"

"Not long. It's hard to function on that little sleep. I convinced myself that to do my best work, I needed to be my best self, and my best self included more than two hours of sleep a night." He seems fine with the words I spoke, but I saw a glint in his eye. "My brain needed a break, things that were obvious became so hard to understand, just because I was stuck in the pattern…did something happen?"

I chuckle mildly and rub the sleep from my eyes, now reeling in the day spent working. "It just hit me that the more days go by, the less clear it is. Yeah, every now and then, I remember a bit more, but it gets more and more fuzzy. And that's just what time does, it makes things less and less memorable. Like our graduation party. I remember not liking the food, but I don't remember what the food was. The memories are there, but they're fuzzy. And that hit me, the realization that I might not find out what happened to me. For all I know, I'm forgetting some important detail, and I'll never know. I keep feeling closer, but it just feels so far."

"I get it," Tristan responds smoothly and stretches his arms back behind his head. I want to snap at him, and tell him that he couldn't possibly understand what I'm going through; I bite my tongue. He doesn't understand what I'm going through because he went through something probably much worse. If something like this happened to him, what would I do? "It's hard." His words sound so simple, but they hold so much. "The hardest part isn't all the work you do, it's taking off all that pressure that you put on yourself."

"I don't know how," I admit, my voice meek.

He sighs out gently and leans back in his chair, holding eye contact with me; I'm fixated on the closed laptop, but I can feel his broad gaze. "Yeah, from what I remember, you were never very good at that. Considering you'd try to go out every night."

"Not every night." I haze back into the days of alien hunting. "I'd forget some nights. Sometimes I'd be too tired."

"You'd talk about going every night, though."

I finally break contact with the intriguing laptop and meet his lovely sage eyes. There is so much that I haven't yet told him about how I feel. I've dropped hints, alluded, but never directly told him. I've been too afraid to tell him in case I'll get rejected. Right now, I don't care what happens. If he can stick with me for five years of potential limbo, we can handle a little bit of awkwardness.

"I still find it weird," I begin, half picking my words carefully, half spewing out the first coherent sentence I can manage.

"What do you find weird?" His head cocks to the side.

"You." Cue the eyebrow arch. "I find *you* weird. This whole situation, NETRAD, the fact that you, Tristan Barnes, made all this possible. The guy who got arrested with me," his cheeks flush, "for helping me hunt for aliens."

My mind rushes back to the memories, recalling the story of how Tristan and I were arrested. The only time he ever made contact with Denton back in those days.

Tristan and I had driven up to Maple Mountain, parked our car as high up as we could, and began our project. A few weeks prior, I had asked Tristan if he knew anyone with any spotlights meant to show up in the sky. I was convinced that I could actually make contact with aliens if I had a giant strobe light, and if I flashed it in a certain way, the creatures would know exactly what I was saying; I don't know where I got the idea, but it was one stuck in my head for weeks.

Tristan didn't know anyone at first but remembered that he had some connections with our high school drama club. The rest was history.

So, we set out to Maple Mountain, hiked up further than the road would take us, the abundant light in tow. I don't remember the specifics, but I know that I was talking non-stop about the potential to make a connection with these creatures. Tristan listened absent-mindedly, I'm sure.

We made it to the peak of the mountain, after only fifteen minutes or so, and spent the next fifteen minutes setting up the light to aim directly at the sky. I remember I had a map of flight patterns from that night, which was surprisingly easy to find, to ensure not to blind any pilots taking off from our airport.

I don't know how I convinced myself this would go off without a hitch.

At some point, at the end of our perfecting the angle of the light, Tristan remembered that he forgot the reflector for the light, something apparently important, so he hiked back down. He didn't want to leave me alone, but I insisted; after all, I would be consistently flashing a huge light. If I stopped, he'd know there was a problem.

The next thirty minutes were spent flashing the light on and off, aimed up towards the sky. I didn't expect Tristan to take so long, considering it's only a ten-minute walk up when one is not lugging a fifty pound magnified theatre spotlight, but when he arrived back up, I knew why.

Chief Denton was in tow.

Denton yelled at me, talked to me about how I could be fucking with flight patterns, which I used against him with my map of flights for the evening, and told me that the park closed hours ago. Apparently, someone living down the mountain alerted the police to my light flashing; I was arrested under a public disturbance.

Contact.

I remind myself of how I tried to create contact, and the word echoes through my head once again.

Contact.

But that voice…

"Yeah, back then, it was pretty surprising," Tristan draws me from the memories. "Now? People think it's awesome."

"Wait, do people know I was arrested?"

He clenches his teeth a little and begins to fidget with his hands, his eyes growing complacent. "They know we were arrested, yeah. A while after you were…after you disappeared, someone found the record. It didn't mean much then, but after NETRAD happened, everyone used it as a sort of 'stick it to the man' deal."

I laugh to myself, attempting to tone down my rouging cheeks and match suit with my own hands. "How very '60's of us," I mock. I almost ask the question; how did my dad take it? I already know the answer.

Contact.

The voice once again enters my head, and I can't quite shake it off. How can something sound so indistinguishable?

"Raleigh?" Tristan takes me from my trance for a second time.

"Yeah?"

Tristan clears his throat, still squirming in his seat. "Look, you should really leave for the night. You need some sleep."

I close my eyes and rest back into my office lounger; I throw a hand onto my forehead, seeping the warmth. "Yeah. I know. So do you."

"Agreed. By the way, how did you get here today? I didn't see your car out front, but I thought I saw you driving earlier…"

My eyes jerk open, dread beginning, but I remember the text from my father earlier. He needed the car for something or other and insisted on picking it up from NETRAD to use it. I didn't care, I was in the zone of sorting through pictures.

"Oh, yeah. My dad needed it. He came by earlier to pick it up. I'm just gonna bus, it's only two buses." The awkwardness radiating from Tristan's pores should have spoken volumes, yet I found myself asking, "What?"

"Raleigh, no buses come here after midnight, the last one is at 11:15."

Panic sets in for real this time, and I squeeze my eyes shut and press my fingers to my temples. *Raleigh, you're an idiot.* "It's fine," I spout, almost laughing from the stress hanging over my head. I thought that this would be the small inconvenience to throw me into a hostile fit, but apparently, we're skipping that stage and diving head first into the 'I have to laugh so I won't cry' stage. Though, I'm feeling the tears sting my eyes; they have been for the past two hours. "I'll stay here. There's a couch in the break room."

"Raleigh, come on."

From his tone alone, I know that he's not going to let that fly. I know that arguing is pointless and futile, but I can't help but try a little.

"It's,"

"No."

I tried.

"I'll call a cab," I counter, feeling slightly more confident in my answer.

"All the way here? That's expensive to get you home." I stare into Tristan's eyes, cautiously optimistic about his next suggestion. "I live pretty close, and I have a spare bedroom, you can sleep at my place tonight."

My heart does a small jig.

"Tristan, that's too much. Really. Let me call a cab."

"I insist," he says, hopefully unable to see my body temperature rise. "Really."

"Well…" For a moment, I ponder my possibilities; seeing where Tristan lives is quite tempting, not to mention the person who lives there. "Okay."

He smiles, his teeth gleaming bright, and pats his hands down flat on the table. "Great. We should get going, it's getting late." He throws himself into action, shooting up from his chair and tucking it under the desk, then snatching up a messenger bag that I didn't know was there from the ground.

I smile to myself, butterflies growing within me, but I don't object any further. That is, until I stand to my feet. Suddenly, my feet are stuck in thick blocks of cement, and my hands are frigid. My shoulders are being held up by wires, the same cables keeping me afloat.

I can't even quiver.

I'm spending the night at Tristan's house, but it's obviously not the same as before. I got lunch with Tiffany today, but it's different. I have a new job, but it feels strange. I know that life is about change, but so much, so quickly...

"You okay?" Tristan asks, a grin on his lips.

"Yeah," I respond way too quickly. "I'm just gonna run to the bathroom first, is that okay?"

"Of course! I'll meet you in the lobby?"

I nod and swiftly sneak past the boy I once loved, back into the bathroom I was in not too long ago.

I don't even bother trying to use the facilities, I only find myself staring into the mirror, hands gripped on the porcelain sink, knees about the buckle at any given moment. Slowly and one by one, the tears begin to stream my cheeks, my nose fading from its pallor to a crisp pink, and the whites of my eyes following suit.

A minuscule part of me smiles, and my mind wanders in the thoughts, *I guess I'm overdue for a breakdown now.*

The thought makes me both bare my teeth in glee and cry some more, a few sobs escaping. I gaze into my eyes with horror, seeing the monster I turn into when I cry, and I brace my hands onto the sink and stare down into the drain. A tear falls from my chin into the sink, and I swiftly wave my hand beneath the faucet to send water after it. It's gone without a trace. I breathe in and out, eyes overflowing with salty tears, lips agape, head confused.

I haven't really cried yet. I've shed a tear or two in moments that plucked at my delicate heartstrings, but I haven't fully let myself go.

Here we go.

I've almost been waiting for one of these, for the bubble to finally burst, and if I didn't know better, I'd say that I'm relieved that it's happening and will be over and done with. The unsettling normalcy that I'd felt for so long feels a little more right to me now, and my mind is brimming with appreciation.

I can't go through life accepting this so easily. It never seemed right. It seemed wrong for me to be even the slightest bit well adjusted after an escapade like this and no memory of it. Now that I'm sobbing in a fairly public bathroom about it…the humiliation and emotions make me feel more human. It makes me feel better.

I take a solid five minutes, draining my body of any possible remaining tears, and I finally look up into the mirror. Nose is still like Rudolph, but my eyes aren't doing too bad.

I could get away with allergies.

I slip into the stall directly behind me, and I paw at some toilet paper on the turnstile, wiping the tears blackened by mascara from my cheeks, rubbing viciously beneath my eyes to erase all of the dark gunk from my face. I stare myself down again and tidy up until any more cleaning will result in further agitation. I throw the clump of tissues into the trash bin, and the staring contest resumes.

Being with him. It's the most real reminder I have of my past. I never had that with my dad. Tiff and I were and still are best friends, but Tristan, he's the star. I don't know what I'll do if…

I laugh at myself, shaking my head.

"You know you'll be fine either way," I comfort myself out loud, and then suck heavily down on my lower lip. *It would just be a lot nicer if…*

I shake my head and throw myself back into the calm and collected Raleigh I've come to know and actually kind of like. After a quick breath, I stride back out the bathroom door and make my way back towards Tristan.

I stroll through the empty office, finding it eerie and comforting at the same time, much like my own predicament. It's always been odd to me to see a place once filled with people, once so lively, empty and alone. It just looks wrong, and almost scary, even though it's just a bunch of desks and chairs thrown together.

I step into the lobby, expecting Tristan, but he's just beyond the glass doors, standing outside. I seem to startle him when the doors open.

"Hey," he says, smiling. He's hopping up and down a little bit, and I quickly realize why; it's freezing. "Ready to go?"

"Yeah. Wow, it's cold."

He chuckles, shrugging a shoulder. "Yeah, it gets a few degrees colder out here, not as many lights or buildings around."

"Makes sense."

Tristan swiftly extends his arm and holds it towards the car. "Shall we?"

I sneak to the passenger side of the car, slipping inside even before he does; he was always much better at handling the cold than I was. I'm surprised he's shivering now.

"Heat?" Tristan asks, already turning it on.

"Yes, please," I mumble, remembering from the last time I was in his car where the seat warmer is.

We spend the rest of the drive in silence, stuck on a radio station playing songs from twenty-five years ago that have a hint of familiarity, but I can't remember any of the words. It is only fifteen minutes of the frustrating sensation of remembering and not remembering, a common occurrence in my present life, and by the time we get to his house, I'm exhausted. Car rides seem to bring out the exhaustion in me, even though I can never fall asleep in anything moving.

I wasn't paying attention to how we got here, or where here is, but judging by the fact that we're entering an underground parkade, I think we're at an apartment building.

"When did you move here?" I speak, feeling more and more fatigued by the minute.

"A few years ago," he replies, pulling through the card activated gate. He pulls into spot number 42. "I used to have a roommate, this guy I met in university, but he moved out a while ago."

"Does he also work at NETRAD?"

"No, he's off doing research in Alaska. Can't remember what for."

How odd.

I step out of the car, now more tired than I was before, and I follow Tristan to a sturdy door. He flashes his key card again, and we stumble inside. I see a sign reading a stairwell, and aim for it, but Tristan swiftly takes my arm and pulls me away.

"Elevator. It's pretty high up."

"How many floors is the building?" I ask while he summons the elevator. I wasn't paying attention when we first got here. The door opens immediately and presents an unexpectedly attractive elevator. The inside flooring is cream and golden marble, and the walls are lined with mirrors. Upon glancing up, there's a small chandelier. *Where the hell does Tristan live?* I then notice the buttons, with numbers reaching up to 24. He is on the nineteenth floor. "It'd be a hell of a workout to walk up all those stairs."

"The fire drills are terrible," he jokes. "But the view is great, it's a very nice place."

I chuckle, holding my hands against my body, twiddling my fingers; I didn't realize that NETRAD had paid so well. But owning any business can provide remarkable riches.

We reach the nineteenth floor, and I follow Tristan down the straight hall, we take a left, and he leads me to the apartment dead at the end of the hall, the last of the five doors. He barges inside, tugging his key from the lock, and extends his arm. "Welcome to my place."

I release a small gasp, glancing around the place; it's impressive, to say the least. The front door leads just to the right of the living room, which extends further than I thought it could, judging on my brief tour of the building. His TV is massive. Directly ahead of the door is the kitchen, which looks like a high-quality furniture showroom. "This is really nice."

"Yeah, I didn't do so bad, considering it's my first place."

I snort, slipping out of my boots where he's slipping out of his. There's a small mat next to the closet lining the right wall of the door, holding a few pairs of shoes. "Wow." I'm not sure if he hears me, but either way, I'm in awe. It's so comely; this would be my dream apartment.

"I'll go grab some extra blankets for the guest room," Tristan mumbles, and yanks on the closet doors next to the front door. Hidden inside, there's a washer and dryer, one stacked upon the other. Beside them lies three shelves, each with different types of blankets. "It gets pretty cold in there."

He struts to the left, past the living room, and disappears into a bedroom. I begin to wander about. I immediately head for the window, taking up most of the kitchen wall that isn't plastered with cupboards and cabinets. The view is dark, only with some lights in the distance, and then a sea of darkness. I can see the silhouette of mountains, but not much else. I think the moon is on the other side of the building.

"It's nicer in the day, trust me."

Tristan appears behind me, peering out next to me. "You can see the sunset from this window, it's nice. Especially on the patio." He points to a door that I hadn't even noticed yet, to the left of his kitchen counters.

"I bet it's beautiful. Do you ever get tired of it?"

He shrugs, crinkling his nose a little. "No, never tired of it. It's one of those things that I'll really miss if I lose have it, though."

"I'll bet." I find myself muttering. I clear my throat and turn around to face Tristan, meeting his sage eyes. "Where's your bathroom?"

"Oh, sure, uh," he turns to face a set of two doors, their corners meeting at a ninety-degree angle. "Door on the right."

"Thanks." I try not to blush.

I stride to the bathroom and take a peek inside the other angled door, into what I assume to be his own room. It looks nice. The apartment is a decent size, but it's really the view and the décor that's getting to me. It all feels very posh. Entering the bathroom only validates my feelings further; there's a separate shower and bathtub next to one another, and the tub is big enough for two or more. There's a glass bowl fixed as the sink, and plenty of counter space, all of it empty, given the toothbrush holder. I'm not sure if he's started being tidier, hired a maid, or this is just an oddly clean day for his place, but it all looks delightful.

I decide to do the cliché thing to do, and I snoop through his mirror cabinets, finding nothing out of the ordinary. A few painkillers, some tiger balm, lip balm, Q-tips, a razor for his almost non-existent beard, though I doubt he's shaved in the past few days, and some eye drops, among other essential bathroom gadgets. I find myself blushing and embarrassed by the sheer fact that I stooped to snooping through my ex-boyfriend's bathroom medicine cabinet.

Ex-boyfriend. That's a whole new reason.

I emerge from the bathroom, hoping that Tristan doesn't sense my naughty morals, but he is undisturbed, still in the kitchen, now holding a kettle.

"What tea would you like?"

I clear my throat and lean against the breakfast bar, facing his back. "What tea do you have?"

"Why don't I surprise you?" I can feel him grinning.

"Okay."

I take a seat down on his couch and bring my knees up with me. His couch is surprisingly comfortable, especially given how stiff it looks, but the cushions soon form around my shape. After a few minutes in sofa utopia, Tristan walks into the living room and hands me a plain white mug.

"Thanks." I had listened to him fumble through his cupboards, even hearing a few tins of tea opening and closing, and was startled by the screeching kettle, but I never once looked over at him. I was too focused on calming my shot nerves. I don't know why I'm panicking so much. Or I'm just convincing myself that I don't know. I always have to be so god damn clever.

He nods, places his own mug down on the side table next to him, and faces me. "Are you warming up? You were pretty cold in the car."

I sip the tea, the mere air burning my lip, and I instead breathe it in. *Yum. Nutty.* "I think so."

Tristan sits down, picks up a remote from the small table and flicks his fireplace on, located to the left of the massive TV. "What do you think?" he asks, not peeling his eyes from the roaring fire.

I let my eyes gaze to the flames, and soon I am transfixed as well. "Too hot to drink right now. Smells really good, though." I fake another sip. I counter, "this place, though, wow. Really nice."

"Thank you," he grins. "It sucked losing a roommate to pay for half the rent, but it's actually working out quite nicely. Living alone is pretty nice."

"That's good." The idea of living alone both scares and calls out to me. I'd love to live alone, my own rules, my own life, no one affecting my living but myself. The thought is great until my irrational mindset creeps in. Out of nowhere, my boldness, for lack of a nicer word, shines through, and I blurt out, "Tristan, can I ask how you've been? With me coming back?" Other than the disaster of tonight, I don't think I'm doing too horribly, especially now that I've finally gotten my breakdown over with. Is that a sign of progress, or am I just insane?

"I'm not sure," he mumbles, readjusting his position on the couch. "It's weird seeing you, the exact same. Just as, I'm sure, it's weird seeing me older." I nod mindlessly. "I'm really just happy that you're back."

I follow his shifty eyes and observe around his TV, all the shelves filled with different glass, metal, and wooden accents, but I focus on the pictures; his mom, dad, the rest of his family, someone's baby, and…me. I lean in a little closer to the TV and find a picture of just me. I've never seen the picture before, so it must be one that he took and never showed me. "Is that me?" I ask before I realize that I externally ignored everything he just said.

"Oh." His eyes dart to where I was looking before I even have to show him. "Yeah. It's my favourite picture of you, I took it when we went to Edmonton." That explains why I don't recognize the background, it's some exclusive store.

"And you have it up?"

He smiles gently. "I couldn't forget you, Raleigh. Even if I tried."

And that's all it takes. It's what I've been waiting for all night, what I've been so nervous for has all been leading up to this moment. The moment where I make my move and see if he reciprocates. It's not as scary as when I first asked Tristan out on a date because it's familiar, but it may feel even more intense. Back then, I had no idea what our future relationship held; now, I know how great it could be. I slowly inch towards Tristan, adjusting and readjusting on the couch, gravitating towards him, until I'm right next to him. I lunge in and take my shot.

Tristan doesn't hesitate before gripping his hands tightly on my body, stroking firmly, and he draws me in closer. It's not long before I'm straddling him, and his hands are fixed on either hip. He tugs me back and forth in time, moving his pelvis along with me.

I've missed him so much. It never honestly occurred to me just how much I missed him until now, now that I'm feeling him again. I run my hands along his chest, tousle his hair, press his cheeks. I love feeling every part of him. I never got the closure for the break up that hadn't happened. Hopefully, now I won't have to. Even today, I wasn't prepared for how I'd truly feel.

"Hold on," Tristan whispers.

Before I can ask what he's talking about, his hands wrap around my waist, and he lifts me up into the air. I squeak a little, my legs flailing to encircle his own waist, and I haul myself up higher to better situate myself. I hope he doesn't notice that I'm a little heavier than the last time he's been so close to me, but I barely notice myself. He carries me into the bedroom, still occasionally pressing his lips to mine, and then collapses down on top of me.

He chuckles. "Hi."

"Hi," I whisper back.

I take off my sweater, and he takes off his shirt. I cave and slip out of my shirt as well. Tristan dives back in and slowly moves down from my lips. He kisses my neck, my shoulders, pushing towards my breasts, and then down my stomach. I glance down, finding that he's stripped down to his boxers; he always manages to do that. He helps me wiggle out of the jeans I'm wearing, and his kisses descend my hips, my thighs, knees. His lips return up my body and rest on my hips. He glances up at me and smiles, and I smile back.

He mounts my body, still in his boxers, and places each of his hands on my breasts. They too slide down my body and find a more desirable position. I moan softly, my eyes fluttering closed, as his hands really begin to get things going. After a few minutes, he strategically places himself, so his pelvis is around where my hands are.

"I think you're ready," he says softly.

I grin.

Half an hour later, the rest is history. I lay next to Tristan, his body too warm to be pressed against him, but I'm sure to hold his hand. I still lay under the blankets, just because of my self-conscious nerves.

"Was that okay?" he asks.

I nod repeatedly. "Yes."

"Better than okay?"

"Yes," I giggle, turning my head towards him. He smiles, props himself up on one elbow, and kisses me again. It feels so right. He throws the covers off of himself and crawls towards the foot of his bed. "I'm thirsty, I'll be right back. You want some water?"

"Sure."

He grins, slipping back into his boxers. "I'll get a big cup." Just like old times.

I chuckle and then flop back down on his bed, staring at the popcorn ceiling. A chill comes over me, and I draw the blankets back up, covering my previously exposed chest. I moan carefully and allow my eyes to drift closed on their own.

My mind is in a calm frenzy of relaxation, seeing bright colours and happy, lovely swirls while my lips trickle into a smile. This is what I've been waiting for since my return, and especially all day today. This is what I wanted. I have the impending doom of discovering my past fate, but I let myself have this one selfish pleasure. I lay in this bed to rest and will deal with everything tomorrow. I have almost never felt so

at peace.
Almost?
I'm asleep before Tristan even returns.

Chapter 18

"Quitting time," Tristan's voice chimes. I glance up from behind my laptop, adjusting my glasses on the bridge of my nose.

"Already?"

He laughs, checking outside the hall, and then sneaks into the conference room, closing the door behind him. "Yeah. And you shouldn't stay late today, you didn't sleep much last night."

I find myself grinning. "Neither did you."

Tristan and I haven't discussed much about last night, but I'm not even sure there's much to talk about. I don't know what we are; all I know is that this morning, he held me while he drank his coffee and that before we got out of his car, just about the enter the building, he gave me a kiss. He told me he enjoyed last night, and I said the same back. I don't know what we are, but I'm okay with that for now. It was just lovely to be with him again.

"Yeah, well, I'll be heading out within the hour," he shoots back, holding firm eye contact. "You, however, get out of here."

I sigh, glancing back down at the computer. I've muddled my way through a lot of pictures, but I kept coming back to the ones Liam submitted. I kept staring, kept observing, repeatedly ran them through Identify, I couldn't help myself. I was hoping that staring enough would trigger some kind of...*something*; no dice. "Soon."

Tristan saunters over around the long table and plops down in a chair next to me. "Anything good today?"

I nod. "Yeah, got a few good authentic ones. One was a different angle of pictures you got about six months ago, so the research guys were pretty excited about that. They said it helped their model." I went into the research lab only briefly today, because I know that if I stayed longer than two minutes, I would have been there all day.

"That's great. And you like the job?"

"I really do."

He leans in close to me, smirking. "Good."

I shut the laptop and gaze over towards the door. I've exhausted myself for the day, staring at these pictures, and forcing myself to stay away from the research lab.

"Hey, maybe go for a walk or something," Tristan adds to the silence. "Clear your head."

I nod mindlessly, but the idea of going outside really sinks in. It just hits me now that I haven't even been back to the corner of Edgar and Caulfield since I first reappeared. I have driven by, on occasion, but I've never actually stopped and gone back there.

"Yeah, that might be good." I don't really know why I haven't gone back to the spot it all happened. I get a small knot in the pit of my stomach when I think about it, almost like a warning. That voice in my head, the one telling me I wasn't ready, disappears. It remains silent now. *I'm ready.* "Well. Thanks." I stand up, grab my messenger bag, and shut the laptop down. I've started bringing the book with me to work, keeping it tucked away inside my bag. Tristan hasn't mentioned it and is probably waiting for me to give it to him of my own volition, but I haven't even told him that it's in my bag. I haven't told anyone.

"No problem." Tristan stands up, places his hands on my shoulders, and gently pecks my forehead. He has a bit of a daze in his eyes, visibly thrown off by how abruptly I became willing to leave NETRAD. It *is* my calling, it's my dream job to work at a company like this. There is still so much I don't know and can't wait to learn. "Have a good night."

"You too," I mutter, finding myself blushing. The quick kiss, in return, throws me off. I slip past him and out of the room, finding myself quivering with anticipation from the thought of returning to that spot. I usher the thoughts of Tristan from my mind; he had his time to shine yesterday. This evening is all about that spot.

It has been too long.

When I step outside, bidding Jack a goodbye, I'm confronted by the night sky; even better. I'm confident that the idea of returning to the scene scares me, even more so in the dark. Laying alone in a public area scares me, not to mention a place where I disappeared from. But I think it's time.

I walk to my car, now parking closer and closer to the building as time goes on. I'm getting used to where other workers park, making it easier to find my own spot; I'm only about ten spots from the door now.

Once I get in my car, I sit still for a moment, picking at the skin around my thumbs. I'm nervous to go back to where it all went sideways, but I guess that's expected.

I switch on the radio to calm my nerves, pulling out of the NETRAD parking lot, and listen to my favourite station for the full half hour until I arrive. It's a mixture of old and new music, and they tend to stay away from the poppy crap.

I drive past the now empty lot at first, almost forgetting its precise location, and I end up having to circle the block to return. I park a few houses away, ensuring that there are no stop signs within twenty feet of me; that trick has had me towed before. I walk the street, clutching my bag tightly, observing what I must have seen five years ago, and I stop in the dead centre of the sidewalk. To my right, a road that leads along Lion's Park, straight to the police station. To my left, the empty lot. I look up; an empty sky. It's cloudy tonight in my neighbourhood, so unlike at NETRAD, I can't see any stars. I keep staring and spot a few stray dazzling gleams, but that's about it. And one airplane. It all feels so serene. My head is pounding with fear and anticipation.

I close my eyes, and I try to go back to that night. I try to talk myself into replaying the act, smelling what the air reeked of, hearing what I was so desperately trying not to listen to, seeing the giant spacecraft in front of me…

After a few minutes, I begin to grow sour; it's been two months. How could I just forget five years? Maybe it's not just because I hit my head or was "struck" by something. Maybe the aliens altered something inside my head, aided me in forgetting what really happened. But I don't remember that.

Maybe that's the fucking point.

"What happened?" I ask out loud. I speak quietly at first but then grow more aggressive, my hands turning into fists. "What happened?!"

I look at the blank canvas of a sky. More clouds must have flooded in because I can't see a single glint of hope. It's a sea of black.

"I can't fucking remember what the point of it all was. Maybe I didn't even have a choice! Maybe I was abducted and experimented on, and I'm just living with all of these changed memories."

I cross the border between sidewalk and grass, and I begin to pace viciously, holding my gaze with the chilled, crunching grass beneath my feet.

"Why? Why?!" My eyes shoot lightning at the clouds. "Why did this happen? Why would you do this?"

I heard a loud crack, and I whip my head around, finding some guy standing behind me on the sidewalk. I glance down to his feet, seeing a broken branch beneath his feet, and then meet his eyes; he's a deer in headlights. He scurries on his way, fixating on the ground, all while casually eyeing me from the corners of his eyes, and makes his way towards where Tristan used to live.

You know things are bad when you're the crazy one of the night.

I sigh, crossing my chilling arms over my chest.

"Just…why."

I mumble nonsense to myself, suddenly feeling exhausted, and I squat down to rest for a moment. My squat turns into a sit, and I plunk down onto the grass, the coolness soaking through my leggings. I stretch out on the small field, my knees bent in the air, one arm beneath my head, the other on my stomach. I stare up at the sky, holding a steady gaze with the darkness, attempting to find any sort of clarity, any cloud movement at all. It just seems like one big puff, stretching out as far as the world will take it.

I press my palm flat against my belly, physically feeling every deep breath I take. It's a beautiful night. It's just a tad too cold, which I like because there's no chance of me getting warm. I may reach a neutral temperature, but right now, I want the chill.

I close my eyes; I don't know what to think anymore. The best that I can do is to continue trying to trigger those lost memories in my jungle of a brain. I twinge and tweak my back, attempting to find the perfect position, but I can't find one. I awkwardly reach behind me and snatch my bag from beneath my back, tugging it out to my side.

My heart almost stops, and I scramble inside my tote, throwing my phone, wallet, headphones, and almost all my makeup from it until I have a firm grasp on the book.

I bring myself back up to a cross-legged sit, and I feel the cover of the book once more, the odd, fabric, gibberish filled book. I hold it in my hands, and suddenly, my head snaps to my bag again. From the corner of my eye, I see a small plastic bag, one that I don't recognize. I tug it out quick and hold my gaze with a small metal sphere.

It takes me a moment to recall the object.

Denton told me they found this with me when I first reappeared. I forgot that I had taken it with me, it must have been in the bag this whole time.

I smooth the ball through the plastic, my fingers tingling when I touch it.

My mind jumps to a place both foreign and comforting to me, and I'm back on the ship. I can't see anything definite, it's almost as if I'm living in a picture. It's a scene I've seen before, with the figure ahead of me, seeming to look at me, though I can't place its features. The creature isn't moving, and neither am I; I'm not even breathing. But something feels…off.

I flash back to my current state, sitting on the grass, clutching the metal sphere.

What…

"…what the fuck?" I scoff, accidentally spitting on my hand a little. "What is that supposed to mean?!"

My hand automatically reaches to my left ear; I almost jump at the touch of my fingers, shocked to find my hand reaching. I stare at the ball again; it doesn't take a genius.

Slowly and carefully, I remove the rounded metal wonder from its encasement, and I move it towards my ear. I ignore the thoughts telling me how strange I'm acting.

I slip the object inside my ear, and I sit there, motionless. It feels the same as it did on my little trip to the past, with the ever so slight pressure against my canal, but everything else is the same.

Until it isn't.

A slow medley of sounds subdues my mind, none of which are familiar or even natural sounding in the slightest. In a single blink, my eyes open to a sea of darkness. But in that darkness, something flickers. Just out of the corner of my eye, out of sight to my left, I see some sort of light. I glance over, my head tilting to rest on my shoulder, and a streak of white drops from the black universe. Within a few seconds, the descending light disappears, but my heart is set aflame.

I gasp, breaths coming short to me, and I swear that I can feel my brain spark.

A massive gust of wind suddenly flushes towards me, and I snap my head towards where it must be coming from, though I can't see anything. I keep thinking to myself how scared I am, that I am terrified and traumatized, but I don't truly feel it. It's all in my head. It's almost a comfort to know that I don't know what's surrounding me, what could be creeping in close. It's almost a relief not to worry.

The moment I place the exact spot of the wind, I'm back in the grass field, and there before me lies the ship. The UFO, the spacecraft, in all of its glory. I sit up, using my hands for support, and throw my body into the air. I stumble to my feet and begin to move towards the colossal object. A sharp split fills my ears, but I ignore it.

The unknown creature is there. He's standing, holding his hand out towards me, the four fingers shining with anticipation in the harsh streetlight. I stand before the hovering craft and slowly take his hand. It doesn't even feel like I'm holding anything; I can feel tickling sensations circling my hand like tiny gusts of wind entwining itself around my fingers. He helps me aboard. I don't know why I decide that it is a he, or that they even have an identifying gender, but in my head, I consider it a "he."

The door doesn't shut behind me; instead, the creature releases my hand and walks further into the ship. I follow behind him. He takes me down an orange-lit corridor, a rounded tunnel, into a domed room, appearing to be some kind of communal area. Three more figures are in the room, not paying any attention to me. I try my best to place the creatures' features, but I find myself out of luck. They only resemble silhouettes, as if permanent light shines behind them, too bright to see anything else.

There are windows all around the round room, about five feet from the ground, only about two feet high. There are four breaks in the windows; two entrances, one which I just entered from and one directly across from it, and two empty spaces. Nothing fills them. To my right, near the opposing exit, I see a sort of control panel, laid across the length of the window, with a partially opaque screen nearly reaching the ceiling. One of the figures is seated before the panel, his fingers not touching the buttons, but swiping above them. He seems fixed to the screen. To my left, at one of the breaks in the windows, lies a plant, but it is a deep, metallic gray. It impossibly looks like it's thriving. Two more creatures are near it, but they are both looking out the window. They seem to be mumbling back and forth in a language that I don't understand.

"Abelsleffin," I catch from one.

"Panashlue."

It's gibberish to me.

The creature whose hand I first grasped turns around and holds his arm out to my right. I follow it, and I discover a small glass-enclosed display case carrying a book.

The book.

He leads me to the book.

I step closer, eyeing the book carefully; the cover is a thick caramel fabric, with words in black font appearing to be handwritten on. I lean my head, first to the right, then to the left, noting the thickness and shape of the book. Unlike most books I've seen, it is a perfect rectangle, however unlike most of what I've seen, unlike all of what I've seen, the pages also appear to be some sort of cloth. They are thin, like sheets of paper, but when I lean in closer, I can see the minor imperfections only a piece of fabric can display; the small, barely noticeable stray strands, only visible to the ones seeking.

I stand back up straight, hearing the creature make a small noise behind me, and my back tenses. A dab of panic sets in. The ship hasn't moved; it hasn't left or gone anywhere. I'm still home.

A black arm stretches past me, its fingers fidgeting, and they suddenly type, as if in some kind of pattern, on the top left corner of the encasement. When I look at it, I see a small keyboard, containing characters that I don't quite recognize, and an amount that doesn't seem quite right. I'm confronted with a list of words drenching the entire glass panel, all of which are in no particular order. The creature behind me makes a sound and then begins scrolling through the words. I promptly follow his lead, though I'm not sure what I'm looking for until I reach the word "English." I quickly tap on the glass, and the what I'm assuming to be language options disappear.

I went past at least forty different languages, only a handful I may have recognized.

After a few moments, some bold black words flash onto the glass and read, "The Book of Hallandor." I hesitate, unsure of what to think of this, and turn back to the thing that lead me aboard. He makes a curt, squeaking sound and then reaches past me once again, demonstrating the possibility of scrolling through text. I watch the page numbers flash by, his hand not even touching the screen. He waves his hand at the electronic book, almost as if he's encouraging me to try it for myself. I follow his lead and return to the beginning. I jump at the sensation of having a grip on the simulated book, my fingers tingle; that must mean I'm connected. I toss my fingers up a little, and the pages scroll down. The entirety of the screen is about a foot down, and eight inches across, a tad bigger than the standard size piece of paper. My hand flicks down, and the numbers shrink. I scroll all the way to the beginning, page 1.

The Book of Hallandor. It's an intimidating read, to say the least, and I'm not entirely sure what to do with this information. *Is any of this really happening?* I feel like my brain is a lantern, the flame almost extinguished, but then a short burst of oxygen brightens it once more.

I quickly discover that the first few pages are a table of contents, in a way. There are about a hundred different points of interest, some concepts I recognize, others foreign to me, all of which are a type of scientific or social advancement. My eyes are darting in a million different directions until I shut them completely; *take a breath. Breathe.*

I count to three, a tip I've heard but never practiced, and I open my eyes again. I decide to start at the beginning. Introduction.

I tap on the word, my fashion of deciding, and I'm surprised when it takes me to that page; page 9.

To whom it may concern, it begins. I clear my throat, shifting my stance, and I rest one hand on the side of the glass while I read, as if to steady the inanimate novel. Really, I'm steadying myself.

If this passage is being read by you, it is likely that our planet has been demolished. I swallow. Hard. *If this is the case, then you have been chosen to learn our greatest advancements. Many years prior, we realized that our planet, Hallandor, would soon perish. We were at war with a neighbouring planet, Avones, and knew that if the war progressed, we would be the ones to suffer. We began this collection as a way to document our most successful and meaningful technological triumphs.*

My hands start to quiver, and my grip strengthens onto the glass, my eyes glossing over. I don't know what I am reading; that, or I can't process it.

Over the years, we added what we feel has aided our society the most. We are a planet founded on peace and share, and we hope to carry that legacy to another existence. We want to share our greatness with others, so they can achieve what we have.

Imagine what Earth would be like with that kind of attitude.

Even the lapses in translation aren't getting to me. Not now.

It has been decided that the non-Hallandor inhabitant to create contact with us will be the one worthy to learn about our civilization and secrets. The fact that you, alien, how odd it is to know that I am an alien to most of the inhabitants ever to live, *have reached out means that you have thought beyond yourself, a root in which our planet was founded. We trust that you will keep our legacy moving forward. We thank you.*

I turn around, my body moving on its own. I stare towards the silhouette, but I'm unsure whether or not I'm making eye contact. "I don't understand," I say, trying to keep it together.

The creature swiftly turns towards the screens and the other being of darkness and marches over to him. He opens a petite drawer, snatches something from within, and walks back to me. He holds out a small, metal ball to me and points to my ear with the first of his four fingers. I study his close hands, overwhelmed by the darkness I see. I can almost see colours swirling within the pit of black. I slip the ball inside my ear, completely, and possibly stupidly, trusting. I hesitate for a moment, but I allow the tiny marble to settle in my ear.

"I don't understand," I repeat.

"What don't you understand?"

I stumble backwards, startled by the voice. The creature isn't speaking; it's merely a voice inside my head. A million thoughts race through my mind, the least of which is how he can communicate with me.

"This must be a mistake!"

"Why do you think that?"

I can't identify if the voice is male, female, old, young, I just can't tell.

"I...we don't deserve this." I glance back at the flat glass and scroll back up to the table of contents. The names themselves excite and terrify me; there are concepts on here that scientists have been working on for years. All the answers, right within this book. I glance at the bottom of the page; over a thousand pages. "I didn't make any contact..."

The silhouette shuffles away from me, back towards the screens, and the only sitting creature. He signals for me to join him. We stand there for about two minutes in absolute silence, while different folders, documents, and words flash across the screens in no particular order;

this must be some sort of supercomputer. The seated creature presses one last button, very forcefully, and darkness reaches all the screens. After a solid fifteen seconds of black, just as I'm about to speak, a blinding white light drenches the dark. I jump back, shielding my eyes, and then return to focus. The camera, I suppose, jostles a little, but then steadies itself strategically alongside the light. It appears to be zooming in.

A setting reveals itself, fit with trees, mountains, a sky, all shrouded in darkness. The trees and one prominent peak are a darker shade of black than the sky, though I wouldn't call the night gray. I'm still attempting to focus on the light, or rather, what's next to it.

I gasp, a hand clasped over my mouth, as the zoom reveals a figure standing next to a strobe light. With unbelievable resolution, considering this ship must have been miles away, *I* become in focus. I'm in my pink toque, white boot warmers, dark pants and coat, staring up at the sky, apparently oblivious to the craft filming me. I'm even wearing my glasses; I'm unmistakeable. I'm standing next to the strobe light, and I begin to adjust it, streaking across the clouds.

The creature presses a button again, and it pauses on my face. A software similar to a facial recognition that I'd seen on TV scans my face, pinpointing many features. I've never seen one in real life before; I'm seeing a lot of things I'd never even dreamed before.

I remember that time so vividly; Denton was about ten, maybe fifteen minutes out. That time must have been when Tristan returned to his car to grab a few extra supplies, and even insisted that I joined him. But I didn't. Instead, I shone my giant, borrowed light; the consideration of being able to make contact humoured me, but part of me didn't think it would ever happen. Now...

"From our observations, no other living creature has ever made contact," the voice in my head echoes. "Not that we have seen."

I shake my head. "No...no, I mean, so many other people, something else must have..."

"We have only seen your attempt."

I look at the creature, searching in the general vicinity of where I think its eyes would be. "How long have you been looking? For someone to make contact?"

"We have different measurements of time than you. But in your time..." the creature appears to do some calculations in his head, "about three hundred and twenty-seven years."

My mind cannot fathom; since just before the break of the eighteenth century. "How? How have you survived so long?"

The creature shifts from side to side, swaying on the ship, and I can see his feet moving rhythmically, too. "We require only the energy of the sun to survive. Which has made our search very difficult." *Solar powered aliens?* "We need to stay within a certain radius of the sun. However, the surrounding planets do not match our regional needs. Like your own species, we require water, and many planets do not have this. The ones that do are not warm enough."

"Oh. I see…" I gaze out of the window, spotting houses nearby; if they only knew what was going on. If it's even really happening. The neighbourhood is rural right now. "But your population,"

"They are all aboard."

I glance around at the four creatures; I don't know what I expected other populations to be, but it was definitely more than this. "Just the four of you?"

The silhouette shakes his head and points to the entrance to the room I have yet to explore. "No. We have millions of our kind in a Cellulis. It is a suspended state." He doesn't explain more, so I'm guessing he's referring to something like a cryogenic state.

"Do you age?" I find myself calming down a bit, enough to ask informative questions, but my insides are still in flames. My brain is exploding, over and over and over again.

"Not in the sense that you are referring to. We start small, like your kind, but we are made from the passing energy of others. Once a Hallandorian passes, from either not enough sunlight, or whatever that reason may be, other Hallandorians are formed in its place. They grow stronger, and soon have the intelligence to think and formulate all of the thoughts of their predecessor. And then they learn more."

"So, you're born with all of this knowledge, and then as you get stronger, you learn how to understand it all?"

The creature, confused by my words, takes his time, and then finally responds with a single, "Yes."

"That's…incredible." I gawk in wonder at all the magnificence aboard the ship, from the creatures to the seemingly supercomputer, to the immaculate flooring, not a speck of dust in sight. It's not exactly what I imagined, but I feel exactly how I thought I'd feel; I feel useful, as if I have a purpose. I feel proud. I feel free.

The skeptical side of me begins to creep in, and I start swaying back and forth, looking around the room; what if it's not real? I'm known to just jump into crazy things… "How do I know it's real?"

"I do not understand," the creature replies, tilting his head to one side. My eyes desperately try to concentrate on anything distinguishable; it doesn't work.

"All of this." I hold my arms out, signaling to the entire spacecraft, even drawing the attention of the two conversing aliens. Now that I have the earpiece, I can tell they are making notes of what they see from the window; the "domiciles" seem of interest to them. "You, this ship, that book." I point to the book. The thought of a book with a bunch of technological advancements that are apparently mine for the taking strikes a bit of an odd chord. My head is spinning. "How do I know it's real?"

"Why would it not be real?" I'm asked.

I open my mouth, about to argue, but I can't think of any valid argument. I find myself blushing, even embarrassed to have asked the question.

"You have made contact with us. The book is yours." He reaches over towards the fragile case and places his hands on it, but I stop him. My hands twitch at the thought of anything touching the delicate placement.

"I can't take it," I reply, startling him to the point where his hands jolt from the display as if it had shocked him. "It's not mine."

"It is yours."

"But, this can't be real…" The creature takes a different approach than my intention.

"If we can prove it to you, will you take the book?"

"…what?"

He brings up the English translation of the book again and taps the glass. "If we can demonstrate one of our accomplishments, will you take our book and share it with your people?"

My body begins to shake, and I stare temptation directly in the eye. My heart is pounding so hard that I'm surprised I'm still standing. My eyes swell again. "I…"

"Please. It is yours. You are the only hope of our legacy being continued."

I can't help myself; possibly because I can hear the hope in his voice, or rather the voice inside my head, or maybe because my curiosity is just too much to bear. But either way, I say, "Okay."

All four of the creatures, even the other three that didn't seem all that interested, expel an aura of relief, and I too find myself relaxing a little. The atmosphere was so tense and frigid, but now, it seems the ice has been broken.

"What would you like to see?"

I approach the book again, slowly scrolling through the table of contents; electricity reaches out to me, considering we too have that asset in our lives. As well as a phone, computer, flying ships. Our civilizations seem relatively similar. That is, until I see that the further down the list I read, the more powerful and complicated their inventions are. *Portals; quick access to different points of any given region. Water Converter; draws the moisture from the atmosphere to create water. Energy Transmitter; a permanent capsule inserted in the body to convert respirations to endless energy.*

The English translation, no matter how stiff, is giving me a straightforward and direct explanation of everything. I don't think that it is so simple in practice, however. I'm feeling as though the translation is almost dumbing it down for me.

Thought transfer; the transferring of one being's thoughts to another. I instinctively touch my ear, considering that I could have that thought transfer inside my own head. I wonder if the other creatures can hear everything I'm thinking.

Air Vacuum; the air vacuum is activated in a location which breathing air is required and clears all toxins; settings are on the device.

Habitat replication; this device is activated in a location and transforms that area into a suitable habitat; settings are on the device.

Extinction accumulator; gathers the remains of an extinct creature and recreates the creature in a suitable habitat.

My heart is clobbering my chest so much that it hurts. I hold a hand to my thumping chest, continuing to list off all of the technologies inside of my head. I could see a mammoth. I could watch them create water from nothing. I could transport myself to China using a portal. Hell, why stop there? I could go to a different planet!

All of the enticements are incredible. But I come across two words that make my heart stop entirely; time travel.

Time Travel; the process of moving forward in time with only minuscule physical reactions to the time that has passed.

The mere concept of time travel has always fascinated me. Not only because no one has ever been able to conquer time, along with all of those "time marches on," "time waits for no one," quotes, but because of the confusion. If I travel back to a time and see myself, will I really see myself? If I have already traveled back, why didn't I remember it? Because it already happened to my past self. Time has always scared me, with our inevitable meeting with death, but time travel is the loophole in a rock-solid contract. There's always one way around it.

"You seem to have found one," the creature's voice announces in my head.

A nod arises, surprising even myself. "I suppose I have."

The alien plants himself next to me and confirms what he must have heard me thinking. "It is not perfected, in the sense that we can only move forward. Not back. We were in the midst of that research."

I bite my lip, feeling nervous and excited all at once. "How does it work?"

The creature begins to explain to me how it works, giving me formulas and equations, describing how it all comes together and forms his perfect explanation. It's overwhelming. What I took from it is that we in this ship travel a certain distance away; in our case, the creature has confirmed Earth hours equalling to the number of years I want to travel. Then, once we've reached that point, we approach the Earth, entering faster than what my mind can comprehend, and begin circling the planet. It almost feels like hopping through different…wormholes. Eventually, after all the circling, we stop and land again, and time has passed faster on Earth than it has for us. The only time I will age, according to the alien, is when we are flying out. When we enter the speed they call "Utranium speed," a translation error that I can't quite grasp, we are in a state of suspension. I won't grow any older, nor will time pass for any other planet, given the few hours.

"Does that satisfy the explanation?"

I nod, rubbing my hands together. I think so. I don't think explaining it again will make it any clearer.

In a sense, I'm almost glad that I don't get to choose whether I go forward or back, just so I don't I have to live with the wonder if I had decided differently. I don't have a choice, on this front. The fact that this is at all possible makes my heart swoon.

"It is all written in the book," he concludes, easing my concerns.

One of the creatures by the windows suddenly disappears into the back entrance of the common room, and the door spirals shut behind them. I try to figure out what's happening until I hear the faint sound of an engine starting up.

"Are you prepared?"

I look back towards the open door. Do I stay? Or do I leave, and chalk this all up to some bad dream?

I knew my decision when I stepped onto this ship.

"Yes."

I watch the platform I'd walked on retract back upwards, and the second entrance spirals shut. I turn to the creature, and he guides me towards the second entrance, the mechanical sounds growing louder. Through another short corridor, we're confronted by more doors that open upon our sensor. We find one of the creatures inside what appears to be a control room. He invites me to the open seat next to him. The creature controlling the ship looks smaller, shorter, and rounder.

"What are your names?" I find myself asking.

Both pause for a moment, motioning towards each other, and the first one responds, "We have only identifiers. Other Hallandorians can identify us by them, but they are unspoken. We do not have names."

"Oh, okay…" I glance out the front of the ship, the entirety of it covered in windows. Only the ceiling and floor are an opaque material, glass floods the walls.

I'm about to ask for a bit more information when the engine sound revs up rather quickly, and I instinctively grip onto the edge of my seat.

"Oh, yes. You may want to hold on to something, for your own safety," the creature says to me.

I look around me, examining the seat, but I can't find any sort of seatbelt. Looks like my clenched fists will have to do. Air gets caught in my throat, and I hold my breath, unable to breathe, but also not really trying to. I sit there, motionless, hardly even blinking.

All at once, the ship is thrown into action.

I grip tighter onto my seat.

We begin slowly, but only for a few seconds before the ship levitates itself into the air, and we start to go faster and faster. It all feels unstable and downright terrifying.

My breath is still caught.

The tops of houses disappear, and soon do the tops of trees.

We're up so high that I can't even see the remnants of my city below. The ship bursts forward, continuing upward, and my mind starts to spin. I'm dizzy. I can't even formulate a coherent thought. The dark sky gradually fades, and a light comes into view, but it too fades right back again. We enter what appears to be a thicket of clouds, appearing so suddenly that I find myself flinching.

I gasp; the shock was enough to get my body going again.

I hold one hand to my chest in efforts of steadying my newly found breathing. The array of clouds disappears, and so does my hysteria. I calm down. All that's before us is dark, and I can hardly feel the intensity of the ship anymore. I feel safe, at ease.

"Are we…" I lean forward, trying to see more out the glass, but I can't see much. "Where…"

"Would you like a better look?"

I nod, hopping up to my feet, and I follow the alien I'd been talking to all of this time. He only takes a few steps before stopping and points to the floor. There's a circle marked on the floor. I step into the ring, and almost immediately, I'm in a different location.

My knees buckle, and I just save myself from falling to the ground. If I didn't know any better, I would say that I just transported from one location to another in less than a blink of the eye.

"This is our observation deck, as you humans would say."

I peek up from my stumbling state, and my jaw drops. I must be somewhere on top of the ship; I'm encircled by a glass dome. I continually turn around, stunned by what I'm seeing. The pictures don't do it justice. No films I've ever seen of any space artifact could have ever done this justice.

The Earth is behind me, far behind me, and I just stare at it. I can't help it. It's cloudy and mostly blue, and there is a lot more brown than I expected, but also a lot of green, and, and…

My heart calms itself. Seeing the planet that I'd been living on, seeing it dazzle in the darkness, and float there like a bouncy ball mid-bounce; it's intoxicating. All at once, my perspective is changed. All those tiny, insignificant instances, they all seem so silly to me. They are all so small. *I* am so small. It's hard to believe that Earth hosts all those buildings, all those roads, all those living creatures. And how little we all are.

"That's amazing," I gently cry out. I'm melting.

All those fights with Tristan. All those moments with my dad, where we just can't quite grasp an ideal relationship. All those feelings of emptiness left by my mom. *This is why I love the idea*, I say to myself. *This is why I started trying to learn more. There are so many greater things waiting for us all, just beyond the surface. One only has to look.*

"I sense that you would like some time alone," the creature says. "I will return. The trip out is the equivalent of four hours and fifty-seven minutes, in your human time."

"Thank you." I'm not sure if he even hears me.

In a moment, he's gone.

I take a quick look around the room, one big ring of a bench against the dome's edges, and I take a seat, facing my home planet. It shrinks as we truck on forward, and warmth fills my entire body, planting me in my place.

I don't care if this is a dream. I've never felt so free.

I flash back to when I first started all of this. The first time I'd researched aliens, conspiracy theories, the whole deal. My dad wasn't home, and I was holed up in my room, and I remember looking outside. And I saw the moon. I remember staring at it for hours until I began to study it. I knew the first man to walk on the moon, but I wanted to learn more. I stayed up until seven the next morning. I went from the moon, to the stars, to the solar system, to planets, and one small word lead me to aliens. Unknown.

Unknown.

The rest is history. I haven't been able to stop since. Even when I tried to stop, it didn't take. I'd find a rational excuse to go out and "stargaze." It was like an addiction. I always felt so free, so alone, yet so comforted altogether. It was a neat little package.

I can't stop staring at my home. I try to see it revolving around, but I can't quite place it; I'm not surprised, though. I'll probably see it once I look away for a while, and look back. Is that how it works?

I don't know how long passes before I manage to peel my eyes from my planet. I look to my left, knowing that the sun has been there all along. I saw it from the corner of my eye, but I couldn't get myself to look away. My eyes start to water within a few seconds of seeing the impossibly big sun. It's funny, since I was first on Earth, that I'm shocked by my planet's smallness, and equally stunned by the sun's magnitude. The irony is there. The sun is massive, to say the least, and appears brighter now than before.

It doesn't take long for the sun to sting my eyes, though. There are many details to observe, but it hurts a lot more to look at it now than on Earth. I can't even see the full sun, only a round edge; it's massive.

I look to my right, finding it easier to stay away from the sun, considering it's burning my eyes from here, and then I spot something else that captures my attention; I don't count them right away, but I have a feeling that the small billiards balls striking the universe are the planets of our solar system. I piece together what they are by size and colour; Mars is red. Mercury is just a spec, and it takes me a little time to find it. Venus is so bright, dazzling like the sun. I expected Saturn to be much more intimidating, with the rocky rings encircling it, but Jupiter is the one that sends chills down my spine. It's massive. Neptune and Uranus linger in the background, beautiful blue spots dotting the otherwise black sky. I can't spot Pluto, despite my searching, but it still brings tears to my eyes.

I settle further into my seat, my back relaxing, and I draw my legs up onto the plum infinity cushions. I cross my legs and sit, resting my hands on my lap. I continue about the sky, finding glimmering stars sprinkled around, almost in orderly chaos. It's beautiful.

As if on cue, the creature I'd been conversing with appears before me, blocking my view of the stellar universe.

"Hello," he says to me, and steps out of my view, allowing me access to the key to my heart. I hold my breath and smile, and he sits down next to me, the sky still visible.

"Hello," I respond, literally star struck. I could live in this little dome forever.

"Are you enjoying being on this ship?"

I nod, biting my dried lips. "I am. It's incredible. I can't even begin to thank you."

"We require no thanks. We owe you our eternal gratitude. You will continue our legacy." The alien pauses for a moment and then reaches to where his ear would be, and draws out his own metallic sphere. In his free hand, he produces a rectangular rock, containing all the edges and grooves stone would carry. There is a round indent near the bottom, and he places the marble inside. The indent shines so suddenly that I flinch in my seat, but the alien doesn't notice. A small screen reveals itself above the tiny ball, and a word quickly flashes before the light disappears entirely. It's gone back to being a brick. He brings his hand back up to the side of his head, and the marble vanishes.

"What is that?" I ask, touching my ear.

"It is a recorder and translator," he replies. "It is beneficial when meeting creatures who do not share our language. It records events and words for our archives in any language we find most comfortable.

"And the brick?" I prompt.

He takes a few seconds to understand, and I point to his hand. "It copies the memories from the device so that they can be watched at any time. Raleigh?" I blink a few times, a little speechless. I'm still trying to wrap my head around how such a petite invention can do so much, I can't remember if I told him my name. "Is that how you are identified?"

"Um…yes," I mutter, but I still can't wrap my head around what he just said. "I–"

"You said they are called names?"

"Yeah…everyone has one. It's what you call someone. So, I'm Raleigh, but there are many different names."

"Does everyone have a different name?" The word name feels unnatural to hear from him, stiff and wrong.

I hesitate a little, feeling a sense of pride. I'm explaining to this creature what names are, and as small as that may be, it does feel good. "Kind of, there are a lot of different names, but some people have the same name."

"Then how do you tell each other apart?"

I smile a little, blushing, and I clear my throat. "We all look different. And Earth is a bit…different. We have these things called 'countries,' which are pieces of land divided and belonging to different regions."

"I do not understand," it says, a peculiar tone entering my mind.

I try to think, but I'm honestly surprised I came up with that decent of an explanation. I turn next to me and point at a cushion. "Say that this is the Earth and all of the land on Earth. I'm not exactly sure how it came to be, but the land became…invisibly separated," I choose my words carefully. "There are no physical boundaries, except for manmade ones."

"And you don't know how it came to be?"

I shake my head. "I know that many years ago humans made up these divisions. But I don't know why…what was your planet like?"

"It was much smaller than your Earth. We were not divided in any way, we all shared the land." I find my eyes welling up once again;

the idea of humans sharing, it plucks at my heartstrings. "We had a conflict with another nearby planet, Avones. They were similar to your planet, they were divided. They wanted to take our planet from us and use it for materials. In the end, they struck a war with us, a war that we would not fight. One of the habitants of Avones then went directly to our leader and informed us that they were going to destroy our planet, because we would not fight, but our technology had them beat. We had defenses to keep them at bay, but not against the caliber of the weapon they planned on using. So, we gathered all of us into the Cellulis, and we shipped off. They destroyed our planet and had no idea that we had even escaped."

"That's…" a million thoughts race through my head. "I'm so sorry. That's terrible."

"During that time, we wrote our book of advancements. The book which is now yours."

Butterflies flutter throughout my body. "How did it come to be the four of you on this ship? Why you?"

"We volunteered. We were close with our leader, we worked with him to ensure the safety of the planet. He himself is in a Cellulis."

"What is a Cellulis?" I finally ask, the question burning in my mind.

The creature holds up his hands, extending two fingers about an inch away from each other. "They are small capsules that suspend life," he says. "Time will not pass for them. They will not feel any emotion or pain until they are released." He pauses for a moment and then nods to himself as if he's learning new information as we speak. "It is like sleeping for humans."

I nod, gazing out into the abyss of stars once more. "Why isn't your leader here with you?"

"He believed himself to be a danger to the planets."

"A danger?"

"Yes. He thought to be too angry at the Avones for what they did to our home and thought that he would only crave revenge. He felt that way when he was put into the Cellulis. We agreed and decided it was best to not make his decisions out of revenge." My heartstrings ache.

"That's very noble of him."

The creature nods gently, managing to steal my attention from the atmosphere. I had my eyes on the vast space the whole time. "Our leader was very noble. A great Hallandorian...I think he would be happy to know that there is another living creature, on a different planet, that feels as he does. He would be happy to know that our legacy will be carried on by you."

I smile softly, staring down at my finally steady hands. "I hope so." I stare at the creature's face, no discernable features. Despite their appearances, their emotional ranges seem quite similar to our own. "I hope one day you'll find a planet to call home again. And I hope that I can meet you all again."

"I as well."

I smile, gazing out into the abyss of darkness, my heartwarming and cooling in rapid waves. I'm about to speak, when the creature opts in, shattering my bliss, "the trip won't be much longer. Would you like to be alone?"

I shrug, rubbing my hands on my thick thighs. "You can stay if you like." I don't remove my eyes from the darkness; I can't even see the Earth's features anymore, it's just a small blue dot. The creature settles into its seat, briefly stretching his arm from his body. "I've never been to space before."

"...but your species have traveled to space before?"

"Well, yes, but only certain people. They have to go through a lot of tests and training to be suitable for space."

"How peculiar."

"Why's that?"

"I suppose because any of us Hallandor can go wherever we please."

"We're not there yet," I joke, feeling an odd, nostalgic feeling towards my home planet. It feels so small and sheltered, and not advanced at all compared to what it could be; I guess that's the fun in advancement, though. It's all this change, slowly, but still all at once, and when you see what's ahead, the past looks primitive, even if it felt like there was nowhere else to go from where we were...

A small light appears above me, flashing blue; how did I not notice the fixture before?

"It is time," the creature says, standing up. "We can return back downstairs. It is time for you to return back to Earth."

I gulp, suddenly feeling very anxious. I don't want to leave. I want to ask if I can stay here, if there's a way I can live in space forever. Only now do I give all the people in my life a real thought; I've never gone so long without thinking of anyone else. Though I'm now realizing how much I miss them, I'm not ready to go back.

But I don't think I have a choice. I want to stay in this moment of limbo, between staying and going back, living both lives I want to live. I open my mouth to say something, but no words come out. My lips lock together, and I take one last look at my tiny planet.

I follow the alien back to the portal. In a heartbeat, we're back downstairs and in the front area of the ship. The creature signals to the seat I'd previously sat in, and I reluctantly take my position. I instinctively reach for the seatbelt that isn't there, and my hands rest awkwardly on my lap.

"We are at the distance to be able to enter Ultranium speed," the creature explains, answering any questions I might have, "and then circle the planet safely. We have to get back into orbit." The creature points to the other alien. "...inputs the speed which we will enter, and the ship will then automatically be pulled into orbit, and we will circle Earth until the time is up." The identifier of the creature, I assume, comes out as nothing in my ear. It's only silence; I guess there isn't a translation of his identifier.

I nod, considering this carefully. Until the time is up. I'm not sure if I merely forgot to ask earlier, or if my brain hadn't caught when the creature told me, but I'm not sure if I'm ready to hear the answer.

"So, what now?" The creature sits down on the other side of the alien who's controlling this ship. It's pushing all these buttons that don't have any unique attributes on them. It must all be from memory. Or maybe it can see something that I can't. The ship, I realized is now stopped, and is pivoting around until it's facing from whence it came.

"Now, we return back to Earth. Are the coordinates set?"

"Yes," another voice, different from the first creature, but still with that unknown factor, responds.

"Then we shall travel back. We will be going very quickly, as before, you may want to hold on."

I bite my tongue, gripping onto the armrests again. I'm scared. I don't know what's going to happen. Part of me wants to call it all off and tell the creature to just take me home at a normal speed, take me back up to the observation dome, let me see myself coming closer and closer to Earth in a timely manner. Part of me wants to go home and see Tristan, and Tiffany, and my dad, and Denton, apparently, and all of my co-workers again, and pretend like this never happened. I bite my tongue even harder, letting it sting a little. If I speak, I know I'll chicken out. I'll take the easy way, the safe way, and I'll miss out on something truly incredible. And this is what I want.

My mouth opens, and even I'm not sure what I'm going to say, but just before I can speak, we are thrown into action. The ship goes faster than before, accelerating at impossible speeds, and my fingers dig deeper and deeper into the fabric armrests. I clamp my mouth shut, feeling my bones rattling within me, teeth chattering, eyes watering. It's almost like a movie, the blue-white streaks of light passing us by, but then something different happens. Orange and pink lights gradually outweigh the blue. I make the mistake of opening my mouth to express my wonder, and I let out a small scream, horrified at what I'm seeing. I snap my lips back shut, and without trying, a smile presents itself to me.

I slowly get used to the speeds, feeling weightless, as if I could float throughout this ship. Just when I think I could actually get up and move around in this speed, the deceleration begins. It lasts much less time than I expected or hoped, and within another thirty seconds, I'm seeing familiar treetops and houses, and a big grassy area that I don't recognize as much.

No. No, not yet.

I take a deep breath, the smirk still plastered on my lips; I don't even feel like I belong here anymore. But it sure would be nice to be back…

The ship lands quickly on the street, no one around, streetlights still on. An orange light glows within the spacecraft, but I'm not sure why.

"That was it," I finally speak, as the alien controlling the ship presses a few more buttons, and then leans back in his seat. I sense he's at ease.

"Yes, we are here. You are back home."

I chuckle to myself. The hours felt like years away from Earth.

My heart stops.

"How long–"

"It is time for you, and for us, to go. I will give you the book now."

The creature exits the room, the doors eating him, and I stumble to my feet to follow. I try to catch up with him, but end up falling in the process. My mind feels like it was just thrown into a blender, cut up into a billion pieces, and is now trying to put itself back together. These creatures seem very blunt and honest, something that I'm not entirely used to.

I push myself up and use the walls as assistance to catch up to the alien. I find him back in the common room, along with the other two space creatures, both still enthralled by staring out the window. This must be just as interesting for them; maybe a little less so, considering they've been to other planets before.

"Here you are," the creature says.

I watch him type something onto the glass, and all four walls slip down into the podium, the top glass folding up onto one of the walls. He grips onto the book and then places the recording brick in its place. Some high pitched, technical sounds ring out, but soon disappear once the four walls reappear. The top goes back into place.

The creature turns around and hands me the book. "It is yours now. Please take good care of it."

"I…" I'm panting from the journey, and my knees are ready to buckle at any second. "I will."

"This is yours as well, I believe" the alien adds, and holds out my broken cellphone, headphones still attached. "You dropped it while coming onto our ship."

I take the broken phone, the small pieces of glass piercing my skin.

It hits me now that everything has felt like it's moving in fast forward, too quick to comprehend, but I don't think it really is; I think it's all going at a normal speed, but my mind feels like it's on crack. Everything is blurry. All of these "abrupt" actions only feel relatively slow. It's an unsettling feeling.

The creature escorts me throughout the ship, and until the capsule is opened and there's a platform assisting me to the ground, we stay in silence.

"This is your first time travel, and your first space travel," he says carefully. "Upon research, I see that your body is not used to such experiences. You may experience some trouble recovery."

"Like what?" I ask, my tongue feeling like mud. I'm not sure that I even know what I'm currently experiencing.

"Weakened   senses,   diminished   muscles,   memory complications, and sensory disturbances."

"That's fine," I brush off, fatigue running over me. My brain is not equipped at the moment to process any of this. Weakened senses, definitely. That's about as much as I can take.

"Thank you, Raleigh. Your contact means very much to us. I hope this book will help your species."

I look up to the creature, and I find it in me to smile, even in my current state. I feel like I've just peaked, and there's nowhere to go from here. It's not a fun feeling. "Your contact means the world to me," I sputter, my tongue sloshing around unpredictably inside my mouth. "It means everything. Thank you."

The creature nods and holds out his hand to me. I take it, and he helps me step down onto solid ground. It feels like I'm standing on spaghetti.

"Where will you go now?" I ask, begging this adventure to stay forever.

"We will continue to search. It will now hopefully be easier to find a suitable planet, now that we are no longer looking for contact."

"Good luck," is all I can seem to think of saying.

The alien begins to walk away, back onto his ship, until I call after him.

"Can I ask one more thing?"

"Yes, of course."

"How long have I been gone?" It's the dreaded question, the one that will make all this real. For all I know, it's only been those precious hours. Maybe nothing has changed.

"How far forward have you traveled?"

I nod again. "Yeah." *Don't tell me…*

"…five years, in Earth time."

My eyes blink rapidly, my brain feels as if it's melting. I don't even know how to feel about it. Five years…part of me hopes that this isn't real and that it's a dream, or some psychotic break. But a stronger part of me wants everything I've seen in the past few hours to be true, no matter what the cost. And that cost might be a lot.

"Five years," I say, taking a look around. The Earth is five years older, which is hardly a thing to the planet itself, but is a full quarter of my life older. So much awaits me; seeing Tiffany again, seeing Tristan, telling Denton about this…there's so much to do. It brings a small smile to my lips.

It's scary. It was scary, to hop aboard that ship, and my new future is terrifying. Everything surely must have changed. There will be things that I broke that I can't fix, and even better things to come. It is scary. But I am proud of my choice. And I don't regret it. No matter what the consequences."

"Why five years?" I ask.

"You told me," the creature says. "When you first saw time travel in our book," I clutch it tighter, "I examined your mind to find the perfect time suitable for you." Using one hand, I reach up to my ear, the metal sphere still sitting inside. "From your history, it was the exact time you wanted and needed."

"Oh." I close my eyes, almost drifting off to sleep while standing. Five years. My decision. No regrets. "Thank you."

The alien nods, and then turns back around, disappearing into the ship. The platform retracts, and soon enough, the door is shut. I hold my arm up, using all of my strength, and I wave to the ship and to its creatures within. I keep waving, my arm numbing, as the craft lifts into the air and slowly propels itself forward, up and away until it is gone again. Within a minute, it is completely out of sight, only a single streak in the sky.

I turn around on my heels, facing from where I was walking, just hours ago, and I hug the book against my chest; the sun is rising. The orange glow that had filled the ship now blankets my surroundings.

I smile, feeling soft smears of salty tears down my cheeks, and I stare towards the rising sun, unable to quite catch it beneath the houses and trees.

And suddenly, the sky starts to turn sideways. My grip on this sacred book isn't so strong. Condensations streaks my cheeks instead of tears. And it all slips away.

■■■

"Raleigh?"

The voice echoes inside of my head, that same voice that I can't place. My body feels exhausted, and I slowly remember why. I just got off a spaceship. I think I passed out...

"Raleigh?"

My eyes twitch a little; I can place the voice. It's male, definitely male. Deep, and gruff, and...*Denton?*

I open my eyes, shocked by a bright beam streaming into my eyes, and then I adjust. A silhouette blocks the light, and I think that I'm back on the ship again, but, once again, I adjust. It is Denton.

"…Denton?" He's propping me up from the ground, keeping me in a lounge position, his arm just around my neck. I quick jerk up, my body feeling perfectly back to normal, and I scan the area. Two police cars sit in front of my van, and two officers are standing around, attempting to subtly check what's going on.

"Are you okay?" Chief Denton asks, holding gaze with me.

I pull my legs up, sitting comfortably on the ground, and Denton leans away from me. He resumes in his kneel, concern flooding his eyes.

"What happened?" he urges.

"How long has it been?" I reply, startled, my brain darting all around to remember if I'd forgotten something again. If it's been another five years… I begin searching his face for signs of aging. I think he has more wrinkles.

"Since I saw you? Like, two days." I'm about to protest, feeling those memories so true and recent, but then I see my van down the street. I remember driving here, and it's still dark, so it can't have been that long ago. I guess his new wrinkles are a myth. Denton, sensing my confusion, adds carefully, "…it's just after ten."

So, it's been a few hours. I bite my lip, peeling the dry skin, grasping firmly onto what I'd just experienced. But I suppose I didn't *just* experience it. It was a few months ago, now. All those memories, the ones finally uncovered, sit comfortably. I don't think I'll ever forget them now. I smile, chuckling. *I remember.*

I draw my hand up to my ear and pull out the tiny marble. Denton looks a little disgusted as I slip it back into my messenger bag, carefully zipping it into a pocket. I rest my hand gently on The Book of Hallandor, feeling the texture on my fingertips. It feels so soft; I now know why I spent so much time worrying about it. I tuck the book away as well, and I close my bag.

Denton arches an eyebrow, skeptical as always, and holds contact with me. He rests one arm on his knee, beginning to look drained from the kneel. "Officer Ables says that you were passed out cold, saw you while he was doing his rounds. What happened before that?"

The night flashes by, conversing with Tristan, with all the appropriate butterflies, leaving work, exhausted, parking my brute of a van, yelling at the sky, freaking out that random guy. Everything is falling into place, and I can feel the pieces fitting perfectly. It's euphoric. "I...I drove here to try to remember what happened."

"What do you mean, remember what happened? What does that mean?"

I smirk, softly, and then meet his eyes. "What happened over those five years." I can see the goosebumps on his forearms rise, his lower lip dips a little, and his entire demeanor tense and relax at the same time. "I remember."

Chapter 19

One year later.

"You're on in five, Raleigh."

I sigh, standing near the plethora of snacks, debating which one to take. I've already eaten five of the crackers and cheese, three of the mini donuts, one of the revolting finger sandwiches, and a four of the store-bought cookies. I don't even like the cookies, it's like I'm hoping that I'll develop a taste for them if I just force them down. It's dumb, the more I think about it.

"Raleigh?"

"Okay," I mutter back, reaching for another gross cookie. I resist the urge. A woman appears from my left, holding a tray of fruit, and manages to fit it on the already packed table. Looking at the snack table next to it, she would have been better off putting it there, but who am I to judge?

I reach for some cantaloupe, nestled between the sandwiches and the pineapple.

The lady in the headset, the one telling me I have five minutes, disappears in a scurry; I imagine she's swamped. She must be, she's the only one wearing sneakers.

I eat three pieces of cantaloupe, and then grab a napkin to clean my fingers, and mistakenly, my mouth. I smear my lipstick.

"Shit."

"There's my star," Audrey's voice echoes from behind me. I turn around, half covering my mouth, half not caring if I look like crap. She steps into view next to me and arches a perfectly threaded eyebrow. "Did you mess up your lipstick?" I let my hand down, allowing her to see. "Nope, you're good."

"Great. How's the crowd?"

She shrugs, placing on hand on her tiny hip. I only met Audrey a few months ago; we'd emailed back and forth for a few months before that before I finally decided on her as my agent.

"Not bad," Audrey replies, swaying side to side. "And by that, I mean, totally full. I'm not surprised."

"Can't believe it's only a few months away," I mutter, reaching for a piece of out of season watermelon.

"You always wanted to be a writer, right?"

I nod, gazing behind me towards the murmur of the crowd. Since I was fourteen years old, I've enjoyed writing, and I've always dreamed of being published. I feel like I cheated, though. I just got lucky; I became a national, *global*, sensation from one decision I'd made. I never specialized in non-fiction, I liked fiction. I dabbled in romance, horror, even some fantasy. I didn't think my first novel would be a sort of autobiography of something that happened to me. It felt like writing an extensive journal and then flaunting it for the world to see.

"It wasn't supposed to be this easy," I joke mildly, holding my hands together. I straighten my skirt, observing my neat clothing.

"Everybody loves a survivor," Audrey says, eyes fixed on her phone.

"Girl missing for five years and returns." The headlines still bother me.

"Everyone loves a tragedy." I cringe. "By the way, your people are here. Four of them, anyway."

I definitely didn't choose Audrey for how emotional she could be. I'm honestly not sure why I decided to go with Audrey. A lot of agents who approached me, upon hearing that I wanted to publish my story, confided in me about their own experiences; most of them were fake. Audrey, on the other hand, knew just how to get me. She told me she wanted to share what I had to say with the world, she didn't talk about how when she was five, she thinks she saw a UFO and has had that image stuck in her head ever since. She talked about how she feels I had an interesting life story, and that she wants to share it with others. That got me. Growing up, reading other people's experiences, that always interested me. Now I have my own experience to share. It only felt right that I write a book.

"Who?" I ask, dragging myself out of my trance.

"The cop, two girls, and the kid."

I strut past her, towards the stage, and look past the panel; there are two tables set up for me, with seating for four; Audrey, me, the publishing company's CEO, and some other guy. I'm not even sure who. I didn't even know that first-time authors had book tours, if one city even qualifies as a tour, let alone what the tour is supposed to look like. I look like a panelist at ComicCon. Who knows, maybe one day I will be. I could talk about aliens, astronomy, and flying space crafts all day.

I look to the right of the stage, finding the five reserved seats. Tiffany is sitting there, talking to Denton, waving her hand in the air as she explains something. She rests it back onto her lap and begins twisting the engagement ring on her finger; she told me a few weeks ago that she's still not used to it, even though Cole proposed months ago. I think it's a comforting thing.

Denton nods along to Tiffany, but his mind looks like it's somewhere else. Even though he is much more lenient towards this "sci-fi" kind of world, he definitely looks out of his element. It brings a nasty smirk to my lips. Meanwhile, Michelle and Liam both look starstruck. She's in a trance between all the posters holding my book, the dozen or so photographers, and the people waiting anxiously in their seats, while he's just vibrating in his chair. He blurts something out to Michelle, and she nods viciously. I'm not surprised they get along so well.

"I don't know where the guy is."

"Probably still at NETRAD," I mumble back to Audrey. Tristan is almost definitely still at NETRAD. He's even worse at tearing himself away from work now. He's recently opened a new department about the history of extraterrestrials, even receiving a government grant, and his mind is going crazy. History and aliens? His brain is exploding. He, however, assured me last night that he would be here today. He knows how long I've dreamed of being a published novelist, even if it's not in my field of expertise. Then again, who knows my life better than I do?

As if on cue, the back door of the room is thrown open, and in enters Tristan. He races to the front in a flash, and sits down next to Denton, waving hello to the Chief, Michelle, Liam, and to Tiffany.

"Oh, so, your boyfriend did show up," Audrey teases from behind me.

I shake my head, rolling my eyes. She knows as well as I do that my and Tristan's relationship is not simple. Even now, well over a year since reuniting, we're still trying to slip back into the regular rhythm of us. It has definitely been interesting. We are dating. We call ourselves boyfriend and girlfriend. But neither of us know if it's going to last. Five years were thrown in between us, *I* threw those five years in between us. It's quite trying to conquer. All I know right now is that, despite the work, we're happy, and maybe we won't always be, but we are right now. And that's what matters.

"Ready?" headset lady asks, appearing from thin air.

I take a deep breath. The Book of Hallandor is occasionally on display at NETRAD, but only for the time being. It is being analyzed by the research department and helped along by me. Knowing the title of the book is making it a lot easier to decipher the letters and interpret the text, but there's still a long way to go. Thousands of more pictures have been sent in over the past few months, thanks to NETRAD being in the news circuit. I should be thanking Audrey for that one; she's an incredible agent, and she does her business very well.

NETRAD has skyrocketed in popularity, not that it was struggling before. It's becoming recognized as something even more legitimate, and the hype around both my book and The Book of Hallandor is only helping. The possibilities of the technological advancements only heard of on paper or seen on TV is sending everyone for a spiral. Once the book is fully deciphered, then NETRAD will be donating it to a museum. We have a lot of offers, so we're not sure which one yet, but preferably one nearby so I can still visit it; I still have the protective instincts of it.

I'm trying my best to keep on the legacy of Hallandor. I wanted to protect it from the people who only want to profit from it, or who want to steal it, but I realized that if I didn't put it out there, the good and honest people wouldn't get to see it either. The ones who actually want to make the world a better place wouldn't get that chance.

I think about Hallandor a lot, and about my experience. The book wasn't a means to get famous, I don't care about that. My book is about remembering what happened, and having that detailed log, and sharing it with others. That's the legacy I want to keep.

"Yeah," I conclude, looking to Audrey, who also nods along. She's used to my moments of pause and doesn't think much of them anymore.

"Ready," the lady repeats into her headset and takes us a few feet back from the stage.

A man, reaching just under six feet tall, braces the stage, microphone in hand, smile on his lips. He is wearing a suit, along with a very loud orange tie. He's pulling it off. He extends his arm, signalling for silence, and the crowd falls to a hush.

"Thank you all for joining us today," he begins. "We are very pleased to have you. Today, on our stage, we have Mr. Barney Hobblestead, founder of Pen and Ink Publishing, as well as the acting CEO, his son, Gregory Hobblestead. And we have the great honour of presenting Raleigh Carlise, author of," chills roll down my spine, "'*My Choice*,'" another chill sneaks through me; the name still kills me. The book could very well suck, but it's too late. I made my choice, "and her agent, Audrey Trent."

The crowd's applause gives me butterflies, and headset lady ushers me onto the stage, Audrey close behind me, and the Hobblesteads approach from the other side of the tables. I avoid almost all eye contact with anyone seated before me, on the pure basis of me trying not to trip in the high heels I'm wearing. Surprisingly comfortable, but still a hazard. I shake hands with the two men publishing my book, and then we all take a seat at our assigned spots. I finally observe my audience, and I see all sorts of people. The press has been pushed to the back, leaving room for the diverse people before me. There are business officials to men and women bearing *The X-Files* shirts, or the classic alien patch on their bags, and everything in between. It's heartwarming.

"Ms. Carlisle, would you like to say anything before we start?" The announcer asks me.

I nod, clearing my throat, and I tug my microphone a little closer to me.

"Thanks," I say. "I just want to thank everyone here for coming in the first place." I'm met with applause, and so I wait patiently for it to subside. "I want to thank Pen and Ink Publishing, for taking a chance on an unknown author." Both men give me a single nod, grinning softly. "And I want to thank all the volunteers and workers for arranging this press tour today." More applause.

My stomach starts to feel a bit funny, and I gently press my palm to it, subsiding the butterflies within. *Deep breaths, Raleigh. You practiced this unwritten speech before.*

"If you don't already know, this book is a work of non-fiction of my encounter with unearthly creatures. I have only recently finished writing it, and it is being edited as we speak. In *My Choice*, I talk about all the days and weeks, leading up to the two months where I was constantly fighting with myself, trying to remember what had happened. It was nerve racking and nearly threw me into insanity, because I knew, at the end of the day, I didn't have much say in whether or not I remembered. I could only try techniques that were recommended, and my brain and time would have to do the rest. Looking back, I didn't realize how lucky I was to even have remembered anything. Some people lose time and never get it back. Maybe not five whole years," a few chuckles arise, but not very many, "but nevertheless, I am one of the lucky ones."

I meet eye contact with my five guests of the night. Tiffany has finally stopped fidgeting with her ring; I hope she accepts it soon. Denton is entranced, but still a sore thumb by a mile. Michelle almost looks like she's in tears, beaming, with Liam dangling on my every word. And Tristan is just smiling.

I lick my lips and scan the room.

"My point is, is that it was very intense. And it was scary, not knowing, and only remembering bits and pieces. It is still scary. Before everything happened, I was in a world where anyone who even talked about aliens was weird, and we were just kind of shunned away. It has been over six years since then, and it's still a culture shock, but I'm happy that I actually have the chance to share my story without being immediately disregarded. Growing up, I never really saw anyone taken seriously about this kind of stuff, but it seems like that's changed. A lot."

I chuckle a little, staring down at my blouse, ensuring that no buttons have popped open. It's my biggest fear of button-up shirts. I open my mouth, about to mention my parents, but I shut my mouth again. I almost say how my mom left, and how it sparked my passion. I almost bring up how my dad and I haven't talked in over three months. But I don't. I sit there in silence, lips pressed together. There are things you can't change. I tell myself that every day.

"Anyway." I release all the feelings about my parents and look at the front row of people, the five people sitting before me. I smile; that's enough. "I am here today to talk about my story, my truth. *My Choice* is about my alien encounter." I take a deep breath, breathing in the clean air being breezed in from the one open window to my left. There's a vague scent, possibly only in my mind, but it reminds me of the ship I was on last spring. I finally feel happy again. "This is *My Choice*. And this is my story of time travel."

About the Author

Kaitlyn Johnson is a new up-and-coming author in the young adult genre. She has been writing for nine years with her short story, Cake and Coffee, as her debut into the writing world. She has since published a poem, Sail, but has spent the past few years on publishing her first novel.

Made in the USA
Middletown, DE
06 April 2018